Margaret Roberts

Mademoiselle Mori

A Tale of Modern Rome. In Two Volumes: Vol: II.

Margaret Roberts

Mademoiselle Mori
A Tale of Modern Rome. In Two Volumes: Vol: II.

ISBN/EAN: 9783744786379

Printed in Europe, USA, Canada, Australia, Japan

Cover: Foto ©Andreas Hilbeck / pixelio.de

More available books at **www.hansebooks.com**

MADEMOISELLE MORI:

A TALE OF MODERN ROME.

'D'abord je suis *femme*, avec les devoirs, les affections, les
sentiments d'une femme; et puis je suis *artiste*.'
MADAME VIARDOT GARCIA.

'Come, make a circle round me, and mark my tale with care,
A tale of what Rome once hath borne, of what Rome yet may
bear.'
MACAULAY.

IN TWO VOLUMES.

VOL. II.

LONDON:

JOHN W. PARKER AND SON, WEST STRAND.

1860.

MADEMOISELLE MORI.

CHAPTER I.

O patria mia, vedo le mura, e gli archi,
E le colonne, e i simulacri, e l'erme,
Torri degli avi nostri,
Ma la gloria non vedo.

LEOPARDI.

IT was so unusual for Contessa Clementi to pay a morning visit, that when she and Gemma appeared in Casa Olivetti the signora was immediately prepared to discover some important cause.

The appearance of the contessa and her daughter did not betray their poverty ; they were splendidly dressed, for appearances must be kept up, and nobody could tell how they saved, and pinched themselves in food and fire to buy those silks and velvets, or that, if Gemma's shoes should get wet, she had not another pair to put on in their stead !

The ladies met with the usual embraces and salutations, and the two elder ones settled down into a quiet chat, while Gemma took a place by Imelda, holding her hand affectionately, and remarkiug, ' You look pale, dear little one ; what have you been doing ? Have you been to St. Peter's to see the bride and bridegroom ?   You heard how the Principe Allori and his bride went there this morning to pay their devotions before St. Peter?'

As usual in the case of this religious ceremonial the bride had been magnificently attired, and all Rome had flocked to see her jewels, and behold the new-married pair kneel before the statue of St. Peter and at the chief altars; but Imelda had not been present, and said, 'No, I hardly ever go to see such things; mamma likes staying at home.'

'So does my mamma, but I made Pietrucchio take me. Mamma always says, "Wait till you are married—then you may go where you please." When are you to be married, dear Imelda?'

'I do not know.'

'Oh, you are in mourning now, and must wait. Is Ravelli very much vexed at such a delay?'

'I do not know.'

'How sadly you speak! What can be the matter? I saw Ravelli yesterday; he spent the evening with us, and *he* was not at all melancholy.'

'Was he with you?' asked Imelda, not feeling or comprehending the full sting which Gemma meant the words to convey, but glancing towards the seat in the window with a sigh, as she recollected Ravelli's early departure, on the pretext of an engagement. 'He was here for an hour?'

'Oh, that was why he looked so gay, of course; how good of him to come to us at all! What do you talk to him about, Imelda?'

'I don't know.'

'Books and music, I daresay? Of course you know all about such things, as Irene Mori is such a friend of yours, and your mother knows so much.'

'No, I cannot talk of such things at all.'

'But what do you say to him then? He is so

ridiculous; he talks to us women, just as if we were men, about politics, and I don't know what besides, as if that was what we cared for!'

'Does he do so, except to Irene?'

'You ought to know best, I should think. I really wonder you are not a little jealous of Irene, Imelda—he is so often at her house, and talks to no one else when she is by.'

Imelda only smiled; her trusting look was for Irene, but Gemma fancied it included Luigi, and was provoked at being unable to make her innocent rival feel that he was the property of another.

'What is the signora contessa saying to mamma?' said Imelda, glad of an opportunity to approach her mother's side. 'A robbery in St. Peter's?'

The contessa was relating how, in the crowd assembled to see the bridal pair, a gentleman had found a boy picking his pocket, and being an Englishman without education, had seized him, and conveyed him down the aisle to give him into custody; but happily a priest perceived him, forbade the policeman to touch him, and insisted on his being released.

'To lay hands on him in a sanctuary!' said the contessa indignantly; 'could you have believed such a thing? But these English heretics are mere animals; they know not how to behave. There was a scandal impossible to be imagined!'

'Indeed!' said Signora Olivetti dryly, her liberal views not quite inclining her to take the same view of the matter. 'It truly was scandalous.'

'Certainly, certainly; as Monsignore Clementi says, from attacking the throne to attacking the altar there is but one step, as we see in the history of that poor English king, and also Louis XVI. of France. He spoke so admirably about it one evening; I wish you could have heard him. But I must not say these things to you, my dear; you and your husband are liberal, I hear, and I don't know what made me think of it now—' said the contessa, much confused in her mind, as to what had recalled to her Monsignore Clementi's wisdom apropos of the robbery, 'but I am sure I had some reason for it—yet he could not have said it on hearing of this sad business, because that had not happened.'

'Doubtless it was apropos of the municipal council, or the civic guard,' said Signora Olivetti, with secret triumph and satisfaction; for these long-contested points had been gained by the Liberals at last, after a mighty struggle with the *Gregoriani*.

'I daresay it was, dear Gigia; I really know nothing about these things;' and the contessa trembled to think that she had nearly betrayed, that her son and his uncle had had some intercourse of late—a fact which her brother-in-law had impressed upon her was never to be mentioned, and she obeyed implicitly, though not at all understanding the motive for secresy. 'I live so retired—I hear nothing.'

'Your son should convert you, contessa.'

'Ah—Pietrucchio,' said the contessa, nervously. 'Yes—no—I wish instead of meddling with politics he would marry. If your dear little girl were not affianced, Gigia! And now there is Gemma still on my hands—such a charge; what a thing that was! I shudder to remember it. Dear friend, if you should hear of any one that would do for her,

you will let us know? A thousand thanks! you
are too kind!'

'I assure you, my dear contessa, I am as anxious
she should be well married as you can be,' said
Signora Olivetti, gravely. The reason of the visit
was out now.

'Thanks! thanks!' repeated the contessa; 'she
loved your poor dear cousin so truly! we must
try to console her, must we not? Her uncle
already has proposed her, through a third person,
to a certain cavaliere, but I fear this signor will
not marry again yet; he has daughters as old as
she, and his wife has not been dead six weeks. A
man of such feeling! I have reason to believe he
still weeps, if he hears her name. How is your
husband, Luigia mia?'

'He is exceedingly busy; this case of the Fias-
coni has employed him incessantly.'

'Ah, no one has so much business as he! There
is no one I would so gladly trust with my affairs.'

The contessa paused to give her friend an
opportunity of offering that Signor Ravelli should
serve her if he could; but his wife had no intention of burdening him with business to be performed gratis, and which would doubtless be
troublesome. She appeared to expect Contessa
Clementi to speak on; so there was nothing for it,
but to add, 'If he had an hour to spare some
evening, I should be so happy to see him.'

'He would have been too happy, but his affairs
speedily call him to Germany.'

'Really! then this little one cannot be married
yet. Are you not anxious to see her settled?
Daughters are such a care!'

'Not my Imelda,' replied Signora Olivetti, involuntarily drawing her child closer to her; but instantly resuming her former guarded tone. 'If I hear of anything that can be of interest to you, I will certainly advise you of it.'

'Thanks indeed, my dear friend! Now, Gemma, I cannot spare you any more time with Imelda; we must go. My respects to Signor Olivetti. *Mia cara*, could you not come to us on Sunday evening?'

'Impossible, dear contessa; it is my week at the Trinità dei Pellegrini. *Addio, addio.*'

When the visitors were gone, Signora Olivetti drew a breath of relief, and looked for Imelda, whose pensive attitude caused her to observe her long, and then ask what she was thinking of.

'Mamma, do you think I can have vexed Luigi?'

'No, my dear; what makes you fancy such a thing?'

'He was so grave last night—he has been so different lately, and went away so soon.'

It was true. Since his reconciliation with Gemma, he had been intensely annoyed by the recollection of the confidence he had reposed in Imelda, and had altered into coolness and constraint; Luigi never did anything on calculation, and followed his present impulse without remembering what the effect of the last week or two might have been on Imelda, who could not so easily forget his affectionate looks and words—signifying in truth but a passing mood, but most anxiously watched for and treasured. Her mother had marked it all, and now said, 'My dear, you must not think too much about a man's moods: he may have a thousand things in his mind which you know nothing about. All you have to do, is to make his home pleasant, and be cheerful and trustful; but never insist on knowing what is in his mind, nor expect him to think of you continually.'

'Yes,' said Imelda, submissively; but she was not satisfied, for she added, 'a man must find it tiresome, if his wife cannot care for what he does.'

'A good wife always does, my dear.'

'But she cannot, mamma, unless she has learnt how. I know nothing of politics nor of books.'

'My dear child, a husband wants rest and peace at home, not a learned wife. It is of much more importance that you should be able to teach your cook, than to read German; Luigi would not find that your being learned made his dinner comfortable!'

'But when dinner was over, mamma, he would perhaps talk to me if I were clever enough,' said Imelda, with diffidence, as if she felt that her supposition implied great vanity. 'Signor Nota reads his poems to Irene.'

. 'Or to Vincenzo, more likely.'

'Oh, to Irene, too; I know he once said she was his best critic.'

Signora Olivetti mused. Perhaps Imelda might be right; she had overheard what Gemma said, and though she did not believe that Ravelli talked of books or politics to her, yet it might be well if Imelda were more of a companion for him, and knew more of the world; but this was a discouraging game, and the means taken to secure Imelda's happiness threatened it more and more.

Therefore, Signora Olivetti said, 'Imelda, you think too much of what Luigi wishes.'

Her little daughter looked exceedingly surprised, and the mother continued, 'Till he is your husband, there is no need to think continually whether

this and that will please him.   I am afraid if papa
said you were not to marry him, you would find it
hard to obey cheerfully.'

'Oh, mamma, has he said so?'

'No, my dear, and I do not suppose he will; so
you need not look so frightened, but you see I
was right.'

'Mamma, I don't know what else to think of.'

'Your music, for instance; sit down and prac-
tise something—that *notturno.*'

Imelda obeyed instantly, but in the midst of her
piece she turned round with tearful eyes—

'Indeed, I cannot help it, mamma; I was
thinking then that Luigi says he is tired of this.'

'Well, never mind, my child, and don't cry, for
it is not worth anything so serious; come here and
tell me if you would like to go next Easter to
the Pellegrini, and see the *Lavanda?* When you
are old enough, I hope you will be a sister there,
and help to nurse the poor sick people.'

'Oh, how pleasant that would be, mamma!' said
Imelda, nestling down by her mother's side; 'when
I am eighteen I may be admitted. By that time
I shall be ——' she paused abruptly.

'Yes, I suppose you will be married then,' said
Signora Olivetti, suppressing a sigh, and perceiving
that it would be unwise indeed to make this a forbidden subject. 'I shall have lost my little one.'

'Mamma! but you know you only say that as
a joke. You know, not even dear Signora Ravelli
can be quite the same as you are, though I love her
so very much. I cannot think why people say that
a mother and daughter-in-law are hail and tempest
in a house.'

'All mothers are not like Signora Ravelli, my

child; but no doubt it is often the bride's fault. You must try to make your husband's family love you; your own do so by nature, but one must win the husband's.'

'But you were very happy, mamma?'

Bitter were the recollections aroused in Signora Olivetti's mind by that innocent speech; but she replied, 'My father chose my husband, and I was quite willing to marry as he wished. You remember how kind grandmamma was to you, Imelda?'

'Oh yes,' said Imelda, quite satisfied; 'and did you read a great deal after you were married?'

"Yes, my dear.' Signora Olivetti did not add that she had taken to study, as some of her country women do to flirting, to occupy her mind and aid her to forget disappointment and annoyances. Yet it might have been a useful lesson to Imelda had she heard, how at last Signora Olivetti had fully won the esteem and affection of her husband, though not till after the death of her mother-in-law, who hated her, misrepresented all she did, and exercised over her a petty tyranny which Signor Olivetti never guessed.

'I must wait then,' said Imelda.

'What books do you want to read?'

'Oh, mamma, if I might have Signor Nota's poems; they are all printed now, Irene tells me.'

'My dear child, most of them are satires, if you know what that is; you would not understand a word. Well, never mind, you may try; but I have not got them.'

'Luigi has—he can say them by heart, and so can Vincenzo and Irene. How glad I shall be when Irene comes home, and how much she has to see ! Our guard !—do they not look well in their dark blue uniforms, and the belts with each man's initials in front ?'

'Yes, our civic guard make a very reputable appearance, now that they have managed to buy the uniforms ; they were hardly so at first.'

' Only for a little while, till the rich ones helped the others ; Luigi says that Government gave only arms, and so the poorer could not buy the dress. What a feast it was when the guard was instituted —lights, and flags, and crowds everywhere !   And is it not beautiful, mamma, when the Pope blesses the people from the balcony at the Quirinal ?   We used only to have the benediction at Easter, but now I don't know how many times he has given it ; it was so good of you and papa to take me last time.'

' It was a fine sight,' said Signora Olivetti ; but there was a certain coolness in her assent, as if the name of Pio Nono no longer excited the same enthusiasm as of old.

' I shall never forget it as long as I live !' said Imelda ; ' the whole piazza was a sea of people, all looking up to the palace, and among all the thousands there not a sound was heard—only the fountains.   Every one seemed afraid to breathe while the Pope spoke ; one man near me pushed another, and the people whispered, " Hush, hush, we are in Pio Nono's presence !" as he appeared in his white dress and scarlet mantle with all the flambeaux like an illumination round him, and then there was a shout like thunder !   It was a wonderful night, mamma !'

' I wish we may never go to the Quirinal except to be blest,' said Signora Olivetti ; ' they say Padre

Rinaldi has lost favour of late with the Pope, and that his advice is no longer taken. Well, all this does not matter to us two; would you like to go and see the guard exercise ?'

'Oh yes, yes, *cara mamma*! *Madre mia*—will you please ask Luigi for those poems ?'

'Yes, I will recollect. Let us get ready.'

The institution of the civic guard in July, 1847, had been a great boon to the Roman ladies, who, instead of walking in the Corso or on the Pincio, went to see the guard drilled at its various quarters ; and as nearly every one had a brother, a husband, or a lover in its ranks, the ladies took a personal interest in it, called it 'Our guard,' and were never tired of rushing to their windows to see the blue uniforms and red plumes go by. The children, instead of playing at ball, and *campana*, and *maroncino*, put paper helmets on, and played at '*la Guerra Austriaca.*' Rome resounded with martial music and measured steps ; in certain piazzas the echoes must have been weary of repeating the word of command, and the clang of muskets striking on the ground. But one thing was apt to make the drill somewhat unmartial ; the soldiers could never by any possibility be got together till at least an hour after the right time, and a wet day was apt to send them home under umbrellas, or keep them away altogether; it was so hard to be obliged to soil the new uniforms which they had bought for themselves. They had not yet had any experience of real war ; though how gallantly they fought when it came all the world knows; and that the Romans were no fairweather soldiers when they fought for house and hearth in the siege of their city. The spirit which both Mazzini and the

Papiste had secretly fostered for their own purposes, and which had threatened to break into rebellion, now took its legitimate direction; the Romans looked eagerly forward to joining in the war of independence, and the party of whom Leone had in past years been the leader, and had in fact created, to a man were eager to join it at once. To this all his labours had long been directed, and a universal hope was springing up that the Pope would formally send his troops to aid in the good cause. This was a hope in which all men might join—even the *Papiste* could be patriots here.

An animated scene presented itself to Imelda and her mother. The piazza was full of troops, volunteers from every class in Rome, mostly gallant youths rejoicing in this outlet to their martial ardour. Many were of high rank; the colonels of several regiments were princes, but the substantial middle class furnished the greater number. They turned proud, laughing looks to the bevy of ladies who walked up and down outside the piazza, or stood in groups, talking to each other, watching the manœuvres, and exchanging in the pauses smiles with their friends among the guard. Each passer by, man, woman, or child, lingered to watch the beloved civic guard, and exclaimed, ' *Quanto son carini! quanto son belli! belli, belli, davvero!*' and similar expressions of delight, as if all derived a personal gratification from the gay and gallant aspect of their soldiers.

' *Halte!*'

The exercise ended, the soldiers dispersed; Clementi, Leone, and Ravelli all came up to Signora Olivetti and Imelda, and stood talking for a while. Imelda heard with joy that Irene would very speedily return, and said to Leone, 'I had a letter from her last week, and she says she is going to sing at the Teatro Regio. I am half sorry; I do not like her to appear since that terrible night.'

Leone's face darkened at the recollection. 'Vincenzo wrote me word of it, signorina; he is satisfied, and if Mademoiselle Mori did not sing here, she would go elsewhere, and you would lose her.'

'And you are satisfied too?' asked Imelda, shyly and low. 'She never told me, but people say you have a right to object if you choose.'

'I do not mind confiding our engagement to you, and I only wonder she did not,' said Leone, while his peculiarly sweet smile banished his previous quiet, stern look, and replaced it with sunshine. 'We merely do not announce it, because long engagements such as ours are so unusual.'

Imelda forgot to answer, because she heard her mother saying, 'Why should you send the book, Luigi? Can you not bring it this evening?'

'I and Clementi are going to Circolo Nota, and then into the Trastevere.'

'Bring it to-morrow, then. Perhaps Signor Nota will give us the pleasure of his company?'

Leone willingly agreed. He too was going to the Circolo, a kind of club which had several meeting places in Rome, where the members read the newspapers and discussed politics—a very great novelty in Rome. It had been instituted with the full approval of Government, who would now gladly have put it down, had they dared; but these were not days for taking away a privilege once granted. Nota had planned and founded the one which bore his name, and its politics were guided by him, and therefore much more sensible and moderate than those of some others, which were fast becoming mere hotbeds of sedition.

As the young men were about to bid Signora Olivetti good day, a sound began to rise, full half a mile off, indistinct yet full, like a flood, coming from the direction of the Vatican, and a multitude of voices blended into one all along the streets— '*Pio Nono, Pio Nono—il Papa—viva, vi-va !* '

' Oh, we shall see the Pope,' cried Imelda, and presently, surrounded by the usual escort, appeared the coach of the Pope, who leaned forward with a serene, well-pleased aspect, and raised his hand to bless the people, all kneeling as he passed. A hurricane of applause pursued it, and every one looked delighted and cheerful, as if the sight of Pio Nono had brightened the whole day. His popularity had little decreased as yet with the populace.

Nota and his two friends entered the Circolo together, and were warmly welcomed by the assembly, which was large and increasing. Reforms and popular education were the subjects brought forward by Nota, and warmly discussed, taking, at last, the turn of arguing what future Government might be desirable for Rome. A lay element had been introduced by Pio Nono into the hitherto strictly ecclesiastical ministry, but so slowly and partially, that it rather tantalised, than satisfied, the unruly and impatient people. The discussion grew vehement ; Leone rose and spoke with effect and moderation ; Clementi followed.

' My friends, I am about to draw a picture of a certain century ; it matters little which or when.

It was spent in terror, suspicion, pain. No man could trust his friend, his wife, his servant; all or each might be a spy, might deliver him to death, or imprisonment; was encouraged to do this, and profited by it. There was a spy in every chamber, and an executioner at each man's door. A word, a look, a false and anonymous accusation brought death on high and low. This man is rich; he seeks popularity; he would rebel. Let him die and his estates be confiscated. This one lives retired; he studies unlawful sciences—he is a magician—he is discontented. Let him pursue his meditations in prison! Anguish and dread filled Rome. My friends, do I see you imagining that I speak of a time within your own recollections? that I can mean a Christian century, when the Vicar of the apostles sits on the throne of St. Peter? Out on such profane thoughts; no holy prelate, or abbot, or friar could exist in such days as those; we know well how meek and lowly, how wedded to poverty they are, and ever have been. We know how closely the successors of St. Peter have copied his great example. Fie! my friends, are you dreaming, that you apply my words so rashly! Leave it to the heretics to say

> ' " Quegli ch' usurpa in terra il luogo mio,
> Il luogo mio, il luogo mio che vaca
> Nella presenza del Figliuol di Dio!
> Fatto ha del cimiterio mio cloaca! "

It cannot be a Christian, who has had fair means of knowing the truth, who says such scandalous words; it must be some Catharo, or Hussite, or Lutheran! Far from me be such profanity! I spoke of the reign of Domitian!'

The whole assembly was thrilled by the auda-

cious irony of this speech, and of the description
which, if not applicable to the mild rule of Pio
Nono, might have served without altering a word
for the reigns when Sanfedism triumphed; and
another speaker instantly started up to point out,
that where the whole power was concentrated in
the hands of one man, the safety of the people
must necessarily be in peril—a Commodus might
follow an Aurelius, and safety belonged to a republic alone.

Again Nota replied, and the witchery of his
eloquence silenced the malcontents, and called
forth shouts of applause; and the discussion
closed, but the stinging speech of Clementi was
reported all over Rome.

'Come, Leone, before we separate, improvise
us something!' was next the cry. He looked
round, smiling; the poet felt himself a king.
Many voices proposed subjects for his muse; he
chose from them 'Orlando Avogado at Genoa'—
leant his head on his hand for a moment in
thought, and then looked up with the kindling
expression of one whose soul is full of a great
subject. He sang of Genoa, ready to perish
among nations, racked with divisions—of the
alarm bell, which suddenly called her citizens by
night to the great piazza, where they found no
enemy, but their venerable archbishop and his
clergy, who, holding aloft the crucifix, bade them
be at peace together for His sake who died for
them. The measured rhyme grew low and mournful, and then rose into passionate earnestness, as
Leone told of Avogado, standing weeping before
the throng, while he declared that the honour of
his dead ancestors forbade him to forgive their
and his hereditary foes—ay, though all Genoa

should perish by his refusal. After a moment's pause, the *improvisatore* continued speaking in the person of Genoa, in words that must lose half their force and beauty when translated from their own idiom : 'Son, thou refusest life to thy mother ! thou wouldst slay her who gave thee birth, for thou hast no mother so near to thee as I; and I bid thee go to the tombs of the dead, and hearken what their voices say to thee, and then return ! And he went, and listened in thy Campo Santo and the bones of the dead were stirred, and their voices bade him be no more an Avogado, but an Italian !'

'Oh, my friends !' Leone continued with energy, 'is there no lesson for us here ? Are we but Romans—but Florentines—but Sardinians? When shall we learn to call ourselves Italians ? Our country calls us, once the queen of kingdoms, long a bondslave—she holds out her chained hands imploringly to her children ! Let us lay aside our feuds, our miserable private interests, let us forth and fight for her ; little matter whether the crowns we win be laurel and parsley—wreaths of victory, or the hyacinth and cypress—garlands of the dead. Let Italy's children answer her voice ; let Rome as of old be foremost in the combat, and the patriot's heart shall beat faster, and the tyrant tremble in his stronghold, as he hears the multitude advancing to deliver her. But O friends, O brethren, beware lest false hopes, meaner motives, dazzle you and lead you aside ; be generous, and salvation is at hand ; be self-seeking madmen, and these amber and rosy lights which flush the horizon will prove no dawn of a glorious day, but the treacherous splendour and the gorgeous colouring which pre-cede the sunset and the storm.'

Leone's voice was exquisitely melodious as well as powerful, and always exercised a singular spell over his audience. While he recited, there was intense silence, every face turned towards him; each sentiment, each passion he described, reflected on the countenances of his listeners; and as he ended, out burst applause, unanimous, deafening, on all sides. Oh southern audience and southern poet, where are now the hearts that beat so high at the name of Italy? Are those charmed lays quite forgotten, or do some yet cherish their remembrance and murmur them, as they pass a lowly grave in the Roman Campo Santo?

Leone left the *Circolo* in company with Ravelli and one or two more, to seek a less refined *réunion*, at a *locanda* or tavern in the Trastevere, frequented by the lower class, hitherto the bitter enemy of the *bourgeoisie*, with which it had always been at war, and had derided at every possible opportunity. But the middle class had of late studiously conciliated it, and mingled as much as possible with it; and a friendly feeling sprang up which has lasted ever since. Leone improvised for the populace as willingly as for the *Circolo*, and was literally idolized by the Trasteverini, themselves orators and poets by nature. Clementi did not accompany them; he sought a small secret meeting, where were Cecchi and a few more of the same politics, whose debates were carried on in mystery and darkness—a secret society very unlike Leone's. These men met, and exasperated themselves by recalling past wrongs and predicting future oppression, and the dream of a republic was ever in their minds.

Their movements were duly reported to his

uncle, who thus was kept well acquainted with the views and purposes of both the moderate and ultra-liberals, so as to be able to forge, with his colleagues, means of opposition to them, counteracting their schemes on the one hand, and the measures suggested by the Pope on the other. Monsignore Clementi and his party formed, as it were, a dense resisting atmosphere, through which the reforms commanded by Pio Nono, and ardently desired by the liberals, could not penetrate, or at all events struggled so slowly that they had more the air of tardy concessions than wise and original measures. The Pope and a few enlightened counsellors, such as Padre Rinaldi, might debate and suggest reforms, but they were suffered to drop, or strenuously resisted, by the Ministers who should have carried them out ; and the Romans began to wonder whether Pio Nono were sincere, or whether the blame rested with those about him, and a cry had more than once been heard of ' Long reign Pio Nono, but Pio Nono *alone !*' words equally unpleasing to the Ministers and to the gentle Pope, whose timid conscientiousness was ever taking alarm, and was ever appealed to by men who sought to terrify him from the paths of reform.

Ravelli told Leone, as they walked together, of Signora Olivetti's request concerning the poems, and confided to him that he had given a copy to Gemma, which by some chance had fallen into the hands of Monsignore Clementi, who had carried it off. Ravelli was brimful of delight at the idea of the little volume being submitted to an assembly of Monsiguore Clementi's friends, and drew an imaginary sketch of their aspects and their comments as the worthy prelate read them aloud, having first sprinkled them with holy water!

A copy was duly sent to Casa Olivetti, and Imelda passed an afternoon between studying it, and a MS. collection of proverbs, that she might be well prepared for the evening, when there was to be a *società*. It was Signora Olivetti's usual evening for receiving guests, and the younger ones usually passed the time in some game, now and then of *oca*, or *gatto cieco* or blind man's buff, but more often in what was quieter and more instructive, said their mothers—namely, proverbs.

The party always met rather early, and seldom staid long, on account of Signor Olivetti's known dislike to late hours; and seldom any but the same set met together. They were all intimate, and nearly all of the middle class, with the exception of the Clementi. There was frequently dancing, and always more or less of card playing, and those who assembled here every Thursday, also met continually at each other's houses on the remaining days of the week.

The room began to fill; Imelda was soon surrounded by friends of her own age; Leone entered, and exchanged a pleasant look and a few confidential words with her respecting a letter from Irene—their friendship had progressed wonderfully since the day before. A wave of sound, in which particular voices were absorbed, began to rise, but still Ravelli had not come, though his father and mother were there, and when he appeared, his look did not promise much for Imelda; nor did he approach Gemma. Signora Olivetti perceived that there had been a quarrel with her, or else a battle in Casa Ravelli; she could not decide which.

He stood conversing with a knot of gentlemen about a late riot, peremptorily put down by the civic guard, and then began to inquire whether Signor Olivetti really intended to go to Germany.

'If I had any choice, I should not go now, especially for an indefinite time,' said Signor Olivetti; 'it is the last place where a Roman is likely to be welcome; but this is business which ——' the rest was inaudible beyond where they stood. Words floated round by which the general tenor of conversation through the room might be guessed—'young Italy,' 'Mazzini,' 'the municipal council,' 'deputies,' 'Austrians,' 'Jesuits,' with the pantomime and vehemence inseparable from the conversation of Italians, especially at such a time, when all Rome was in the utmost excitement, resolute to expel the Jesuits, and looking breathlessly for great news from Sardinia.

When Signor Olivetti turned to speak to a new comer, Ravelli threw himself into an ardent discussion on Neapolitan policy, and the ever-burning offence of the Austrians in Ferrara. Imelda was near enough to hear, and he suddenly perceived her extreme interest in the debate, and, breaking it off, soon came to a seat by her side. It was very soothing to perceive that he was welcome—very refreshing after a stormy interview with Gemma, who had delighted in trying her power over him to the utmost, from the day that he had returned to her a willing slave. He was always lured back after every quarrel; but, when angry and out of patience with her and himself, the innocent, unconscious flattery in Imelda's glad looks was irresistible.

'So you are patriotic enough to like politics,'

said he, with a smile, half guessing it was only because he was one of the speakers.

'Sometimes,' said Imelda. 'Oh, I like listening very often; you know papa and mamma talk a great deal to each other about the times. Luigi, I have read Signor Nota's poems.'

'You! what could induce you? you don't mean that you understand them?'

'I like this,' said Imelda, laying her finger on a page of the volume.

'Oh, that—I forgot it. Yes, it is very pretty,' said Ravelli, turning the leaves, and looking at one poem after another, while his eyes sparkled as he recognised each familiar war cry, '*Italia Ancella*,' '*Italia libera*,' '*Il Bilancio della Morte*.' 'Ah, this is grand!' he broke out, repeating verse after verse by heart—'that is strong—one could fight on that!' then, recollecting to whom he was speaking, he laughed, and said, 'I forgot that they could not be much in your line.'

Gemma had perceived that the two were in conversation, and took a chair by Imelda; but her aunt called her to sing, being thereto instigated by Signora Olivetti, and with a clouded brow she went to the piano. Imelda said, 'I did like those verses, Luigi; Gemma told me you often talk of such things, and indeed I care for them too.'

'When did Gemma talk to you of me?'

He asked so quickly and sternly that Imelda was thoroughly frightened, and replied entreatingly, 'I did not mean to say anything wrong.'

'I did not say that you had,' answered Luigi, disarmed by the pleading voice, and unable to help smiling. 'How are you to go through the world, silly child, if you think so much of a hasty tone?'

His manner was almost caressing, and she answered gaily, and repeated what Gemma had said. Luigi's mental comment was that no woman could resist tormenting another, but he resented, inconsistently enough, Gemma's conduct towards Imelda. Perhaps the reason of his displeasure might be the one he gave to himself, that he had the same regard for Imelda, as for a sister.

She was happy now, yet there was something wanting to her; he spoke of her, never of himself. One word of confidence would have been worth all these attentions, but she hardly knew what it was that she missed. When Gemma had finished her song she approached again, but was intercepted by Leone, who quietly enjoyed the knowledge that she was furious at being detained by him in conversation, and that he was giving Imelda some more happy moments. He met Signora Olivetti's eye, and the mutual slight smile which they involuntarily exchanged, showed that each comprehended the other's tactics; and that Leone had made her his fast friend.

In a little while all the party were summoned to play at proverbs, and the dialogue between Imelda and Luigi ceased; all the groups were merged into a circle, every one took the name of a flower or fruit; and Leone began the game by throwing a handkerchief to a lady who had chosen to be a lily, with the words—

> ' From my hand, my bird has fled
> To this lily's breast, and said—'

'*Cosa disse?* what did it say?' demanded the lily; and Leone answered quick as light, '*Veronese, bella mano*,' quoting a well-known proverb, amid

great applause; for the lady was of Verona, and
really had a pretty hand. Without losing an
instant she passed the handkerchief with the same
form of words to Signor Olivetti, and in answer to
his '*Cosa disse ?*' maliciously alluded to his proposed journey with 'a rolling stone gathers no
moss;' and the war of proverbs and laughter grew
so fast and furious, that the merits of the game,
as far as quietness counted, were extremely pro-
blematical.

CHAPTER II.

Those lips are thine—thy own sweet smile I see,
The same that oft in childhood solaced me ;
Faithful remembrancer of one so dear !
O ! welcome guest, though unexpected here.

COWPER.

ON his way home from his business, the evening before Irene returned to Rome, Leone was joined by Count Clementi, as he turned into a street full of shops, where old furniture, curiosities, and pictures were sold. They lingered to look in at the windows and to laugh at the vile copies or worthless originals, which were exposed to catch the eye and empty the purse of unwary foreigners.

'Alas, Beatrice Cenci !' said Clementi, ' if you had committed all the crimes of which you are accused, sufficient punishment is it to be caricatured in every picture-magazine. And, behold Titian's unwearied daughter still holding her casket, of which no charitable person comes to relieve her. And who shall say our prospects are not cheerful, when Guido's Hope looks out from every corner ! Here is a variety, Heaven be thanked—a martyrdom ; a wretch with his mouth open and frogs tumbling out ! No, I am wrong ; it is an exorcism, and doubtless the frogs represent the evil spirits of covetousness and ambition, which the priest is about to appropriate to himself.'

' Martyrdom ! exorcism ! don't you see the likeness ?' exclaimed Leone.

'Likeness! to what imp of darkness?   Dante might have seen this unfortunate, perhaps ; but I do not own him as an acquaintance, for he surely is in purgatory, and my visit to that region is yet to make.'

'Are you blind, count? look here—this painting far back !'

'I see,' cried Clementi, approaching closer. 'Irene! this is no chance likeness! extraordinary! the same, and yet no, this face is less noble, more beautiful, perhaps.'

'It is doubtless the portrait of her mother ; see ! the Sora costume ; this is one of the lost pictures,' said Leone, entering the shop in haste. The owner civilly gave the painting into his hands, but observed that he had sold it that morning.

'Sold! I must have it at any price ; see here is the name, V. Moore, and the date—how came this into your hands ?'

Even the tempting offer of any price was vain, to the extreme and visible regret of the dealer ; an English gentleman had bought it, and it was to be sent the next day to the Hôtel de Russie. It had been bought from the Monte di Pietà, and hung long on hand—only that morning the picture dealer had esteemed himself in special luck at having sold it, and here was Leone come to embitter his satisfaction with his 'any price.'

'It is a good picture; the colouring so rich, and the handling free—a valuable work, indeed,' said he, regretfully, his estimation of it rising every moment.

Count Clementi asked the Englishman's name, and obtained his card.

'What brings him here at this time of year? If he had come in the spring he must have heard Mademoiselle Mori sing, and no doubt would in courtesy have given this up,' he remarked ; but the colour came into Leone's olive cheek, and he said quickly,

'It is not a gift to Mademoiselle Mori, it is the picture of Irene's mother that I desire.'

'Is it really the portrait of Mademoiselle Mori's mother?' asked the dealer with great interest. '*Per Bacco!* had I known that, I might have sold it long ago ; it should have been where all could see it, instead of in a lumber room whence I only brought it yesterday. I would have offered it to Mademoiselle Mori myself. Ah, signori! What a voice! what grace! what sentiment! Unfortunate that I am to know the value of this picture too late!'

Count Clementi frowned : he would have gladly hidden Irene from all eyes save his own, and each time, that he was forced to remember she belonged to public life, caused him a sharp pang, while Leone was proud to hear the talents of his promised bride acknowledged, and said cordially, 'At least I will tell her of your good wishes, my friend.'

'Stay,' said Clementi, looking at the card, 'let me think—I believe I know a way of getting at this man, if you will trust me with the matter.'

Leone gladly acquiesced, and Count Clementi lost no time in calling at the Hôtel de Russie and explaining as much as was necessary of the story to the Englishman, who had only bought the picture because he wanted two or three to furnish his walls in England, and readily gave it up, assuring the count he did not value it in the least, with true English bluntness, contrasting amusingly with the Italian's polished courtesy. The painting was carried to Cecchi's abode, and hung up by Leone under the delighted superintendence of the padrona.

How did Leone guess the exact hour at which Mrs. Dalzell's carriage would drive into the quadrangle of Palazzo Clementi next day? or, if he saw it at a distance, how could he manage to be at the foot of the great staircase, ready to receive Irene as she sprang lightly out? Madame Marriotti had been deposited at her own residence; Mrs. Dalzell alighted after Irene, and lastly Vincenzo, and they stood exchanging welcomes; but Leone saw that Vincenzo was leaning against the wall for support, and that he looked very thin and invalid-like, though the meeting had called a flush to his cheek.

'Come, we shall talk better upstairs,' said Leone, putting his arm round him; 'I am going to take you there. What have you been doing to yourself, Vincenzino?'

'This naughty boy has been ill, or we should have been here a fortnight ago,' said Mrs. Dalzell; 'he was so anxious to come that the doctor and I could hardly manage him; as for Irene, she had the strongest persuasion that he required his native air.'

'Why did not Irene tell me, Vincenzo?' said Leone, looking at him with a mixture of affection and reproach in his bright hazel eyes. 'I would have been with you long ago.'

'I would not let her; I meant to get well

forthwith,' replied Vincenzo, smiling, as they slowly ascended the stairs, and stopped to rest in the first corridor. 'There is no great matter amiss.' But before they reached the third, Leone's support was increased to almost carrying him. Irene had sprung upstairs many minutes before to see that the door was open and his room ready for him, and being espied by Carmela, who, defying all rules, was chattering at the door to the baker's boy, and by Menica, looking out of the kitchen window; both ran to meet her with joyous and familiar welcomes, to which was soon added Madama Cecchi's, as the up-raised voices reached her in her bed-room.

'Ah! my signorina! *ben tornata*—welcome back! welcome as rain in August! How well she looks! where are Vincenzo and Lady Dallay?' her nearest approach to Mrs. Dalzell's name. 'Pieces of macaroni, that you are! go along—' this was to the two maids, who, however, did not stir a step. '*Gazze ladre*, magpies! always staring about; ah, here, here they are!'

'Now you are not to let Vincenzo stop one minute,' said Irene; 'he is sadly tired;' and her bright face became over-clouded, as she watched his slow progress along the *loggia*.

'*Ma cos'è!* what is it? ill!' exclaimed Madama Cecchi, in dismay. '*Cos'è, signorina mia?*'

Vincenzo was not too weary to pause and answer the welcome of the two girls; and Mrs. Dalzell also stopped to speak to them, for she had grown sufficiently Italian to comprehend that servants consider themselves part of the family, and entitled to share in its joys and griefs. Before Leone knew

what Madama Cecchi was about, she had pounced
on Vincenzo, and conveyed him into his sitting-
room, laying him down on the sofa laughing and
submissive, and then vanishing with a promptitude
that showed some further scheme for his benefit
to be in her mind. He lay, tired and happy, on
the couch, which felt so comfortably familiar, and
let Irene arrange it as she liked. She was so
much occupied with him that at first she had
eyes for nothing else; until standing behind his
sofa, while she softly put the hair away from his
forehead, she was commencing something which
ended in a breathless 'Leone! Leone!' The cry
made Vincenzo look up hastily to follow her
glance. He actually started upright! '*Il ritratto!*
our picture!—our mother!'

'Leone, this is your doing,' said Irene, with
glistening eyes. 'It must be—don't let it be
any one else's—'

'Mine in part, Irene; but you must thank
Count Clementi, too; I must tell you how I
found it.'

'Eh, eh! what do they say to this fine *beffana?*'
asked Madama Cecchi, returning with a tray of
coffee; 'there, I had to give up seeing the dis-
covery because I can't trust that *figliaccia* Carmela to make a cup of coffee, though I set it to
boil myself. Now, signor, I made it, and speaking
with respect, it is very good—so drink.'

While the travellers ate and drank, Leone told
the history of the picture amid an interest more
easily imagined than described. All the circumstances were told and retold and commented on,
while the brother and sister looked at the portrait,

as if they could think of nothing else. Something
of both father and mother seemed restored to them.
Not till the first excitement had passed could they
let even Mrs. Dalzell share their rejoicing ; and she
did not attempt to mingle in the rapid questions
and answers, but silently convinced herself that, in
this work at all events, Vincent Moore had shown
himself an excellent artist. Both his children bore
a little likeness to it ; Irene now resembled it more
than she had done as a child, but her countenance
was of a nobler cast, with more soul, more intellect, and less actual beauty, than that of her
young mother. It was strange to think that the
daughter was now older than the mother had been,
when that lovely face was drawn ; hard to believe that
an original had existed and passed away without
leaving a trace in the world, which had gone on
without her ; for though we all know that we
shall die to be forgotten, it is almost impossible
to realize oblivion, and utter separation from the
world.

'Now, I shall not say a word about the civic
guard or anything else to-night,' said Irene, 'or
Vincenzo will get excited, and be too tired to sleep ;
so you must say good night, Leone.'

'I suppose I must not be selfish, then,' said
Leone.

'Yes, indeed ; I don't want her—Irene, if you
did read to me to-night, I could not attend.
Don't come—and why should I go to bed? You
are growing intolerably tyrannical! you will be
busy all to-morrow with the theatre affairs, and
not have a moment for Leone.'

'Meanwhile time is passing, Vincenzino.'

' It has been doing that ever since the flood.
Well, I will submit, if you will stay with the
signor here.'

' The signor is going to be your valet,' said
Leone; 'I shall not let him excite himself, Irene.'

' Oh, I can trust you,' said Irene, with a bright,
confiding look, and, while Leone helped Vincenzo
to his room, which opened out of the one where
they sat, she staid and listened as Mrs. Dalzell
talked.

She said, ' He is less tired than I expected;
this journey being over is a great weight off my
mind; I quite dreaded it. Now, Leone will look
after him, and no one is more gentle and handy
with an invalid, and it will be a relief to you
to know he will look in and cheer Vincenzo when
you must be busy. How well Leone looks!
I always like seeing him with Vincenzo; the
friendship of men, when it is real, always strikes
me as singularly beautiful. When I was a child
there was no Old Testament story I loved so
much as that of Jonathan and David.'

' I do not think though that it is really " passing the love of women," ' said the betrothed
bride.

' Of women for women, perhaps, Irene; but after
all, it has a feminine element in it. You will not
quarrel with me for what I am going to say now,
at all events—that Ravelli and Leone are another
pair whom I particularly enjoy; Ravelli is such
a fine fellow—so completely the perfection of
animal health and spirits—while Leone is like a
picture of Titian's or Morone's—just one of those
southern faces, dark complexioned, with such a

vivid, intense expression, and yet almost melancholy in repose.'

Leone deserved all that she said; he had that suppleness of limb which makes every motion graceful; the middle stature and the taper hands of the southern nations of Europe, and the look of power—of intellect—that indescribable air which gives to the paintings of which she had spoken, their individuality, their patrician look. Irene's eyes thanked her, and induced her to add, 'Do you know, Leone has often reminded me of Raphael; I think he has just the same brave, gentle, generous spirit, the same power of winning love; I could fancy that it might be said of him also, " that he never had an enemy." '

'Ah, signora, the world is worse now than it was in Raphael's time; Leone has a great many enemies.'

The outer bell rang, and there entered Count Clementi.

'Irene!' he exclaimed, with a flash of unconcealed delight; then, turning to Mrs. Dalzell—'Unreasonable that I am, signora! but I could not wait till to-morrow to hear how my friends are. Where is Vincenzo?'

Irene explained, and something passed on the events which had taken place during her absence. All concerning Gemma's marriage had been reported by letter, but still seemed so dark and mysterious, that she wanted to ask innumerable questions. Clementi enlightened her very little, though he had long since wormed out enough to show him the truth; he was so acute, that a single word was enough to reveal to him a whole plot. He paid but a short visit.

As he rose to take leave, Irene said earnestly, 'There is something for which Leone tells me I must partly thank you, count, if I only knew how'—she glanced at the painting.

'I too have a mother,' replied Clementi, with feeling, 'and I knew this portrait must be inestimable to you.'

'It is, and that is all the thanks I can give you.'

'Sometimes think of me as well as of Leone, when you look at it,' he answered, with one quickly-withdrawn look, which told her that the attachment which he had never named to her since she had confided to him her engagement to Leone, was as fervid as ever. She could not be angry at that unconscious betrayal—unconscious she deemed it—and knowing, deep in her own heart, the bliss of love returned, what could she do but pity him? His feelings towards her were, indeed, intense and genuine, and his usual entire suppression of them gave them double emphasis when revealed. Both ladies were silent when he was gone; Mrs. Dalzell confirmed in an old suspicion, Irene pensive. She looked up with glad animation when Leone returned, reporting Vincenzo to be asleep.

'You are a capital nurse,' said Mrs. Dalzell; 'he has had miserable nights of late from incessant restlessness, almost worse than pain; and now, after the journey which we all dreaded, you have mesmerised him into going quietly to sleep. Now, Signor Nota, let us hear how public events are progressing; even Tuscany was growing disquieted before we left it, and I quite pitied an Austrian when he appeared in Florence.'

'Leone! I have something to show you!' Irene went away, and returned waving a green banner, whereon were embroidered the Papal arms. 'See, my contribution to your Circolo; I chose the colour of Hope—do you approve? Mind you carry it yourself the very first time that Circolo Nota marches out in procession.'

All that Leone had to tell showed how much the popular movement had deepened and widened; how strong was the love of independence, the national spirit awakening throughout Italy, one that would not merely break out in partial revolts to be quenched in blood, and leaving no traces except in heavier chains and broken hearts; but a strong, united, vigorous effort in a great cause, which should swallow up minor jealousies. Irene brought Tuscan news to compare with Roman, and asked eagerly how the endeavour to conciliate the *basso ceto* prospered.

'Our alliance is striking root deep and wide,' said Leone; 'there are noble fellows among that class; it is the wealthy—who care for nothing but getting more money—that are our plague spot; men who calculate whether they shall gain a farthing, or lose it, by some event on which a nation's destiny depends—who live in the midst of earthquakes, and buy, and sell, and eat, and drink without so much as knowing that men's houses are falling on their heads, and the judgment is at hand. We cannot touch such as these. If we tell them we are starving, they will give us no gold; if we bid them rise up, for we do battle for life, will they arm themselves? No, for they cannot comprehend what we say.'

'They have taken no interest in Italy's past, so they cannot understand the present,' said Irene.

'Exactly—a man cannot put his heart into a cause that he knows nothing about—the present would be a blank, or rather we should seem madmen, if we were set down in the midst of it without the past, out of which it has grown. We must turn to the people, for those above them are deaf and blind.'

'The people! fickle as the waves! Your own proverb says, "He who builds on the people builds on the sand," ' said Mrs. Dalzell.

'There is rock below. No great change was ever effected by rulers alone; Rienzi freed Rome, so did Arnold of Brescia, but only because the hearts of the people were with them.'

'Ah, Leone, what ominous examples!'

'No, Rienzi did not fail till the masses distrusted him; our Romans only want a leader—they have a gallant spirit in them still. Unmanageable fellows!' said Leone, smiling, as a recollection occurred to him; 'I'll tell you what happened the other day, Irene; Luigi and I were in the Trastevere at a *bettola* [a tavern], such is the company I keep in your absence. The Trasteverini came dropping in, with their wives and *dame*—fine brown hardy fellows, and women to match—and they made us signori very welcome; one sang and played the mandoline, then another —then I must improvise something. I thought of a legend I had read somewhere of armed warriors in a magic sleep, spell-bound, till the drawing of a sword and blowing of a horn should wake them '—

'"Woe to the coward that ever he was born,
That did not draw the sword before he blew the horn." '

quoted Mrs. Dalzell.

' Yes, that was the moral, as we blow our horn pretty loudly just now ; but the pith of the story was the warriors sleeping till the hour to serve their country should come. In the midst, a stone was flung through the window among us. The whole party had been listening as if they were spell-bound too—one woman would have made a fine study ; her great black eyes wide open, her finger on her lips, gazing, panting with excitement —but that stone was worse than the horn ; up they all started infuriated, vowing it was an insult to us, the signori, and rushing pell-mell towards the door. Ravelli was next to it, he threw himself against it, and barred the way like a rock, while he shouted out above the uproar, that it was only a sign that some fellow was jealous of his mistress coming without him to the *bettola*. I made them a speech, and all sat down, and began to talk again, seeming pacified ; but first one slipped out, then another, and another, and returned as if nothing had happened. I saw they had fetched their knives, and kept them ready up their sleeves, but nothing more happened that they could twist into an affront to us, and I thought it was all over ; but somehow they discovered who had flung the stone, and that night there was such a fray that the guard had to march out and interfere.'

' Well, now I must bid you good night,' said Mrs. Dalzell, ' and Irene must rest, I think.' She shook hands and went to her own apartment, attended to her door by Leone ; but he could not resist coming back for a few last words with Irene, who asked if he had lately seen his married sister, and if her husband had been less overbearing to him.

He shook his head and a cloud of unspeakable sadness overshadowed his face. 'These politics make a terrible breach in families. You remember the sort of welcome I used to receive in that house?'

'Oh yes—whoever might be there—however large the society might be—-there was always a clapping of hands and rejoicing when you came in.'

'It is not so now. He idolizes Assunta, or I should have been forbidden the house long ago. There was a moment when I thought it had come to that, but I kept silence for Assunta's sake and it passed over, and now they never name politics when I am present—you may guess how easy and agreeable the conversation is—and always a crowd of priests there. But for Assunta's sake I should never go near the place, and even she has been taught to look on me with grief and doubt. Some day she will think herself only too fortunate, if she may disown and forget her brother altogether. But I have my Irene! Ah, Irene, you little know how hard it was to keep silence those long two years, when every day showed me more and more what you were worth!'

'We could not spare those two years,' said Irene, 'and at the time I hardly felt what danger we were all in, though they were dreadful days; sometimes I had to go to my singing lesson, while I was wondering why you had not been near us, and longing for Cecchi to come in and assure us that nothing had happened. If I had foreseen all the suspense and anxiety beforehand, I should never have had courage for it!'

'Irene *mia,* how many of us would have courage

to live, if we could foresee what our lives would be?   But I never contemplated burdening you with our secrets, only Vincenzo could not keep a secret from you!'

'Do you remember that evening when I had been making so many copies of your essay on the " Unity of States"—and one could not be found! I never knew what terror was till then ; I counted my copies till I was bewildered, and still one was gone!   I was convinced that it had been left about, and seized by some spy.'

' I found the poor little conspirator nearly rigid with terror,' said Leone, with affectionate playfulness; 'not daring to alarm Vincenzo, and waiting for Cecchi's return to confess.'

'And you comforted her, and found the sheet of paper crumpled up by Tevere in his basket !' said Irene. 'It does not sound much in the telling, and yet what misery I felt !'

' I very nearly betrayed myself that night,' said Leone.   ' there was nothing for it but to fly, and hear no more thanks.'

' I often wondered how I could forget everything but my music, when my lesson time came,' said Irene. 'All the haunting fear and anxiety—'

' By the same power as that which makes you a good actress,' said Leone; ' you throw yourself entirely into whatever you are doing.'

Irene's holiday was over.   The next day brought a multitude of affairs ; household matters, theatrebusiness, and a visit to Madame Marriotti to see how she was after her journey, and tranquillize her nerves, much disturbed by anxiety regarding a hundred trifles, which were finally entrusted to Irene's care, while Madame Marriotti sat up in

bed, her beloved ermine cloak round her, and a
handkerchief of cardinal's lace on her head, direc-
ting, questioning, and fidgeting, and more than
occupying both her maid and Irene, who could
hardly contrive to get released in time for luncheon.
She found Vincenzo just up, and taking a survey
of his plants; Velvet Cap, over the way, had already
spied him out, and was exchanging a pantomime
of welcome with him across the street; and the
canary, which had gone with them to Florence,
sang loudly, as if in challenge to his friends, and
the songsters opposite were not slow to answer.
Vincenzo was soon weary, and let Irene help him
to the sofa, and give him what he called 'an idle
book,' though he ejaculated, 'What a thing it is
to be so good for nothing!   I wonder why people
are glad to have one back!'

Leone thought him so much less well than when
he left Rome, that he lingered in the evening, till
Vincenzo had gone to bed, to have a private consultation about him with Irene, who said,

' He is less well; the Florentine doctor said he
had worked too hard at his carving, and must give
it up, for the present at all events.   He was so
good and patient about it—Mrs. Dalzell said it
was a beautiful lesson to every one; but it was a
hard trial, and the worst of it is, he has not been
able to begin again.   I thought how terrible it
would be to me to be forbidden to sing—I should
not have been as good about it as he!'

'I think there is but one thing that he allows
to harass him,' said Leone, 'the fear of becoming
dependent, and that must be doubly strong now,
poor dear fellow!   I know he sometimes troubles
himself on the score of being an obstacle in the

way of our marriage. This miserable money, Irene !'

Irene gave one deep, suppressed sigh. Their marriage seemed a very distant prospect. Leone looked at her, his lips unclosed, then shut again ; and, whatever it were that he had been about to say, it was not spoken.

CHAPTER III.

A voice rang through the olive wood with sudden trumpet's
    power:
' We rise on all our hills! come forth! 'tis thy country's
    gathering hour.
There's a gleam of spears by every stream, in each deep,
    winding dell:
Come forth, young man! bid to thy home a brief and proud
    farewell!'
And a maiden's fond adieu was heard, though deep yet brief
    and low;
' In the vigil, in the conflict, love, my prayer shall with
    thee go.'

MRS. HEMANS.

Ire gran furie ho meco.
Ira di patria oppressa, amor de'miei,
E vendetta la terza; si, vendetta.

MONTI.

ANGRY voices were raised outside the sitting-
room door—uplifted—vehement—those of
Madama Cecchi and Carmela, one in accusation,
the other in justification. Evidently the baker's
boy had been detected in holding converse with
the damsel. Tevere might have been used by
this time to similar domestic hurricanes, but his
temper appeared upset by the noise, and he
barked loudly at a distance.

'I tell you it shall not be done,' was distinctly
heard; 'here is Menica, who is twice as pretty as
you—what am I saying! you know you are as

ugly as sin—and when do you see her chattering to any one? If she sees a friend, she salutes and goes by, but you—you have friends among the *vetturini*, the milkmen, the lacqueys—'

'It is very hard,' was returned in sobbing accents, 'if I may not speak to a friend; I wish I were in my own country, where Battista came to talk to me every night for a year under my window, and no one cried scandal; it is the custom there for *promessi sposi*, signora, and I never—'

'Don't talk to me of *promessi sposi*, evil jay— my house is a monastery, and next week you shall go. Menica, Menica, where are you? is not that girl come in?'

Madama Cecchi retreated towards the kitchen, and then a shout of amazement resounded, and the next moment she dragged Menica into Vincenzo's sitting-room, laughing, blushing, and shorn of the shining fair tresses, which had been her glory, and the envy of all her female friends.

'Why, Menica!' cried the two occupants of the room, in amazement, 'what has happened?'

'She has sold them,' gasped Madama Cecchi, between tears and laughter—'the foolish thing has sold her hair! Tell them, Menica *mia*.'

'I had nothing else to give, signor; nothing at all signorina,' said Menica, addressing herself alternately to Leone and Irene; 'they offered me really a folly for my ear-rings, and I must have something to give to the war, and there is the money, Signor Nota,' and she handed over a few pauls to him. I hate the Austrians, and I could not bear to hear that the religious orders had given thousands of pounds, and our nobles were

bringing ever so much more, and Emilia sold her
necklace, and Sigismunda her *spille*; and one this,
and another that, while I had nothing for Italy.
I only wish I could fight; it would do me good to
kill an Austrian;' and therewith she retired,
smoothing down with one hand the short thick
golden hair, which was all that remained of her
long plaits, and followed by the padrona.

Some laughter followed their departure, but it
was, like Madama Cecchi's, allied to tears; the
girl's sacrifice, of what was most precious to her,
touched these Italian hearts, and Leone said,
'Would that we had a few more as devotedly in
earnest!'

He leant his head upon his hand, and Irene
waited, her heart beating slower as she divined
what was coming. Both had looked serious all
the morning, though Leone usually had great
enjoyment of a holiday, and Irene had been telling him good news; the Academy of St. Cecilia
had offered her a diploma, an honour always
welcome to musicians, and giving them a certain
prestige, yet she relapsed into silence and pensive-
ness, and Leone seemed inclined to follow her
example, till the entrance of Menica had roused
them both, only to make them more thoughtful
than before.

'We always said, that our individual happiness
should not interfere with our duty to our country,'
said Leone, as he met the eyes which always had
such a true, confiding expression to answer him
with—'we knew then, that our words would be
put to the proof—'

'I know,' said Irene, seeing that he shrank
from inflicting a blow upon her, for which, how-

ever, she was already prepared; 'you do not think I would hold you back?'

'No, I know you would not. You would have worked me a banner, and buckled on my armour, had we lived in the old times, in spite of your peace-meaning name, my Irene.'

'I did work you a banner,' she answered, with her sweet, brave smile, 'and you shall take it with the volunteers if you like, Leone. '*Segui tua stella.*'

He did not know that she had heard a whisper of the fact that the volunteer corps was really formed, and speedily to go; he asked, 'Who told you, my dearest?'

'Cecchi named it last night. You were the first to enrol yourself, Leone!'

'Did he tell you that too?'

'No, I guessed it, because I should have done the same. I will not be afraid, Leone; I know we shall triumph, if only we are brave and self-denying. We women cannot fight, but we will not hold back those who can.'

'No man ought to think of himself in these days,' said Leone; 'and if he were the veriest coward, the spirit of the women might inspire him. Irene, I *could* not hear of Milan rising, of all Lombardy struggling for freedom, and sit still here! I have been hoping and planning for this corps for months; it was proposed again last night, by Stefanini, and settled in a few minutes; he had proposed it a few hours before to the Ministry. But there is a point that I have kept to discuss with you. All that I have is yours—yesterday, news of an unexpected legacy reached me—a considerable one, enough to make us independent—how much of it can we spare for our soldiers?'

'All, if necessary. Government is too poor to supply half that is wanted. We must not be like that duchess in the siege of Naples, who hid all her gold and jewels till every one was starving, and then repented and brought it—and Queen Joanna thanked her, and said, a bit of bread would be worth more!'

'And our marriage, Irene?'

She looked up, and met the look fixed on her face; but her eyes sank, she blushed deeply, and silence ensued. It was hard to put away happiness indefinitely, hard to feel that they had not enough for themselves and for Italy.

'Irene, you must help me,' said Leone, hurriedly, 'I have hardly dared to think of this.'

She could not summon an answer at first, then she exclaimed, 'Oh, Leone, where would your esteem be, if you found that I thought of ourselves first and of duty last? You might be happy for a little—a very little—while, but soon you would feel that you had not acted up to your own standard, and that I was the cause, and the end would be misery. Whether you let me see it or not, I should know it; but what folly to talk in this way! if you wanted me to help you to decide, you would not be Leone. I know how it must be.'

'Thank you, my dear Irene, you are always true to yourself,' said Leone, with proud, yet halfmournful affection. 'But after all, how long are we to endure this uncertainty? I have shrunk from letting you share my poverty, but I have not courage to wait an indefinite time—poverty or riches would seem alike to me shared with you, but I am asking you to give up fame, Irene.'

Her smile said he might ask what he would, and he eagerly pursued—'When I return then, rich or poor, you will be my wife, Irene? If it were only not the forbidden time now—'

'It is impossible now,' said Irene; for Lent had come round again, and not only would no Roman willingly marry in that season, but a union between a Roman Catholic and a Protestant was illegal in the Papal States, and could not have been solemnized nearer than Florence.

They talked on with the perfect confidence in each other, that only entire esteem, as well as love, can give; and she sat thinking, long after he had discovered that business called him away. There was a blank feeling, now that the excitement was lessened, but no regret; she had not reluctantly yielded what she knew she could not keep; two noble hearts had freely sacrificed their brightest hopes to Italy that day.

Vincenzo presently came in with a part which she was to perform, when the *Teatro Regio* should re-open, and called her attention to a point which had struck him; and she attended, and tried at the piano the effect which he proposed; but when he was satisfied, and, having settled himself on the sofa, asked, 'And what have you and Leone settled this morning? Is the table-cover to be green or red?' she felt that she must tell him what had passed. She would gladly have hidden from him a sacrifice which she knew would grieve him, but she had never had a secret from Vincenzo, and could not begin now. Perhaps it was not easy to speak steadily, but her voice was so serious as she replied,

'We cannot afford luxuries for ourselves now,' that he laughed heartily.

'Luxuries, my dear? are we to have no cloth to our table? I suppose you will soon call the table itself a luxury, and insist upon our dining on the floor!'

'Not quite, but we have been agreeing that every one who can, ought to contribute to the war. Do you know, Menica has actually cut off her beautiful hair, that she may have something to give.'

'Why, I call that heroic, considering who did it?'

'We should have had almost as little to give, if Leone had not just had a legacy left to him.'

'Leone! My dear girl, why did you not tell me at once? Irene, I should be so happy if I knew that he had a right to protect you—you little know how anxious I have been lately. This is the legacy he once spoke of to me!'

'I think it would be as wrong and selfish to think only of marrying and buying and selling now, as ever it was in old days,' said Irene, striving to speak composedly.

'What!' exclaimed Vincenzo, raising himself up hastily to look at the face bent over her sheet of music.

'He always said that our own hopes should come second to Italy,' said Irene, looking up, with dew on her long eyelashes, but with a brave countenance. 'I know it is right—I wish it— it must be so.'

'Second! you shall come second to no one, with my leave!' said Vincenzo, with a spark of impatience; 'if Leone do not know how to value you—but what nonsense! Is Don Quixote going to contribute his whole fortune to the war, or what?'

'If necessary; but that is not all, Vincenzo, the volunteer corps is really organized.'

'Ah, I understand.' Vincenzo sat silent, beating his fingers on his book for some minutes, and then resumed in a different tone. 'Irene, I beg your pardon and Leone's too; it is only that I had not the sense to admire him. He could not do otherwise, being Leone—he is always consistent. Yes, he has lived for this day. I should have felt at once that he was right, had any one but you been concerned. Tell me all about it ; I suppose the matter is to be laid before the Pope?'

'Leone has been asked to head a deputation to the Pope, and Padre Rinaldi says Pio Nono approves; and of course he must know. He told Leone privately that he should go too, as chaplain. The Ministry have decided on forming four regiments, and on offering the command to Durando.'

'When do they go?'

'The time is not fixed ; they were to discuss it again to-night. Leone and Luigi were the first to offer themselves when Prince Stefanini proposed the corps at the Circolo.'

'Ah, Luigi would be ready enough ; he would be delighted to face death any day for the mere excitement ; but Leone would walk up to the cannon's mouth in cold blood for conscience' sake—I guess there is a difference! I wonder whether Signor Ravelli consented, or found that his consent was not asked.'

'Oh, Vincenzo, he is a very fair liberal.'

'Ay, I know, but he may not be ready to spare

his son. What good luck Luigi will think it! But what will Gemma say?'

'She has spell-bound him, and if he wake one minute, he is entranced again the next,' said Irene, impatiently and despairingly; 'if they could be married for three weeks, he would find out how astonishingly infatuated he is.'

'Clementi will not be able to go unless the contessa gets better; poor fellow, he has looked so much harassed since her illness, that I would give anything to comfort him. Have you heard how she is to-day?'

'The same—a bad night. Poor Imelda can hardly have heard yet that Luigi is going. I shall make time to see her to-day, if Mrs. Dalzell will leave me there when she goes for her drive. There she is—will you tell her, Vincenzino? I really must study this part, and I had better take it to my room, for some one else will be coming presently.'

There must have been something unusual in Irene's face, for Mrs. Dalzell asked, as soon as she was gone, what had occurred. Vincenzo told her; and, when Irene returned, she could speak quite calmly about it.

She went to the padrona's sitting-room in the afternoon, and found Cecchi acting carpenter, and nailing up the white window-curtains; he turned round on his elevation half way up a ladder to greet her, asked if Leone had been there, and described the animated scene in the Circolo Nota when the volunteer corps was proposed; his wife added her voice, and Irene found it was well that she had taught herself to feel on this subject as Leone felt, for it was in every mind and on every mouth; nothing was heard of but preparations and contributions; volunteers came forward from every rank, princes, nobles, and commoners; 12,000 men were speedily collected, and two nephews of the Pope were among them; prelates who could not join in person gave large sums, and provided horses for the troops; the Pope publicly expressed his approval, and published a beautiful address to the Italian people, which raised his popularity again to the highest degree; and Rome and her States were in a perfect effervescence of fervour and patriotism. Well might Austria tremble for her power, when Italy rose up as one man, with the gallant Charles Albert at her head, in a war of independence; well might all hearts beat high, and foresee a glorious future!

All private affairs became necessarily of a secondary interest, and yet went on much as usual, since nothing claims attention more tyrannically; and men went to their business, and women attended to their households in the midst of all the excitement, having to turn from the great, and all-important public events even to some such matter as the finding a new servant.

This was an affliction which came upon Madama Cecchi amongst others; Carmela was dismissed, and another had to be found in her place. Carmela recalled one evening to Mrs. Dalzell's mind that she was going, by exchanging the customary '*Felice sera, signora; non occor, altro?*' for '*Addio, signora, non ritorno più!*' She looked very merry; leaving her place in disgrace did not seem to weigh on her spirits. Cecchi came in later, with the tea-kettle, attired in a long dressing-gown and velvet cap—his

E 2

usual in-doors costume, and was invited to stay to
tea with Mrs. Dalzell, which he laughingly declined,
but lingered to exchange a few words with his lodger,
as he always liked to do, but never had a chance
of effecting when his wife was near. Mrs. Dalzell asked if they had found a servant in Carmela's
place. He lifted his shoulders by way of reply,
and arched his eyebrows, saying, ' My wife saw a
woman this morning, who says that she lived
eleven years with a family here, was treated as
their daughter in a long illness, married from
their house—she wants a place.'

' That sounds very promising.'

He gave a peculiar half laugh. ' If it be true,
signora ; who can say ?'

' But she gave you a reference ?'

' Yes, yes, she gave us a reference, but masters
and mistresses do not like to tell the truth; they
are afraid. The best thing would be to oblige
every servant to bring a written character from the
police; we shall pass that measure some day.'

' I suppose this person cannot have invented such
a story ?'

' Who knows ?' repeated Cecchi, with the same
laugh. ' We shall see.'

' Where is Signora Cecchi to-night ?'

' In society.'

' Alone ? You never go, signor.'

He shook his head. He had been mixed up in
some past political troubles, and marked out as a
victim. His employment had been taken from him,
the fine imposed on him had made him almost a
beggar; and the suspense, the terror, and indescribable harass of the whole affair had thrown him
into a long illness, from which he rose a dangerous,

embittered man, brooding over his wrongs, and cherishing a sullen, intense hatred against the Government which had ruined him. He refused pertinaciously to enter into society again, and for more than a year after his misfortunes had fled to his room at the first sound of a visitor's voice. A friend had succeeded in finding for him some employment, which had saved him from both starvation and becoming a monomaniac, a state to which enforced idleness and fear of the future was fast bringing him. He had a cowed look as if the iron hand of power were still griping him; ordinarily he would not speak of the past, but sat silent, taking no part in any conversation; but sometimes a chance word would rouse him into such fierce passion, that even his wife, herself a fiery spirit, was terrified, and had privately besought Mrs. Dalzell never to name politics to him, if any one were present.

'I go to fetch my wife,' was his reply to Mrs. Dalzell; 'that suffices.'

'Have you heard this article in the English papers, signor? Pray sit down, and as Irene is not here, I must translate it myself. What do you say to this?'

'Italy can act without foreign aid,' was Cecchi's comment as she concluded. 'She must rely on herself; we want nothing, but that the other European Powers should not interfere; we have a right to be governed as we please. We want no Kings or Popes here—let us have a republic, say I. Popes—every abuse that we groan under arises from the Popes; how much blood has their temporal power cost! and as for the spiritual, the Popedom is a worn-out mass of deceit and iniquity, which is crumbling down from its own decrepitude.'

'But you need not reject friendly foreign interference,' said Mrs. Dalzell, who had by no means
intended to rouse the Red Republican spirit.

'Intervention—intervention! we had the same
thing in '31—fighting. Childish weakness, treachery! What became of Menotti? where is
Zucchi? They put their trust in princes; ask
the Austrians where they are—the Austrians, I
say, who have always played us false; ask the
French, to whom we are eternally trusting! Italy
must be her own deliverer and protector, if ever
she is to hold up her head among nations. We
have been like serpents too long; they have said
to us, "Dust thou shalt eat," and dust we have
eaten, and have crawled before them; but a day
of account comes, and our tyrants shall learn that
we can sting as well as crawl. Then let those
beware who lurk among us to betray—traitors like
that turncoat Pellegrini Rossi; it would be a good
deed to end that man's course!'

A fierce and evil spirit gleamed in the eye of
this man, usually so subdued and silent. Mrs.
Dalzell answered seriously, 'I know what some of
you say of Count Rossi; but the reason of your
prejudice I cannot understand, though I have
heard you and Signor Nota argue the point.
Exiled for Italy's sake, liberal, brave, he returns
here under the most favourable auspices—'

'French, French, he is French at heart; it will
soon come out plainly.'

The door-bell rang; Menica opened it, and
Leone was heard speaking. The slight interrup-
tion cooled Cecchi at once; he relapsed into his
usual quiescent mood; the fire was quenched, the
menacing accent gone, he rose, courteously wished

his lodger good night, and went back to his accounts and his pipe in the kitchen, where he habitually sat, never entering his wife's sitting-room till an hour when all chance of visitors was over.

Madama Cecchi went to inquire the new domestic's character the next day; when she returned she came to Mrs. Dalzell.

'Ah, signora! I hear you have rung twice, and Menica was out *a far le spese*—to buy some little matters, and I was absent, too; it is not once in a year that I leave the house, as you know, and it lacerates my heart to think you should have been inconvenienced.'

'It does not matter, I assure you.'

'I beg a thousand pardons for myself and Menica, but I went to get this woman's character; ah, Heaven! Heaven! these servants! Not a word of truth—she lived three months with these people, and left them because she was a thief.'

'Is it possible?'

'Too true, signora; that is the way with them all. She supposed, no doubt, that I should not take the trouble to ask her character. When I see her to-morrow—ah! see, I bought this silk to make me a dress; does it please you? I shall send for Maria, the milliner, to-night, and make her bring her patterns. Hark—there's our guard!'

She rushed to the window, flung open its two valves, and leant out; Menica had already flown to that in the ante-room; Vincenzo nodded to Madama Cecchi from his; heads had crowded to those opposite, as if the roll of the drum and the long lines of soldiers marching by were a novelty.

'There!' said Madama Cecchi, withdrawing half her person which had been extended forth, and heaving a sigh, 'soon they will be gone! I shall ever regret that Signor Leone's marriage cannot take place at present, but our country must come first; is it not true?'

'Yes, and happily Irene quite agrees with you.'

'*Che brava giovane*—what an angel she is! a man for understanding, and a nun for modesty! What talent! and a character! Say Mademoiselle Mori, and you have said everything! Ah, may she never suffer what I did when she is married! I loved my husband too well—I suffered whatever he did! I never speak of it now, but I feel the pain of that time always—here!' she said, sorrowfully, pressing her hand on her heart. 'These men—they strive, and they labour, and they are occupied; but we women sit at home and weep! Signora, no one can imagine what I underwent from seeing how it would end; and at last he grew morose, harsh, thin as a spectre; he would tell me nothing, but I knew that our affairs went ill. Finally, he was summoned before the tribunal; he came home as white as my chemise, his cousin with him; Nino shut himself up in his own room, and Sandro came to tell me the sentence. When I heard it, I fell down as if I had been dead! And then, how I went from friend to friend, seeking to get some one to help us, but none—none—all failed me. I waited in ante-chambers, I walked miles, I wrote, I entreated, I prayed—in vain! *Sordo come una campana*— and I dared not for my life let my husband know what I was doing; he lay ill, he asked no questions. I was out at dawn and at dusk; I moved heaven and earth, but to no purpose—we had an enemy. Ah, that cardinal, that wild beast who drinks the blood of the Roman people—Heaven reward him as he treated me! I went to seek him with friends, and alone—(I who never had crossed the piazza by myself)! and at all hours! Once I thought I should be admitted, but at the last moment the head of the Collegio Romano entered, and we were all dismissed, I and the other aching hearts that were waiting and trembling in his ante-room! I say no more—we will not speak of this,' concluded Madama Cecchi, her flashing glance quenched in tears. 'Never speak of it to me, signora, and never, I beseech of you, tell my husband that I named it. He knows nothing of all that I tried to do. Who is this coming? the Moorish lady, Madame Marriotti?'

She went to meet 'the little Moorish lady,' as she always called Madame Marriotti from her Spanish complexion. Madame Marriotti was by birth an Andalusian, and her singularly dark complexion formed a great contrast to that of the blue-eyed matron, who was truly Roman in her portliness and dignity.

Madame Marriotti came to inquire why she had not seen Irene for two days, though she had written a note to summon her. Mrs. Dalzell said that Irene had been very busy packing a knapsack, and providing all that it was to contain.

'Ah! now her head will be fuller of young Nota than ever! I am thankful he is going away, however; for I do believe she would have been so excessively foolish as to marry him—and then, adieu, Fame!'

‘ You will have to make up your mind to that, at last, madame !’

‘ We shall see.　I know that you think me more like an old raven than a song bird for croaking my forebodings, and that child, Irene, only smiles at them ; but I am old enough to remember the beginnings of several Popes’ reigns. Take Gregory XVI.—there was nothing talked of then but “ the new Era ” that was beginning ; and what came of that ?　Now, I dare say matters might go on improving ; Pio Nono seems sincere ; but there is no truth in the clergy, no patience in the people !　They are mere parvenus in liberty— don’t know how to bear it meekly ; they were not born to it.　My belief is, that we shall have a re- volution, things will be turned upside down, and then settle just as they used to be ; there will be exiles and fines on all sides ; Nota will certainly be a marked man, and may think himself lucky if he get away before he is clapped into prison. Irene will then have an engagement at Vienna or London ; and he may join her, if they really must marry.’

Mrs. Dalzell could not help laughing at the coolness with which Madame Marriotti settled this agreeable finale to reform and romance, and asked if she had mentioned it to Irene.

‘ Yes, I did,’ said Madame Marriotti, pensively. ‘ Yes, I told her that I was negotiating an engage- ment for her at Vienna, as she would want one when her present one at the Teatro Regio expires. Yes, I am sure that I told her.’

‘ And what did she say ?’

‘ I do not know,’ said Madame Marriotti, in a very dreamy tone ; and Mrs. Dalzell thought it probable that she had only half expressed her meaning to Irene, and had taken it for granted that her auditor knew the whole of the train of thought by instinct, which she was very apt to suppose, thereby often creating remarkable confusion, and always amazed at the stupidity of those who were perplexed by her.

Irene, coming in while she yet spoke, answered all reproaches with a smile, but the next instant, tears filled the girl's eyes, she knelt down, and, hiding her face on Mrs. Dalzell's neck, said, in a broken voice, 'They go next week—I have just heard it.'

'Ah, child, child, why did you fall in love!' said Madame Marriotti, reproachfully yet sympathizing, while Mrs. Dalzell caressed and soothed Irene, and said,

'Irene could not have loved any one nobler or better worth these tears, dear madame! She does not regret having given her heart away!'

Irene raised her head and pressed her kind friend's hand, and perceiving that Madame Marriotti was regarding her with moistened eyes, she said, 'I am not going to be so foolish again; it is over now, you need not scold me, *cara maestra!*'

There were few houses in Rome where a parting was not impending, and scarcely any parent or lover sought to hold back son or friend, but in Casa Ravelli was war; its master would not hear of his son joining the volunteers. Vainly did Luigi urge and implore, declaring that he should be marked as a coward for ever did he draw back after having taken such part in the preparations; Signor Ravelli was obstinate, stormed, menaced, and besought him that he would be content to

stay at home, finally going to bed, there to shed a
flood of tears, quite despairing and '*avvilito*' like
a child, but stubborn as ever; and to make sure
of keeping his son, he cut off his allowance, and
bribed all the authorities to refuse the youth permission to leave Rome. Luigi's high spirit always
found home life tame, and now it was unbearable
to lose this opportunity of seeing the world, putting patriotism out of the question; and when he
saw other young men about to march to the war
of independence, and heard the hopes, fears, and
praises that resounded on all sides, he grew desperate with vexation. His mother could not bear
to see his rage, she secretly pledged her ear-rings
to fill his purse, and gave her consent to his
departure, though it almost broke her heart to part
with him; but still his father remained obstinate.
Luigi sought Signor Olivetti and urged him to
use his influence; Signor Olivetti laughed at
him, and asked if he did not know his father
well enough to be aware, that no one could talk
him over. There was no help to be had in this
quarter. Luigi fairly stamped with vexation, and
vowed he would turn brigand sooner than not go,
and Imelda forgot her own terror in the prospect
of losing him, and said, 'I am so sorry, Luigi; I
know how you want to go!'

'All the walls of Rome shall not keep me here,'
exclaimed Luigi; 'stay idle here and be branded
for a coward? I will turn priest if I stay!'

He betook himself to the authorities, but his
father had been beforehand with him, and all the
answer he got to his impetuous remonstrances
was, '*E impossibile, impossibile, impossibilissimo!*'

Irene had need of all her spirit as the day of

parting approached; she was thankful that Lent had closed the theatres, and made this a season of comparative leisure, for it would have been a severe task to attend rehearsal, and to appear in public night after night. Her perfect health enabled her to shake off the effects of wakefulness, a new thing to her—or of sleep so full of dreams as to be little refreshment. From one of these she woke one morning feverish, breathless,—feeling, before her mind was collected enough to think, that the day of departure was come. Vincenzo remembered it too, and made an effort, of late unusual to him, to rise early, that he might breakfast with Leone, who presently came in, looking so cheerful and soldierlike in his travelling costume, that Vincenzo's spirits rose, he ceased to watch Irene anxiously, and breakfast passed amid much talk of even a gay kind.

The muster call sounded suddenly, Leone started up—Vincenzo grasped his hand. It was a parting as of dearly loved brothers; Vincenzo murmured low, ' Leone, Leone, I ought to be going too !' and Leone's last word to him was, ' Think of her !'

Irene had turned away that she might not see or hear; she waited for Leone at the door. That was a hard parting; a strange beating filled her ears, her voice was lost. He clasped her hands in his, and gazed in her face, as if he could not let her go, and she could make no answer to his ' Irene *mia !*' A whole volume of love and trust was contained in those two words. The muster call sounded again, one close clasp, one kiss, and he was gone, while yet she stood with her hands locked together; without word or sign—he turned at the end of the corridor, looked back, and sprang again to her side. 'Irene! one word! I cannot part in this way!' Then she found strength to say, 'It is for our country—good-bye!'

Madama Cecchi and Menica came out to add their farewell. Leone had not another instant to spare; he waved a hasty adieu to them, gave one last look to Irene, and darted down the stairs.

He saw Irene again in the throng in the Piazza del Popolo, now with a bright smile for him. So sanguine were all, so ardent in the cause, that, though nearly every one had relations among the volunteers, yet when the hour came for them to set forth, all Rome assembled in the piazza, as if for a feast. There was barely room for the soldiers when they marched in, and halted to listen to an oration from one of their chaplains. It was a grand scene, and it passed in a beautiful spot.

Already the light green of spring foliage began to clothe the Pincian Hill; the belt of cypresses, on the other side of the square, rose up against an intensely blue sky; the fountains sent gushes of clear water into the air. The three long streets leading into the piazza, at all times arteries of traffic, poured in a dense crowd, which struggled to enter the square, already so full that not a single additional spectator could press in among those already swarming there. The windows, and roofs of houses, and even of churches, were lined with gazers, all hushed into profound attention and silence, as through the piazza rang out the voice of the preacher. It ceased; the word of command to march was given—then the tempest of feeling broke loose, and amid *vivas*, waving handkerchiefs, tears, and a tumult of sound that pursued them far on their way, the volunteers marched out of Rome, every note of their martial music, every flutter of their banners, every sunbeam that glinted on their weapons, accompanied by prouder and yet prouder steps, and hearts beating higher with exultation, as each moment seemed to bring them nearer to their destination of Ferrara— Ferrara, soon to be set free from the foreign invader! Afterwards—the Pope indeed had ordered that his troops were not to fight except in a defensive war; but neither general, nor soldiers, nor even chaplains, realized that they were not speedily to join the brave King of Sardinia. The gentle voice of Pio Nono was lost amid the beatings of Italian hearts, burning to join in the general war for freedom, and too eager for considering whether he who called himself the representative of the Prince of Peace could send his subjects to dye their hands in the blood of men whom he regarded as truly his children as themselves.

No one had seen, though many had looked for, Luigi Ravelli in the piazza, and speculation was rife among his friends as to what had become of him. The enigma was solved ere they had gone many miles by the appearance of a rider dashing across the Campagna on a magnificent horse. The headlong speed and the noble animal instantly revealed the rider, and almost at the same instant as when many voices together were proclaiming it, Luigi galloped up and waved his hand triumphantly to his friends. As he could not get leave to join, he came without it; and he was so general a favourite, and the eager desire to join Charles Albert was so universal, that both the general and the officers of Luigi's regiment shut their eyes to his escapade, and he took his place joyously among the volunteers.

His was not, however, a thoroughly light heart, for the thought of Gemma weighed upon it. If he had had stormy scenes with his father, those with Gemma had been worse; at the first hint of his intention she broke into entreaties, reproaches; she even threw herself on her knees as she implored him to remain, and vainly he now soothed her like a child, and then appealed to her reason; all she knew or cared was, that he meant to leave her. He could hardly endure to face her misery; she thought he was wavering, but she was mistaken—she could make him wretched, but not faithless to the cause in which he gloried; and she recognised the limit of her power, and her tears were replaced by a sullen mood, which ended in a parting on both sides in anger, equally soon repented of; but Luigi had no means of letting her know that her image was with him in the march and the camp and the battle-field, nor she of telling him that she had tortured herself into absolute illness, and was almost wrought up to the desperate design of flying from her home to seek him. In absence, all her power over him revived; he forgot how she had exasperated him, and forgot, too, the tearful eyes, the trembling lips that he had kissed, and bade remember him, when in the height of his anger with Gemma he had sought Casa Olivetti to bid Imelda farewell.

She did remember him. She thought of him in all her occupations by day, and whispered his name in her prayers each night. There were heartfelt supplications uttered for dear ones in peril that Lent by those who could but remain behind and pray for them.

A great preacher was missed from the pulpit, which he had filled in former Lenten days; Padre Rinaldi was gone as one of the chaplains of the volunteers, and his very presence was enough to raise their enthusiasm to the utmost; but sorely was he missed at the Roman Court, where his opinions and advice had been constantly sought by Pio Nono, who was left to the contrary influence of the *Gregoriani*.

Padre Rinaldi was one of the few priests to whom the reforms were welcome. When others opposed a silent, stubborn resistance, suffering the new measures to drop unheeded, he seized and carried them out unflinchingly; he saw in them a commencement of other reforms, not temporal, but spiritual, calculated to restore his Church to her ancient majesty, and to give back to her ministers that pure and unworldly spirit which of old had rendered their enormous power a benefit to the world, who, feeling they were better than itself, had bowed before them. No man felt the corruption of his class, of his Church, so strongly as did Padre Rinaldi; none contemplated such sweeping measures of reform, nor cherished such magnificent visions of what the Roman Church might again become, with her purity restored, and all the world again united in one faith.

Dreams of the anchorite! dreams only; but had others been as stern to themselves, as holy as he, different indeed would have been the fate of Rome. His eloquence all knew, but at the extent of his austerity and sanctity men only guessed. They regarded him with reverence almost as great

as that felt in the middle ages for the celebrated
Dominican of Vicenza, at whose bidding tyrants
laid down their arms, prisoners were freed, laws
altered. Like that Fra Giovanni, Padre Rinaldi
would have rebuked undaunted an *Eccelino* in his
own hall. But those who lived at ease, those who
were rich and luxurious among the clergy, would
gladly have silenced this stern monitor, who
seemed to the people a very prophet, and whose
life and doctrines were a thorn rankling in their
sides. In earlier days Padre Rinaldi might have
shared the fate of Arnold of Brescia or Savonarola;
luckily for him the stake had gone out of fashion,
and the friend of the Pope could not be lodged in
the dungeons of the Inquisition; but could the
feelings of the whole body of the Florentine clergy
towards that rude Fra Girolamo be compared with
those of the Roman abbots and priests towards
Rinaldi, little difference would be detected in the
shades of dread and hatred. But the people listened
to him gladly.

All the chaplains were not like him, and strange
indeed was it to hear one (whose name became
afterwards but too well known) preach turbulent
communist doctrines, declaim against the rich,
abase rulers, from the King of Naples to the pe,
and lead and urge the people to revolution. The
political storm thickened and spread; the Italian
Governments were neither strong enough to pardon nor to punish, and skilful had he need to be
who stood at the helm in that tempestuous year
1848.

CHAPTER IV.

Conrad.—What dost thou, daughter?
Elizabeth.—I have been washing these poor people's feet.
Con.—A wise humiliation.
Eliz.—So I meant it.

The Saint's Tragedy.

SIGNORA OLIVETTI was a wise mother. She did not discourage Imelda from speaking of Ravelli, but she tried to give her new subjects of thought. She obtained leave to take her occasionally to the hospital for convalescents of the Trinità de' Pellegrini, to which sisterhood she herself belonged, and attended in her regular turn one week in every month, going there for many hours each day, remaining all night if wanted, and assisting at all other times when an unusual press of work called for additional nurses. Ladies of all ranks belong to the sisterhood, and men of all classes to the brotherhood of this institution, which is intended for patients newly dismissed from other hospitals, that they may there recover strength ere they return to their homes; and, likewise, as the name imports, as a resting place for pilgrims. Imelda could not be enrolled as a *sorella* until she was eighteen, but meanwhile her mother asked, and obtained the favour of being allowed to take her to the Trinità, and encouraged her to assist the patients after they had left the hospital.

She likewise did all in her power to encourage
her daughter's intimacy with Irene, for whom
she had a high esteem.   Her friendship and
countenance were valuable to the young cantatrice, for Signora Olivetti was a person of con-
sideration in Rome.   Imelda joyfully availed herself
of every opportunity of meeting her friend, and all
through Lent Irene was comparatively at liberty,
and could accompany her and Mrs. Dalzell to
many churches and galleries which she had never
before seen.

Mrs. Dalzell was to return to England immediately after Easter, and though she had lived
in Rome long enough to consider it almost a
home, she still found much that was new to her,
and almost as much to visit and revisit, as though
she had been the merest stranger.   The *lavanda*, at
the Trinità de' Pellegrini was a ceremonial which
she had never yet witnessed, and Imelda, who had
grown very fond of her, besought her to attend,
and see all the sisterhood assembled to wait on
the pilgrims.   Mrs. Dalzell promised to go on
Easter Eve, on condition that Imelda would come to
Palazzo Clementi to accompany her; and Signora
Olivetti gave a ready consent, for she had assured
herself long before that there was nothing but
good to be gained from the English lady, and that
neither Mrs. Dalzell, Irene, nor Vincenzo ever
approached the subject of religion with her child.

Imelda arrived, on Easter Eve, under the care
of a servant, who saw her safely into the hands of
Madama Cecchi.   It was Mrs. Dalzell's tea time,
but her sitting-room was empty.   '*Ecco eccoli*,'
said the padrona, opening the door of Vincenzo's
apartment, and there accordingly Imelda found

her friends, standing in contemplation of three paintings, intended for what is technically called a diptych. The brush that executed them might still have been stiff with paint, they were so evidently new; but for sentiment and delicacy of colour, they might have been the work of Fra Angelico. There were three compartments, the two side ones intended to close if necessary over the centre, where the Virgin Mother was depicted, holding her Child; herself a perfect model of womanly grace, modesty, and humility—the Infant Saviour nestling His little Head against her with childlike love, amid which the expression of something divine was beautifully given. On each of the outer compartments an angel in pale blue robes was drawn; on the panel, which would be placed above the centre one, another angel knelt, bending forward and scattering flowers.

The three persons looking at these lovely paintings turned as Imelda came in, and welcomed her; she noticed immediately how animated Vincenzo looked, and exclaimed, ' Oh, Vincenzo, are these yours? How very, very beautiful—*quanto è caro quest' angelo!* Where did they come from?'

' Mine! No, an old friend, a Sir Arthur Laurie, who was at Rome last Easter, has had them painted for him by a German; he is just come back—he gave me some work last year. Are they not exquisite? Well, they are to stand over a small altar, and I am to carve the canopy and frame—is not that good? He brought them here, because (he says) he knows they will inspire me!'

' He seems to have been right,' said Mrs. Dalzell.

' What a long time it is since you undertook a

long piece of work, Vincenzo! You are a great deal better to-night, are you not?' said Imelda.

'Quite well, to-night. See, I shall have a pointed canopy to throw into shadow this angel scattering flowers; the middle panel is to have a slender border of leaves, I think, and the emblematic dragon bound among them—where is that bit of paper, Irene? Thanks. You see, Imelda, so; I have not devised any more, but all the front of the altar is to be carved too, and the words *Fides, Spes, Caritas*, introduced: it is a votive offering—I wish I knew its history.'

Vincenzo's artist spirit was all awake; his delicate, thin hand was playing with a carver's tool as he spoke, his face lighted up brightly. Irene looked equally happy; and, when they took their places at the tea table, the conversation maintained the same course, and Imelda inquired how a rosary was progressing, which had been his amusement for a long time, whenever he was too ill to attempt work on a larger scale. Each bead, though no bigger than a nut, contained a perfect subject; one was a bunch of acanthus, another the Annunciation, a third the Salutation of St. Mary and St. Elizabeth. It was Imelda's delight to examine it whenever she came, and Vincenzo's pleasure was to puzzle her as to its destination, amusing himself with her unconsciousness that it was intended for herself. He half rose to fetch it when she inquired about it, but Irene forestalled him, and put it into Imelda's hands.

'Three beads since I was here last!' said she. 'Oh, Vincenzo, you have not been well!'

'You all use this rosary as a thermometer of my health,' said Vincenzo; 'but not another

[illegible]

[illegible]

[illegible]

[illegible]

[illegible]

[illegible]

[illegible]

[illegible]

[illegible]

[illegible]

things ?' said Imelda, wonderingly; 'they believe what we do? It puzzles me very much. No, it cannot be the same; Irene does many good acts, but not as a penance, nor to gain indulgences. You know, every one who washes the pilgrims' feet to-night gains an indulgence.'

'I hardly understand what an indulgence means,' said Mrs. Dalzell; and Imelda found it difficult to explain.

'I am not sure,' she said, 'why, by a good deed, such as washing the pilgrims' feet, we get forgiveness of small sins—not mortal ones, of course. Some people say that an indulgence is of no good unless you are in a state of grace; and who can be sure of being so? Indeed, I don't know what it is—but my confessor says that good works ought to be done.'

'I suppose so,' said Mrs. Dalzell.

'Oh, then Protestants think so too; and I know how kind Irene was to that poor Catarina Bresca. Was it only because you had known her, Irene?'

'Well, was not that reason enough?'

'Oh, but I think there was another; please tell me.'

'Why, would you have had me let her starve, cruel child?'

'Ah, I was mistaken then; I thought perhaps you had a Protestant reason.'

Irene smiled and answered in lowered tones, 'If I had, it was that our Lord told His people to help all who are in want of help.'

'Ah! not to obtain anything for yourself—*capisco*—I see! But a great many people—Roman Catholics as you call them, do good without *egoismo*.'

'Yes,' replied Irene, 'but we ought not to talk in this way.'

'I forgot!' said Imelda, with a look of alarm; 'but we have not been arguing, have we?'

'Not much,' said Vincenzo, laughing; 'we have not been trying to convert you; but, lest we should, suppose we talk of something else.'

'Or get ready to go,' said Mrs. Dalzell, 'unless you will have another cup of coffee. Is a veil the proper head-dress, signorina? I see you have one.'

'Almost everybody wears one at the *lavanda* instead of a bonnet; I don't know why. May I get ready?'

'Imelda, do you mean to be a little white dove all your life, with no will of your own? Shall you ever learn to say, "Let us," instead of "May I?"'

She laughed at Vincenzo's saucy question, and said, 'Impertinent! Mamma says a woman's will should be the same as her father's, or—or—'

'Or as her husband's?'

Imelda looked up at him with smiling yet moistened eyes; an allusion to Luigi was always so welcome, but it recalled the thought that he was absent and in peril. She ran away to Irene's room, and Vincenzo said to Mrs. Dalzell, 'Will she be a child all her life?'

'I could almost hope it, Vincenzo; I should regret to see her lose her simplicity as one does to find a pet child losing its childishness, and becoming too old to be petted.'

'I wonder if she ever will turn into a woman!'

'Yes, if ever she discovers that Ravelli does not love her. What shall you do this evening? Draw designs for your carving?'

'And read Gioberti. That man writes with a pen of fire! I shall have a visit from Cecchi, too, and perhaps Clementi.'

'I give him infinite credit for not joining the volunteers; it must have been such a sacrifice! but he told me yesterday that the bare idea of his going had made Contessa Clementi so much worse, that he has quite given it up. He certainly is a thoroughly good son, as I think most Italians are.'

'Yes; Ravelli, for instance, is devoted to his mother, and in any other case would have obeyed his father, I do believe; but I was certain that nothing would keep him from Ferrara. You know our proverb—"My home, my mother, those are the two best things that man can have." Good night; here they come, and I hear the carriage in the quadrangle. Irene, give me my journal before you go.'

She arranged for him the thick volume, and his pens and ink, and lingered to read the last entry. It was such a journal as many people in Rome kept at that time—a minute record of all daily events in which politics had any share.

'It will be material for history some day,' said Irene. 'Anything else before I go?'

As the ladies went out at the entrance of the palazzo, Count Clementi came in. His almost daily visits were very welcome to Vincenzo; he was one of the threads which connected the secluded invalid with the tumultuous world without, whose stir and swell Vincenzo heard as a man on the other side of inaccessible rocks hears the surge of an ocean, invisible to him, break in thunder on the shore. Clementi had become necessary to him of late; Leone was away, Ravelli was away; Cecchi was a democrat, engaged in schemes of which the uninitiated knew nothing; Vincenzo was on excellent terms with him, but knew little of his views, and had no sympathy with them. Count Clementi was now the most intimate friend whom Vincenzo had in Rome; a visit from him was always cheering, and Irene, even if she had not liked him for his own sake, must have received him cordially, because she knew how much pleasure his visits gave to Vincenzo. As it was, she could meet him frankly and warmly, grateful for the entire suppression of feelings which she well knew still existed, and for the friendly manner in which he invariably brought her all tidings of the volunteers, and shared in Leone's letters to Vincenzo, when a hurried one chanced to arrive. She could leave home contentedly this evening, secure that Vincenzo would have a pleasant companion, and she exclaimed, involuntarily, 'Oh, I am so glad you have come! Vincenzo has been so well all to-day, and he has some good news to tell you. *A riverderla!*'

Clementi passed on, but Cecchi looked out from his domains, and called him in a whisper, and a political discussion of some minutes took place, in subdued but vehement tones. Count Clementi was no stranger to the plans of the ultra-faction; no speeches spurred them on in their own little club so fiercely as did his. He did not look like a conspirator, with his calm air and inscrutable face; yet there were darker secrets in his breast than those of which Cecchi had the keeping. Somehow or other, Cecchi never was ten minutes with Count Clementi, without being lashed by the remembrance of his wrongs—a word, an allusion so slight as to be almost imperceptible, would be sure to recal them. He was not a patriot, but a man bent on revenge; longing to trample on those who had injured him, and classing all rulers together as tyrants. His former experience of conspiracy had not cured him; on the contrary, its excitement and peril allured him, as the passion of the chase allures the chamois hunter, though he knows how many have fallen victims to it, and that he himself will become another. It was only when Cecchi thought of his wife, that he shrank back for an instant, and saw the whirlpool into which he was plunging. When Clementi left him, the most restless agitation took possession of him; his features contracted, he walked up and down, listening to every sound. Once or twice, a sort of bitter laugh escaped him.

The sound of his wife's entrance forced him to compose himself; she came in full of excitement; she had been with friends to the *lavanda*, and had seen the Princess B—— wash a pilgrim's feet, and several *nuovi Cristiani* had obtained special leave to assist in the *lavanda* to show their devoutness; Lady Dall was there (viz. Mrs. Dalzell), and the two *signorine*—in short, Madama Cecchi was overflowing with the history of her evening, to which he listened nearly in silence, and, as soon as she would let him, plunged into a large book of accounts.

Irene had put aside all anxieties for this evening, and devoted herself to make the economy of the hospital clear to Mrs. Dalzell. They found a throng of carriages and ladies at the door of the side appropriated to females; the entrance to the men's side being equally crowded with gentle-men, for the *lavanda* is one of the few sights which attract the Romans. Following the feminine throng, Mrs. Dalzell and her companions passed up the staircase into a long, large hall, where so many ladies, old and young and of all ranks, were running in and out, that their number confused the eye and defied computation, like a multitude of ants on an ant-hill. They all wore dark dresses, with a picturesque scarlet skirt, defended by a little white apron, with a bib, as it would be termed in nursery language, and adorned by a badge with a picture of the Crucifixion, surrounded by the name of San Filippo Neri, the founder of the order.

Long tables occupied the sides of the room, divided from the space in the middle by rails, within which the younger sisters hastened backwards and forwards, bearing huge baskets of bread and trays of boiled fennel, apples, fish, and fritters, The elder ladies superintended, amid much laughter and chattering, greatly increased by the crowd of spectators pressed together in the centre of the room. There were a few foreigners, but the staple of the throng were black-veiled Romans, amongst whom a general acquaintance seemed to prevail, and who were greeting each other joyously. Presently, Imelda exclaimed, ' There is mamma!' and one of the black and scarlet ladies saw, and came to speak to them, and to give the information that the *lavanda* would soon begin. Mrs. Dalzell had not at first recognised Signora Olivetti in her unfamiliar costume, becoming to all, with its spirited contrast of colours and neat little white sleeves and collar —and particularly so to Imelda's mother.

Signora Olivetti had not a moment's time to spare
for visitors, but she admitted them within the
rails, out of the crush, where they stood more at
ease, though in some danger of being run over by
the agile *sorelle*.   Imelda smiled to her acquaintance; Irene gave Mrs. Dalzell information.

'It is a Roman edition of what we call a school
feast,' said the English lady; 'and it reminds me
of another thing. We have an institution for poor
old men, called the Hospital of St. Cross—these
brethren [looking round at the grey-haired old
men who occasionally entered the room] in their
peculiar dress remind me of the Brothers of St.
Cross. I see only old men here, but I suppose
there are young ones in the masculine depart-
ment.'

'Oh yes, both Leone and Luigi belong to it,
and many others that I know.'

'But the young men do not come here,' said
Imelda, very simply, 'or all the girls would fall in
love.'

'See, Mrs. Dalzell,' said Irene, drawing her
aside to allow two girls, carrying a large tray, to
pass; 'the supper is arranged in sets of four—four
little pipkins for wine—four plates—four everything. It is a fast day, so they have no meat.
All pilgrims are taken in for three nights, who
come from a distance of more than sixty miles,
with a recommendation from their parish priest,
and they have a supper, but that is all; so they
generally keep part for the next day, as you will
see presently.'

'Oh, we can go on now,' said Imelda, as a general movement towards the end of the room and
a lessening of the crowd showed that an outlet had

been made. They followed in the stream, past
one room, where sat the female pilgrims, clustered
as thick as bees, waiting till they were summoned,
to another large room on a lower floor, along
whose walls ran stone benches, below which stood
a goodly array of tubs.

Here there was no barrier; visitors and
'*sorelle*' mingled together, and a general Babel
of sounds arose, in the midst of which the train
of pilgrims began to enter, each led by a lady
to a place on the benches. They were of all
ages and very unequal ranks, from all parts
of Italy, and even from Germany, speaking
dialects, various and unintelligible, to the great
amusement of the younger *sorelle*, who laughed
more than was quite proper for sisters of charity.
Old and young and middle-aged were these pilgrims; one wore a heavy black coif, which marked
her as a widow; another was a beautiful girl,
scarcely sixteen; a third withered and bent, with
a child in her arms fast asleep. Side by side they
sat, looking patient and weary, and a little em-
barrassed by their novel position. The laughing
and talking went on all around them, nobody
paying them much attention, till a priest entered,
carrying a book; an attendant followed, with a
candle, a bell, and a desk, on which the book—
a Latin Bible—was placed; the priest opened it,
the bell was loudly rung, and the chattering
ceased for a moment, while each lady knelt down
and prepared to wash the feet of a pilgrim, both
reciting a Pater Noster, and the priest read aloud
in Latin the chapter which tells how our Lord
washed His disciples' feet. Silence for an instant
—then whispered requests for towels, water, this

and that, rose in gusts, soon louder, more general; the hum had recommenced, the voice of the reader was drowned; he signed for silence in vain, then rang his little bell vehemently, and turning to the crowd, exclaimed in despair, 'Sisters, sisters, hush! it is scandalous, scandalous, most scandalous!'

With one accord all the throng cried hush, and there was a brief pause, during which the unintelligible Latin lecture again proceeded, only to be overpowered anew by the mirthful throng, who, like birds let loose, darted upstairs again, as soon as the *lavanda* was over, to aid in the second part of the entertainment, namely, supper.

'I see that only a small part of the sisterhood shared in the actual *lavanda*,' said Mrs. Dalzell, as they went upstairs.

'It is permitted, not obligatory,' said Irene; 'they do it or not, as they choose. People consider it as a humiliation; I heard an English lady downstairs saying it must be a severe penance; but really I think the *sorelle* only consider it very diverting.'

'I should have allowed a little soap,' said Mrs. Dalzell. 'It strikes me that the pilgrims rather submit to the washing than like it.'

'Yes,' said Irene; 'did you hear that lady— English from her accent—who asked one woman if she did not feel grateful for the kindness shown to her by the young lady? She answered with such a droll look!'

'I heard her,' said Imelda; 'I thought of what you were saying before we came. She answered, "Not in the least, dear signora; the young lady gains an indulgence by it—I am of advantage to her, more than she to me, since spiritual things are more valuable than earthly ones."'

'A reply that my countrywoman hardly expected,' said Mrs. Dalzell. 'I often think the lower classes of Italians and Irish alike in their ready answers.'

The supper was laid out in three long rooms, and soon the pilgrims were marshalled in, and took their places ; grace was said in Latin, and they all responded in the same language, standing reverently. The meal began ; it was a very ample one ; there was plenty left for the next day, and each woman spread her pocket-handkerchief to receive the fragments. Probably Mrs. Dalzell was right in thinking the supper to be more to their taste than the washing, though both were equally needed after their long journeys on foot. The *sorelle* waited on them briskly, and the visitors stood by, and looked on. Towards the end of the meal, the pilgrims produced their bottles, to be filled with part of their portion of red wine—bottles made of skin, of iron, or of wood, curious and often beautiful in shape and material, each peculiar to the district from whence its owner came. A collector of curiosities would have emptied his purse on the spot to acquire them ; as it was, no one was present except Mrs. Dalzell who took any particular notice of them. One took her fancy so much that she asked its possessor whether she would sell it. The old woman looked up in wonder and doubt ; Mrs. Dalzell thought her Italian was in fault, and looked round for Irene, but both she and Imelda had been absorbed into a group at a little distance.

'Irene !' She did not hear. Mrs. Dalzell repeated the call. 'Irene ! Mademoiselle Mori ! will you come here for one moment ?'

She now heard and came; the reason of the summons was explained to her, but when she interpreted it to the old woman, she found a pair of kindly shrewd eyes fixed on her face, and was answered with, 'Are you Mademoiselle Mori, signorina?' in an unfamiliar, but still quite intelligible, dialect, and the younger *sorelle* pressed round, exclaiming, 'She has heard—she has heard of Irene—of Mademoiselle Mori. Where did you hear of her, good woman? Where do you come from?'

'I come from Reni, a village beyond Ferrara, *signorine mie*, and I bring her a message; but I do not know that I am to give it to all the world.'

'Oh yes, yes, yes, may she not, *cara* Irene? it cannot be a secret; may we hear, Mademoiselle Mori?' cried a dozen voices. 'She comes from near Ferrara, and she has a message for Mademoiselle Mori—only listen!'

'Oh, you may hear,' said Irene with amusement and surprise. 'But Ferrara!'

'Oh, Ferrara! Ferrara! she must have seen our troops! Did you see our soldiers—the Roman soldiers?' cried every voice, and the crowd thickened momentarily, and all the pilgrims within earshot suspended their supper, and leant eagerly forward to catch what was going on. The old woman had a pleasant, good face; she seemed greatly entertained by the general interest, and commenced readily with a touch of poetry.

'I have come from a country laid desolate, ladies; our vineyards are cut down, our cottages are burnt, our fields are trampled like a road; I sent my two sons to the war, and I vowed a pilgrimage if the cause prospered; and when good news came from Piedmont, I went to our priest, and got a letter from him, and set out with my youngest grandchild, who is asleep on my lap now. He is my own child, ladies; for his mother died at his birth, and I had him from that day, and his father is in the war. Holy Virgin, protect him! I have come a shorter way than many here to-night. When I set out, I often thought of Rome and how I should tell my friends when I got back what I had seen there (none of our people have ever seen Rome, and all wish to hear what Pio Nono is like); but I am old, and the child fell sick, and I had to carry him every step, and many times I thought I should lie down and die on the way. One afternoon I was toiling on; I had not a half *baiocco* to buy a supper or a night's lodging; the child did nothing but moan—he had grown like a waxen image, and hardly seemed to know me. Saints forgive me! what bad thoughts I had! Just as I was going to give it up and turn back, I came to a hill-side where soldiers were resting under the trees. First I saw one alone, with his horse bending its head down to him as he lay on the grass—'

'A black horse?' asked Imelda, eagerly, and when she heard that it was black, she felt certain that this was Ravelli's noble Auster, and clasped her hands with joy; but 'Go on, go on,' was exclaimed on all sides, and the old woman continued:

'There were but a few troops here; doubtless the rest had gone on further; soon I saw some half-dozen men lying asleep; next thirty or more sitting and listening to one who told them some story. I came among the trees to listen too, and I do assure you, *signore*, I forgot all my trouble while I hearkened to him. It was the history of a brave cavalier who loved his country, and is now in Paradise. I never recollected where I was till he stopped, and all the men began shouting and clapping their hands like demons.'

'Oh, Nota! Nota! Nota!' ran from lip to lip. 'Was he handsome? What was he called? Did you speak to him?'

'I shall tell you presently, *signorine*,' said the old dame, nodding her head; 'he got up and walked away smiling, and passed close by me— then, seeing me standing, he stopped, and asked whence I came, and such like questions; then, when he had heard my story, he turns to the rest, and says he, "Friends, here is a good woman who has sent her sons to the war, and is going to our Rome to pray for them—what shall we give her to make her remember us there too?"—and the silver showered into his helmet! I was made rich in a moment, ladies, and that was not all— he would not leave me there with the sick child; he took it into his arms and carried it a mile or so to an inn, while the other soldiers were halting; and, as he was about to go, I asked him what I could do to reward him—I knew it was but words, for what could such as I do for him? but I could not help saying it. First he laughed, but soon I saw a pleasant thought come into his face, and he gathered a bough from the nearest tree, and said, "Here, dame, you shall take this to Rome, and go to Palazzo Clementi, asking for Mademoiselle Mori—remember—and tell her that this has come too late for Palm Sunday, but she must wear it on Easter day!" I asked him who, I should say, sent it; but he only smiled, and said she would know. I should have brought it last evening, but I and the child got along like a procession, stopping here, stopping there, though he grew better from that blessed day, and it was too late, so I thought to find Palazzo Clementi early to-morrow. However, if this be Mademoiselle Mori, I can give it to her now.' And regarding kindly Irene's flushed, smiling face and glistening eyes, she took, from within her peasant bodice, a branch of olive, dry and withered; but what were all the fresh olive woods on all the hill-sides in Italy to Irene, compared with this little bough ? She took it with fingers that trembled, but held it very fast.

'Come to Palazzo Clementi all the same,' she whispered; 'I too have something for you.'

'She has seen our troops—she has spoken to Signor Nota—she heard him improvise,' circulated like a breeze through the rooms, and brought an increasing crowd round the old woman, regardless of orders to be quiet, and not to block up the way. The Renese was the heroine of the evening, and questions poured thick upon her; every one was anxious to prove that she had seen their own par-ticular friends among the troops; and much was Irene envied for possessing an actual message from one of the volunteers. Imelda had clasped her hands with unselfish joy and whispered, 'I am so glad!' and longed, but dared not to inquire, more about the master of the black charger, which she had entirely made up her mind could be only Luigi's gallant and gentle Auster. The general excitement only lessened when the time came for the pilgrims to go to their beds, a

ceremony as public as the *lavanda*, but Mrs.
Dalzell did not stay to see it. She was weary
with the long evening, during which she had had
no opportunity of sitting down, and Irene was
eager to be at home and tell Vincenzo all that had
happened.

CHAPTER V.

When shall we three meet again ?
Oft shall glowing Hope expire,
Oft shall wearied Love retire,
Oft shall Death and Sorrow reign,
Ere we three shall meet again.

'YES, my dear Irene,' said Mrs. Dalzell, 'I really must ask Signor Cecchi to take a place for me in the diligence next Wednesday. Sir Arthur Laurie is going then, and has offered to see me safely on board ship at Cività Vecchia, and that is too good an offer to be rejected. I must not linger here any longer. Do you know it is more than eighteen months since I was in England ? But now, tell me something about your plans ; I believe that many people say, a celebrity like Mademoiselle Mori ought to have a grander dwelling than your apartments here.'

' Oh, I know they do, but we cannot leave our dear old rooms.'

' Even Madama Cecchi, in her profound admiration for you, declared the other day that though, if you left her, her heart would be found broken into little pieces, yet she was not worthy to have you here. She will insist on your going, some day ! What a levee you had last night !—two of the guardia, an abate, the maestro di capella, an American, three Englishmen (I suppose I must not count Vincenzo's friends, the German artists), all raving about the voice and the beautiful eyes of Mademoiselle Mori! By the bye, I should like to see the abate's sonnet again.'

'I dare say he got the letter writer in Piazza Montanari to compose it for him,' laughed Irene. 'Vincenzo wanted an *allumette*, so I made one of the sonnet. Really sonnets are very useful things—they quite keep us in *allumettes*.'

'Irene, your engagement to Leone has been a great safeguard to you.'

'Yes, signora,' she answered from her heart. 'Oh, no one can tell what a shield his love has been to me. I have thought so often of that, and what my fate might have been, had I become a singer without the home you gave me. Poor Catarina Bresca taught me to realize what cause I have for gratitude. Do you know, once, years ago, before I appeared in public, a bunch of flowers and a note were sent me through Nanna. I fancied then, that they came from Count Clementi, but I never knew; for Leone made me return them, without reading the note or asking Nanna whence they came. I did not know then how important that first step was.'

'My dear child, it was well indeed that you acted rightly. I cannot tell you how shocked I was to learn the kind of Don Juan character that Count Clementi bears.'

'Oh, signora, it is like that of half the young men here! I sometimes wonder if any good can be in store for us Romans, when there is such a corrupt state of society. You don't know half—one learns it in such a profession as mine; things come before me that make me feel absolutely con- taminated.'

' Nay, dear child;—you have read *Comus?* Well, it seems to me, that you are not unlike the lady, fearless and pure among all the rabble rout, and unharmed by the magician's spells.

Irene kissed the hand which she held, and Mrs. Dalzell looked fondly at her noble, truthful countenance, and rejoiced to think that not a shadow of blame had ever fallen on the fair name of the young cantatrice, who had now all Rome at her feet ; but the boldest of her adorers ventured on none but the most respectful homage. Irene's return had been a triumph. Not only had her cause become identified with that of the liberals, then at its height of prosperity, but the public missed her sorely, and were indignant at the risk which they had run of losing her. The uproar on the night of the *Caio* had been the work of a clique ; the tide had turned in Irene's favour, and, had Madame St. Simon reappeared, she would have been received with a storm of hisses. But she was at Paris, strong in long-established popularity, and missing no opportunity of contemptuously crying down the young rival, whose fame reached her even there.

Irene received an ovation on her first night in the Teatro Regio ; she was recalled half-a-dozen times amid tumultuous applause, and half buried in garlands, nosegays, and bracelets ; ever since, her door had been besieged by foreigners and natives, eager to be introduced to the star of the day. She enjoyed the success for which she had worked patiently ; it was not a sudden glare, but well and gradually earned fame ; she enjoyed her triumph, too, and her levees, laughed at her adorers, and charmed all who approached her ;

for, as Madame Marriotti once said, she had that gift of fascination which is distinct from beauty, but full as powerful. There was a great course open to her, if she chose to enter on it, but—

'No,' she said, in answer to something mentioned by Mrs. Dalzell, regarding the engagement at Vienna which Madame Marriotti wished to obtain for her; 'no, I could not accept it; if I once began that life, I could not draw back; my place is here. I do not see, however, why I should not go to Naples, or Milan, or Venice, in the intervals of the season here; some day that will be for Leone to settle. I should certainly have accepted that offer from the San Carlo Theatre at Naples this Lent, and then returned here; but I could not leave Rome, and I don't think those six weeks were wasted; I wanted some more lessons, and Herr Z. has certainly improved me. Madame Marriotti likes no style but one, and I wanted to understand others. She is too exclusive, too severe, in her taste; no modern music satisfies her, not even Mendelssohn's, which I now feel to be magnificent.'

' Unquestionably those weeks were well spent; Madame Marriotti herself said so, and you act and sing all the better for having had a rest,' said Mrs. Dalzell.

' I must go,' said Irene, as she looked at her watch; 'I shall never be dressed in time, if I linger any longer. It is the *Cenerentola* to-night. You must come and hear me before you go, signora. Ah, *carissima amica*, when shall I see you again in Rome ?'

' I have promised to come back for your marriage, you know, dear child, if it does not take place till the autumn.'

'I shall miss you so much in every way. I wanted to ask you whether Vincenzo is chaperon enough at our *società?* Madama Cecchi is often there, and yet—'

'I think if I were you I would make Madalena come in, if Madama Cecchi cannot. Madalena looks staid and respectable enough for a dozen chaperons.'

'I have a great advantage in being a native of Rome,' said Irene; 'for I made some friends before I became a cantatrice, who give me quiet, refreshing society still. Had I come here as a stranger, I should only have known men. As it is, there is Casa Olivetti always open to me, and I am not asked *there* merely to sing.'

She went away warbling a cadence with a gay and saucy expression, which signified that she was quite aware that certain great ladies cultivated her acquaintance, because it was advantageous to have such an attraction at their parties, and economical to be able to invite her without payment.

Many English were leaving Rome, alarmed by the unquiet state of Italy and the revolution of Vienna, which had caused a tumult of joy in Rome. It was hailed by illuminations and processions, every bell in the whole city pealing; the streets were thronged by crowds who shouted and danced for joy, let off their guns, strewed flowers, and displayed flags from balcony, roof, and tower, till the popular excitement breaking all bounds, the crowd rushed up to the Venetian palace, the residence of the Austrian ambassador, tore down and trampled on the detested arms of Austria, and then in a vast throng of half-frantic men, women, and children, rushed up the broad steps of Ara Cœli, above the Capitol, and burst forth into a

Te Deum of gratitude for the downfall of *i barbari*. None present can have forgotten the sermon then preached by Padre Gavazzi, whose deep voice resounded through the church, uttering vehement, heart-stirring denunciations, which found a ready echo in the breasts of the people. Then, as night came on, out poured all Rome into the streets again, and the same mad revel and fire-fly dance, of *moccoletti* began, which is the crowning delight of the carnival, but had not been indulged in, before, this year; for on the right day all Rome was in agitation, and mourning over the blood shedding at Milan, afterwards so well avenged.

This was on the 21st of March. Some of the visitors at Rome were so much alarmed, that they left it at once: but more remained till after Easter, when, as usual, they went off like the *girandole*, 'north, south, east, and west,' as Madama Cecchi expressed it. Naples was in no inviting state, Upper Italy still less so, France in confusion; so that nothing remained for the English but to hasten by the shortest way to their own country, which was itself feeling the influence of the general convulsion and somewhat affrighted by Chartist risings.

Mrs. Dalzell was an experienced traveller, and preferring the risk of going alone to that of finding every bed at hotels and every berth in steamers occupied, she delayed her journey until the first rush of departing tourists was over; though she thus lost the chance of going with several friends. It turned out, however, that an Englishman with whom she had become slightly acquainted was also lingering after the rest, and she gladly accepted him as her escort. This was Sir Arthur Laurie, first a patron, and afterwards a friend of Vincenzo's—a man of about thirty-four, wealthy and unmarried, a perfect specimen of a high-bred English gentleman. Like every one else, he had gone to hear Irene, and his admiration for her (not so much as the cantatrice, but as the charming girl whom he saw in his visits to Vincenzo), though quiet and undemonstrative, was so evident, that Mrs. Dalzell early perceived it, and had thought it right to mention before him that there was such a person as Leone Nota. It was difficult to say what effect the information of her engagement had on him; he still came frequently to see Vincenzo, and not seldom appeared at Irene's levees, where he sat silent, observing her arch and animated manner or listening when she sang; but he spoke no Italian, and his conversation was almost always addressed to Vincenzo, who learned from him much that interested him greatly of the habits of thought and of politics in England, always so perplexing to foreigners. Of politics he had never been able to glean much from Mrs. Dalzell, who, like most other English women, knew and cared little about them. The society of a member of the House of Commons, with a large estate, accustomed both to country and public life, was valuable to Vincenzo, in whom there was a great deal of the Englishman in spite of his foreign birth and breeding; he readily sympathized with anything English, unlike Irene, who was heart and soul Italian, and thoroughly believed that

> ‘While stands the Colosseum Rome shall stand,
> And when Rome falls—the world!’

Sir Arthur sometimes listened to her enthusiasm

with a smile, but always with interest, and he once said apart to Vincenzo, 'Your sister might be a Corinne. I wish her a happier fate; but I can hardly imagine her ending in calm commonplace.'

'I hope she will have happiness which is too rare to be commonplace,' said Vincenzo. 'I often think how little my father could have foreseen her course—his little Nightingale, as he used to call her.'

'She has found her vocation,' said Sir Arthur, pausing, and looking at the eloquent, liquid eyes of Irene, which kindled and glowed as those around her spoke of Milan and Venice. 'It is strange how prejudiced we English are against anything like public life for a woman.'

Mrs. Dalzell heard and thought that this was the strongest proof she had yet seen of how far Irene had captivated the reserved and fastidious Englishman.

'It was fated that she should be a cantatrice, I suppose,' said Vincenzo; 'everything has tended that way; but her public career will, perhaps, end with Nota's return.'

Sir Arthur made no reply, possibly because Irene and a young German artist began to sing. Vincenzo's, as well as Irene's, friends came to these evening meetings; for he had acquired a few acquaintances of his own craft, and enjoyed heartily the artist talk which they brought with them.

Madama Cecchi's sharp eyes had long ago found Sir Arthur out, and she privately asked Mrs. Dalzell whether in England men of rank could marry beneath themselves.

'We do not hold to rank as the Romans do,' said Mrs. Dalzell.

'That cavaliere—*quel gentleman Inglese*—he is of rank, and doubtless opulent!'

'He is of a good family, and has a fine old house in Northumberland.'

'In Nortomberlano!' said Madama Cecchi, strenuously attacking the long name so unlike her soft Italian ones. 'Where is that? near London? Ah, it matters not. And could he marry our signorina? would his family allow it? would the Queen consent?'

'Nobody could object, if he chose to do so.'

'*Cosa stupenda!* see what a thing it is to be free! But rank is rank, and Heaven made it; the plebeian is not a Cæsar,' said the padrona, whose democratic predilections by no means did away with her respect for long descent. 'Still Cupido is a liberal, a *Carbonaro*, is it not true? He does not ask if Psyche was born of a beggar or a duchess. And *quell' angiola* might be a *miladi*, and she gives it all up for the sake of Leone! What constancy! may she only be rewarded! I said to her yesterday, "There is that piece of northern ice—(speaking with respect, signora)—that piece of northern ice dissolving beneath your eyes, and you will not see or hear; yet it is serious, oh very serious, when these Englishmen fall in love! They do not sigh nor weep like us Italians, but they shut up their sentiments in their hearts; and if they are unfortunate in their love, they shoot themselves." And she only laughed! But is it not true, signora; will not that be the end of this poor gentleman?'

Mrs. Dalzell knew not whence the padrona

derived her belief of the desperate nature of English love, but assured her she did not think Sir Arthur's life in danger.

'Ah, I feel for him, signora! it tears my heart to think of this gentleman; the northern nations are slow to feel, they do not love fiercely and swiftly; they do not die abruptly as we do; but they are as iron—it grows red hot and is bent, and ever after keeps its shape. I have had many lodgers, and I have always observed that to be the English character. But we could not spare our signorina; she is all Italian, *è tale quale come la Giulietta*. What a play—what a play! Signor Leone translated it to me from the prose of Guglielmo Shaksperay, an English author, who derived it from our so touching opera of *I Montecchi e Capeletti*. I wept, my heart beat fast, Nino wept—we sprang up, and assured *il Romeo* that she was not dead, but alas! in vain. Oh, that tragedy is truly Italian, *Italianissimo!* Thus we love. But to return to that gentleman; you doubtless know his friends! all the English know each other; persuade them to get him a wife speedily, signora.'

The case did not appear so desperate to Mrs. Dalzell as to the padrona; but she did think that Irene might have been Lady Laurie, had she willed it.

Packing-up and leave-takings are rarely cheerful things, especially when those who part are to be separated by long distances; but Mrs. Dalzell was returning to her own country and dear friends, while Irene was being left behind in anxiety and suspense, the future of Rome uncertain, and Leone in the wars. As usual, the one left was far more to be pitied than the one who went.   Mrs. Dalzell faithfully promised to return in the autumn or spring for Irene's marriage, and though she said it with the proviso 'If nothing should happen to prevent me,' it was merely the usual commonplace acknowledgment of the uncertainty of human affairs; she did not really suppose that any event was at all likely to interfere with her plans.

The diligence started in the evening.   Madama Cecchi provided coffee for Mrs. Dalzell before she went, and bade her a tearful adieu.   Vincenzo, too, parted with her in the palace, even the short walk to the diligence-office was an effort beyond his power; and she saw them both waving her a farewell from the window as she went to the office, escorted by Irene, Cecchi, Menica, and Count Clementi, who courteously issued forth from his domicile, as they went downstairs, on purpose to accompany her.   Cecchi carried a small basket full of cakes, which he offered to her when she had taken her seat, saying that his wife had made them, and begged she would eat them, '*per l'amor suo.*'   Menica had the care of a flask of orvieto, also a gift for the benefit of Mrs. Dalzell, who gratified and astonished the damsel by promising to take the pretty bottle all the way to England.   It was a fine evening, very welcome after the constant rain of that wet winter and spring.   There was a little crowd as usual in the piazza, just as there always is in England round a stage coach, consisting partly of idlers waiting to see the travellers start, and partly of officials, and of the travellers themselves.   In the first of the two vehicles about to start, an English family had just established themselves, with the

exception of the father, who had been transacting
some business within the office, and now came
out, anxious to see that wife, daughters, maid, and
trunks, were all safely stowed away; but while he
was gazing earnestly up at the laden roof of the
diligence, a hand seized on his, and a bearded face
saluted him with a kiss on each cheek. It was
the farewell of the Italian with whom he had been
lodging, and was evidently altogether unexpected
by the Englishman, who, probably during the whole
of his residence in Rome, had not realized the existence of his landlord, except when he came to
receive his rent; and the ex-tenant's countenance
expressed such blank astonishment, not unmingled
with disgust, that the heads of all his family were
suddenly withdrawn from the windows of the diligence, and suppressed sounds of laughter issued
from within. The leave-taking between Mrs. Dalzell and her party was interrupted by the appearance of an American in angry distress, utterly ignorant of Italian, and outrageous at the stupidity
of the officials who could neither comprehend
his native language nor his attempts at French,
though he continually raised his voice, shouting
as if they were deaf, apparently under the belief that
they must understand if he only spoke loud enough.

'Could you ask what he wants, and I will translate,' said Irene to Sir Arthur Laurie, who had
just come. He politely addressed the irate gentleman, whose wants Irene made known to the
officials, while they murmured, 'Such as he should
not go about! People should learn to speak before
they travel!'

No one who had heard the flow of wrathful
language which the American had been indulging

in could help laughing. He was to be a fellow-traveller of Mrs. Dalzell's, and took his seat, leant back for a moment, then putting his head out of window, gave an admiring look at the curtain of purple cloud which seemed to hang from the sky and close in the long narrow street, and exclaimed, ' Well, I call that handsome !'

' Think of us sometimes in England, signora !' said Count Clementi; ' see, day departs with you !'

' *Buon viaggio*, dear signora ! Madonna look favourably on you !' cried Menica.

The conductor mounted to his seat, the postilion sprang on his horse ; Irene had only time to give her friend one last close embrace, before the whip cracked, the bells jingled, and the two diligences rattled over the stony streets. Mrs. Dalzell leant from her window and gazed back ; she caught another glimpse of the group she sought, still standing in the piazza, looking after her—the houses all aflame with sunset lights, and great purple clouds floating in a golden sky, where one large star already shone. Sir Arthur did not look ; she fancied she heard him sigh, and he remained silent long after they had crossed the Tiber, passed Santo Spirito, and made the customary halt outside Porta Cavaleggieri, while every one's passport was examined—a delay which caused much grumbling from the other occupants of the diligence. Darkness came on rapidly, even before they resumed their way ; there was only a kind of half light prevailing, which dimly showed that now they traversed open country, and now ascended hills ; tall asphodels crowned the banks on either side, making a very ghostly-looking *chevaux-de-frise*, behind which brigands might easily have lurked.

But the diligences rattled on unmolested, keeping close together for protection, and no sounds were heard, except some which one traveller declared to be the song of nightingales, and another less poetically to be the croaking of frogs. It was a wearisome night, as most nights spent in travelling must be ; but Mrs. Dalzell at length fell asleep and did not awaken till daybreak, when the Campagna was sparkling with dew, and glittering with golden cytisus, above which rose myrtle-bushes and the stately white asphodel. The sun was just rising in a saffron sky above the Mediterranean close by, and Cività Vecchia rose in the distance, melting into a background of pink and golden cloud. Not a wave broke the blue expanse of sea, but a white speck floated slowly along which might have been a nautilus.

A few hours had yet to be spent on Italian ground; the steamer did not start till noon, but soon Mrs. Dalzell was on board ; and a few more days saw her back in England, wondering to find how ignorant her countrymen were of Italian affairs, and how remarkably indifferent to them— back in calm, sober England, where every one was occupied by his own affairs, and too much accustomed to liberty to be in the least enthusiastic about it.

CHAPTER VI.

O holy knowledge, holy liberty,
O holy rights of nations!   If I speak
These bitter things against the jugglery
Of days that in your names proved blind and weak,
It is that tears are bitter.

E. B. BROWNING.

PIO NONO had doubtless begun his reign as a sincere reformer, probably with the fair vision of Italy freed from the Austrians, and himself at the head of a league of all the Italian states. But the long accounts of misgovernment left him by his predecessors were not to be so easily liquidated.   He had granted much in the short period of his Popedom, and it no doubt seemed far more to him than it really was.   'Well, Count,' said he to the French Ambassador, Rossi, 'are you satisfied, now that you have got your lay element in the Government?'   But the working of this lay element was hampered at every turn; the clergy, who had hitherto possessed exclusive power, looked with an evil eye on the secular intruders.   The new form of government was very unlike that of free states; every law proposed by the two chambers (the Alto Consiglio consisting of members named by the Pope, and the Chamber of Deputies chosen by the people) was submitted to the Consistory of Cardinals, who deliberated in secret upon it, and had the right of a veto. The Parliament discussed all its measures openly; the Consistory, like the Criminal Court, sat with closed doors. Moreover, Parliament was forbidden to enter on 'mixed affairs,' under which innumerable matters—even certain taxes—were included. These were reserved for an ecclesiastical court. To have a Representative Parliament at all was, however, much; the usual rejoicings had followed when its concession had been announced, and a deputation, of whom Leone Nota had formed one, had been sent to offer thanks to the Pope; who had made them one of his beautiful, striking speeches, which was greatly admired; but there was much quiet laughter in Rome at his assertion therein, that 'all the Sacred College had gladly and unanimously consented to the reforms.'   His subjects knew better!

The war had worked both ill and well for the reforms. It had given a vent to the excitement ready to break into revolution, but it had taken away many moderate liberals, whose influence now no longer checked the ultras who remained behind to thunder in the Circolo Popolare. Nota, all-powerful with his own party, and restraining and captivating by his eloquence even those whose views were the most narrow or most extravagant—Nota was absent, and so were many of the truest patriots. Vincenzo was doing his best to supply Leone's place; he had undertaken to overlook the printing of a work on *The Present and Future of Italy*, which the mitigated censorship now allowed to be published; and he also conducted his friend's newspaper, and though Vincenzo's articles had not the energetic fervour of Leone's, they were strong and sensible, and went some way towards counteracting the radical papers. His room became the resort of all who were interested in the paper and the views it supported; and round Vincenzo's couch gathered men whose aspirations were so lofty and pure, that for their sake, Rome might almost have been spared. Fate had dealt strangely with the invalid boy, who was now fast becoming a man, and as influential in the battle of life as those who could go forth at pleasure to confront it. What *zingara* would have ventured to prophesy the future of Irene and Vincenzo at the time when Mrs. Dalzell found them in the dreary old palazzo ?

Vincenzo's spirit kept him up, when bodily weakness and continual tracasseries combined to overpower him. The editor of a political newspaper has a life nearly as full of cabals and vexations as a popular cantatrice. Irene knew what the latter life was, and Vincenzo experienced the former, and, perhaps, his was the more trying. When was moderation popular ? The favourite newspaper at Rome was the *Contemporaneo*, whose editor, Sturbini, had the reputation of keeping himself out of danger, while he urged others into it ; but he was mighty in the *Circoli*, ever fond of a vehement orator. Later came *Dom Pirleone*, a satirical paper, with woodcuts, published daily, to the huge delight of great part of the witty and laughter-loving Romans.

Political agitation and riots increased perceptibly ; the provinces as yet kept quiet, and believed in Pio Nono, who was now, however, beginning to tremble and waver, terrified by insinuations that he was encouraging revolutions, and by the retirement of the Jesuits, who fled from the general outcry raised against them, taking, however, high ground, and declaring they went because they would not be made a pretext for sedition. Few things had so intoxicated the Romans as this triumph over the detested *Gesuiti*, concerning whom they whispered tales surpassing anything related in *Le Juif Errant*.

Every ear was now intent for tidings of the war, and all hearts bounded or sank as the uncertain rumours of good and ill arrived, and kept the whole city in agitation. Durando had put himself into communication with Charles Albert, and had been ordered by him to pass the Po, w' ·h was by no means confining the Papal troops to a war of defence, as the Pope had intended; but the Pope, in agonies of indecision, would neither consent nor forbid, while the volunteers were burning to join the Piedmontese army, and outrageous at the cautious delays of Durando, who knew better than they did what stubborn enemies they would encounter in the Austrians. Radetsky's army had long been trained to war and hardships, while the Roman soldiers had had no previous experience, and were peculiarly liable to sudden fatal illnesses. The Roman has none of the tenacity of life which northern nations possess; and their gallant spirit alone would not enable them to cope rashly with such formidable enemies. Modena became the seat of war; the Friuli was ravaged by fire and sword. Then came the triumphant news of the victory at Pastrengo, and that Naples had sent 14,000 soldiers to the war. For a time even King Ferdinand was popular.

But amid the general rejoicing (for even among the *Neri* there were some who loved Italy), Pio

Nono was sad, knowing that the Austrians abhorred him, and racked by his own undecided mind. His nuncios in Germany sent him awful reports of the hatred there felt for him; a vision of new schisms haunted him, and finally he was thunderstruck by the famous proclamation of Durando turning the war into a kind of crusade.

Indisputably it put Pio Nono into a false position, and was an enormous blunder. The war was holy—a war of independence ever is such—and the Austrian barbarity was notorious, and will be a stain on their name for ever; but religion had nothing on earth to do with the matter. It was assuredly not befitting the priest who called himself Father of all Christendom, to encourage one half of his children to destroy the other half. And so felt Pio Nono. Just at this time stories, partly true, partly false, were rife of the violences and brutality of the Austrians, framed so as to exasperate the Romans to the utmost—tales as dreadful as those unspeakably terrible ones which maddened England during the Indian rebellion. And these tidings reached Rome just when a speech made by Pio Nono to the Consistory became public; combined together, this caused such a ferment as made all previous agitation seem tranquillity.

It was first announced to Vincenzo and Irene by Madama Cecchi, who entered their sitting-room pouring out broken and incoherent exclamations. 'The butchers—the heathens—and he, that false, deceptive coward, that Bengal tiger—only worthy of those barbarians; he dares to say our soldiers shall not fight; he declares he never blessed our banners! He is worse than Gregory—

at least *he* hated the Austrians! Worse? Ay, a million times worse; Gregory never pretended to be a liberal. Ah! the traitor—the double, treble, fourfold traitor!'

'But who? what?' demanded Vincenzo, looking up from his writing, Irene at the same time turning round from the piano in amazement at the abrupt entrance and violent demeanour of the padrona, who replied in almost a shriek, while her eyes flashed through wrathful tears.

'The Pope! this traitor, who says our soldiers shall not fight! says it in so many words in his allocution to the Consistory! All the world knows it by this time. He might well say it in Latin; our Italian would have refused to come to his tongue to utter such treason. What will the world say? What will my husband say? Ah, the fox in a Papal mantle, the wolf in sheep's clothing—from lying princes *libera nos, Domine.* And at such a moment—at such a moment, when we hear how those murderous villains have conducted themselves in the Friuli—'

'Stay, I do not comprehend a word; tell us what has really happened; Donizetti and Martino were here last night, and knew nothing of all this,' said Vincenzo, while Irene listened breathless, but Madama Cecchi hurried on unheeding—

'Those infamous ones—those Austrians—say "Austrian," and you have said all—my tongue will not tell what they have done; was not Milan enough? All the saints reward them as they merit! I will tell you but one tale; a peasant woman took in one of *i nostri* [our soldiers] who was sick, and fed and sheltered him; she sees a body of those demons approaching, and warns him, cup of gold that she was! He fled into a wood of chestnuts, and thence escaped; but they come—demand him, for they had heard that one of our men was there; they threaten to bayonet her infant, unless she confesses where he is—still she refuses, she does not believe such infamy possible; it is snatched from her arms and cut to pieces before her eyes—all are deaf to her prayers, her shrieks; and she—I dare not think of her fate—oh Heaven, Heaven! *Basta!* when her husband returns at night he finds wife and child massacred, and a heap of white ashes where his cottage had stood. It is true!'

'Impossible, impossible; the Austrians are men. It is some lie.'

'Men? impossible, forsooth? They are not men nor Christians; they are demons; do you think that is half what I have heard? Do you remember Lucio Naldi, that young painter, that lamb, that innocent boy? He was sketching in the Friuli this year, you recollect? He met with our soldiers, he put on the uniform, like a good patriot. Well, he is dead, and how did he die? Ask the Croats who seized him, and hung him by the neck to a chestnut tree, with a writing on his breast, "Thus fare the soldiers of Pio Nono." Is that enough?'

'Good heavens!' said Vincenzo, confounded by this report, 'Lucio Naldi, that gentle, light-hearted fellow—I cannot believe it.'

'I speak of the Croats,' said Madama Cecchi, with emphasis. 'Ah, Holy Virgin, I seem to hear that poor boy's gay laugh now; I see his blue eyes and long fair hair—alas! who has told his mother?' and she threw herself into a chair, and burst into a flood of tears. Irene, too, was weeping silently and bitterly; the dreadful fate of one whom she had known might well affect her; and, besides, which of the volunteers was safe from like barbarity? Vincenzo at last spoke again, trying to assume a confidence that his pale lips belied. 'We have repeatedly found these miserable reports to be exaggerated—enormously exaggerated; why should we believe this more than the rest, till we have some proof? What did you say about the *allocution?* What has that to do with it?'

'I tell you the Pope disowns our soldiers; he says they shall only fight on the frontier, the false poltroon. Saints, what do I say? yet he is, he is; we shall see if his word can hold them back. *Ahimè!* idiots that we were to believe in him. Nino, Nino, is that you? come in, I am here, have you heard? Come, quick—you have heard of the Pope's speech.'

'Yes,' replied Cecchi, briefly, and he looked round at the dismayed group with a gleam of triumph so sinister that it struck them all, and silenced even his wife's volubility. 'Yes,' he repeated, 'did I not tell you long ago how much a Pope's professions were worth? Long ago I prophesied that he would turn against us at the critical moment. A priest, a reformer! It has been a grand parade, truly. Miserable farce! only a generation of moles and asses could have put their trust in a Pope. Ah, ha! he has found our reforms becoming too earnest; Silvani was too wise, too honest, and he is dead. He breakfasted with kind Cardinal Antonelli, excellent Cardinal Antonelli! and found his chocolate unwholesome.'

'True, true, if he had lived, things would have been otherwise,' chimed in Madama Cecchi, catching at the allusion to the sudden death of the eminent lawyer who had been appointed to revise the code. Cardinal Antonelli was supposed to have borne a grudge against him, and popular prejudice laid a death, easily accounted for by natural causes, to the prelate's door. Vincenzo contented himself by taking up the defence of Pio Nono, and left the cardinal's character to clear itself.

'I only see that the Pope is a timid, scrupulous man in a most difficult position,' said he; 'but I do think this step so ill-advised, so frantic, that I expect that it will be retracted.'

'Ay, the ministry, too, think it ill-advised. They have resigned. We shall see what comes of that.'

'Why a republic—no more traitors to rule us . . . . Madonna Santa Catarina! what am I saying? I did not mean it; pardon me!' said Madama Cecchi. 'See, I must be Italian; count it not against me; and this Pio is really a traitor.'

'With or without the saints, we will have a republic,' said her husband, vehemently, but with a singular rapt look coming over his face, as like that of a dreamy mystic, carried away by a vision. 'Away with all this pomp of Babylon, fire is already kindled upon the earth, the sword hangs over Rome, Elias is come, the cry of the saints is heard in heaven!' He paused, with suspended breath and intent, abstracted gaze; Vincenzo and Irene watched him as if fascinated; his wife anxiously seized his arm. 'What is this? what do you say? are you mad, Nino?' He turned his eyes upon her, but did not seem to see her; then, starting, gasped and asked hurriedly: 'Did I speak? Why, I said—I said—we would have a republic—ay, that was it; now is our time, we are hopeless fools if we lose it.'

'You are wrong,' said Vincenzo: 'don't you see that this is no time for founding a new government, which must creep before it can walk; there is some strength in this one: work with the tools you have at hand, my friend; the present is worth more than two futures.'

'I know your doctrines by heart, Signor Vincenzo. You moderates should talk them to the angels, who neither rebelled nor stood firm, but were only for themselves,' said Cecchi, with a sardonic smile on his thin lips. 'Rome will never be Rome till she has swept out all the abominations of Pope and priest, and the lobsters of the German college, and the rooks of the English, and all the heap of them. Rome is for the people. We want no priests or kings; when the war of the kings is over, that of the people will begin. By and bye you will see what Charles Albert is made of. Don't talk to me of the Pope's conscience. If he cannot reconcile his temporal with his spiritual power, let him abdicate.'

'His duty is to govern to the best of his ability; he has no right to abdicate,' said Vincenzo.

'Hark, hark to the uproar!' cried Madama Cecchi, flying to the window, and gazing into the street, where a crowd were rushing along, shouting and gesticulating. 'Hear how they cry out! only hear!' and they could plainly distinguish the shouts of 'Treachery, treachery! death to the cardinals! death to the traitor Mattei! down with Lambruschini!'

'Signor Cecchi, you belong to the civic guard,' said Vincenzo, eagerly; 'all this is frantic; it should be put down instantly; why are you still here?'

Cecchi shrugged his shoulders, smiled, and leisurely went to assume his uniform; but others were more prompt, and the threatened riot was quelled. His strange unconscious speech haunted Irene, who long speculated on it, while it likewise occupied her brother's thoughts. The looks and language befitted a religious fanatic; and Vincenzo had long suspected Cecchi of an abhorrence of the Romish Church, but was at loss to imagine with what sect he could have connected himself, since apparently there were no Italian Protestants in Rome, though it was whispered that some existed in Tuscany and North Italy, holding lonely meetings in woods and caves where no persecutor could track them. Was Cecchi connected with any of these? Vincenzo had noticed before, that a strong tinge of mysticism pervaded Cecchi's speeches when he was excited; and now divined that he combined enmity to the Government that had injured him with the zeal of a religious enthusiast.

Rome was on the very brink of revolution, shipwrecked on that rock over which Pio Nono had vainly tried to steer, the difficulty of governing both as prince and prelate. In granting a constitutional government, he had done all he could; to go a step further would be to compromise the sacred dignity which it was his charge to keep. He had not in the least foreseen the effect of his energetical letter, which affected all Italy, dispiriting Piedmont, and above all, enraging Bologna— Bologna, haughty in comparative independence, proud of her antiquity and her great men, and for ages at variance with Rome. One revolution had failed in a former reign because Rome and Bologna would not act together; but now that the common cause had swallowed up these unworthy jealousies, Bologna had held out friendly hands, and not only welcomed the Roman volunteers on their way, but sent many of her own citizens to the war. At Rome the agitation became excessive; the *Circoli* were besieged by crowds flocking to hear Sturbini and others; the civic guard were disaffected, and the Pope was so much alarmed as actually to meditate taking refuge at Milan. Like others of his projects it ended in nothing, and after much disgraceful disorder, a new Ministry was formed by Mamiani, a man in ill odour with Pio Nono; for he was one of the few who had refused to take the oath of allegiance when he availed himself of the amnesty, and had written works prohibited by the *Index.* Pio Nono was bent on peace; his Ministry on war; Mamiani took his own way, and the Pope alternately murmured and submitted. In fact, from this time, the revolution may be said to have begun, and the idea of a republic grew more and more familiar.

The Pope lost no time in publishing an address intended to calm the Romans, but he had himself broken his magic wand; they had loved him as the patriot, they now abhorred him as the traitor; they thought he had deceived, juggled, betrayed them—and he thought them guilty of intense ingratitude. Alas! he and they suffered for the sins of his predecessors. Had former Popes accustomed them to liberty they would have known how to use it in the days of Pio Nono.

CHAPTER VII.

Glory to Thee in Thine Omnipotence,
   Who dost dispense,
As seemeth best to Thine unerring will,
   Which passeth mortal sense,
The lot of victory still;
Edging sometimes with might the sword unjust,
And bowing to the dust,
The rightful cause; that so much seeming ill
May Thine appointed purposes fulfil.

SOUTHEY.

ILL news began to thicken, and the gloomy forebodings of the alarmists in Rome were fully justified. Disasters and mistakes checked the victorious course of Charles Albert. King Ferdinand recalled the troops which the pressure of popular feeling had compelled him to send to assist the Piedmontese army, and thus fatally crippled its operations. Each account from Upper Italy was worse than the last; from time to time a volunteer returned to Rome, wounded, sick, haggard, a mere shadow of the gallant, confident soldier who had marched out amid music and huzzas a few months before. Many, many a Roman had fallen in battle or died of marsh fever, or been shot like a dog by the Croats when taken prisoner, and a voice of weeping that could not be stilled arose in Rome. Distrust in their leaders, and in the noble Charles Albert, was studiously sown in the Piedmontese army by Austrian agents, or by miserable men who preferred seeing Italy enslaved to seeing her owe her independence to a king— men who denounced Azeglio and Count Balbo, because they were true-hearted royalists, as they had proved by their wounds. Reports of treachery were spread in the army; a rumour got abroad that the Pope had excommunicated it; the men were so discouraged that the unhappy engagement of Corunda broke the spirit of the whole army; many of the soldiers deserted, others were disbanded; step by step the Austrians regained all the ground they had lost, and those who loved Italy best saw with eyes wet with indignant tears, that the campaign so glorious when it commenced had ended—like how many Italian hopes—in a miserable failure. It had not been the brightness of the steady dawn, only a false meteor. That manifesto of the Pope's served the Austrians better than if he had sent them a new army. Do any wonder that his people found it hard to forgive him? He was a disappointment incarnate to them. But in spite of reverses, and manifesto, and traitors, the high-spirited Romans for the most part stood firm, held to Durando, and betook themselves to Padua and Vicenza.

Direct communications from the volunteers came seldom to Rome; but occasionally Leone succeeded in sending a few lines to Vincenzo or Irene—missives waited for with breathless suspense, few and far between; and how many heart-aches were there in the intervals for Irene! The first enthusiastic glow of hope had quite faded, and all Rome waited in inexpressible anxiety for future events. A far longer time than usual elapsed, and still no news came to Irene—then worse than none, for a hurried despatch from Ravelli to his mother named Leone as wounded—the brief fact was stated, and no more. Irene could hear nothing. She had never known what anxiety was till now; she even began to sympathize with Gemma, whose worn face showed what she suffered. She was less happy in one respect than Irene, for Ravelli had no means of communicating with her; she was dependent on others for all news of him.

Irene's time was not her own; she had still to attend rehearsal, to appear at the theatre of an evening, to study hard, and combat all the difficulties and vexations which seem inseparable from the life of a *prima donna*. It was well for her; the suspense might have driven her distracted, had she had nothing to divert her thoughts from the one great trouble. She was better off assuredly than Gemma, who had nothing but her embroidery to occupy her, till ennui well nigh ate her heart out. But it was such a strain as must sooner or later tell on mind and body, and only the strong will, and the habit of public life, could have enabled Irene to endure it; and night after night she sang gloriously, with all her powers excited by mental pain, and then left the theatre, her eyes over-flowing with scalding tears, utter prostration taking the place of excitement. The fever of her mind only added power and pathos to her acting; never had she seemed so inspired as at this time; the public little guessed how different their favourite looked when she left the theatre yet ringing with applause, and sought the carriage where Maddalena waited for her. For Mademoiselle Mori was now too celebrated to go and come in her old unobtrusive manner; she had her own carriage. Often when she had entered it, she would sink back too much exhausted to speak a word, and Maddalena only manifested her sympathy by looks, putting her strong arm round her, and almost carrying her upstairs when they reached the palace.

Count Clementi watched for her one night when she had been singing with boundless applause, and sprang after her into the carriage. 'Irene, you will allow me?   I must tell you how gloriously you sang to-night—you might have represented Italy herself, as you stood there with your violet crown!   Who would not be a patriot who heard you?'

But she was lying back with closed eyes; their lashes rested on a colourless cheek, and she made no attempt to answer him, or to withdraw the ice-cold hand which he had taken.

'Is she ill? is she often thus?' he asked of Maddalena, who looked sorrowfully compassionate but in nowise surprised at the state her young mistress was in.

'No, *eccelenza*. It has often been thus of late,' she briefly answered.

'She should see a physician—does her brother know?   Are you mad to see this so tranquilly?' exclaimed Clementi.

A faint smile unclosed Irene's lips; it seemed so singular to hear herself spoken of as if she were not present, and to be too weary even to remind them that she could hear.

'It is the long waiting for the absent, signor,' said Maddalena, in a low voice; 'she kept up till she heard of his wound.'

'Irene! speak to me! I cannot bear to see you

suffer thus,' said Clementi, passionately; 'I would give my life to comfort you. You are wearing yourself out; have mercy on yourself, if not on me, and give up this profession which is killing you.'

'The profession is guiltless enough,' she answered, rousing herself and trying to smile. 'I could not live without it. My thoughts are occupied when I am in the theatre. It is at night—oh, what dreams haunt me! Night is very terrible—very cruel. I see Lucio Naldi for ever before me, or Angelo di Rosa, who was shot in cold blood by Radetsky's soldiers, and I fancy—' she broke off with one of those deep, gasping sighs which exhaust rather than relieve.

Count Clementi was gazing at her with what she took for sympathy. At that moment he hated Leone so intensely, that even if it were to have killed Irene, he would have rejoiced to know him to be in the young painter's place.

The carriage stopped at the foot of the great staircase; Irene alighted and took the arm which he offered to assist her upstairs, but paused to say earnestly, 'Say nothing to Vincenzo, I entreat of you; he is far too anxious already, both for me and for Leone,' and she spoke the word lingeringly, as if she loved to utter that name.

'I must, Irene. I cannot see you in this state without warning him.'

'You have not the smallest right to interfere,' she answered with the impatience of an overwrought spirit. 'It is my own affair entirely.'

'True,' he replied, and voice and look told that he was deeply wounded.

'Forgive!' said Irene.

'What have I to forgive? That you love another?'

'I do,' she answered, stopping abruptly and clasping both hands on her breast. 'If you could take my heart, and hold it to your ear like a sea shell, you would hear Leone's name—nothing else—that always, always murmuring there.'

'I doubt it not, Irene. Long ago you showed me that I was to be nothing to you; that my life was wasted for your sake. I would have thrown it down at your feet; you cared nothing for it. I could not win one thought from you, to whom I gave all man has to give. You were another's. I loved you before he did—but that counted for nothing. I have not forgotten, Irene; you need not remind me.'

'Oh, this is not generous,' murmured Irene, much agitated by the suppressed passion with which he spoke, and by his keen reproaches. 'Forgive me if I was ungrateful—he is away— I cannot listen to such words as these.'

'Were you generous, Irene? But enough of this, it is in vain.'

She was shaken from head to foot by her agitation, for she had used up all her strength of late; she could not answer, and he supported her to her own door without another word, and led her in. The voices of Cecchi and his wife were heard in some distant room in eager consultation; Menica opened the door and began a hurried '*Signorina mia*—' which the count cut short with a sign, and opened the sitting-room door.

Late as it was, two figures sat within, Vincenzo, who raised himself in haste as they entered; another, in a soldier's uniform—his eyes were bright but sunken; there was a feverish colour on the thin dark cheeks, it was a mere spectre of that

Leone whose name burst from Irene's lips; but he *was* returned, he *was* returned, and with a cry she fell into the arms stretched out to her, and was clasped close to his breast.

She rested there for awhile in speechless happiness, and no one spoke; but raising herself at last, she looked up in his face, and uttered his name. He replied by a caress, and now fully realizing what had happened, she exclaimed 'Leone, Leone, tell me it is really you! how came you back? Is the war over? Make me feel that it is really you—that you are here.'

He smiled and clasped her closer. 'My Irene, I should not be here with my own good will now, but I was wounded in a skirmish, and Sturbinetti was in as bad a plight; so Durando sent us back to Bologna together, while I was too ill to know what they were about, and thence we were ordered here by a despotic commander in the shape of a doctor, so you will have to nurse me.'

She looked at him and saw now what Vincenzo had dreaded would both shock and startle her, how ghastly Leone looked, reduced by fever and fatigue, his brow disfigured by a deep sword-cut.

'Leone!' she exclaimed in alarm; but quickly recovering, 'Ah, now you will be so well nursed that you must get strong directly. You will not be able to help it! You are really come back! you were here an hour ago, and yet I was fretting. Oh, can it be the same day?'

Count Clementi had stood a mute spectator, his white lips quivering, but now he advanced and took Leone's hand. 'Welcome, friend. What news of the war?'

'I know nothing new; I was carried in a fever

to Bologna, and as soon as I could move I was
ordered on here.   There is little to tell that is good.'

'And Vincenzo was the first to welcome you!
Leone, can you tell us anything of Luigi? his
mother is very anxious,' said Irene, so happy
herself that she could not resist the wish of letting
Gemma have a chance of hearing good news.

'When did you hear of him last?   I left him
in the highest health and spirits; he has turned
out a splendid soldier.   I have often thought of
your padrona's description of him—*è una saetta
scatenata* [an arrow let loose.]   His course was
nearly ended though at a little village which it
was necessary to take: we were ordered to advance;
a concealed battery began to play upon us out of
a mulberry plantation.   The command to capture
it was given; we galloped at it, the grape-shot
hissing over our heads—Luigi discovered a path
which led, clear from trees, right to it—he dashed
forward, all the rest following—cut down an
artilleryman who was making ready to give us
another discharge, and the same instant the Croats
were upon us; the officer in command cut at
Luigi, and a dozen men pressed round to drag
him from his horse—he fought like a madman,
but if Auster had not fought as desperately as his
master and fairly bounded out of their hands, we
should have been too late to save Luigi.'

'I must tell Signora Ravelli to-morrow—and
Imelda!   Leone, tell me about your wound.'

'I got it in a skirmish.'

'It must have been a terrible one!'

'That and marsh fever did the business for me
between them.'

'What news of the Cardellas?' asked Vincenzo.

Leone's face saddened. He put his hand into the breast of his coat and drew out a book of prayers; the pages were stained with blood. 'There!' he said in a deeply moved voice, 'Ercole Cardella gave me that for his poor old father. It is all that is left of the two brothers. We lost young Francesco in Castelnuovo; he fell close by Ercole's side; those two were no more apart in war than in peace—Damon and Pythias to the last—poor fellows! Ercole knelt over him while the shot was falling as thick as rain about us—men dropping on all sides. The poor lad was dead— we could do nothing but advance and leave him; but, when we halted for the night, Ercole asked me if I would go back with him, and we went and found the body—we dug the boy a grave with our swords in the churchyard, and there he lies. Ercole took this book from the poor lad's breast—stained with his life blood. It was their father's gift just before they left Rome. God help him—he has no child left. I shall not forget in my lifetime the look with which Ercole said, " He trusted the boy to me!" I knew he had made up his mind that he should not long outlive his brother, and so it was; he was dashed to pieces by a shell next day. Nothing can give you an idea of the horrors of Castelnuovo; a literal massacre; not a thing was spared by the Austrians but a goat which rushed among them out of the flames. The ground was covered by half-burned bodies of men, and women, and children—the place was a pest-house. For weeks I had the shrieks for mercy ringing in my ears; we saw, and could not help the poor wretches!'

'Horrible!' said Irene, shuddering.

'One hardly dares to ask after any one,' said Vincenzo; 'but Guidi?'

'Gloriously killed,' Leone answered; then kindling with the recollection; 'yes, that was a death to envy! He charged, at the head of a handful of men, a Croat battalion as they crossed a bridge, dashed through them and seized their colours, sabring the man who held them, and fell himself, pierced by a hundred shot. I caught the colours from him, and was knocked over the next moment, and that was when I got my wound. It was our best time, for except Verona and Mantua the Austrians had not a stronghold left that was worth anything. If orders had been transmitted rapidly, we should have had Verona—the army came up by mistake in three divisions and at different times, and that ruined us.'

'But you, Leone? what became of you?'

'Well, I had had all the sense knocked out of me, and was left for dead; the first thing I remember is waking up to a consciousness of pain and intense thirst; it was moonlight, and I heard a stream somewhere, but could not crawl to it. As I moved, I touched something cold, a dead hand. There were four or five of our men, and of the Austrians lying about, dead and dying. I got delirious; I imagined myself in Castelnuovo again, and that the groans of a poor fellow near me were Francesco Cardella's, and then the Croats came on the scene in my vision dancing and shouting among dead bodies, as they did at that doomed place, while all the town was wrapped in blue smoke, with flames bursting out here and there from a burning house, and cannon thundering. It was that scene again and again, all night long, and always the craving for water. At last I found myself on a mattress in a tent, and Padre Rinaldi beside me.'

' Ah, every one whom we have seen has spoken of him.'

'Well they may. Unwearied in preaching—ever by deathbeds and by the sick—I owe him my life; he came to the place where he heard I had fallen, expressly to see if there were any life left in me. I have seen him repeatedly where there was most danger, confessing a dying man or binding up wounds. Strange! though all that night is like a wild horrible dream, I seem to recall his pale face bending over me, and holding a lantern to mine. I escaped while many brave men perished—perished in vain!'

' Ay,' said Clementi.

' Now, Leone, not another word to-night! you are my prisoner now; you must stay here, especially as you have no lodgings now anywhere. I am going to talk to Madama Cecchi about it.'

' I will not be art and part in keeping him up any longer,' said Count Clementi, and he bade them all good night. Irene looked up at him anxiously; he had entirely recovered his self-control, and bade her a very kind, but calm good night. She sought Madama Cecchi, who was waiting to congratulate her, and had already planned to give Leone Mrs. Dalzell's vacant room, and had arranged all for his comfort. Cecchi went to assist him, and the tired soldier was soon installed in his apartment, too weary and excited to sleep, and scarcely wishing it, so pleasant was it to feel that he was again among friends. Irene lingered in the sitting-room above till Cecchi

came to assure her he had taken every possible
care of his guest. She looked up at the portrait
of her mother, when again left alone, as if she
would have asked her to share her happiness; to
her excited fancy there seemed a smile on those
pictured lips.   'Ah, mother, you have never
looked so since he went!' Irene said aloud, and
she went to Vincenzo's room; her happiness was
not complete until shared by her brother.

'Yes, we are very happy, thank God, my darling,' he said as she leant over him, and pressed
her lips to his. 'Good night, my own dear sister,
my dear Irene!'

CHAPTER VIII.

Campagna, che di te me ne fidavo,
E tutti i miei segreti a te dicevo:
  E tu eri innamorata del mio damo,
Ed io meschina non me ne avvedevo!
  Campagna fosti, e campagna sarai:
E lo mio Damo me lo renderai.

RISPETTO.

AT noonday in August, Rome is literally asleep. The shops are shut, the gay awnings over their windows hang motionless in the sultry air, the green persiani outside the windows of private houses are closed; pavements and walls reflect the burning heat, not a creature is seen abroad, except here and there some threadbare figure standing idly, hat in hand, with nothing to do, lounging in an archway, or on the shady side of the street, or sitting at the door of a *café*, drinking lemonade at a stall; or perhaps two lads may be seen playing at *mora* or the equally beloved *maroncino*— (pitch and toss), or a fat and bearded monk goes by, fan in hand.

At three o'clock some life reawakens in the city, the hours of the *siesta* are over, the shops re-open, so do the churches, the sultry heat slightly abates; but there is no real freshness till after sunset, when the glare vanishes, the baked ground and walls become cooled, the sky assumes its deepest purple, shrubs and plants drink in the dew and lift up their parched leaves, and the Romans pour forth to inhale the evening breeze.

Once a week, however, Rome is alive at a much earlier hour, when the citizens refresh themselves with a kind of bath in Piazza Navona, and thither Irene and Vincenzo drove one August afternoon. They called for Imelda at Casa Olivetti, according to a previous appointment, and she came dancing to meet them, and sprang like a bird to her seat by Irene's side, with Tevere for a *vis-à-vis*, sitting upright by Vincenzo. 'I am so glad you have come!' she exclaimed. 'I have watched for you this hour past! Mamma has gone to the Trinità, and I had nobody but Crescenzia to talk to. When we have been to the piazza, you must take me to St. Ignazio ; I told mamma I knew you would. How is the padrona to-day?'

'*In villeggiatura* at Frascati.'

'Oh! I forgot—is pretty Menica gone too? What a nice carriage! Irene, do you know, people still wonder very much that you live so quietly. They say nobody in Rome lives so quietly and dresses so plainly as Mademoiselle Mori, but mamma says it is quite right and does you credit.'

'We are not extravagant, certainly, Imeldina ; suppose I were to lose my voice!'

'Oh, what an idea! I should pray every day to Santa Cecilia, if I were you, to preserve it. Why did not Signor Nota come? Is he not well enough?'

'His sister, Signora Bianchi, came in just before we left home,' said Irene, returning mentally to a speculation which had occupied her as they drove along as to whether Assunta's husband had intended this visit as a step towards reconciliation.

'Assunta talked him into it,' said Vincenzo, guessing her thoughts.

'I suppose so.'

'I wish Signor Nota would get well faster; he still looks so ill,' said Imelda.

'If he wished it less himself, he would be much better than he is,' said Vincenzo; 'he is enough to throw any one into a fever with his impatience to be gone again! He informed me to-day with triumph, that he had walked four times round our *loggia!* Can you imagine, Imelda, why a man who is comfortable at home with his friends, can want to go back to a place where he got a wound and a fever?'

She laughed, and answered, 'He is a soldier.'

'There are some who would not comprehend that logic,' muttered Vincenzo, as he thought of sundry volunteers who had taken the first opportunity of returning home, on the strength of the Pope's speech, and who now trumpeted their loyalty at every opportunity.

'I shall be glad when this hot weather goes,' said Irene, involuntarily drawing a deep breath, as she thought how it oppressed Leone.

'Is it true, that he and Signor Bianchi are not friends?' asked Imelda.

'Who says so?'

'Oh, many people have talked about it at our house.'

'About as good friends as Count Clementi and his uncle.'

'Assunta is very anxious to make them friends again,' said Irene; 'and she said to-day that, if Leone would make the first step, her husband would most likely meet him half way, and procure another appointment for him, as of course he has lost his old one in the *Dateria*. But he expects a sort of apology from Leone, who has put up with a great deal already for Assunta's sake; and really he is not in the least called on to beg pardon for his liberal views. Besides, he hopes to be in Lombardy soon.'

'You will let him go again?'

'Why, I must,' said Irene, half playfully, half seriously; 'but we shall keep him till he is well. He knows it would be useless to go yet a while.'

'Piazza Navona,' announced Vincenzo, as they drove down one of the streets leading to the square, where a busy market is held of a morning. One day it is of piled-up fruit and vegetables, where Roman housewives, or oftener their husbands, argue, cheapen, and buy; for it is the husbands who transact all the household money-matters of the middle-class. Another day the market is of china, provisions, old iron, and old books, which cumber the stalls and the ground—a motley, noisy scene; but now the whole piazza was converted by closing the pipes which usually carry off the water from the fountains into a lake, wherein carriages drove up and down, the occupants exchanging mirthful greetings with their acquaintances. Bare-legged boys splashed about, chased each other, and played pranks; a crowd stood to gaze from the streets which led into the piazza; a band of music performed lively opera airs in a balcony; and a shabby-looking poet stood reciting on the steps of the church of St. Agnese, where the market women go to pray for chastity. His theme was the 'lake in piazza, more limpid than Como, more sunny than Maggiore; more blessed than all the lakes of Switzerland since it reflected the dome of St. Agnese and the sky of Italy!' and the passers by threw him small coins from their carriages, and laughed at his allusions to each as they drove past him. The water splashed beneath the wheels, clamorous voices filled the air; Irene and Vincenzo entered heartily into the spirit of the scene, and Imelda clapped her hands with delight, while Tevere, sitting with silken ears erect on the seat by his master, barked with all his might, as if to add to the manifold sounds.

'Drive slowly—let us hear what he is saying,' called Vincenzo to the coachman as they approached the poet, who probably had seen Irene at the theatre; for, bowing low, he immediately produced a couplet about the Syren of Piazza Navona, more witching than any heard by Ulysses in the grots of Sorrento. This won great applause from all near, together with a shower of silver coins, while Irene laughed and returned his profound obeisance; but Tevere, actuated by some unknown canine motive, bounced out of the carriage; snatched the poet's greasy hat out of his hand, and conveyed it to Vincenzo amid universal laughter and applause. Vincenzo took the hat, but refused to readmit the dripping dog, who retreated up the steps of the church and waited there. The poet did not miss so good an opportunity, and his admiration for the young *prima donna*, and Tevere's adventure with the hat, figured in a new stanza, till Vincenzo, thinking they had had enough, bade the coachman drive on; and, when they next came near the steps, Irene handed the hat, and a donation to the fortunate owner—'unspeakably fortunate,' so his next verse ran; 'since his unworthy hat had been sanctified by the touch of Mademoiselle Mori, it had become an immortal laurel crown!'

There were none but natives present on this afternoon; Rome tempts not the foreigner in August, and even of the Romans, a great number were in the country, keeping *villeggiatura*. It was a thoroughly Roman scene, and thoroughly enjoyed by those who partook of it; but, after an hour or so, Vincenzo found himself wearied out, and Irene quickly perceiving it proposed to go home. So they drove out of the *lago*, to the church of St. Ignazio, where Imelda's maid was waiting for her, and there Irene left her.

The church of St. Ignazio, as its name imports, belongs to the Jesuits, and is dedicated to their founder, Ignatius Loyola. It displays all the lavish colour, light, and ornament, the precious marbles and the gilding, the style of architecture, especially patronized by them, and which exactly suits the Roman taste. In Sant' Ignazio is the chapel of San Luigi Gonzaga, on whom not a few of the young Roman damsels look with something of the same kind of admiration as did Clytie on Apollo, whom he and St. Sebastian, those two young, beautiful, graceful saints, very fairly represent in Christian mythology. His *festa* falls in June, and then his altar is embosomed in flowers, arranged with exquisite taste; and a pile of letters may be seen at its foot, written to the saint by young men and maidens, and directed to Paradiso. They are supposed to be burnt unread, except by San Luigi, who must find singular petitions in these pretty little missives, tied up now with a green ribbon, expressive of hope, now with a red one, emblematic of love, or whatever other significant colour the writer may prefer.

San Luigi Gonzaga was the patron saint of Ravelli; Imelda seldom failed to pray daily at his altar for her absent betrothed; and, if the truth were known, a certain little note laid before the altar that year directed 'to the angelic youth, San Luigi Gonzaga, in Paradiso,' contained an entreaty for Ravelli's safety in the campaign, and was written by Imelda. She was not the only one who sought this altar for Ravelli's sake. As she and her maid rose from their knees, they saw Gemma Clementi approaching. The Contessina's cheeks became scarlet as she recognised Imelda, who timidly saluted her, and asked if Signora Clementi, her aunt, were there also.

'Yes, she goes into *villeggiatura* to-morrow, and she wished to confess first. Are you going this year?'

'No, mamma says she had rather not, as papa is away; she never goes anywhere without him. Are you going?'

'No,' said Gemma, discontentedly; 'we don't go anywhere—my uncle and aunt go, but as for mamma, she is like Signora Olivetti, and stays at home; but you do go out, when Signor Olivetti is at home—I never go anywhere.'

'You know we do not go to Albano or Frascati, only to papa's *masseria* [farm] in *il Regno*. It used to be my uncle's, and when he died papa had it, and we have gone there nearly every sum-

mer ever since I can remember. One year, when
I was not well, we staid there six months.'

'But that must be dull—don't you wish you
went to L'Arriccia?'

'Oh, there is no place that I like so much as
the *masseria*. We have three rooms when we are
there, and the tenants have the rest, and I help
Annunciata to spin, and see to the silk-worms, and
feed the poultry. There is a court with a well,
where it is always cool, and a garden—olives and
orange trees—and a shady path close to the edge
of the cliffs; the sea is below, and you can get
down to the shore directly by a winding way.'

'I did not expect to find you here,' said Gemma,
whose thoughts were elsewhere than in the *masseria*. 'I thought you always came very early to
mass.'

'I do, generally, with mamma, but she is at the
Trinità to-day, and Crescenzia was busy all the
morning,' said Imelda, looking at her attendant.

Gemma gave a guilty glance at the mild face of
San Luigi depicted above the altar, as if she feared
that Imelda must divine the motive that brought
her there. 'I must wait for my aunt,' said she,
hoping to get news of Ravelli by detaining Imelda,
but inwardly enraged at having to seek it through
such a channel. 'Will you stay a few minutes?
we can sit on this bench.'

Imelda was too timid to refuse, little as she
liked her companion, and sat down. Gemma
continued, 'You don't confess here? Oh no, I
remember now who your confessor is—are you
not afraid of him? he is said to be horribly strict.'

'He is so kind,' answered Imelda; 'mamma
sees my confessions before I make them to him;

I write them out and she helps me; thus I know exactly what I ought to tell him, and he is so patient with me.'

'But people say he is the most particular confessor in Rome. That would not please me, and it is the reason why he has so few penitents. Our confessor says he has at least four times as many as yours, and hears so many confessions that I am sure he has not time to ask about every little folly; and, besides, he knows he should lose his penitents, if he were too severe.'

'I understand,' said Imelda, not entirely satisfied.

'But you can't have many sins to confess,' continued Gemma; 'that you thought of Luigi Ravelli at mass, I suppose, or said his name instead of an *Ave Maria? Approposito*—has his father forgiven him yet for going without leave?'

' Oh, he pretends to be very angry still, but he cannot help looking happy and proud when they hear of him; and Luigi has distinguished himself so much, that he is made captain. Signora Ravelli came to tell us, and afterwards the signor came in, and though he would not be the first to speak of it, he was longing all the time for mamma to begin.'

' When did you hear of him last?'

' Signora Ravelli had a little letter, just after the armistice was proclaimed.'

' Armistice?' cried Gemma, with flashing eyes.

' Have you not heard?'

' Nothing! Pietrucchio does not speak of public news to us women—I hear nothing! What armistice? is the war over?'

' Oh, I fear so,' said Imelda, seriously.

' Fear! Then he is coming home!' said Gemma,

pressing her hands on her heart to still its violent throbbings. 'Ah, San Luigi, I ——' she stopped herself just in time, but Imelda was already looking at her with wonder.

'How can you feel glad, Gemma? it is terrible news; Milan is given up again to these evil Austrians, and our army is defeated! Poor Luigi must be so grieved!'

'Oh, he will be comforted by coming home— Are you not in Rome, Imeldina? where else would he be? When do you expect him?'

'I cannot guess; he has joined Garibaldi, and we heard that two little steamers had been surprised by Garibaldi's men; and that they had fought for a long time in the mountains of Lago Maggiore, and were now at Arona.'

Gemma gazed at her with pale, menacing looks. 'What do you say?'

Imelda repeated her statement, and there was a pause, during which Gemma summoned all her self-command to her aid. She succeeded in asking presently with calmness, 'Do you ever hear from Ravelli?'

'I had one letter after they reached Bologna.'

'Only one?'

'Only one; he cannot possibly have time to write, and besides so many letters get lost.'

'Oh,' said Gemma, sharply, piqued by her confidence in Luigi, 'you really are very trustful;' and her black eyes glanced daggers at her innocent rival.

As the two girls sat side by side, even a cursory glance told that Gemma had the advantage of Imelda, as far as striking figure and features went. Her face recalled those of the bold, handsome women of no good repute, whose likenesses sculpture has preserved for us—the women of imperial, degraded Rome. Not a few busts in the Vatican might have passed as more or less correct likenesses of the young contessina. Such as it was, her beauty appealed at once to the senses; while the little shy, graceful Imelda, with no beauty except the eyes which contained such wealth of liquid softness in their brown depths, might steal into the heart or touch the imagination, but were more likely to attract women than men. She seemed to shrink out of sight, and be *effaced*, to use a French expression, by Gemma.

Signora Clementi now appeared, greeted Imelda, and asked her to walk home with them, as her way to Casa Olivetti lay past the palazzo. She could not refuse, and thus Gemma had the opportunity of resuming the subject of Luigi, and of tormenting Imelda a little more.

'Do you think he loves you very much, Imeldina?'

'I believe so,' was Imelda's naïve answer.

'Why?' demanded Gemma, ready to flame up at this unexpected reply.

'Mamma has often said that she and papa never would let me marry any one who did not love me.'

'How are they to know?'

'Oh, mamma would know, and besides ——' Imelda stopped; for though, like most Italians, she was very naïve and frank in expressing her feelings, something checked her when she was about to tell Gemma of his affectionate farewell, and her conviction that he could not possibly be so dear to her, without his loving her in return. False logic, alas! It was quite as well that she

did not address it to Gemma, who remarked next,
'If I were you, I should be afraid to marry him,
lest he should turn out a tyrant like his father.
You know that old Signor Ravelli is as jealous as
a Turk; they say he used to threaten to beat his
wife if she even looked out of the window, and he
never lets her stir out without him.　One might
as well not be married as that; one would be freer
in a convent; and yet nearly all husbands are as
bad.　Mine shall find that I am not to be treated
like a doll or a baby; I mean to have my liberty
and spend my money as I like.　Signora Ravelli
has to tell her husband how she spends every
penny.　One might as well be a *zitella* [an old
maid] for ever.　But one must marry or be a nun.'

'Yes,' assented Imelda.

'My aunt and mamma are always preaching to
me that I am getting old—and so I am, almost
twenty! but perhaps I may marry and surprise
you all yet, Imelda.'

'What are you talking of, Gemma?' asked her
aunt.

'Of Piazza Navona, dear aunt,' replied the
niece, with unblushing effrontery; 'have you been
there yet, Imelda?'

'This very afternoon, with Vincenzo and Irene,
and it was so amusing! and we saw Signora de
Romanis, and Marchese Allori, and Count Rossi;
he was there for a little while with two Frenchmen, and there was a *poeta da dozzina* who made
verses on every one.'

'I see Count Rossi now,' said Gemma, standing
still; 'look, he reads a newspaper in the French
library; stay a little moment, aunt; do you see
him?　What a hard, proud face! and how his

lips curve! I should like to know what he is reading.'

'He lives in Palazzo Buoncorsa just opposite,' said her aunt; 'I should like to know what keeps him here; everybody knows he is half French, half Austrian at heart.'

And possibly the gazette which he was reading conveyed the same unpleasant hint to the ex-ambassador, who, though a native of Carrara, had been made a peer of France, came as a French minister to Rome, and was looked on very dubiously by the Romans in general. He had none of the Italian suavity, and disdained popularity; but he was a true patriot, and the Pope and the moderates had the justest and highest esteem for Pellegrino Rossi.

A bright-eyed boy came by with a springing step. 'Ha, Imelda!' said he, stopping; 'where are you going?'

'Home, from St. Ignazio. My cousin Filippo,' said she to her companions. 'How is my aunt, and Lalla, Pippo? and *la pupa?*'

'*Non c'è male*—very well. I cannot stop.'

'You look quite a little soldier, Signorino Filippo,' said Signora Clementi.

'I am a soldier, signora,' said the boy, proudly, with a glance at his uniform. 'I belong to the *Speranza.*'

'The *Speranza?* Ah, I remember now—the children's regiment. And are you on your way to parade?'

'Yes, signora; excuse me, I must not linger; a soldier's duty is punctuality, and there are some who set an ill example,' said Filippo, full of impatience, but still showing the courtesy of a little squire of dames. '*Addio*, Imeldina! they say the Pope himself will be present to-day! that is magnificent! though people declare now that he is no *Carbonaro*, but a black *Gregoriano*. *Non mi vale*—if only the war lasts till I am old enough to volunteer. *Addio* once more, signore.'

He darted away. Shortly after two of the Pope's guard appeared, preceding his coach; every one paused as he passed, and some knelt, but there was no enthusiasm manifested. Times were changed indeed; cold looks and a contemptuous murmur followed him; and strangely must the reception he now met with in the streets of his capital have chilled him when he contrasted it with the rapturous acclamations with which he formerly was welcomed.

'Your cousin will be disappointed,' said Signora Clementi to Imelda; 'the Pope is doubtless going to Villa Patrizzi; it is said he frequently plays billiards there. And so your mamma sometimes lets you go out without her, little one?'

'*Alle volte* with Irene, and with Crescenzia. She has lived with us these nineteen years.'

'Ah, happy is Signora Olivetti to have such a treasure! Well, my dear child, I must bid you farewell here. My respects to your mother; tell her that my husband and I go immediately into *villeggiatura* at L'Arricia.'

'I like the signora much better than Contessa Clementi, Crescenzia,' said Imelda to her maid as they walked on. 'Did you hear what Gemma said to me?'

'She is capricious and a *stravagante*,' said the duenna with austerity; 'do not think of her folly, my child.'

‘ Oh, I know it is nonsense; I shall tell mamma,’ said Imelda, reposing herself in that resolution, and quite satisfied as soon as she had confided the conversation to Signora Olivetti. Happy child, who did not yet know a grief that her mother could not caress away !

CHAPTER IX.

He must serve who fain would sway, and soothe, and sue,
And watch all time, and pry into all place,
And be a living lie, who would become
A mighty thing among the mean.

Manfred.

ONE Sunday evening, a couple of months later, Count Clementi sat locked up in his room, absorbed in looking over a heap of papers, which he glanced at and arranged, with pauses of deep thought. Those papers contained notes of all important discussions at the *Circoli*, and the secret meetings which he and a few of the ultra-republicans held in profound secresy; also there were minutes of his mission to France and Germany, as a delegate to such exiles as, having refused the oath of allegiance, could not benefit by the amnesty. Even in those early days, a few in Rome, and not a few in other parts of Italy, had cherished the vision of a general republic; Count Clementi had been selected as their spokesman, and sent to levy supplies, and concert measures in foreign parts. He had conducted his mission ably; he held the proofs of his success in his hand at this moment. In those papers was enough to bring ruin on nearly every family in Rome; for, whatever might be the politics of the fathers, there were few families which had not a liberal among the younger branches—often a member of the secret society, calling itself *Giovane Italia*. If ever the tide should turn, Monsignore Clementi and his party held a net ready to throw over their enemies at one swoop. The young count had done such good service that there were few things which his uncle could have refused him—even if he should demand permission to marry a heretic cantatrice.

Count Clementi sat meditating on the state of public affairs, and of his own private ones; it seemed to him that a crisis in both was absolutely necessary to him. Should the war end and public affairs become quiet, there was nothing to prevent Leone's marriage with Irene. It was clear, that this dangerous rival must be got rid of; but the idea of a stiletto did not please him, especially as in the event of Leone's sudden death, Irene would probably leave Rome. There was a second chance; Leone might fall into such danger, that she would seize on any hope of saving him, even by marriage with another. What more probable, nay certain, than that the *improvisatore*, the most eminent man in his own party, the one most odious of all to the *Gregoriani*, would be marked out for special vengeance at the first opportunity? And then she——

'Yes, it is possible,' mused the count, 'possible: there are some whose nature prompts them to grasp at an opportunity for self-sacrifice; she has that nature. Yes, Irene is truth and unselfishness itself—strange that, after all I have seen and known, I should find myself believing entirely in any one, and most of all, that that one should be a woman! Yes, I could work upon her, but Vincenzo—ah, Vincenzo!—no romance

there ! The fellow takes his stand, and is no more
to be moved than a rock—confound his island
obstinacy !—common sense, as those English call
it.   He would never let her sacrifice herself.
Pazzie! would she ask him ?   What girl would
listen to a brother when a lover is in the case ?
Stay—Nota out of the way, say—Vincenzo in
danger.   Ah, ah, Englishman though you are,
young Mori, you are too much mixed up with
Roman politics for that defence to serve you,
once let the other party have the upper hand.
Irene, I have waited long, but my time will come;
I feel that I shall win you yet.'   And so calmly,
proudly confident, did the schemer look, as he
reviewed his chances, that it was impossible not to
believe that he would succeed.   He sat still now,
laying the papers from his hand, and gazing, as if
it were into futurity with dark, steady eyes.
Presently his features contracted ; he made a
movement as if a thought had stung him.   ' Consent ! he shall consent ! Have I no right to demand
a reward ?   If not, then secresy for a time—he
must consent at last ; I am sole representative of
our house.'   Then again a pause, and a new train
of thought arose.   ' Our time must come speedily
if it come at all.   That weak fool, Mamiani, will
not be much longer in office ; then let us suppose
that Rossi comes to the helm.   Destruction ! that
man would ruin everything with his strong hand,
and his lay government ; no chance of an uproar
with him—he must be got rid of.   Let us see
what monsignore has to say on the subject.'

He rose, gathered and locked up his papers ;
took a thick book, in which names were arranged
alphabetically, with comments opposite to each,
and turned to the letter C.

' Cecchi: that man hates Rossi as he does Antonelli—would stiletto either if properly excited. He aims at universal republicanism in Church and State. There are three or four more of that stamp. Count Rossi, your reign may chance to end even more speedily than Mamiani's.'

He put the book in his pocket, opened his window, and stood listening. The tones of a deliciously sweet voice came to his ear; a little crowd was standing in the street below, attracted by it. Irene was singing parts of the *Elijah* of Mendelssohn to Leone and Vincenzo. Their window, too, was open; the thrilling notes floated through it; even the words were audible, so distinctly were they articulated. As Count Clementi stood and listened, his lips relaxed, a look of tenderness came over his face, he stood motionless till the voice ceased, and Irene's fingers dropped on the keys in the sweet and sighing harmony in which Mozart implores ' *Dona nobis pacem.*' Then a sigh escaped him; he roused himself, and slowly left the room. If ever man loved woman with all his soul, Clementi loved Irene.

The hour was near the *Ave Maria;* the Pincio was already nearly deserted, but the Corso was full of foot passengers in their best attire, jostling each other off the narrow *trottoir*, and a double file of carriages drove slowly up and down, as usual on Sunday afternoon. It was no easy matter to cross; Count Clementi had to wait with many others, till a carriage stopped somewhere in the ranks, and obliged all the rest to halt also. Those who had been waiting for this opportunity instantly rushed across, taking advantage of the short pause, and Count Clementi found himself able to continue his way unobserved, for there were few people in any but the main streets. His way led to a lonely, little-frequented church on the outskirts of the city with a convent near it. It was almost on the edge of the Campagna, still clad in the brown and orange tints which it assumes in summer, and does not put off till refreshed by the rainy season. A group of cypresses raised their heads above the convent wall ; a barren, neglected tract of ground lay before the church, which was too distant from the city, and too gloomy, to attract many worshippers. There was not even a beggar sitting at the door when the count entered, and a sort of half light prevailed within, but feebly dissipated by the lamp burning before a shrine, and casting tremulous gleams on the marble steps, the porphyry columns, and the old mosaic which looked so spectral and grim in the obscurity.

Count Clementi found himself absolutely alone ; he knelt before the altar for a while, perhaps in order to explain his presence to any worshipper who might chance to enter. Unlike most of the young Roman nobles, he was little in the habit of attending the services of his church, and was in this somewhat singular; for though many may believe as little as he did, the outward practice is usually devout. When he did appear in a church, he had invariably some mundane reason for it. A not very creditable assignation had taken him to the *Pastorale* where he first saw Irene, and now his object was, unseen and unsuspected, to meet Monsignore Clementi. The uncle and nephew never now acknowledged each other in public, but the latter had ready means of communicating information to his uncle, and sometime they met, as on the present occasion. As no one came, the count rose from his knees, and was studying with great devoutness a shabby print of a monk, which was hung on the wall above an inscription inviting all the faithful to contribute alms towards the beatification of the venerable Agostino Modena; when a sound in the sacristy told him that Monsignore Clementi had come, having entered by the convent private way. Accordingly after a glance to see that no one else was there, the nephew sought his uncle.

He first offered a report of the last private meeting which he had attended; a report of some importance, as it showed how outrageous the desires of the ultra-republicans were becoming, and that they were combining with the men of their own stamp in Tuscany. He next asked if the report that Count Rossi was to be the new Prime Minister were well founded. Very mournfully did his uncle assent, adding, ' This is the heaviest blow that the evil spirits could have aimed at us. That man is infected with reform; he has it in him to carry out all his diabolical plans. I have heard them from his friend A. B., in whom he places great confidence. He makes no secret of his opinions. Up to this time all has gone admirably; matters must soon have come to a crisis; then Austria would have interfered, and all would have been restored as it was formerly. Now, if Rossi has his way, we shall become like France—nay, even like heretic England, where priests have no share in the Government, and their Church is a state machine.'

' Rossi's course will not be a long one, my uncle; he is unpopular, and the people suspect him; the *Contemporaneo* has done its work; look here,' and he produced a number which violently denounced Rossi.

'That is well, that is well,' said Monsignore Clementi, slightly glancing it over. 'Sturbini acts as if he were in my pay. Cardinal L—— was bent on having him arrested the other day— Conceive such folly ! these divisions are life to us. Had Mamiani's Ministry lasted longer, what with the papers and with the *Circoli*, we should have had the rebellion we had counted on; but, if the Ministry changes, no one can tell the result. It is possible, however, that Rossi may refuse to take office.'

'Possible,' said the count, dubiously.

'I hear that Nota—the *improvisatore*—is returned; I thought I recognised his pen again; that is a pestilential fellow, the soul of these moderates.'

'A small and diminishing party, monsignore.'

'Ay, but dangerous, dangerous ! You made a mistake, nephew, when you objected to the banishment of young Mori and his sister; their saloon is the very focus of that party, and there is no enemy like a woman, especially with such gifts as I hear *la Mori* has. Now we dare not attack her ; she is too popular.'

'Through them I learn the projects of the moderates.'

'So you urged before, my nephew,' said the old man, stroking his chin, and fixing his astute dark eyes on the count; 'but I have an idea—an idea, I say; I am told that—' and he made a significant pause.

Count Clementi never changed a feature though he saw his secret was well nigh divined. He said to himself with a thrill of virtuous indignation, 'What! does he set spies upon me ?'

Obtaining no answer, except a look of surprise and a slight smile, the uncle continued, 'You deserve some reward, Pietrucchio, for what you have done for me; I do not count such slight recompenses as I have been able to give; they are nothing, nothing at all. Had Gregorio lived!—' and he glanced at his violet stockings, and sighed profoundly. 'A few weeks more and I had been a cardinal. Fate willed it otherwise; and until the old order of things be restored, which may Heaven grant speedily, I can do nothing important for you.'

He paused, but the count was too wary to be entrapped into a confession.

'I have never asked for a reward, my uncle.'

'You threw away the best chance I had for you, nephew—that marriage! Such a dowry—and influence! Yet you must marry.'

'Possibly the reward I shall claim may be to choose my own wife, monsignore. I have lived so much among liberals that they have infected me with their doctrines. In this matter I could hardly submit, even to you,' said the count, anxious to discover how far this doctrine would be palatable to his companion.

There was an odd, dissatisfied look in Monsignore Clementi's face as he replied, 'One of your name would never choose unwisely. Any wife less noble than yourself would be a disgrace to us— a disgrace, nephew; it could not be.'

The count bowed submissively, and decided that a secret marriage must be his resource. He folded up his newspaper, and said, as if it had re-called the subject to him, 'If you cast your eye over my minutes of the last meeting, you will see that three men swore to poniard Rossi, should he accept office and play false.'

'These republicans are true demons,' said his uncle, with pious horror: 'but Heaven overrules their evil deeds for the good of the Church! Theirs is the sin, but we benefit by it.'

'These are fanatics, but there are others who owe Rossi a private grudge—one in particular, but he disappeared lately; I suppose the police got hold of him. Tito Campana.'

'Eh! Tito—Tito Campana! the fellow who brawled with Rossi's valet! I remember it all now; he is a *protégé* of Marchesa Gentile's, and would have been let off had Rossi been reasonable; but nothing would satisfy him but the galleys. *Gia, gia,* and he was pardoned afterwards. Let me think, what was he condemned for again? I do not remember, but the marchesa petitioned for his pardon again lately; I had her supplication lying on my table yesterday. So the man has a grudge against Rossi!'

'I fancy that Rossi would have experienced it, had not Campana been so speedily re-imprisoned. Will he be released this time?'

'The Pope is merciful, and the matter has been strongly represented to him; Marchesa Gentile is powerful. So Rossi has other enemies!'

Count Clementi opened his book, and pointed to three names in different pages.

'Cecchi —— red republican —— unbeliever —— desperado — hum, hum,' said Monsignore Clementi, muttering over the names and comments to himself, 'Michele Arpione, hum —— excommunicated villains! tell me no more about them, nephew.'

The count smiled imperceptibly, as he reflected that his uncle had taken care to know all he wanted before any scruples seized him, and did not appear likely to arrest the course of events, however much he was scandalized by the actors in them. Taking back the book, Clementi said, ' A crisis is not far off; the moderates hoped to convert the ultras; on the contrary, the ultras have cajoled more than half the moderates, and will speedily split with the rest. Nota is not the popular man he was. Then comes the battle.'

' Once get them down, and Pio Nono will not burn his fingers with reforms again. Already he repents; the Jesuits made a master stroke when they retired voluntarily; he has never had a moment's peace since, and is dying to have them back.'

Some further discourse followed on the events of the day before the uncle and nephew separated. They went out by different doors and at different times, satisfied with their consultation, but both secretly uneasy on one point—namely, Irene. The uncle suspected an attachment which might lead his nephew into some entanglement, perhaps even deprive himself of his invaluable spy; the nephew was indignant at finding that he, too, was not free from his uncle's surveillance, and disturbed by this first encounter with prejudices which he knew to be almost invincible. A heretic, a cantatrice, for the bride of the sole representative of the Clementi in a position to marry! But some day Monsignore Clementi would have to make up his mind to it; and Irene—yes, Irene, would not refuse, if Leone were out of the way, to save Vincenzo, even at this price!

The count walked slowly towards the more inhabited part of the city, passing along a deserted road, between high walls, over which a locust tree here and there spread its arms, and ere long he reached a wild region, where vineyards, and gardens, and heaps of nameless ruins, were mingled together. A deserted villa stood, shadowed by gloomy stone pines; and, half buried in masses of ivy and brambles, the broken arches of an aqueduct were overtopped by dark cypress spires. A wall shut in this neglected spot; it was green with moss and tufts of maidenhair; climbing roses, mounting from within, trailed over it; there was a closed door in it, near which a man evidently belonging to the lower class was loitering. A hesitating guilty glance, as though the sight of a stranger of rank were alarming, attracted Clementi's attention, and while apparently sauntering onwards, he turned his head, when he was at some distance, and saw the man pausing at the door and then passing through it. The count turned and walked slowly back again. A second man now came from another direction; his dress showed him to be a bargeman of the Tiber; he too went in, after the same momentary pause, as if some one on the other side had asked for a password before admitting him. Two more came soon afterwards, but they were clearly suspicious of the count, who advanced and asked whether they had seen a gold seal lying on the road. Both denied hastily and curtly; he bowed, thanked them, and continued to walk up and down, as if searching for it. They loitered, and hesitated, and seemed to consult; and when he had gone nearly out of sight they too entered the garden.

He now felt no doubt that he had lit on some political meeting, and felt extremely ill-used at the bare idea of such a thing taking place unknown to him. His curiosity was strongly excited; he waited for a while, but no one came, and he turned to the door, and gazed through the bars of the upper part. Nothing was to be seen, but long grass and giant nettles growing rank beneath the trees. He drew back and looked up at the wall, speedily determined that it was too high to be scaled, and made a circuit, examining it narrowly. A door leading into a neighbouring vineyard was unlocked; he went through, and came to the side nearest the garden. Here he again found the wall, but one part of it was low, and a bank of earth rose against it. The ground in the garden was considerably higher than that in the vineyard. Count Clementi stood considering with a muttered ' *Oh, adagio!*' speedily made up his mind, spied out a place where his foot could rest beneath a bush of strong old golden-berried ivy, and scrambling up by it like a cat, he dropped into the garden below.

He alighted in a clump of prickly aloe and cactus, which made him wince and stamp, but he suppressed the oath which sprang to his lips, and glided noiselessly into the shrubs, eye and ear alert, for well he knew what the fate of a spy would be if detected among conspirators. He did not want for courage, or he would not have been there; and he had a sense of excitement, even enjoyment, in the perilous adventure, which quickened his pulses, and roused every sense into double activity, while he advanced towards the centre of the garden, where, amid a jungle of tall reeds and further sheltered by the drooping boughs of a pepper tree, he crouched down and observed the scene.

Evening had fully come, the October moon was up in an intensely purple sky; her beams lighted the ruined stately arches, but could not penetrate the cavernous shadows beneath them, silvered the reeds, danced on the ripe fruit of the orange-trees, and stole into the little empty Belvedere, showing the frescoes dropping in decay from its walls. The ilexes and cypresses seemed blacker than ever under her light. There was perfect stillness; except when a bird woke and chirped, or the bell of a convent somewhere near tinkled. All was tranquillity and desolation; the owners of the villa, which stood white and cold on the rising ground, had left it to solitude and malaria; but others had taken possession in their place.

In an open, grassy space some nineteen or twenty men, and a very few women, were assembled, all of the poorest classes; their careworn faces and anxious eyes looked from beneath the broad grey hats of the men, and the shawls which the women wore drawn over their heads. As the night wind sighed among the trees they started and looked round, and if a few words were exchanged among them, it was under their breath.

Something was said after a while by one who might have been an artizan, and the assembly immediately composed themselves into serious attention; the speaker proceeded in fervent words, which Clementi from his lurking place could only indistinctly catch, the rest stood round and as with one voice uttered, when he concluded, a deep '*E così sia.*' Another man now gave some order, and all at once began in subdued tones to repeat a Psalm in Italian verse. '*Presso al fiume, al fiume di Babilonia*' was borne on the breeze to Count Clementi's ear. He did not recognise—perhaps he heard it for the first time—the mournful lament which the captive Jews once sang by the waters of Babylon, and which the poor Italians were now applying to themselves; but it flashed upon him that this was no political meeting, but an assembly of some who had renounced the Roman Church, and were attempting to form a worship of their own. It was so; these were men who met, at the peril of life and liberty, to pray and read the Bible in their own tongue—men who, with the errors of Romanism, cast off, alas! much that is essential, and, oppressed and persecuted, renounced by all parties alike, and waging war against all ecclesiastical authority, had in the very search for truth become ' in endless mazes lost.'

Count Clementi recalled tales which were darkly told of similar meetings elsewhere, but he had little expected to witness one in Rome. He took note of it for possible future use, and drew nearer to hear what might come next. The Psalm concluded; several of the congregation produced Italian Bibles, and a chapter was read aloud. A new speaker prepared to address them—Clementi's eyes opened wide with amazement, and he had almost laughed aloud between surprise and amusement, as he suddenly recognised Cecchi in the congregation; the man whom he had fancied at times slightly mad, but no more a believer than himself; but whom he was only right in supposing a disbeliever in the Roman Church. Cecchi's eye lighted up with wild enthusiasm as the preacher began, taking for the foundation of his discourse, the text, 'The disciple is not above his master,' probably in allusion to something that had lately occurred among the little congregation; for, as he declaimed on troubles and persecutions, a faint sound of weeping broke from the women present. Taking a different tone as he proceeded, he warmed into rude eloquence on the subject of the lives led by the Roman clergy.

'Behold our Popes and cardinals, our canons and abbots, priests, friars, and monsignori! Christ forsook worldly glory, and they seek it; they sit in their marble palaces far from sun and wind with their proud train; they go not on foot, but in gilded coaches; and they curse, and bless not. Did John go in gilt coaches, or Paul wear purple and silver, mitre and ring, albe, cope and rochet? I think not. Was Peter an ambassador, a senator, a secretary of state? I think not, brethren. Did James fare sumptuously every day? Did he break the commandments from the first to the last, and buy absolution by taxing the people? Oh, generation of vipers! the true church mourns, like Rachel, for her children whom Herod has slain, but her Spouse is at hand; yea, He comes quickly, and His coming shall be an abyss of wrath to swallow up her persecutors. How has the rebellious city filled up the measure of her sin? Yea, and verily she shall be rewarded fourfold!'

The address now rose into a strain of mysticism intelligible only to the initiated; it lasted perhaps half an hour; the congregation stood the whole time, and dispersed separately and mutely. Something between a smile and a sneer curled Count Clementi's lip, as he listened to the unflattered picture of the Roman hierarchy. He waited long after all was perfectly quiet, scaled the wall again, and got back into the road as he came.

'Not one of even the *mezzo ceto* there, except Cecchi,' he reflected; 'hardly a woman either—women always stand by their priests. Those men would welcome a revolution ; hatred of the clergy is the moving spring with them. This is a new element, on which I had not counted. *Mona Luna*, you see strange things,' said he, taking off his hat in a sort of grave mockery to the moon, which rode high in the heavens ; 'how many tales could you tell if you chose ? but you are discreet, you see all, and say nothing. So my friend Cecchi is an enraged fanatic instead of a simple heretic ! *Va bene*—I shall know how to have him. Low be it whispered how I have spent this evening. Ah ha ! a heretic meeting under the holy noses of the Pope, the police, and all the cardinals !'

Two days later, Count Clementi learnt that the Mamiani Ministry having resigned, Count Rossi had, after much hesitation, accepted office.

A few days later Tito Campana was restored to his anxious relatives fresh from the galleys, animated with inextinguishable hatred against him whom he considered as the author of all his woes.

CHAPTER X.

I have lost the dream of Doing,
And that other dream of Done.
E. B. BROWNING.

'O LIBERTY! Oh, lovely liberty!' sang Irene, as she entered the sitting-room, whence she had been called to consult with her milliner on a matter important even to the best singers and actresses—namely, a costume. Irene knew that her dresses must be not only appropriate to her parts, but becoming, unless she would risk her success; and, perhaps, there is nothing in her profession so trying to a sensitive mind as the necessary familiarity of the public with the personal appearance of the cantatrice and the actress. She cannot influence it as the author, or the painter may, and remain unknown the while; she must present herself before all eyes, and even challenge observation. Irene felt this keenly at times; her sensitiveness had not yet become blunted; her art was no mere trade; her crown was still fresh and budding round her head; she entered into her parts even more fully now than when she had first become a cantatrice; and her gay, mounting spirits, after a comic part, or the depression and lassitude that ensued after performing in a highly wrought and tragic one, showed how much of herself she threw into each.

Her present engagement soon terminated; it remained to be seen whether she would renew it or not. Her own wish was to do so; but Leone earnestly desired to obtain such an employment as should put them beyond any need of Irene's salary. He would fain have withdrawn her into private life. She had not yet confessed this to Madame Marriotti, whom she saw as often as usual, but always found bent on taking her speedily to Germany. Irene felt very guilty when she visited her, and longed for Mrs. Dalzell, especially when her heart failed her, because Leone's health so slowly improved.

His recovery had been far from the speedy matter she had anticipated; though cured of his wound, the exhaustion left by illness hung wearily about him; his anxiety to rejoin his regiment but increased his feverish weakness; and added to this, was the critical position of Roman affairs, and the increasing ill news from Upper Italy.

Lombardy lay under martial law; her noblest and best were exiled or captive, and every ruler, save the true-hearted King of Sardinia, was hastening to revoke his concessions. To make matters worse, the ultra-republicans chose this moment for urging their claims louder than ever. Leone had returned only to find his own small party well nigh crushed, as all must be which attempts to stand between two great forces; the public mind so highly excited, that the moderates were hooted as absolute traitors, and his own popularity threatened to give way. He and his little knot of friends had for years sought secretly to educate the people for liberty, should its time ever come; but their work was now scattered to the winds. He had lived to hear himself accused of being at heart Austrian—himself and others whose lives had been spent for Italy!

Leone found that men must head public opinion if they would be popular. Once try to restrain its course, and renegade will be the mildest name for the once idolized leader.

Yet when he spoke at Circolo Nota, the club which he himself had founded, he carried away his audience, for the moment at least, as usual; but the man who rose to reply to him was even more loudly applauded. Irene dreaded the name of *Circolo*, for Leone suffered severely after every exertion, and his fever perpetually returned.

He remained at Palazzo Clementi, for his old lodgings were no longer to be had; while those which Mrs. Dalzell had occupied were vacant. They had been let early in the season to an American family, who, alarmed by public events, had forfeited three months' rent rather than remain. Cecchi was personally attached to Leone, though opposed to his politics, and made him heartily welcome. Doubly welcome was he to the padrona, who seemed to have obtained a dim inkling that her husband, usually so quiet and submissive at home, was not in secret what she had imagined, and she would privately beseech Leone to endeavour to keep Nino out of danger.

' That man !' she would say, alluding to her husband, ' he seems a lamb ; he opposes me in nothing ; yet if he says a thing is to be done—enough ! so it must be. Rarely, truly rarely, does he do so ; but when he does—I assure you, I tremble before him at such times. And of late I hardly know him ; I could figure to myself, that he is indifferent t what I say because he has other things in his head. How does it appear to you ? he hardly hears me, obliges me to buy all things that we require myself —unheard of ! I dare not confess to my friends, that if I want a new lamp, or require this or that, I have to buy it. What woman in my station conducts the household expenses? He is mad, it seems to me. These politics, these politics, they are nothing but a *crepacuore*, a heart break, to us poor women!'

And Leone would reply with the jesting Italian proverb which deprecates interference between husband and wife: '*Non entre tra fuso e rocca, chi non vuol esser filato.*' (He who would not be spun off, must not come between the distaff and spindle.)

About this time Leone became acquainted with Count Rossi, whom he had hitherto only known in his public character. He entertained for him—unlike most of the Romans—a profound admiration. Perhaps the Minister had occasionally relaxed his habitual reserve, and allowed Leone a glimpse into his heart; for Leone implicitly believed in him, and regarded him with personal friendship, which was far from increasing his own popularity amid the general distrust and dislike of the ill-fated count. Whence the mistrust arose, or who plotted against him, has never yet been really known—perhaps never will be. The priests cast the sin on the liberals, the liberals fling it back to the priests. Certain it is, that to the welfare of Italy, to the hopes and views of the moderates, his continuance in office was indispensable; while it was equally fatal to the retrograde party and the ultra-liberals.

Leone had of course lost his post in the *Dateria* when he volunteered, and he did not desire to resume it. It had only too well taught him the corruptions of the Government, and thoroughly sickened him; he looked forward to obtaining honourable employment under the present rule.

While waiting for health enough to undertake it, he turned to the pursuit which he would always have chosen, if a man could have lived by it in Rome—literature. He felt this interval of comparative tranquillity to be fleeting and precious, and used it diligently. The oppressive censorship barred the way no longer; authors need not fear that jealous board of ecclesiastics who were certain to expunge every striking passage, or to refuse permission to print at all. There was now no need to smuggle books secretly into the city, and conceal them in the roof, or in some nook in a wall. A bookseller even offered to publish all Leone's former poems, which had floated about so long anonymous and perilous to author and readers. This offer was a noteworthy sign of the times; but Leone, who acceded to it, could hardly review those early, hopeful effusions without a sigh. Others were to be added, which had wandered round the poet's sick-bed, or haunted him during tedious march and short halt, and now in this time of leisure found their way to paper. Irene and Vincenzo took the utmost delight in this work; it was their chief pleasure and refreshment during those restless, anxious days. A verse of one was on Irene's lips as she came in singing, ' Oh, lovely liberty !' She went up to Leone, and looked over his shoulder: ' You have not got on much this morning.'

' Assunta came.'

Assunta, Leone's married sister, visited him occasionally, but fond as she was of him, she always seemed to have an uneasy feeling that it was wrong to come, and that he was by no means a creditable connexion; and she evidently dared not invite him to her house, lest he should come in contact with her husband. Leone would have been slow to exchange the peace of Palazzo Clementi, or the society of Vincenzo and Irene, and the friends who assembled in their *salon*, for the company of his brother-in-law, who had occasionally used his influence for him in old days for Assunta's sake, but who regarded him and all liberals as reprobate vagabonds. Irene knew that Assunta's visits were apt to be painful to Leone; his sister repeated the lessons taught her with parrot fidelity, and all her love for Leone only made her more anxious to detach him from his party. He could not argue with her, for she did but repeat what her husband had impressed upon her.

Irene sat down, with a roll of music in her hands, between Leone and Vincenzo—who was carving a lectern—and began to read it through in silence; but often she glanced at her companions, comparing the settled invalid look of Vincenzo with Leone's countenance. She was accustomed to see Vincenzo always ailing; it was an old, fixed anxiety; she felt it without thinking about it; Leone's slow recovery and fluctuations between better and worse were a new one, continually coming before her. All were occupied and silent, till Leone's pen paused; he looked up, and smiled in answer to Irene's smile, passing to her the manuscript.

' "A Patriot." I know what suggested this, Leone.'

'Let me see,' said Vincenzo, stretching out his hand.

She gave it, and he read the poem aloud, and

returned it, with a sign that he also recognised its source.

'The man whom they call alternately Austrian and French!' continued Leone with enthusiasm, as he thought of Rossi. 'All Rome should have heard him speak as I did that first time I ever was in his company. "Italy and Greece," he said, "are sisters, differing in age, alike in beauty, equal in glory, both dead. When the last began to revive, could we look without anguish on the first, lying cold, inanimate, though lovely as ever?"— and then for once his noble heart spoke out—I still see his gesture, his kindling eye—he said, "Thank Heaven, we have seen the breath return to those lips, her cheek has flushed, her arm has raised itself. Women wept for joy when they heard this—I, a man, wept too." '

They were interrupted by Menica's entrance with a note for Irene. 'Is there an answer, signorina?' she asked, standing still before her.

'Yes, wait a *momentino*,' said Irene, holding it out to Leone. 'From Signor B——. Madame —— has sent to say she is too ill to sing to-night. Really her fancies are intolerable, and such short notice! She was displeased yesterday, I saw.'

'The manager is in a difficulty,' said Leone, passing the missive to Vincenzo, who read it, and said, 'Of course he could not ask you to take a secondary part to Signora D——; but he evidently hopes you will volunteer.'

'Oh, I would take any part with Signora D——,' said Irene; 'I never can be grateful enough for having found true, firm friends in her, and Grassi, and Sarti. But for them I should think unselfish-ness and friendship impossible in our profession.

Well, we must show Madame —— that we can do without her. She will like me less than ever, I should think!'

While she spoke she was writing a reply to the perplexed manager of the theatre, and another little note to Signora D——, with whom she was on the best of terms.

'You must make my excuses to our guests this evening,' she continued, gaily; 'if they wish to see me, they must come to the theatre. Here, Menica.'

Menica took the notes, but returned to say that the messenger had not waited.

'Oh, stupid fellow! Then you must take them, Menica, if the padrona will spare you. But what is the matter?' asked Irene, perceiving that the girl's eyes were brimful of tears; 'what is it, *poveretta?* speak!'

'*Non c'è nulla,* nothing, *signorina mia,*' sobbed out Menica, 'except that it has pleased Heaven to afflict my family, and I do not know where to turn for help. My brother—you have seen him, Signor Nota! You know what a cup of gold he is —how honest, how simple. He was in the service of a rich Russian lord, who gave him such wages! Oh, the man has gold mines in his own land, without doubt; he spent with both hands—so—I assure you,' said Menica, flinging out her own, expressively. 'He gave magnificent entertainments twice a week, and amused his guests with what Peppino calls Living Pictures—you understand! a marvel, indeed, I hear! and one represented the Holy Family, after a picture by Raffael d'Urbino; that old Capuchin with so long a beard, who came here one day, was St. Joseph, and Clelia Brocchi,

the model, she who sits with the others on the
Spanish steps—she was the most Holy Virgin. It
was most beautiful, I hear; but it caused a scandal;
the police interfered.'

'So I should expect,' said Vincenzo.

'That was the end of this entertainment; and
then the Russian had plays acted; but that was
worse, for in one, was a priest in love; yes, like
Cassandrino himself!' laughed Menica, as she recalled the numerous adventures of that hero of
the Roman puppet shows; 'and also it is said
that some of the characters had sacred names,
such as Saint Simon and Saint Pierre. Doubtless
it was a sin—'

'Nonsense, my girl, those are common French
names!' said Leone, laughing.

'Signor, this I do not know, but I can assure
you that the police admonished him severely; and
he has taken offence and left Rome, and all his
domestics are out of place; and where will they
find employment? All foreigners are provided by
this time, and we have so few this year! Alas!
this Russian made many to live! and now my
poor Peppino is without a situation.'

'We must try to find him another: do not cry
for that, *carina!*' said Irene.

'Oh, it is not all, Signorina Irene; surely we
have offended Heaven, for my mother, that poor
woman, I have named her to you! since the evil
times when the silkworms have failed and failed,
and we could no longer gain a living in our village,
she has gone into service, and I also, leaving my
eldest sister with my father, and the *creature* at
home—four of them; but she had not strength
for a service, so she took a profession, and sewed
umbrellas for Pietro Sanzi—'

' In Piazza St. Eustachio ?'

' *Signor, si*—but even that has failed her; and she is so ill, so ill, that she desires to go to the hospital—imagine that, signori! I sought for a certificate from our priest to-day. No, thank you, signor! not he! not the least shadow of one; and why? Oh, that I cannot tell you, but my master looked as black as—as—King Balthasar—when he heard it, and said the true reason was, because I was the servant of a liberal. And so my mother, poor soul, must lie in that old garret without food or nurse, because I live with Signor Cecchi. It is not just, signori—no, indeed!'

Her audience exchanged glances, which vividly expressed the same opinion.

' Give her money to get a nurse,' said Vincenzo to Irene; ' see what we can spare.'

' I will visit her to-day; she shall not want, *figlia*,' said Leone; ' why, you should have come to us at once, silly one !'

' Madonna reward you, and those you love! *signori, signorina mia !*' said Menica, kissing Irene's hand. ' Every one knows how kind you are. I always say, dear signorina, that, though you are not of our Church, still I know you are a good Christian, and so I always tell our priest when he questions me about you—better than those who let a poor woman starve because her daughter lives with liberals; as if I cared or could choose. One must live! and there is no other house with two young men in it where my brother would let me live,' she added, with Italian *naïveté*. ' There is not a better master than mine anywhere; no, nor mistress either, in all Rome, that is certain. I go to take these letters, signori; do you command anything else ?'

'No more—thanks. Take Tevere with you.'

'Yes, signor. Come! Come along, *amoretto mio!* Come then!' and caressing the dog, Menica went away again, her tears quite banished by the sympathy she had met with.

'Petty tyranny! Without doubt Cecchi divined the truth,' said Vincenzo, and Leone made a sign of assent, but no more verbal comments passed.

Nota resumed his writing, and Irene came to look over him again; she was standing behind him watching the course of his pen, when Cecchi and Clementi entered together.

Clementi never saw Irene now without a fierce, tiger-like feeling leaping up in his heart, a resolve that very soon this game should end—she must be his at any cost, and the life that stood between them must end. The thought of this happy family party, the knowledge that she and Leone were constantly together, nearly maddened him. He greeted them all, and took up a position near Leone, saying, 'The poet at work? what now?'

'You shall see very soon; there are but a few lines more,' said Nota. 'Part of the volume is already printed.'

Clementi took up the loose proof sheets. The first he lit on tried his self-command; it was a little poem written long before, but never hitherto published; its date showed that it had been composed soon after Leone first knew Irene. '*Il Primo Amore.*' The count laid it down with a frown, and looked out of the window. In one corner a spider was spinning a delicate web, examining and strengthening each thread as it progressed. In that web Clementi saw a great deal; he made it a map wherein he pictured to himself the grand crash in which his rival must perish, his own treachery remain unknown (for his uncle might be supposed to relent and save him); the appeal to Irene to become his wife, that he might rescue Vincenzo as his brother-in-law, though he could do nothing for the mere heretic stranger who had meddled with Roman politics. There were other thoughts too; he knew that exile and confiscation of property was the penalty for marrying a heretic; but he knew also how much interest can do at Rome, and how loth the Roman Church is to drive her children to extremity.

'Do you like it? that is one of my favourites,' said Irene, and Clementi found that in his musing he had taken up another leaf, and was apparently studying it intently. It was one of the slighter poems, modelled on those graceful, innocent canti, which are chiefly composed by the peasant and the mountaineer, and float about the Apennines and along the Roman Campagna, joined to plaintive, passionate airs, which only Italians can sing as they should be sung. Leone's little poem was so congenial to the spirit of the canti, that it became popular immediately; nay, it may be heard yet in the mouths of the Roman people.

> 'I saw him in a dream to-night—
>   Brocaded was the dress he wore;
> He had a sword, 'twas gold and bright,
>   A velvet cap and plume he bore.
> With his dear smile he said to me,
>   "I cannot live apart from thee;
> Parted I can no more remain—
>   I come, I leave thee not again."
>
> And when I woke, how did I weep!
>   (My eyes are red you still may see,)
> I prayed that I again might sleep,
>   That he might speak once more to me.

> Would I had never oped mine eyes
>   Until I woke in Paradise;
> There would I wake with him, and then
>   We two should never part again.
>
> They tell me that I trust to lies,
>   But I—I know 'twas truth he said.
> He looked at me with angel's eyes,
>   And on his heart his hand he laid;
> And if he does not come—oh, then,
>   My angel's gone to heaven again.
> Unless to heaven he has gone home,
>   I cannot fail—I know he'll come!'

Count Clementi smiled, and sang a verse in his rich voice, adapting it to a remarkably sweet and touching air, and Irene said, 'That shall be its air henceforward; where did you hear it?'

'In a mountain cottage where I once was driven to take shelter from the rain during a shooting excursion.'

And when Irene sang it that night, it was encored for a second time; and thenceforward *The Dream* was always sung with the air to which Count Clementi had set it.

He put it down to take the poem which Leone had just finished, and his flexile lips took their most sarcastic expression: '*The Patriot?* Ha! Count Rossi, *mi pare!* Well, poets have different eyes from other mortals. Did you see him yesterday? I heard he sent for you.'

'I did; he said he wanted some one who fairly represented the wants and aims of the middle class, but the interview was very short.'

'Interruptions, no doubt?'

'A messenger from the Quirinal; then Cardinal L—— insisted on seeing him, then a courier arrived from France, and he received a deputation from the weavers at noon; so my interview was little more than an order to be ready for another, next week.'

'Next week—ah, the Chambers will be open then. You have heard the rumour that Rossi meditates strong measures against the heretics, who are said to hold meetings in Rome? It is reported that he has had already a very serious consultation with the Holy Father on the subject.'

Vincenzo saw that Cecchi, who had been standing talking to him, was listening intently.

'Heretics! folly! Roman heretics! where will he find them?'

'How should I know? but I can tell you it is whispered, that he has obtained some strange information. If there be such meetings, they must cloak political designs.'

'Where did you hear this?'

'It was told me in confidence,' said Clementi, who had invented the tale with a view to alarming Cecchi; 'and though you disbelieve, I know as a fact, that the prisons of the Inquisition are already being filled. You heard that strange story of a Waldense disappearing lately?'

Cecchi's lips grew compressed; Clementi now spoke truth. A member of the heretic congregation had mysteriously vanished.

'I do not believe it,' said Leone, decidedly, and they spoke of other things.

CHAPTER XI.

Thou shalt have fame!   Oh, mockery! give the reed
From storms a shelter, give the drooping vine
Something round which its tendrils may entwine;
Give the parch'd flower a raindrop, and the meed
Of love's kind words to woman !

MRS. HEMANS.

'ZENAIDE!' called Madame Marriotti in the quick imperative tones which were a sure sign that something had ruffled her; 'Zenaide! where is that large letter which I was reading in bed this morning ?'

'*Non saprei dire*—I could not say, signora.'

'I had it less than an hour ago, and now I can't find it—where can it be gone ?'

'*Anima mia!* who knows ?'

'Be so kind as to look for it,' said Madame Marriotti, growing momentarily more excited and nervous, but preserving the almost invariable courtesy with which servants are addressed in Italy.

Zenaide made a feeble attempt to find the lost letter, by lifting a book and a handkerchief, and casting a glance around, but no letter caught her eye; and, crossing her hands on her apron, she said resignedly, 'It is lost, dear signora; it is the will of Heaven that we should not find it.'

'*Cara mia!*   I tell you it must be found; it is

of importance; I had—— why, here it is! how could it—ah well, it is all right now. Go and fetch my dinner. What's the matter now?'

'It is not the hour yet, signora.'

'*Benedetta te!* did I not tell you I would have my soup at noon to-day?'

'No, signora.'

'Not, *sfacciatella?* I told you so distinctly this very morning.'

'I did not hear you, signora.'

'Well, well, go along, and get it ready this instant, if you please; make haste, *via—via.* It is surprising,' said Madame Marriotti, subsiding again into her usual plaintive and reflective tone, 'it is really very surprising, that she should have the moral force of character to tell me such a falsehood, when she knows that she heard my orders, and knows that I am certain she did hear me. By the bye—Zenaide—come here for a moment; I mean to have refreshments to-night, enough for some twenty people; you must see about it; coffee, and ices, and cakes, do you understand? and you must get some man to come and wait on us.'

'Yes, signora. Raimondo Lopez is an excellent youth; you could trust him in the house.'

'True; see if he can be had.'

'I think not, signora; he serves an English milord at present.'

'What an animal this girl is! What's the use of naming him then?'

'The signora has had Sigismondo Romanis—'

'Well?'

'He waits at a *café*, but he can easily get leave of absence this evening by saying his wife is ill, or some such little lie.'

'Yes,' said Madame Marriotti, taking it as much for granted as Zenaide, that Sigismondo might and would lie if it suited him. 'See about him immediately.'

Madame Marriotti looked through her recovered letter with an anxious and thoughtful expression, called Zenaide again to know if she had taken a message to Mademoiselle Mori, re-arranged the various articles which she had tossed about in her search, went to the window, and looked out.

'There she is!' said she, perceiving Irene coming along the street with her maid. 'Now then! what is she stopping for? a beggar?'

Irene had paused to speak to a woman who had vainly applied to several passers-by for relief, receiving from the foreigners no reply at all; from the natives the more courteous, but scarcely more satisfactory, 'Go in peace,' or 'May Heaven help you.' Madame Marriotti, watching from her window, could see that Irene had asked a question, probably whether the woman were a widow, as her dress seemed to denote; and the answer was a shake of the head, hands clasped on the breast, and a look upwards. Irene gave her a trifle, was thanked by the touching benediction—'The Holy Virgin and the saints bless all whom you love,' and then came quickly under the great archway, and up the staircase, leaving her bonnet and mantle with Maddalena in the anteroom, while she herself entered Madame Marriotti's *salotto*. She wore a black silk dress; her dark hair was plaited like a tiara round her head in the becoming fashion learnt from the Grecian maidens in some remote period by the peasants of South Italy; silver pins confined its coils at the back. Nausicaa herself could hardly have looked more entirely the daughter of a Greek race than Irene, whose pure oval face, soft dark eyes, and sweet and serious dignity, marked her at once as a descendant of one of those Grecian colonies planted some two thousand years ago on the shores of Italy.

Madame Marriotti looked steadfastly· at the elastic, graceful figure, and the face so endowed with nobility and intellect that all mere prettiness sank into insignificance beside it—there was something solemn in the gaze, and Irene asked, ' Dear *maestra*, what has happened ?'

' My child, if I asked you to do something to please me, would you do it ?'

' Ah, *maestra*, ask nothing which I must refuse— it would grieve me too much.'

' Read that,' replied Madame Marriotti, putting the letter, for which she had searched, into her hands. It was an offer, through a third person, of an admirable engagememt for Irene at Dresden. She watched the young *prima donna* narrowly as she read, and saw her eye kindle, her breast heave, the soft colour come vividly into her cheeks—she paused, read on, looked up, and shook her head.

Madame Marriotti was not daunted; she had expected opposition and counted much on her own influence. She shut Irene's mouth with, ' Not a word now; think it well over. We will talk about it to-night, when my people are gone. This is the turning-point in your life; you have as yet won popularity, but not fame ; the world is before you now; lose the opportunity, and you will repent it as long as you live. No, I am not going to hear a word now; take the letter home with you, and consider. Vincenzo is a reasonable person—show it to him.'

'And Leone?' said Irene, with emphasis.

'Child, long ago I prophesied that that entanglement would bring you nothing but grief. You cannot marry him at present, I suppose; and, if you could, he would cause you to throw away all your opportunities for his sake.'

'He asks nothing, he is ever himself, the most generous man on earth; I stay here by my own wish.'

'That is enough now; recollect, however, you have a duty owing to your art—perhaps a little to me. Now go; I shall see you again by and by. Irene! my child—'

Irene had turned to go, but she came back at this appeal, and Madame Marriotti took both her hands, and looked up beseechingly into her face—'You will not break my heart by refusing this? I am old, and have few to love; your success is what I care most for on earth.'

'Dearest *maestra!*' said Irene, much moved, and she stooped and kissed her old mistress, who clasped her close with a suppressed sob—then pushed her away, muttering,

'What folly—what possesses me to-day? Go away, child.'

Irene obeyed and walked home pensive. Arrived there, she found Vincenzo reading over an article just sent in for Leone's newspaper; Leone himself was talking to a friend on the threatening aspect of public affairs, and the alarming unpopularity of Rossi. Fresh news of misfortunes in Lombardy had arrived and saddened every one, and Rome was inclined to vent her wrath on the Prime Minister.

The conversation was suspended with instinctive

caution as the door opened. When they perceived who was come, they changed it to less gloomy topics. When the visitor was gone, Nota exclaimed, 'I would give much to know that the civic guard was to be depended on; nothing can save Rossi, if he will not take warning. I must see him to-night; it will be madness, if he ventures to the *Cancelleria* to-morrow. This strange rumour that he is to be assassinated cannot have sprung up without foundation. Those insane fools, who will be satisfied with nothing but their own crazy visions, are at the bottom of it all; and the priests, whose power he had diminished daily—was there ever mischief without a priest being at the bottom of it?'

'Ay, every one of his measures has been a blow to the priesthood; he has continually taken more and more power out of their hands,' said Vincenzo.

'A firm hand, a clear head, the Pope's entire confidence, all that a Minister most wants; he knows Rome, he knows more of public affairs, in short, than any man amongst us; he was destined to give Italy freedom and justice—and is this to be the end?' exclaimed Leone.

'You say he has been warned?' asked Irene, her own affairs forcibly driven out of her mind by the excitement and alarm which she caught from her companions.

'In vain! He is too proud to listen—too noble to believe in treachery; he trusts in the troops. His one chance is to be surrounded by friends as he enters the *Cancelleria* to-morrow. If I could address the people before he arrives—if I could get a hearing, I could save him,' said Leone, whose eloquence had indeed many a time calmed the populace. 'We should concert measures instantly; but the vagueness of this rumour—'

'If there be a plot, Cecchi knows of it,' said Vincenzo.

'Vincenzino! you do not think him an assassin!'

'No, Irene, not in his sober senses; but the man is strangely changed of late, and we have heard of secret societies, where men are sworn to obedience and assassins are chosen by lot.'

'Oh, it seems too dreadful!' said Irene, turning very pale.

'See him I must instantly,' said Leone, starting up, but recollecting that Cecchi was engaged in his business at this hour, he paused to reflect. 'I must trust to seeing him this evening then. I could not find Donizetti or Galilei at home either, this evening—yes, I must wait. There is just a chance of my seeing Count Rossi again; I may be able to give him one more warning. Nothing on earth could be so fatal to us as his death—nothing so play into the hands of the *Papiste.*'

Menica entered with a dish of macaroni and another of vegetables, which formed the abstemious Italian dinner. Vincenzo had to clear away his books and writing, and the girl's presence of course put an end to the conversation. When they had sat down to dinner, Irene said, ' It is almost wrong to think of personal affairs now, but I ought to show you both this letter. Will you read it aloud, Leone ?'

He did so, and a silence followed; for all were full of thought, all conscious that this was a turning-point in Irene's career; the way to fame and wealth lay open before her. She had already acquired a name, but she was yet comparatively unknown; she had only appeared on the Roman stage, which is little celebrated, and pays its cantatrices ill. To go to that land of music—Germany, to hear and see the high priests of her art, to rank, perhaps, highest of the great singers of her day—these were not slight temptations to Irene, whom nature had created a cantatrice, with as little choice in the matter as she allows to her predestined artists, poets, and men of science. Irene's whole education had been musical; she had learnt to look on music as the purest, noblest thing on earth. The painter, full of yearning after Italy and her treasures of art, feels somewhat as Irene did, when she thought of Germany. It was in her power to go there now.

On the other hand, there was love, and there was patriotism, which, perhaps, in Irene's case was nearly the same thing, since she had learnt to be patriotic from Leone Nota. With a woman patriotism is apt to become a personal feeling— an affection; it was so, in a measure, even with Irene, though her views were wide and just. Too many ardent discussions had been held in her *salon*, too many of the best and wisest patriots frequented it, for Irene's love of her country to be merely the desire that her lover should have his wishes. Irene foresaw that evil days were coming for Rome; she could not desert her birth-place. It might be long before she returned, and where would Leone be meanwhile!—and the marriage, which, were they rich or poor, was really to be in the spring!

Another weighty objection was Vincenzo.

Where would not Vincenzo go if she wished it? But in Rome he had friends, was known by his carvings, was deeply concerned in public matters. Could she ask him to leave all this, and be dependent on her? Vincenzo would not have made this objection, but Irene thought of it for him. And there was another reason, stronger still. Like a distant Eden, Germany offered itself to her view, but close at hand was Nota. She met his eyes with their deep, mournful gaze—smiled, and asked, 'What do you say, Leone?'

He paused, took her hand, and answered in tones which he forced into steadiness, 'Irene, here you alone are judge.'

She looked at her brother, and there was a smile in her dark eyes, a sort of glad triumph in her countenance, as she felt that here was a sacrifice to be made for Leone's sake, and yet that, made for him, it was no sacrifice at all. Vincenzo looked at friend and sister alternately, and for once was uncertain what Irene's sentiments were; and he felt strongly for Nota, whose features betrayed by how great an effort he prevented himself from influencing her.

'Leone is right in saying that this is for you to decide, Irene.'

Nota spoke now low and calmly, and with authority, though his voice faltered as he concluded. 'Irene, I have offered you all that a man can—his love. All the rest is nothing; we may put riches and poverty out of the question. Choose between me and fame, but choose deliberately. Heaven only knows what kind of fate you will meet as my wife; there are dark days before us. There is nothing so precious to me as your happiness

—you know it. Choose freely; I give you back your promise. Irene, many may call you great! to me you are dear; but remember that my happiness and your own will be lost for ever, if too late you find that you regret fame and fortune.'

Vincenzo held out his hand to his friend; his feelings were divided; the grand future offered to Irene dazzled him, but his heart went with Leone, who had not looked at Irene while he spoke; their eyes met now. 'Did you really doubt what I should choose?' she asked. 'Ah, Leone, what would fame be to me without your love? Now, every plaudit seems something to offer to you. You little know how mockingly it used to sound to me when you were in Lombardy—all my life was empty and worthless. And now—now—you are come back. I could bear or do anything now. Choose freely? You must teach me not to love you first, Leone!'

At that moment even Vincenzo was nothing to her in comparison with Nota; they had both forgotten that there was any one in the world except each other. Vincenzo knew it, but his sigh changed into a look of almost womanly tenderness, as he watched the two dearest to him on earth.

When Irene became more composed she foresaw with dread how intense a disappointment her decision would be to Madame Marriotti. She pictured in thought the probable scene; summoned her arguments, braced herself up to meet all the surprise, grief, and anger which she knew she should encounter, talked the matter over with Vincenzo, and finally went and sat for an hour or two in the gardens on the Pincian, to have time for quiet reflection. Scenes that she had almost forgotten rose up out of her past life before her; from where she sat she could see the Bosco— rising high above the iron-grated door of the academy—she had never been there since Vincenzo's accident; the name of De Crillon came, she knew not why, into her mind, though she had not thought of it for years—could not have re-called it the day before had she wished to do so. How much, how very much, had happened since that day; how entirely were her affections, her fortunes, become bound up in Rome!

Looks of interest were cast by many of the foreigners, loitering in those pleasant gardens, on the young Italian girl, who sat so lost in thought that she never perceived their notice; while the staid Maddalena sat by her, knitting ceaselessly, her grave, dark face, long golden earrings, and the silver pins in her hair attracting the notice of strangers almost as much as the pensive Grecian features of her young mistress. A band was playing in one part of the garden; carriages drove up and down, or waited while their owners sauntered in the shady walks or sat to listen to the music, nurses with their bright ribbons and silver pins paraded up and down; crowds of children skipped, ran races, drove their hoops, or played at different games; the rosy, blue-eyed English or German children contrasting with the slender, dark-eyed, sallow little Italians. The air rang with clear laughing voices.

Some little boys, near Irene, had invented a new version of the popular '*Lupo;*' one sitting on the ground, feigned to be ravenously gnawing something, and the others with great eagerness sur-rounded him, and entreated to be told what it was.

The usual answer would have been, 'The bones of your sister,' and then ought to have followed a pantomime of threats and flattery by which the 'wolf' should be finally cajoled out of the relics, but in the present instance the game ran:

'Wolf, wolf, what are you eating there?'

'I eat the bones of an Austrian,' lisped Lupo in reply, lifting up a little mirthful face, and, instead of the outbreak of horror, came a grand clapping of hands, and a cry, 'Let us see, let us see, dear wolf, good wolf—wolf, the core of my heart!'

Lupo growled in answer to these endearments, gnawed ferociously, and replied, 'You are yellow and black Austrians yourselves.'

'No, no, no, we are patriots, we are Italians; out with the barbarians, down with their banner—show us the bones, the bones, the bones!'

Another little fellow presently took the character of Lupo, and improved the game by asserting he was eating Radetsky; and inspired by the burst of applause, he added, 'all the cardinals.'

'Cannibal!' was heard in a tone of profound disgust; and a boy of some seven or eight years, advanced into the midst of the group with dignity, and said, 'You are all miserable *Carbonari*; I am a *Papista*, and I will have you all excommunicated.'

'Oh, oh, the traitor, the priest!' shrieked all the others with veritable rage, for both they and the new comer were in thorough childish earnest.

'My papa says that Radetsky has beaten Charles Albert and your Durando into little bits; so there!' said the small champion defiantly, amid such a storm of shouts and hisses, and hands brandished as if they held sabre and dagger, that all near stopped and looked on with surprise and amusement; and the youthful *Papista* was suddenly captured and dragged away by the nurse with whom his two little sisters were demurely walking. Such a scene was not without its significance. Irene was roused by the noise, and, looking at her watch, discovered that it was time to go home.

It was with a beating heart that she went to Madame Marriotti's house in the evening, and the affectionate look which the *maestra* gave her as she entered, caused her a fresh pang. Though many foreigners had left Rome, there were French and Germans present as well as Italians, and Madame Marriotti went from one to another, stopping to converse for a few minutes with each in their own languages, which she spoke with perfect fluency, though with a slight accent which betrayed that the rich and sonorous Spanish was her native tongue. She was, in fact, a cosmopolite —now, perhaps, more of an Italian than anything else; her chief friends were in Rome, and her beloved art found too little scope in Spain to tempt her back thither; but she retained traces of her origin in her swarthy complexion, her vivid black eyes, soft accent, and fairy-like hands and feet, and a sentence of Spanish would at all times awaken her out of her dreamiest mood. As a girl she had probably been too dark and meagre to have any claims to beauty, though at all times she must have fascinated by the bewitchingly sweet and gracious manners which she could assume when she pleased. Probably she looked better than in her full prime on this evening in her black velvet dress, with a *fazzoletto* of costly lace on her head, her fan in her hand, and a Cachemere shawl, a royal gift, draped round her. She had gathered her wits on this occasion, and instead of letting them wander in the dream-land where she was so apt to dwell that it had become far more real to her than the actual present, she gave her mind to entertaining her guests, and, after some persuasion, was induced to sing to them. She had given up singing for several years, but those who knew her age, stood amazed at the sweetness and expression with which she gave a popular *canzone*. The once magnificent voice was, indeed, almost gone, but the execution and sweetness remained, and the old lady, evidently gratified by the general admiration and thanks, consented to sing now a litany to the Virgin which she had picked up by ear from the boatmen of Sorrento ; then a Russian air ; next one of her native *canciones*.

Irene stood listening, and wondered if ever she should sing to a party who remembered her glory as a thing of the past, and look back on her life as something laid aside—and then she smiled, and remembered that her fate was decided ; she should never wander from Rome, never be a world-famed cantatrice, but instead—ah, what a vision of a happy home rose up! As she looked at Madame Marriotti, lonely and childless, amid the recollections of past fame, she clasped her hands together in the fulness of her silent acknowledgment, that to a woman the sunshine of home, the love and protection of one stronger than herself, is the best lot that life can offer. ' Women and vines both need a prop!' she whispered to herself with a happy smile. Madame Marriotti now rose,

and bade her sing with a German professional,
who afterwards expressed his delight at hearing
the music of his native country so perfectly
rendered and appreciated by an Italian; and she
had some interesting conversation with him about
living German composers, and the characteristics
of modern music.

'You never hear my native music properly in
Italy; the Italians do not love it; you are the
only exception that I have met with; you might
belong to us; you ought to come to Germany,
mademoiselle.   Why remain so long in this narrow
sphere?'

Madame Marriotti was near; she looked round—
Irene shook her head, and her heart beat painfully.
The German, fairly launched on his hobby, proceeded, not heeding her silence. 'The indifference to our masterpieces is surprising; nothing
but music that works on the passions will be
listened to at Rome.   Now this majestic piece by
M——, madame without doubt knows it?' said he
turning to Madame Marriotti, and playing a few
bars on the piano to recal to her the composi-
tion he meant.

'Oh yes, I have heard M—— himself play it;
or let me see, was it somebody else?   Ah well, it
does not signify; I know it was some celebrated
man, but then there are such heaps of celebrated
men; at all events it was very wonderful and dull.'

'Dull!' exclaimed the musician aghast. 'Dull!
his style is colossal; it may be likened for grandeur
and massiveness to a Gothic cathedral; it is infinite;
how calm, how majestic, yet how human; how full
of *schauerlich süsse* harmony!'

'Yes,' continued Madame Marriotti, not in the

least aware of his indignant disbelief of his own ears, and pursuing her recollections in her usual erratic style; 'yes, I know I thought it heavy; he played it to give me an idea of the style of the thing. It was at that party when Sontag and Malibran first sang together.'

'Madame was so happy as to hear those two first sing together?'

'I knew both well—ah, poor Malibran, half zingara, half sybil, and wholly enchantress! Who would have foretold her death in gloomy England who saw her that night!'

The guests pressed round, for Madame Marriotti possessed in perfection that delightful art which can only be expressed by the French word *'raconter;'* that indefinable talent which lends point and grace to the slightest anecdote. They entreated her to describe the meeting between the two great singers.

'I have told it to you fifty times,' said Madame Marriotti, with the silvery laugh which had something of childhood's unrestrained joyousness about it—'don't try to flatter me into telling it again.'

But they would not be satisfied until she had related how the two queens of song had, up to that time, shunned a meeting, as if afraid of each other's powers; how an innocent conspiracy entrapped them into an interview and a duet, in which each sang as if inspired; and how at the end each gazed at the other as if amazed by the excellence of her rival—then by a common impulse they embraced, and were fast friends ever after.

Irene greatly enjoyed this evening, though she dreaded its close; it had refreshed her to hear the subject she loved best discussed with feeling and science, and she was glad to forget politics entirely for a time. She was weary of the miserable tidings from Upper Italy, and of the violence and egotism of the democratic party in Rome.

The guests began to go; the German was the last; he said to Irene as he took leave, 'We shall meet yet in my own land.' Irene and Madame Marriotti were left alone. The old lady sat down, held out her hands to Irene, and said, using one of the caressing phrases of her native language, 'Child of my soul! come to me. How is it to be?'

Irene came, knelt beside her, took her hands, and said, while she looked up in her face, 'Forgive me, dearest *maestra*. It cannot be!'

'And why not, my child? Let me hear,' said Madame Marriotti, with gentleness that showed how entirely her heart was set on this scheme.

'There are many reasons, *maestra*. First, I have promised to be Leone's wife in the spring; he would hardly choose me to leave him in the summer; next, I cannot ask Vincenzo to go. He loves Rome with all his heart; you have heard him say, that he could not live elsewhere, and then, there is his profession. I could not bear him to be a mere appendage to me; and, if my voice should fail, what should we have to live on?'

'True. On the other hand Heaven has made you a cantatrice, has given you great powers; your vocation is as clearly marked out as that of any missionary or martyr. Heaven will one day say to you, "Where is the work that I gave you to do?" it says now, "Show the world what my noblest, most spiritual gift may be made; make your profession honoured by your life; interpret for the great musicians whose works lie mute till one comes who can give them voice." Is this nothing? Child, I never told you your path was strewn with flowers; I warned you long ago, that hands and feet—ah, heart too, would bleed in the path you had chosen; but your choice has long been made; you must go onward, and fling away whatever hampers you in the ascent.'

Irene was mute; she felt strongly the dignity and authority with which Madame Marriotti spoke —speaking out of her own life and conscientious practice.

'You must, you must do this, Irene! What city was ever built, what work ever done, without blood and tears to water it? Mark me, I do not talk of happiness; I only say, that you must account for the great gift that Heaven has given you; cage it, or cast it from you, and it will return to be a terror and a burden; you will have no scope for your energies, no sufficient interest in life, if you throw yourself into a sphere never intended for you. "Do your work" is the command laid on us all.'

'And Leone?'

'Ah me! child, you would not listen when I warned both you and one who was older and should have been wiser; Mrs. Dalzell is an excellent, calm Englishwoman; she knows nothing of the passion and the strife of souls filled, like a pythoness, with some great perilous gift; she would bid a tiger copy the manners of her drawing-room cat. She knows no more of the matter than one who has only seen the blue sea under the cliffs of Sorrento when it laughs in the sunshine, knows how the Atlantic thunders on the iron-bound coast of Galicia. But you, Irene, you should know the impulse which hurries us on, and masters us—don't tell me you cannot understand me.'

'I do, dearest *maestra;* I will tell you the whole truth; I was almost overcome with the wish to accept this proposal; but how can I? When every day darkens for Rome, could I leave Leone?'

'Let him find a home ready made for him in Germany, by the time he is exiled.'

'He will never leave Rome,' Irene answered, very seriously, a dark shadow falling on her face; 'free or a prisoner he stays here. His are not opinions, but convictions.'

'What can you look forward to, if you remain? an audience, fickle as the waves, will weary of you—what are you doing for your profession?'

'Improving the public taste, and our *corps dramatique;* I hope, indeed, dear *maestra,* you will not deny that the operas of this season have been better put on the stage, and sung with more truth of style and taste than they ever were before?'

'As if that were worth all the plots, and calumnies, and cabals that you have gone through this year!'

'I am not artist only, you must remember, signora. Rome is my birthplace; in her all my hopes are centred. I could not go now—leave Leone now! my heart and thoughts would be all here; and, after all, I could not be true artist without being true woman.'

'You are woman enough, silly girl. Are you throwing all away, because you are too proud to ask to be free?'

'Free! Ah, what a desolate freedom! *Maestra*, these were his words, "Many may call you great, but to me you are dear."'

'Then you throw away an opportunity that will never return, for love, as you call it?'

'I love him, signora,' said Irene, rising; 'yes, no words can tell how I love Leone Nota, or how proud I am of his love for me. All possible fame would be worthless if I did not feel that every acclamation was delicious because he felt it as his own triumph. Offer a woman fame instead of love! nay, give her the rosy apples of the Dead Sea at once!'

Madame Marriotti sat listening with a melancholy, abstracted expression. 'So you refuse?' she said.

'Yes,' said Irene, decidedly; but a rush of remorse for the disappointment she was inflicting came over her, and kneeling down again she caught her friend's hand, and exclaimed, 'Oh, forgive me! how can I help it?'

'You really refuse? you have decided?' said Madame Marriotti; and then after a long silence, she added in a low murmur, unconscious that she spoke aloud, 'So it ends thus—it ends thus! well, try the experiment, then; you may be right; I had all the glory once that woman could have, and I sit lonely here now. I shall die alone, unless Zenaide has courage to stay till the last. I had a selfish motive in this scheme, no doubt; I thought to be remembered a little longer through my pupil. "*Le monde usé n'a plus rien qui me touche;*" some one said that who knew life well— it's a desolate thing after all, this life; but it ends, it ends; nothing lasts, neither joy nor sorrow. I

did not think once to grow old without husband
or child, with nothing but memory left to me. Do
as you will, Irene.'

'Dear, dear *maestra!*' exclaimed Irene, amid
fast-falling tears, while she clasped and kissed the
withered hand that lay passive in hers.

'I don't urge you any more, child; I have no
claim on you or on any one. There's not much to
take me anywhere, but I think I shall go to
Dresden; I have one old friend there, and Rome
is no place for quiet people now.'

'To Dresden! not really! you will not undertake such a journey alone?'

'Oh, Zenaide will go, I dare say, and I have nothing to keep me here. Your carriage must be
waiting, my dear; it is late. Good night.'

'Say you forgive me all this pain, signora.'

'Yes, I forgive, if there be anything to forgive.
Good night.'

Irene clung round her and kissed her, and the
kiss was returned, but she felt tears on the old
lady's cheek, and was half broken-hearted herself
at having caused her such mortification. She
could not rouse her from the depression into
which she had fallen, and noticed with great pain
how feebly she rose from her chair, and how
ill she looked—most unfit certainly for a journey to Dresden. Irene could not have retracted; even in the midst of her trouble her
heart bounded at the thought that she had made
her fate one with Leone's; but she would have
almost given even her voice, to be able to console
Madame Marriotti, and be assured that this plan
of setting off to Germany would vanish into air.

CHAPTER XII.

Calphurnia.—What mean you, Cæsar? Think you to walk
    forth ?
You shall not stir out of your house to-day.
    Cæsar.—Cæsar shall forth. The things that threatened me
Ne'er looked but on my back; when they shall see
The face of Cæsar, they are vanished.

Julius Cæsar.

GEMMA had good reason to suppose that Clementi had had some news of Luigi Ravelli, of whom she only knew that he had joined the gallant little band with which Garibaldi was keeping up a guerilla warfare against the Austrians. She was quite sure that her brother would offer her nothing without an equivalent; and, as she had no tidings to offer him, she had little chance of buying the intelligence she wanted. It struck her that Vincenzo might also have had a letter; and she was about to slip away, when her mother observed the movement, and interfered. 'Where are you going ? Stay here.'

'I want to see Irene Mori.'

'At this time in the evening! Nonsense, you are too intimate with her; you forget that she is a heretic and a cantatrice. Your brother is always urging me to make her acquaintance, but I tell him I don't mean to do so; I have not done it all these years, and why should I now? I may

let lodgings to this sort of people, but as for
knowing them—*giusto!*' said the contessa, with a
characteristic mixture of reserve and pride.

' If you will permit me to make an observation,
mamma; you allowed the American lady from the
first floor to visit you.'

' *Altro!* a woman who pays such a rent! would
you have me affront her? I do not mean to see
any more of her, however; you can tell Filippo
to take my card to her rooms to-morrow after she
is gone out. She is sure to go somewhere; these
foreigners are never still; they come and spy into
everything, and admire with open mouths, as if
it were any business of theirs. Rome is ours after
all; they do not enter into the matter, the im-
pertinents! They spend their money amongst us,
therefore the Holy Father tolerates them. Where
is Pietrucchio? it is time to repeat the rosary.'

He entered while she spoke, kissed her hand
affectionately, and asked if she felt better. The
querulous voice softened, and the fretful brow was
smoothed immediately. ' *Benino*, pretty well, *non
c'è male*, Pietrucchio. Are you going out again
to-night?'

' Let me go and see Irene—*she* objects,' whispered Gemma, with a glance at her mother. He
nodded, and, the evening prayers having been recited by the family, he bade Gemma, significantly,
good night, and occupied his mother with an account
of his evening, which had been spent with a friend.
He would have sacrificed anything to forward his
plans, even laying aside for this object the almost
Turkish jealousy with which women, especially
unmarried women, are watched in Rome, which,
however, does not prevent the existence of a very

dark side to Italian life, conventual as well as secular; but scandal in the former case is hushed by
authority, and the matter is, if possible, '*coperta.*'

Gemma ran to Irene's rooms; the outer door,
much to her surprise, chanced to have been left
ajar; no one was in the sitting-room; she held up
the lamp which she had taken out of the passage,
but it illumined only vacancy, and she perceived
with disappointment that Irene could not be at
home. In fact she was at Madame Marriotti's,
and Vincenzo had retired to bed. Leone was not
to be seen, but a sound of vehement, though low
voices, attracted Gemma's attention. It came from
the Cecchi's sitting-room, which was divided from
that of the Mori by a thin partition and a cupboard.
Against this she leant and listened to Cecchi and
Nota in fierce argument. She caught only detached
words, ' Rossi—*Cancelleria*—accursed murder—'
Then came a pause, while she listened in breathless curiosity. Nota spoke again emphatically
but very low; there was no answer at all,
Cecchi seemed to have entrenched himself in
dogged silence; then a movement followed as if
Nota had left the room, and he entered the one
where she was, so hastily, that she had only time to
rush behind the curtain which hung over the door
leading to Irene's bed-room. The idea crossed
her mind that he meant to remain until Irene
came home—a most unpleasant notion. He made
a step towards Vincenzo's room, checked himself,
caught paper and pen towards him, and wrote a
few lines at speed, half standing, half leaning over
the table, as if time were wanting to sit down,
folded and threw down his note, wrote Irene's
name upon it, and went out; and Gemma issued

from her hiding-place, exultant at her release and at the discoveries which she hoped to make. She heard the house door close—he was really gone, and his mind must be very much pre-occupied, for he never noticed the lamp which Gemma had left on the table when she fled behind the curtain. She softly opened the note; it contained a very few words, bidding Irene not expect him till she saw him; he was gone to Palazzo B———. Gemma could not supply the remainder of the name, but she took it for granted that her brother could. 'Ah! I can buy Luigi's letter now! And I owe you some return for that speech in Villa Borghese, Mademoiselle Mori!' She crept out into the passage; all was still; opened the outer door, and darted home. Her brother was waiting for her, and admitted her. 'Well, what took you over there to-night?' he asked.

'A good reason. Would you like to know what Cecchi and Nota were saying?'

His eyes sparkled, and he made a quick movement.

'News for news, Pietrucchio.'

He took out the letter she wanted, but did not give it till she had repeated the fragments of conversation, and the contents of the note. He was at no loss to supply the name of the palace— Rossi's abode. She snatched the letter, and sprang away to her own room with it, while he stood thinking, and he let her take it; she had earned it. Nota's probable plan of operations quickly occurred to him; he must have obtained information of the intended assassination, and have sought to learn more from Cecchi, whose known principles made him almost certainly an accomplice. Doubtless he had argued with him in vain; Clementi had means of exasperating all the ultra men, as being both aware of their plans and able secretly to direct the police ; and he had taken care to irritate and alarm them of late to the utmost. Nota's next step would be to warn Rossi; Clementi did not fear the result of that.

'But he may appear before Rossi at the *Cancelleria* to-morrow—he will harangue the people. Confusion! That may ruin all if he should gain a hearing—this must be looked to.'

And Count Clementi issued forth, and did not return till a very late hour.

When Irene came home she was admitted by Menica, who began, '*Ahi*, signorina! have you heard ——' but the words were taken out of her mouth by Madama Cecchi, advancing out of her own domains, her blue eyes flashing light, and an angry pink spot on each cheek, as erect and stately she marched forward. Her dress was disordered, her hair falling loose. 'Up at this hour!' cried Irene, '*ma cosa avete ?* what is it ?'

'It is—it is—a—a—ah, the *uominaccio*, the *birbone*,' burst out Madama Cecchi, her words hampered by her seething indignation; 'that Rossi! *mi fa una rabbia*, I am desperate, I could murder him with my hands! Imagine, the old days are returned! a search, a *sbirro* here, searching my husband's person, turning over everything —it is enough to distract all the saints.'

'Yes, signorina,' interposed Menica, 'after you were gone there comes a ring ; we are at supper, we naturally do not hurry ourselves—again, furious! I open, and a police officer enters, demanding how we dare keep him waiting, and must see all books and papers——'

'And my husband,' broke in the padrona again, 'my husband sits there glaring like a wild beast, and I ready to faint—what did I know they might not find? and distraught lest Nino should act in some ruinous way. I ask why they come here, and that *scelerato* of an officer replies, that they have had orders to examine certain houses, and inquires where Nino was yesterday, and yesterday week, every hour of the day, and Nino hissed out some answer to each question, I know not what. This *maladetto* Rossi has devised some new scheme. My husband asks politely if all this is under Count Rossi's orders (I shiver, when I see that look in his eye, and hear him speak so smoothly); he gets a grimace for answer, as if the *sbirro* were an ape; then out must come papers and books, all must be explained, and, ah, heavens, what ill luck, and yet how comic it was! you remember the book that Leone bought at a stall in Piazza Navona?'

'And the portrait, so like Gregorio XVI. that it was a marvel!' added Menica.

'Well,' once more interrupted Madama Cecchi, 'that *stravagante*, that young madman Ravelli must needs put a beard to it one day when he was here, before the volunteers went—it was bearded like an owl, as hairy as a thistle. I never beheld Nino laugh as he did that day! and my young gentleman writes under it " Mauro Cappelari, General of the Carbonari." '

'*Si ricorda*, signorina, Gregorio was a Cappellari.'

'Yes, yes,' said Irene, 'go on; where were Vincenzo and Leone?'

'Oh, Menica called them, but that *sfacciatello*,

brass-faced *sbirro*, said he had nothing to do with them.   Well, this unlucky book is in my sitting-room—out comes the picture, torn in half. Leone declared it was his property and the blame too; all in vain, to him the *sbirro* was courtesy itself. So it goes on for two hours, then half my husband's papers are carried off, and he, who sat mute all the time, except when an answer was dragged from him (and I had to push him and implore him in his ear before he would speak), then at last the fire breaks out, and he is *matto perfetto;* blasphemed like a Lutheran, and walked up and down the room swift as thought.   Doubtless this traitor of a Rossi intends to bring back the time when without permission of the police, we could not have more than nine people to dinner, when, if we gave a ball, the *sbirri* must be present !   *Vi pare !* I am like a maniac when I think of it.'

'Where is Leone ?   What can this mean ?'

'Eh! who can say ?   Traitor of a Rossi with his French heart! and that Pio Nono of ours—*ehi !*'

'I hope nothing dangerous was found !' said Irene, with new alarm.

'He says not, Nino tells me not; he has gone out I know not where.   I was so ill with alarm, that I had to lie down in my room; but I could not sleep, such things will not let one sleep.'

'Vincenzo is in his bed long ago, I hope.   Where is Leone, did you say ?'

'I know nothing; I heard voices below, as I lay on my bed—his and Nino's, it seemed to me; but I have a mill in my head,' said Madama Cecchi, clapping her hands over her ears; 'feel my hands, I tremble still, I am as cold as a cat's nose.'

'And I too!' chimed in Menica; 'a knife went through me when I saw that harpy of a *sbirro* with his ugly face at our door; he pushed me aside, thus, and came in while I was too frightened to stir.'

Irene felt perfectly bewildered, so much had happened this day.

'She looks quite weary, the poor darling,' said Madama Cecchi, who began to have leisure to perceive Irene's tired aspect; 'she has been singing like Santa Cecilia all the evening at the little Moorish lady's, and here we keep her still. Excuse, my dearest signorina: in these cases one is ever egotistical, one has eyes only for one's own troubles. I heard your carriage, and hurried down to make you know what had happened. If I could but guess where Nino is! But good night, sleep, and do not dream. As for me!'—and sighing deeply, Madama Cecchi retired, ejaculating once more: '*Maladetti sieno tutti i tiranni!*' and Menica followed, murmuring the comment so often made deep and low in Rome, 'But what would you have! we are under the priests.'

They little thought in what peril was Leone. After hastening to Palazzo Buoncorsi, where he did not find Rossi, he sought several friends to warn them of the dark menaces he had heard, and then bent his steps homewards by a narrow, desolate bye-street. In that street was a mean, inconspicuous house, belonging to a weaver. The police probably knew something about it, but they never interfered with the meetings which, during the last year, had been held by night within it. There assembled the handful of men who guided the revolution, unseen, but influencing the fate of all

Rome, and, with her, of all Italy. Here they concerted their plans, received deputies from their
own party in other States, and assigned to each
man his post and his work; men of various ranks,
one a *Sanpietrino*, or workman at St. Peter's;
another a man of highest rank; their plans were
various, but their aim the same; one and all were
resolved on a republic. One made patriotism a
pretext for gratifying private enmities, another,
like Cecchi, might have a still deeper object than
mere change of an oppressive government; but
they worked steadily together, regardless of life
or death when aught came in their way. Rossi
was that obstacle now, and they could have told
whence sprang that fatal popular belief, that he
had betrayed Pio Nono; a belief which the
priesthood, equally jealous of him, encouraged
rather than checked.

Leone Nota suspected the existence of this
conspirators' den; but he little imagined himself
near it, as he walked slowly homewards, thinking of
the appeal which he should make to the people next
day, and refusing to believe the fear which suggested to him that eloquence may rouse but rarely
restrain the masses. He suddenly became aware
that he was being closely followed by two men,
who had drawn nearer and nearer, and even as the
conviction occurred to him they sprang upon him.
He was unarmed, but with a soldier's quick eye
and presence of mind, he stepped back against the
wall, and flinging his cloak round one arm as a
shield, defended himself by lightning-like blows
with his clenched right hand. It was an unequal
contest indeed, but a new comer appeared in the
street, recognised his voice as he shouted to him

for help, and was instantly by his side. It was
Cecchi. The combat ceased an instant, but the
assailants were evidently known to Cecchi, who
exchanged rapid, low, astonished sentences with
them ; then he turned to Leone. ' I cannot help
you here, Nota ; no harm is intended to your life,
but these men have orders to arrest you, unless
you will give your word of honour to make no
more attempts to see Rossi, nor to appeal to the
people to-morrow. Don't refuse rashly ; what can
you do in this place ? and I tell you honestly there
are those within call who will side against you.
There are some who would gladly know you safely
out of the way.'
  ' What if I refuse ?'
  ' You are wasting precious time,' said Cecchi,
low and urgently ; a refusal leads straight to a
prison.   Are prisons so easy to get out of here ?
Hear me, stormy times are coming—Irene may want
a protector—you can help Rossi not one whit now.'
  Leone knew himself overmatched.
  'You require my promise that I will not harangue
the people to-morrow ?'
  ' That you will not seek to assist Rossi directly
or indirectly. I will answer for it,' said Cecchi
to the men, who eagerly interposed words which
Leone could not hear.
  There was nothing to be done ; he saw that
Cecchi was straining his influence to obtain permission that he should go free. He gave the promise with a proud pang at his heart, and was
allowed to go.
  Cecchi's orders counteracted those of Clementi,
but he did not guess that the count had a much
deeper end in view than merely detaining Leone

for a day. Cecchi said truly that Roman prisons hold their captives fast.

It was too late to return to Palazzo Clementi; in these unquiet times the great gate was always locked at night, and Leone preferred seeking a friend's house to rousing the sleeping porter. His note had told Irene not to expect him.

Feverish and heart-sick with her own affairs and those of others, she lay long awake, listening and starting at every sound, at last scarcely able to restrain herself from rising and seeking Vincenzo, but always checked by her fear of disturbing him. He was invalid enough to suffer severely from a wakeful night. She saw the stars grow dim before the flush of amber which stole up the sky and heralded the dawn, and the little white clouds float like spirits in the blue sky—the day had begun, the 15th of November. Slumber came, however, unquiet and troubled, and broken soon by the entrance of Madama Cecchi, her face as white as her floating dressing-gown.

' Excuse, signorina,' she said in hurried accents, glancing rapidly round, ' I must speak to you, I have a secret to tell you that our life depends on; I cannot keep it to myself; remember it is a secret that I would not tell any one else, no not my confessor on my death-bed, Heaven forgive me!— Nino came home late, very late; he was sullen, and said little, but—listen!—he dreamed!—he spoke in his sleep—and I fear—I fear—how shall I say it? Is there no means to keep Rossi from the *Cancelleria* to-day? He must not go! I know not what they intend; I must tell you, I dare not have the sin on my soul—perhaps I might be led to tell it in confession, and the Holy Virgin only knows what would come of that; if he goes, he will never come back alive—*capite ?*'

'Yes,' said Irene, aghast. 'But no, Cecchi an assassin! Romans guilty of such a deliberate crime! I will not believe it.'

'It is as true as the creed! I dare not repeat to you what Nino said last night. Oh, we have suffered already so much; has he not been *ammonito?* Does he not now obtain employment merely under the rose? and that he should plunge again into conspiracy! I would warn Rossi myself if I could go out.'

But Irene's horror was for the crime, while Madama Cecchi feared chiefly for her husband.

'Leone; where is he?'

'He is not in his room . . . . who knows if he has been able to see the count? Rossi is a traitor—but this is too dreadful; what will be the consequences!'

'The consequences!' repeated Irene. A few minutes saw her dressed and by her brother's bedside, asking, in quick imperative tones, 'Vincenzo, what were Leone's plans last night?'

'What has happened? Where is he?' exclaimed Vincenzo, greatly startled by her look and sudden entrance.

'Where is Leone?' she repeated.

'I left him sitting up, waiting for Cecchi.'

Irene shuddered, and said, in tremulous tones, 'If I did but know whether he had seen Rossi—where he is; Vincenzo, you must ask me no questions, but I have learned something of the plot against Rossi. They mean to stab him in the *Cancelleria.* There seems but one thing left to do, to warn him myself!'

'You, Irene!'

'I must try—I know this thing; I should feel like an accomplice if I let it be done without one effort to save him—Heaven will desert our cause, if this crime is done. Don't object, Vincenzo; I will —I must.'

'Stay, I must know what you are going to do. Irene! come back. I will not interfere, if there is a shadow of hope that you can do anything. Be calm, what can you do in such agitation?'

She stood still, that he might see that she had self-command enough to be trusted.

'I would put Maddalena's shawl over my head, and go to Palazzo Buoncorsi, waiting there till he came down to his carriage; he would stop, when he saw a woman waiting to speak to him.'

'And if any one should recognise you, alone, in the streets; it is madness!'

'We cannot help it, Vincenzo; we must risk it. *Could* we sit idle here, and let this thing be done?'

'You must go. Oh, to be able to go myself— I am more helpless than a woman!' said Vincenzo, with keen mortification; 'I must let you run this risk, while I—yes, go, but it will be in vain. Brave, high-hearted Rossi! you will never turn back one step through fear. The dogs, to act such an execrable part; once do this thing, and Rome is lost—all our work undone, perhaps for centuries.'

Irene had found Madama Cecchi waiting breathlessly to hear what had been resolved on; she was horrified when she heard that Irene was going out alone. Even in this conjuncture, she was meek as a lamb before the laws of custom. But this was no errand to share even with the trust-

worthy Maddalena; Irene was deaf to all remon-
strance, wrapped herself in a large shawl which
concealed her effectually, and glided into the street.
Had her nerves been less highly strung, she would
have felt alarmed at her strange position, and
dreaded remark or recognition; but, as it was, her
whole thought was to reach Palazzo Buoncorsi
ere the Minister should leave it.

An old woman sat crouching with her *scaldino*
at the entrance; Irene asked anxiously, if the count
were yet gone. 'Not yet,' was the answer; and
there was something so sinister in look and voice,
that it made Irene thrill all over, and demand if
she were waiting to speak to him.

' *Eh, figlia!* of what are you thinking?' was the
reply in a dialect which marked her as a dweller
among the Monti; ' a poor woman like me have
anything to do with a great Minister! He knows
nothing of us poor folks, unless he sends us to
prison.'

' No one need fear injustice from Count Rossi,'
said Irene, looking anxiously at her; sure that this
old hag had a personal grudge against the count.
And so she had; she was Michaela Campana, the
mother of that Tito whom Rossi had had sent to
the galleys for an attempt to stab his valet in a
quarrel.

'There is his excellency's carriage,' said the
crone; ' *accidente!*' she added lower, but from
her very soul, and the imprecation meant, ' May
you die suddenly, unconfessed!'

Irene went rapidly to the foot of the great staircase and waited. Several servants were standing
about, and asked what she wanted. ' Excuse me,
I have something to say to your master,' she

answered, and voice and manner must have betrayed that she was of higher rank than her dress denoted; for, with a look of curiosity, the man replied, ' *Perdoni, signora,*' and molested her no more. Now a step sounded above—Rossi came down the staircase, calm, noble, impassive as usual, lifted his hat to Irene, who had gone up a step or two, and would have passed on, but she made an eager movement towards him. ' Count Rossi,' she said, low but very distinctly, ' do not go to the *Cancelleria.* Nay, hear me—you are an Italian, *Italianissimo,* you should know our proverb, " The vengeance of a priest endures to the seventh generation!" They hate you; you have enemies among the people—if you go to the *Cancelleria,* you leave it a dead man.'

' The people know me,' he replied calmly, scrutinizing his companion narrowly, and more occupied with speculating on who she was, than with her urgent warning.

' They have been misled—blinded; besides, you have personal enemies—how many deadly foes may a Minister make unconsciously! Do you know why the old woman at your gate muttered " *Accidente !*" when she saw your carriage? Count Rossi, is mine the first warning you have had ?'

He smiled coldly and proudly. ' No, signora, and I thank you, and all my well-wishers. Permit me to pass; the Pope expects me.'

' He would be the first to implore you to beware, did he know half—his safety, that of all Rome, depends on you. Count, I am one of the people myself, I know the general feeling—I beseech of you do not go.'

A faint and gentle smile now came on the lips of

the Minister. 'Are you indeed one of the people, signora? However that may be, I thank you again, but no man shall say that fear ever influenced Rossi. The cause of the Pope is the cause of Heaven. Farewell, kind friend.'

He got into his carriage, and it rolled away to the Quirinal, where he saw the Pope ere he proceeded to the *Cancelleria*. Irene stood watching it with clasped hands, then she went into the nearest church, and offered up agonized prayers for him, for Leone, and for Rome. Her cheeks were still bathed in tears when she reached Palazzo Clementi unobserved.

There were knots of people talking of public affairs in the streets, but no sign of general excitement. In the *loggia* of her own floor she saw Leone, leaning on its low wall, immovable. Her impulse was to spring to his side, but she stopped, reading at once in his countenance and attitude what that night had been to him. She had seen him in many moods— when his brow was lighted, and his eye glanced with the inspiration of the *improvisatore;* she had seen him in earnest thought musing on the present and the future, on his fellow workers and principles, on a great cause and on the enormous obstacles in its way; she had seen him too when harassed with anxiety, or calmly resolute in the teeth of lowering danger; but when had she seen him look as he did now? with that stern hopeless aspect, that brow dark with wrath and grief, that attitude so listless, so expressive in its dejection! There was nothing to be done, all hope was indeed gone, or Leone would not wear that look, would not linger here inactive. There was no need for words;

she knew that, like herself, he had failed, and looked on this day as dealing a death-blow to the hopes of Rome.

She stole to his side, and laid her hand on his arm. He turned quickly. 'Irene! you here! alone ?'

'I have been to Palazzo Buoncorsini.'

'Ah! you saw him ?'

'All in vain. And you ?'

'Failed—utterly, entirely failed—should I otherwise be here ?'

'But last night ?'

'Ask me nothing: I am pledged to secresy. But you, alone! What induced you——'

'I too have a secret to keep,' she answered, smiling sadly ; 'there is very little I can tell you. But come in, Vincenzo must be anxious.'

Madama Cecchi admitted them ; her eyes questioned Irene, whose shake of the head replied plainly enough. They entered the sitting-room ; Vincenzo drew a long breath of relief on seeing Irene ; a question was on his lips, but it was arrested by a long cry in the streets, a sound of many feet—windows were flung open in all the houses, and voices called to know what had happened. But Leone, Vincenzo, and Irene did not stir, they looked mutely at one another ; and even through their closed windows pierced the horror-stricken cry, 'Rossi is dead—they have stabbed Count Rossi !'

It was so indeed. The lifeblood of the true-hearted patriot stained the marble steps of the *Cancelleria*, and Rome's best hopes lay murdered with him.

CHAPTER XIII.

There hath been in Rome strange insurrection; the people
      against the senators,
Patricians and nobles.

Coriolanus.

IN every house in Rome there was dismay, alarm, or guilty joy on that fatal day; but, from the strange tolerance of assassination which exists in Italy, there was, perhaps, less horror of the crime than fear of what would come next. The crowd poured out of the *Cancelleria*, bearing the terrible news with them. Cecchi entered his dwelling with haggard, yet exulting looks; in which horror and triumph were strangely mingled. 'The tyrant is dead!' said he to his wife, who rushed out upon him, gasping, 'Is it true? Husband! not by your hand?'

'No,' he said, putting her briefly and sternly away, and passing on; while she sank down upon the sofa in her sitting-room, choking with the hysterical sobs pent in till now by suspense and terror. So Irene found her, and with great difficulty calmed her, listening to her broken exclamations, and making such answers as she could, while thoroughly dispirited and sick at heart. Cecchi presently came in, and seeing his wife's state, addressed her with kindness, and approached to take her hand. She grasped his, and her sobs returned, uncontrollably, as she saw the horror

with which Irene shrank from him. 'He did not
do it, he is innocent; tell her so, husband! I am
a fool to weep in this way! I never believed that
you had done it! Signorina, believe him!'

Irene stood aloof from him, and looked at him
with her serious eyes.

'I cannot take your hand,' she said, drawing
back indignantly as he held out his own; 'there
is blood upon it!'

He started and looked at it with a momentary
horror, as if he thought to see the stain there.

'He did not do it, I tell you; he assures me so,
signorina!' cried the wife.

'He knew that it was to be done.'

'What if I did!' replied Cecchi, impetuously,
disregarding his wife's desperate attempts to silence him; 'Rossi was fated to die, but not by my
hand. Your woman's judgment holds no death
lawful save that which a venal judge and court
have decreed. I hold that he who rids his country
of a tyrant has done a noble deed, and that the
blood on his hand purifies it. Rossi threw himself on his fate; he was warned, warned, warned,
many times—you know it! but no man can escape
his destiny. He died a traitor's death—as he
deserved.'

'The traitors are those who murdered him!
Oh, be satisfied; you have your will; you have
cast down in him the last barrier between us and
revolution.'

'And my Italy, for the first time for centuries,
is free!' exclaimed Cecchi; 'free to enter on her
glorious future, unfettered by tyrants, trampled
on no longer by a corrupt priesthood and a false
Church. The way is open before us; the day is

at hand. I see the fire kindled to consume, and
the sword unsheathed to sever. Thine elect,
thine elect, shall be known at last!'

So wild and exulting was his look and tone that
Irene doubted whether insanity had not seized him;
and his wife grasped his hands with all her might.
' Are you a lunatic, husband ? what are you saying?
For pity's sake be reasonable—you are only fit to
be sent to the mad hospital.'

' Look here,' he said to Irene, regardless of
his wife's terror, ' you and your party thought
that a few concessions, a soft speech or two, a
shadow reform, was all we wanted. Do you suppose that a handful of dry bones would satisfy a
starving lion? We have been starved, and caged,
and beaten ; and, now that we have broken loose,
do you ask us to return to the cage, and fawn on
our keeper? Let him beware that he be not rent
in pieces.'

' I hear,' Irene answered, struck in spite of
herself by the energetic conviction with which
he spoke—' I know what Rome has suffered—all
the tyranny and grinding misery of past years ;
but I believe, as you do not, that all would have
been well had we but had the courage to wait.
Now—oh, who has cause to lament this deed as
we, who see in it the ruin of all our hopes, and a
sin which calls down Heaven's vengeance on our
cause! The *Papiste* will point to it as the result
of liberal opinions ; and we, who abhor it, shall be
confounded with you in men's eyes.'

' A woman's judgment! If Rome is to be
regenerated, it must be amid tears and blood,'
returned Cecchi, who had attempted repeatedly
to interrupt her. ' Our time is come. What!

shall we hold back, because human weakness makes us shrink from shedding blood, though the spirit cries to us to hold not back? Have I not fought and striven, even as did Paul? Did I not shrink back, when visions of the night bade me do this thing, and a horror of great darkness was upon me? My traitorous heart, my cowardly spirit! How often have they turned against me, telling me that I should stand alone upon the earth, renounced by all men, deserted by my own people, marked out as the shedder of my brother's blood. Has life been smooth and sweet to me of late? And I was unworthy, I smote feebly, like the weak Israelitish king, and the lot was taken from me and given to another.'

'Signorina, go away, if you love me; he is not himself, he does not know what he says—forget all this, I beseech you. Nino, Nino, if not for your sake, for mine!'

Her voice of anguish recalled him to something like self-command. He was silent, and looked down upon her with a sigh. He loved her dearly; but if even she had been an obstacle in the path which he had chosen, he would have swept her instantly away. Irene kissed her, and turned to go. The movement recalled a thought to Cecchi; he asked quickly, 'Is Nota safe?'

She turned abruptly. A conviction flashed upon her, that he had protected Nota during some danger, and she exclaimed, 'Were you with him last night?'

Cecchi's face wore an indefinable expression, which convinced her that she had guessed right; but she felt stifled in his presence, and went hastily, without asking another question. She breathed with difficulty as she recalled the wild fanaticism which had been poured into her ears. If she believed that a touch of insanity coloured it, perhaps she was not far wrong, and what was more likely than that one who had brooded over his wrongs for years, should take the promptings of a mind naturally mystic and exalted, for inspiration? The mental strife which he had undergone since the impulse to murder Rossi had taken possession of him, had further unsettled it. He said truly that 'his own people,' the little Protestant congregation, would renounce a murderer. Their doctrines, though wild and vague, taught peace and submission; Cecchi would have found no supporters amongst them.

Leone hastened to the Quirinal early on the following day, namely the 16th. He obtained admittance, for he knew more than one of the few who rallied round the Pope in that hour of danger. He brought bolder counsels than had yet been heard in the panic-stricken assembly; urged instant, stringent measures, and advised leaving the Quirinal for the Vatican, with its private passage to strong St. Angelo. One or two caught at these suggestions, but most were utterly helpless and dismayed, sunk in a kind of pious fatalism; and they baffled and paralysed their braver companions. Sighs, accents of despair, incoherent protests, and hurried movements, filled the palace; and the Pope showed the mild and passive courage of an ecclesiastic, without a spark of the decision befitting a temporal prince. So, in wavering, in terror, in contradictory advice, and orders unheeded, passed that day in the Quirinal.

Outside, the agitators were at work; the assassins had laid their schemes deeply; the *Circoli* were thronged, a report was diligently circulated that the Pope had invited his subjects to come and lay their grievances before him; the morrow dawned dark with ominous forebodings. Rome was stupified; a few frantic republicans rejoiced loudly and publicly; but, for the most part, a sullen gloom pervaded the whole city, all hearts sinking with terror, or looking forward with sinister exultation.

Leone did not return home till late in the evening. He brought the first distinct intelligence to Palazzo Clementi, which had been full of uncertain rumours all day long. It was one of Irene's reception evenings; but, instead of a crowd, only a few anxious faces appeared. Leone was surrounded as soon as he entered, and pressed with questions: The Pope? the new Ministry? what had been done? what had really passed? One of those present had been up to Monte Cavallo, and seen the angry crowd about the palace, a cannon dragged up and pointed against it. Leone confirmed this, and told that now all was still, except that little groups of men and women came to gaze at the half-burnt gates, the marks of bullets on the walls—

'All would have been well,' Leone exclaimed, 'had decisive measures been taken at once, but everything was against us. One said this, another that; the Pope listened to all in turn. One man said, "Let us submit, it will be sooner over." Monsignore M—— absolutely told the Pope, in my hearing, that he held Rossi's death as a public blessing. Calderari was summoned, and ordered to arrest certain whose names you may guess; he

shuffled, hesitated, and at last went away, and not
only made common cause with those very men,
but exhorted the Carabineers to do the same.'

'Confound that traitor! he never was a liberal,
thank Heaven! Gregory's darling; the pet of
the *Papiste!*' muttered the liberals who stood
around.

Leone went on to narrate the events of the day;
the march of the insurgents, gathering strength
as they advanced from Piazza del Popolo upon the
palace, where the Swiss closed the gates in their
faces, and bravely resisted—the fatal order to fire
on a throng who might easily have been calmed—
an order given, it was said, by Monsignore Palma.
He expiated the error by his death. The fire was
furiously returned from the roofs and campaniles;
helpless dismay prevailed within the palace, and
treachery both within and without. The Pope at
last submitted, with the sad protest that he yielded
to violence alone, a prisoner in his palace. He
deputed Cardinal Soglia to construct a new Ministry in combination with the chief republicans;
and, as soon as this was known, amid vivas, cheers,
and muskets fired in the air, the insurgents accepted his concessions, and slowly dispersed. It
was a strange end to a frenzied day which decided
the fate of Rome.

And was no voice raised in protest? none to
disclaim these deeds? Here and there one was
heard; but there was a strange palsy of terror
abroad. At Bologna, however, and in some other
places, a cry of wrath and grief was raised, which
showed that the stain of Rossi's murder fell but
on a small portion of the Italian people.

Day by day disorder increased in the city and

terror in the Quirinal, before whose doors the children played and shouted, 'Down with the Pope and the Cardinals!' The broken windows, the charred gates, the marks of shot, told a strange, sad tale; and now, had the Pope had courage to take strong measures, the time for them was past. He was a prisoner; the faithful Swiss guard had been disarmed; no one was admitted into the Quirinal without giving his name to the officer on guard, and the moderates above all were suspected and denied access.

Once before had Pio Nono fled from his diocese when a simple Bishop; he again adopted the same course. All the world knows how, on the 25th of November, he fled in disguise from his capital, to return no more, until a road was forced open for him by foreign bayonets.

The secret of his plans was profoundly kept. That he was gone was not so much as guessed by his people, until a proclamation, which he had caused to be printed and put up in the streets, announced to the amazed Romans that the Pontiff had fled.

CHAPTER XIV.

Marche d'un pas plus ferme au vrai but de ta vie ;
Travaille, souffre, attends, ton heure doit venir ;
    Tu dois laisser un nom à la patrie,
    Tu dois laisser un nom à l'avenir.
A travers les écueils, à travers les orages,
Dirige toi vers ce but de tes jours ;
    Que ton ciel soit serein on chargé de nuages,
    Marche à ton but, marche toujours.

AMPÈRE.

THE news of the evasion of the Pope soon reached Palazzo Clementi, brought by Cecchi, who belonged to the Lower Chamber, and to the party whose chief representative was the Prince of Canino—Citizen Buonaparte, as he loved to be called. The Pope had left an address to the Parliament, on the reading of which a fierce debate ensued, and a proclamation was issued by the Ministry, lamenting the Pontiff's departure and exhorting to peace. There was a violent conflict of feeling in the city, exultation, doubt, or dismay, according to the political creed of each citizen, and deep regret in all the calm and farsighted.

The feeling of the women in general was not ill shown by Menica, who came to her mistress with great, terrified eyes, exclaiming, ' He's gone, signora, he's gone ! what will become of us ? they say we shall all be excommunicated ! And I hear that it was predicted by a poor girl just dead in the hospital ! She saw in a dream Madonna walking out of the city with a golden glory round her head, and Pio Nono and all the cardinals were following her two and two, signora.'

'Yes, truly, like the beasts going into the ark!'

'Dear signora! and my own mother dreamed that Rome would be chastised unless she were more humble and grateful! And besides ——'

'Hold your tongue, silly one!' said Madama Cecchi, assuming indignation, to hide the impression made on her by these portents.

'But listen, dear signora! You saw yourself the dreadful fiery serpent in the sky last week; all Rome saw it, and many like me say that it was a serpent and nothing else; and my confessor told me, when I went to the Caravita to-day, that it was a sign that the city was given up to the power of the evil one! He said so much, so much, and asked me such a number of questions, more than usual, it seems to me; I thought that I should never get home! *Ma cosa avete*—what is it, signora?'

'*Non ho nulla*—nothing, nothing. What kind of questions?' asked the padrona, with anxious jealousy.

'Eh, I don't remember; who comes here, and what is talked of, and such things.'

'And he urged you to leave me, eh?'

'Oh no, indeed, signora; on the contrary, he said that if I noticed all that passed in the family I might be the means of saving you all, and Signorina Irene too. He said it was so sad a thing that so good a lady should be a heretic; and that is true, is it not? it is a compassion to think of!'

'Blessed girl! The raven grieves for the lamb and then eats it!' ejaculated Madama Cecchi to herself in considerable perturbation.

'All the cardinals are slipping away,' pursued Menica, returning to the original topic of her discourse, 'and the ambassadors, and the strangers, and what will there be left for us poor people to do? No buying or selling! And they say the cholera will certainly come to punish us!'

'There! go along! I have no time to listen to your chattering, you grasshopper! Is your master come in?'

'No, signora. Ah, we were much happier when all was quiet; there was a little tyranny, to be sure, but we had our *festas* and processions and the *Girandola;* but how can there be such things without the Pope?   Lisa has had her lover killed in the war, and Monica ———'

'You simpleton! is not that better than Ippolita Rella, whose husband was carried off in the night, nobody knows where, for letting a room to an exile who had ventured back to see his own sky, and hear his own language again?   Has he ever been heard of since?   Is it not better to die for one's country than live in a prison? Eh! go out of my sight, and don't make me think of past things!'

'But oh, signora! do you know what dreadful things are done? The people were pulling the confessionals out of the churches, as I passed to-day, and burning them in Piazza del Popolo! and cursing and vowing they would never marry girls who went to confess! and they said such terrible things of the priests! None will dare to stay.'

'*Manco male!*' said the padrona, divided between superstition and republicanism; 'plenty will stay, I assure you, and nobody will harm them.'

This was true. No one harmed such priests as

ventured to remain openly, but ill fared it with any who were detected in disguise. Most of the cardinals had fled with haste and secrecy, but a few, like Cardinal Tosti, Governor of San Michele, stayed at their posts, unmolested and even welcome. Cardinal Tosti received public thanks for his confidence in the people, and answered with frankness honourable to him and to them, that he was influenced by exactly the same motive as those who went—attachment to Pio Nono.

If the ultra party had hoped to establish a republic at once, they failed; a large faction in Rome would have gladly recalled the Pope on certain terms. There was a kind of pause, filled up with negotiations, difficulties, and debates; the Ministry passed laws, carried out some pressing reforms, and tasted the bitterness as well as the sweets of power. Messengers came and went between Rome and Gaeta, where the Pope had taken refuge, and Naples threw every obstacle in her power in the way of an accommodation between Pio Nono and his subjects. This is not the place for discussing the motives that led him to that kingdom, rather than to his own Civita Vecchia, nor the fatal consequences that ensued from this self-exile. From Gaeta he sent briefs and despatches, that did but destroy such credit at Rome as the Ministry possessed, and made confusion worse confounded. There, Naples, Spain, and Austria had every opportunity of influencing him, and there he remained immovably until his return— a return as mournful as his flight.

During this interval Leone and his own small party remained passive. They found no favour in the eyes of the republicans, nor could they act with men whose opinions differed so widely from their own. With deep foreboding they looked on, unable to stem the torrent, and protesting by their silence and inaction against the course which public events had taken. Whether they were right, or whether those judged correctly, who believed that nothing but complete change could reform Rome ; none can now say, for the experiment was not worked out. Leone could only act on his convictions.

About this time, as he was lingering by a bookstall in Piazza Navona, he met one with whom his thoughts had often been, but whom he had not seen since he had been invalided. Padre Rinaldi had been charged by the Pope with a mission, which kept him absent after the war had concluded; a mission suggested by some of those of Pio Nono's advisers, who dreaded the reforming priest as if he had been the arch fiend. He had since been at Gaeta to report the issue of his mission. His work now lay at Rome. Leone recognised him with joyful reverence. 'Father! would that you had come sooner! It is much to have you even now !'

'I have seen our hopes perish in Upper Italy,' he answered; 'I come to stand by their deathbed here.'

'There is abundant work for you here, father. Many posts are vacant,' said Leone, with an inflexion of voice betraying something like contempt for those who had deserted them.

Padre Rinaldi's thoughts were with the work in which he had laboured before he went away ; the stern ecclesiastical reforms which he had stimulated the Pope to undertake, and prosecuted unflinchingly, armed with the Pope's sanction, and regardless of the host of enemies whom he was creating. How many conferences he had with Pio Nono, when all was fair and promising, and both dreamed of a Utopia! He knew now that his hopes, like those of so many others, were dashed to the ground—knew it by his own farsightedness even before the news of Pio Nono's flight had reached him—knew it afresh from the coldness and ill-concealed triumph which he met with at Gaeta.

'Work that calls for diligent labour,' he answered Leone, ' "for the night cometh when no man can work." Yet a little while, and more than Egyptian darkness will cover Rome. I know Pio Nono well; he will return, recalled perhaps, perhaps restored by foreign arms——'

'*Obbligatissimo!* Sooner let Rome lie a heap of ruins,' burst forth Leone with a glow of anger on his brow.

'Return as he may, it will be to distrust himself, and yield up his power into any hand that may choose to take it. He will seek for peace henceforward in a contemplative life, while every reform will be swept away and his people will groan again in vain in their bondage. Till then let us work. My college—is it prospering? Barberà and Ansoldo at their posts?'

'Barberà is here; Ansoldo went long ago with Cardinal A——. The college has not progressed a step since you went.'

'As I expected. I had not counted on such an absence, otherwise——. Ah, the Ministry will countenance it?'

'Yes; it was discussed, and a subsidy voted for it, only yesterday.'

'That is well,' said Padre Rinaldi, mentally recalling his views for this cherished work, a school for the middle class, free from the vexatious restrictions of the Jesuit colleges and seminaries, and on a much more liberal scheme of education. He had fully planned it before he had left Rome, had submitted his views to the Pope, and obtained full sanction and approbation.

'Nota, you are taking no part in public affairs?' he asked, suddenly turning his falcon glance on his companion.

'None. I cannot act with these men, but opposition would be worse than useless. In Heaven's name, let us not quarrel among ourselves!'

'Take Ansoldo's post.'

Leone looked up rejoiced, 'You think me worthy, father? I have craved for employment, and it is no slight honour to work with you.'

'You have studied geology.'

'How do you know that, father?'

Padre Rinaldi smiled. 'Do you yet need to be told, that the priests and the police know everything in Rome? I can show you a minute report of your proceedings—a police character of you far from flattering. Good—you shall lecture on geology in my school.'

Leone looked astonished—geology, so strictly prohibited! He said, 'Yet you believe that a few months will restore the old *régime?*' and he spoke the words with absolute loathing, his tone expressing to the full how utterly hateful that *régime* had been.

'Let us do what we can till then.' At least, we

will leave a recollection, a precedent, a proof that such plans as mine can be carried out. There is enormous power in a recollection. If a people remember that they once were free, some day they will assuredly resolve to be free again. It is much to plant an idea; even if it be cut down, it will spring up again. Nothing can be done with the old generation, everything with the new; and on this the Jesuits act; they aim at education above all things; they get all the schools into their hands—schools and confessionals,' said Padre Rinaldi, with a slight, sarcastic smile, which betrayed, not the jealousy of a priest of another order, but a much deeper feeling, as he mentally enumerated the 'congregations' under the Jesuits in Rome.

'It is true. No life is wasted which remains as a beacon in men's memory,' Leone added, with a calm, mournful smile, 'even though the objects on which it was spent remain as far off as ever.'

Padre Rinaldi nodded assent.

'Far off as ever! Fair vision of a moment! a star shining through clouds which have veiled it again,' Leone continued; 'liberty, with her fearles· eyes and her pure hands, vanishes to give place to anarchy ending in slavery.'

'Anarchy, called by some freedom,' said the priest.

'We have but obtained tyranny in a new form— the tyranny of the many, a false divinity instead of the true. When will men learn that where liberty is, there law reigns supreme, reverenced and loved as each man's own best treasure. Where her kingdom is, men speak frankly and act fearlessly; none come between husband and wife,

father and child; the poor is not favoured for his
poverty nor the rich for his riches.'

'And in the day when that liberty shall beam,
the Church shall take her own place again, leading
and guiding all nations, a shelter for the weak, a
mother under whose wings science and art and
knowledge shall flourish; and mankind will regard
her as that for which all unconsciously crave—
something so pure, so holy, so mighty, that in its
presence we can but kneel and adore.'

So spoke the reforming priest and the liberal,
both alike dreamers, whose visions were too noble,
too pure for common eyes—two alone amongst
hundreds bent on selfish ends.   Leone was a
devout Roman Catholic; he looked up to Padre
Rinaldi with an intensity of affection and respect,
rescued, by knowing him, from the infection of
that contempt and hatred of the ecclesiastic, so
mournfully common in Italy, and finding in him
all the counsel, the sympathy, and the wisdom
which *should* characterize those who take the souls
of others into their hands.

Padre Rinaldi looked at him again, and asked,
with a complete change of subject, in the singularly
winning tone which made all he said so attractive,
'And when will your marriage take place?'

'In the spring—come poverty or riches, father.
I have shrunk from letting her share my fate;
but I was wrong; I did not then know that
women have some alchemy by which they draw
consolation from care and poverty, when they share
it with those whom they love.   Every day has
taught me to value her more; every anxious hour
—and they are many—that we have watched together, has made her dearer.'

'She is a noble creature—but a heretic!' The tone was very gently reproachful.

'Father, being such, I know that no confessor can step between us.'

Padre Rinaldi sighed, and his brow darkened. He too had found that problem unsolvable.

'My wish is that she should quit her profession,' said Leone; 'she is now judged entirely by politics; the *Papiste* make it a point of conscience to cry her down, and the liberals to praise her. Art cannot flourish in such an atmosphere.'

Padre Rinaldi's eye was suddenly caught by a placard on a wall, inscribed with 'Giuseppe Mazzini, Roman citizen,' in large letters.

'So you have got that arch plotter here!'

'He came the other night, very quietly, on foot I believe; but you see how he is received.'

'Returned like half the exiles, embittered by wrongs and absence, filled with new schemes of rebellion!'

'Yes; such is the lesson taught by exile,' Leone answered; 'and what is that learnt by the many who are "*admonished*," forbidden to exercise a profession, driven to despair, and forced as it were to meditate continually on their wrongs, since they have no other occupation!'

'Ah, madness and delusion,' muttered the priest; 'inaction, inaction! Where are the thoughts of men forced to sit idle, with souls burning with life and energy?—in the world and in the cloister, ill fare those whose hearts' cry is 'let us strive, suffer, fail, but do not suffocate us with this sense of life wasted, power suppressed!' And how many such are there in Italy! The end is heresy, unbelief, and revolution. If an angel came

down from heaven, and called to this people from
St. Angelo yonder, his voice would no more be heard
now, than yours or mine would be beside the war-
ring torrent which dashes down the Saint Gott-
hardt! And yet this Gordian knot was slowly unwind-
ing itself, when one accursed deed complicated it
again perhaps for centuries. Did you ever see a flood
restrained for a moment by a dyke, which at last
tottered and fell, and the waters rushed on, bearing
bridge and dwelling and forest away with them ?
Such a dyke was Rossi! Now, never shall you nor
I nor any living see Rome truly free. Blood is on
her, and her children.'

He spoke aloud, others besides Leone heard, and
he walked the street conspicuous from his tall
form and priestly attire. There was no longer
the old affluence of friar and priest in Rome, but
only murmurs of respect accosted him, though
there was a fast increasing irritation springing
up against the ecclesiastics. Old scores were
remembered against them ; men had learnt to
look upon them as police officers, as tyrants, as
executioners, and now moreover as obstacles in the
way of a reconciliation with the Pope.

Leone returned to Palazzo Clementi in the
dusk of evening. Angry voices reached him as he
approached the sitting-room of the Cecchi ; he
paused, and they were still ; and, when he went
in, there was no trace of emotion ; Cecchi sat
smoking with a gloomy countenance, his wife was
in a languid attitude, and wore a weary, abstracted
look ; scarcely seeming to perceive Leone's entrance. He addressed her husband on some
indifferent topic, in the midst of which her
eyes suddenly brimmed over with tears, and

and with some inarticulate words she hurried out of the room. Cecchi took no notice for a few moments, then looking up with exceeding bitterness he said, ' There, you see what comes of it— Scripture says, man and wife shall be one; the priest says they shall be *three*. That is a good woman, a true, honest, loving woman; she loves me heartily, and yet I had rather face my worst enemy than come home to her. When we married, she was young, gay—she had her friends, her visits, her servants—she laughed at the priests, and piqued herself on being an *esprit fort*. In my troubles she stood by me, and hated the men and the government that caused them. Now, of late, behold what a change! Her confessor has got her into his claws, she repents of the past, becomes devout—'

' Takes refuge in religion. Can you wonder, my friend ?'

' Oh, most welcome as far as I am concerned! But she loves me still; unfortunately, she cannot be content to let me lose my soul if I like. I must go to confess also! I tell her I am a sceptic, a heretic, a Mahomedan, for all she knows ; at all events, confess I will not. Her confessor urges her to tell my secrets—she is too faithful, but she considers that she risks her salvation for my sake. Thus night and day I meet with reproaches, accusations, tears, or silence and gloom. I would rather she would at once tell that priestly spy all that she knows ! Be thankful, Nota, be thankful that your bride is a heretic !'

It was a strange comment on the feeling which Leone had expressed to Padre Rinaldi. When he sought Vincenzo's sitting-room, and his friend held out a welcoming hand, and Irene turned her smiling eyes to him, with, 'Well, what news?' the peace and brightness of the scene gave him a sudden vivid feeling of rest and refreshment. It was as if the clouds had suddenly parted in a stormy sky and had given a glimpse of deep serene blue and shining stars between them.

CHAPTER XV.

Sing on, my nightingale, my songstress fair;
The fame of thy sweet voice, so full, so clear,
Doth reach to France and mount the Emperor's stair;
And if the Pagan king thy voice should hear,
His richest gifts he would present to thee,
And to his people publish a decree,
That to the Faith each Pagan should pass over,
Be made a Christian, and become thy lover.

Canto.

'HERE is a note from Signora Olivetti, proposing that you should go with her to that property of hers at Santa Chiara. You had better go, if you can find time,' said Vincenzo.

'It is a very long drive. She does not name Imelda,'. said Irene, glancing through the note; 'but I suppose. . . . Well, Menica, say that I shall be ready when she comes to-morrow.'

Accordingly Signora Olivetti called the next day for Irene, who enjoyed the prospect of the drive, and told her so as she stepped into the carriage. Signora Olivetti looked care-worn, and smiled but faintly in return for Irene's animated thanks. 'Ah! you look weary, you have been much engaged of late?' she said.

'Yes; but my chief care has been Madame Marriotti; she is going almost immediately.'

'Indeed! I did not believe— My dear Irene, you will find me guilty of egotism, but I asked you to come chiefly to talk to you on a subject

which I have at heart. I want to speak of Imelda.
That is why she is not here. I sent her to spend
the day with her aunt, who will take her to see
Lalla and Antonia at their convent. They are in
education——'

'Yes,' said Irene, between inquiry and assent,
for she saw that Signora Olivetti was lingering,
half unwilling to come to the point.

'I will tell you presently, when we are out of
the city. There, now we can hear each other
speak. People talk of nothing but public affairs
now-a-days, but private ones go on still, even
though the Neapolitan Government will not let
our ambassadors cross the frontier! We must
think a little of domestic matters all the same,
Irene! My husband is not yet likely to return;
indeed, I hope he will not——'

Irene understood. Signor Olivetti was a pru-
dent man, who had long ago made a comfortable
little fortune, and now, though he wished well to
the liberal cause, he had not the least inclination
to mix himself up with it. His wife had higher
views, so she could better bear to see him absent,
than enjoying a selfish security in Rome.

'There is a thing on which my heart has been
fixed for years,' continued Signora Olivetti; 'if I
have ever indulged a dream it was this; I believed
it secure, but now——'

'Imelda?'

'Ah, you divine! What, you know, then?'

'I know that only what concerns Imelda can so
move you, dear signora.'

'Is that all? Irene, I am going to trust
entirely to your prudence, and speak to you on a subject which I have never named even to my husband.

You know Luigi Ravelli well; tell me why he has delayed, perpetually delayed, his marriage with my daughter? Why has he one week returned to his old friendliness, then treated her again with indifference the next?'

Irene was silent.

'Ah, you know, but you will not say. You know it as a secret? Good, I ask no more; but at least you can tell me whether you believe that he will ever fulfil his engagement?'

'Yes, I do.'

Signora Olivetti drew a deep breath and studied Irene's face. 'Your reasons?' she asked, unaware how imperatively anxious was her manner.

'I believe,' said Irene, 'that he will find out, there is no one so loveable as Imelda; that his present feelings will pass away.'

'But when? when? Remember that she cannot waste her youth in waiting for him to come to his senses. Listen; I have had an offer of marriage for her—excellent, perfectly satisfactory. Is it not my duty to communicate it to her father? But if I do so, I must tell him all, and I know he would break off her present engagement, and insist on her accepting this offer.'

'Do not do so, signora; rather let her take the veil, for then she might still without sin pray for Luigi.'

'Ah! you think thus! I know not which way to turn—I, who ask no counsel at other times except from my own conscience!'

'Without doubt Luigi will be in Rome immediately, since the Garibaldi legion are coming from Ravenna.'

'Yes; but what does that advantage me? He

will have grown used to that free, wild, perilous life; he is like a fish which has darted from a quiet lake into a great river. He will never settle down to a quiet, monotonous existence.'

'Dear signora, it ought to have some charm, if half be true that we hear of the hardships the volunteers went through. He must have had enough of wandering, I think. Surely a home must be more precious to one who has tossed about the world a stranger everywhere.'

'You may be right, Irene; Heaven grant it,' replied Signora Olivetti, sighing; ' but it seems to me as if I had planted my little rose-tree on the banks of a rushing stream that might carry it away and break it to pieces at any moment. And yet, if he did but love her, how happy she might be! I have tried to put him out of her thoughts, but in vain; all brings him perpetually to her mind. Ah, love is very weak, after all—I would have given my life to make that child happy, and yet I cannot so much as raise my finger between her and sorrow!'

They were on the Campagna, now fresh green after heavy rain, and girdled by hills which seemed, as it were, full of light, yet which cast long, dark amethyst shadows over the plain. A covered bridge, over a clear dimpling stream, was just before them, a train of pack-horses were descending the bank to drink, and further down, a raft appeared, propelled through the overhanging boughs by a man with a long pole. A butterfly flew past full of vigour and life in the warm sunshine, happier than its kindred who were fluttering over the arid, sunburnt Campagna, in the summer months, and vainly seeking a flower. Overhead the sky was intensest blue, but above Rome it was fast darkening, gathering gloom every moment; a stone pine stood black against the grey sky on the horizon; the mist wrapped it quickly round, it grew dim and dimmer—diappeared at last in the driving rain, and a flash and a growl of thunder, told that Rome was enveloped in one of those almost tropical storms which fill the streets with water, and make the Tiber rise some ten feet in a few hours. Only a few drops reached the travellers, who drove quickly on for several hours, towards the little village, where was the property after whose welfare Signora Olivetti came to look. Santa Chiara stood on the hill-side, picturesque, straggling, and dirty, consisting of a villa, a few cottages, a church, and a small inn; and it looked down on one of those lovely Italian views that witch the heart, and remain there as a joy and a vision of beauty for ever.

Signora Olivetti ordered the coachman to drive to the house of her bailiff, where she intended to rest, but the bailiff came out to warn her that his wife lay ill of fever, and that the house was an unsafe abode. They went to the little inn instead, and while some refreshment was being prepared, the signora visited her vines, poultry and sheep, and heard how all fared. She had made the expedition more for the sake of seeing Irene undisturbed, and unknown to Imelda, than really to visit the farm, where all was going on well.

They returned to the inn, which possessed but one guest room, with white walls and scanty furniture, and a fire of boughs on an open hearth. The landlord met them at the door with equal courtesy and embarrassment; there were two strangers just arrived; he hoped, he trusted that their presence would not incommode the illustrious ladies. Signora Olivetti was a person of great importance at Santa Chiara.

'Of what country?'

'A thousand pardons, excellence; one is French, but the other, he seems to be—to be Austrian.'

Word of abhorrence to the Italian ears that heard it.

'We do not sit down with Austrians,' replied Signora Olivetti, haughtily; and Irene assented with a rapid gesture; 'you must let us have another room.'

'Signora, it afflicts me that there is none that I could venture to offer you except a bedroom up-stairs.'

'That will do.'

The debate had been observed within and partly understood; a gentleman in uniform came to the door and said in Italian with a French accent, 'Do not let us cause these ladies annoyance; my friend and I should much prefer leaving the house.'

'There is no occasion,' said Signora Olivetti, not in the least propitiated, since the courteous Frenchman claimed the Austrian as a friend. 'Brocchi, show us the room;' so sweeping the stranger a curtsey, she passed up the stairs, followed by Irene, who was saying to herself in perplexity, 'I have seen that face before.'

But the Frenchman did not recognise her. He turned with a smile to the landlord when he came downstairs, and asked, 'Who are those ladies?'

'The elder is the Signora Olivetti, monsieur; her family have property here; and the younger —Giacomo, what did you say the signorina's name was ?' he demanded of Signora Olivetti's servant, who was lounging near, observing the foreigners with no friendly eye.

'She is Mademoiselle Mori,' replied Giacomo, in a tone which implied that if that were not explanation sufficient, it was entirely his hearer's fault.

'Mori! ah!' said the Frenchman, with interest; 'the cantatrice?'

'Yes, signor,' said Giacomo, slightly mollified.

'Monsieur knows the signorina?' asked the landlord.

'Ass!' ejaculated Giacomo with boundless contempt.

'I have heard of her, my friend,' replied the French officer; 'her fame has spread into France, though it does not appear to reach fourteen miles from Rome. That was a fine face,' he added to himself, and returned to triumph over his friend, who had sat still and seen nothing.

The bedroom had a vine-covered balcony, still thickly wreathed with rich red and brown garlands, in which the blood of the grape seemed showing itself. Irene stepped out on it from the curtainless window, and looked at the landscape below—the distant mountain peaks which seemed to quiver in light, the undulating plain, the vineyards near at hand, the swift torrent pouring close to the church with its marigold stone window, the ruined casino, approached by a long dark cypress avenue. There was a lonely, deserted, decaying look in the mountain village; and yet, solitary as it seemed, it was not far from a high road along which many travellers passed. Signora Olivetti joined Irene, and they sat in the balcony while the host arranged their dinner. The room afforded only two hard chairs, so it was well that the party was a small one. Its single decoration was a cluster of little prints, representing the Virgin and half a dozen saints, stuck on the wall close to the bed; a few flowers stood in a jar below; and there was a walnut-wood table, a long chest and a bed. The room might have served an anchorite; it certainly had a very monastic air in its extreme simplicity, but the fare offered was by no means ascetic; the table was speedily covered with a good homespun cloth; and an omelet, a dish of roasted kid, bread, dried figs and oranges made a dinner which need not have been despised by more fastidious travellers than the two Italian ladies.

Signora Olivetti's face had lost the haughty look which the name of Austrian had called up; she talked kindly and familiarly with the landlord, and seemed to know and be interested in his family affairs. He came and went, waiting on the obnoxious guests below as well as on the ladies above, aided by his daughter, who went about in the untidy half-laced peasant bodice, and sang snatches of some old ballad about the seven galleys of Spain.

A long absence of both father and daughter presently caused Signora Olivetti to marvel; Irene stepped out on the balcony again, to watch the clear changing lustres steal over the Campagna, and chase the shadows cast by each little hillock and dimple over its wide expanse. She looked out with the artist love of Nature inherited from her father, and was turning to call her companion's attention to the view, when indications of an unusual stir in the village caught her eye. There were women hastily dragging their children after them into the church, hurried passers to and fro, eager voices, a knot of talkers, amongst whom was the landlord, gesticulating on the open space under the trees before the house. Irene tried to read the pantomime; she could not hear the words, but she plainly perceived that the news had brought an extremity of terror with it. Now a new comer hurried to add his mite to the general excitement, then one of the speakers suddenly left the group. The French officer came out, spoke, listened, and looked keenly in a direction pointed out by half a dozen hands, beckoned to his companion, and stood talking to him apart. Irene's comments had ere this brought Signora Olivetti to her side, and they were in eager speculation, when Giacomo and the landlord entered with wide open eyes and mouths, explaining in duet: '*Signore mie!* Garibaldi and his men! the Scarlet Demons! they are at hand, they will pillage us; and as for those foreigners——'

'What! coming here?'

'A woman on her way from the wood has seen them; she flew home to warn the village; half the people are fled already!'

'My good friend, Garibaldi is doubtless on his way to Rome; there is no fear.'

'The signora does not know these men; they are not like our soldiers, who, all the time they were in Lombardy, never stole so much as a dish of polenta—these wear the livery of the evil one —they eat children; they pillage on all sides, and kill whoever resists. Ah, Holy Virgin, there they come!'

And a wild looking troop were now seen riding up the steep mountain road, clad in the red tunics

which had alarmed the imaginations of the villagers,
now appearing, now disappearing in its windings,
their arms flashing in the sunlight through the
cloud of dust which accompanied them.

'The strangers! They will massacre the Austrian,
at all events! Rosa! where art thou?' cried the
landlord, hurrying down, leaving Giacomo trembling like a leaf, with his mahogany cheeks turning nearly white with fear. Signora Olivetti
looked at Irene, not quite at ease, though she had
kept a brave countenance. 'If only by good luck
Luigi is there!' said she.

'Make them welcome; offer them dinner at our
expense,' suggested Irene.

'A good thought. Giacomo—no, stay here; I
will go down myself,' and she descended to the
lower room, where were the foreigners, on their
guard, but cool and outwardly indifferent.

'Brocchi,' said she to the host, 'beg these gentlemen who are coming to accept a dinner at my
expense, and——'

'Signora, what is to be done with these
foreigners?'

'They need be under no apprehensions; they
have Italians to deal with,' said Signora Olivetti,
emphasizing the word *Italians*, as if to recal the
Austrian enormities.

The Frenchman smiled, bowed, and continued
smoking his cigar; his companion appeared not to
comprehend the language spoken round him; but no
more could be said, for the next moment the clatter of
horses' feet was close at hand, the open space without was filled with dismounting soldiers, and immediately the room was crowded with wild, black
bearded figures, clamouring for the landlord. Signora

Olivetti stepped forward calmly, her eyes seeking out the leader of the noisy troop; 'Gentlemen, let a Roman have the pleasure——' she began; but at her voice, a soldier turned quickly round, uttering her name. She knew who it must be, but hardly recognised Luigi in the bearded, bronzed features, further disguised by a steeple-crowned hat with a bunch of flowers stuck in it. The meeting brought order instantly into the troop; all looked on, eager to see what friend their captain had found.

'I suppose it is you, Luigi! this is fortunate indeed! I hardly dared to hope you might be among them, and we heard such terrible accounts of your men!'

'We are used to finding villages deserted, and convents barred against us,' he answered, merrily, and a laugh from the rest showed that certain old adventures were recalled by his words. 'And yet we pay as we go, I assure you, and harm no one but the enemy. Now, my friends, it seems to me there is no room for you here; your dinner shall be served to you out yonder.'

'Remember, these are my guests,' said Signora Olivetti.

They made a universal murmur of thanks, withdrew at once, and settled themselves under the trees, lying on the ground, or sitting on benches, laughing, smoking, singing, and questioning Giacomo, whose fears had vanished at once before the sound of Luigi's voice, and who was now curiously examining the mysterious American saddles, capable of being turned into a kind of tent, which had been taken from the horses' backs.

Just as Luigi was beginning an explanation to Signora Olivetti, the landlord again appeared with a troubled countenance. 'Signora, I have the best will, you know it, but who can dig gold out of a granite rock? what is a net without fish? I have nothing but bread and wine to give these men! I dare not tell them so!'

'Oh, is that all?' said Luigi, and he went out, looked down on an open pasture where sheep and oxen were feeding, and spoke to one of the men, who instantly got up, sprang on the bare back of his horse, and darted off, waving a long cord in his hand. Two or three more made free with the wood stack, and with practised hands built up a pile. The landlord looked on blank with wonder, not diminished by the swift reappearance of the rider, dragging an unhappy sheep after him by his lasso. In a short time it was neatly skinned, and roasting on the fire which crackled merrily, and sent up a cloud of mingled sparks and smoke towards the sky. 'Holy Virgin!' ejaculated the host, and he hurried to prepare whatever provisions he could find, as if expecting to be killed and eaten himself, if his stock should fail. Luigi was meanwhile explaining that Garibaldi's scheme for going to Venice, which was still keeping up a desperate resistance, had been suddenly changed by the summons to Rome which had reached him at Ravenna.

'I am the advanced guard,' said Luigi, gaily; 'what do you think of my troop? They are good children, after all; but their reputation is a famous thing, it is worth more to us than another regiment; it has emptied many a village, where we should have lost half our number, had the poltroons stayed to fight. Two nights ago we found a convent barred against us; there was no other shelter, and we broke it open. Not a living soul in it!

all the monks had fled, locking each separate cell!
That put the men past all patience, and I could
not prevent their turning the whole place upside
down; one fellow came out in a monk's hood,
another in the white and black mantle, another in
an embroidered cope—you would have died of
laughter if you had seen them! and when I called
them together to quiet them a little, the rascals
came to answer to their names in these costumes,
each with a lighted taper in his hand!'

An irrepressible laugh from the Frenchman
betrayed that he understood what was said. Signora Olivetti lowered her voice, and said, ' You
will protect these foreigners, though I believe one
is an Austrian?'

The change in Luigi's face was startling, but he
turned abruptly away. 'They are perfectly safe;
I am not obliged to know anything about them.
Are you alone?'

'Mademoiselle Mori is with me.'

'Irene! where?'

Hearing his voice, she ran downstairs, and
questions and replies were rapidly exchanged. He
was famishing for Roman news; did not even
know of Leone's safety, and his joy on hearing it
made Irene his fast friend for ever. While they
stood talking, the landlord and Giacomo were
briskly serving the guests outside; and a peasant
or two might be seen venturing into sight, and
then approaching with eager curiosity. Presently
one of the men rose, and came in, doffing his
broad hat, and looking at Luigi, while he bowed
deeply to the ladies. He was the bearer of a
message from the whole troop to their captain;
they had heard from Giacomo that Mademoiselle

Mori was a famous cantatrice; would he intercede with her to sing to them?

Irene laughed and hesitated; Luigi laughed too, and pushed the soldier towards her.

'There, plead your own cause, my friend; bright eyes do not usually make you so bashful!'

'Signorina, it is a great liberty that we take,' said the soldier, with a frank and gallant bearing which itself pleaded strongly for him; 'and if you consent, we can only offer you our thanks—the thanks of men who come to fight for Rome.'

'You cannot refuse, Irene,' said Signora Olivetti, some lurking romance aroused within her by the singular scene. 'Come, consent; but we must be gone soon.'

The two foreigners looked on, entertained and curious.

'Tell your comrades that I can refuse nothing to men who ask me thus, friend,' said Irene; and she and Signora Olivetti went to the upstairs room, where dinner was speedily served to Luigi, as it had been to the ladies. Irene stepped out on the vine-trellised balcony again; and, leaning on the rail, with the gorgeous autumn garlands hanging in rich profusion around her, she surveyed the scene for a moment, the glorious landscape, the troop of soldiers in their strange and picturesque costume, lying under the trees around the dying fire, their flashing eyes uplifted to the songstress in eager expectation. Small groups of peasants had gathered here and there; at the door of the church, the women and children were clustering, eager and timid. It was a scene to inspire the dullest, much more an artist soul like Irene's, as she thought of all that this gallant band had endured for Italy; how readily, too, they had responded to the call of Rome, menaced by perils as yet uncertain, but daily more threatening—perils which could only be averted by a steadfast, united spirit; and as she thought thus, there came to her lips a song of Leone's, which had been such a favourite among the volunteers, that it had reached both the Lombard battalion and the Garibaldi legion. It had been sung on bleak Monte Suelo, and by the watch-fires over Lago Maggiore. Every man there knew it, and greeted the first notes with scarcely suppressed enthusiasm. Translated into English it might run thus:—

> Princes of Rome, sons of gallant old houses,
>   Sprung from the heroes of days that are passed,
> Come from your revels, and leave your carouses,
>   Prove you true heirs of your fathers at last.
>   Good-sworded band, take ye your stand;
>   Who but Rome's lords should fight first for
>   their land?
>
> Burghers, away from your goods and your chattels;
>   Has not your country been bought and been sold?
> Show yourselves changers of blows in the battles,
>   Dealers in steel, and not dealers in gold.
>   'Gainst their fierce horde, play with the sword;
>   Is not a burgher as good as a lord?
>
> Priests, close your volumes of musty old learning,
>   Leave each good saint all alone in his shrine;
> No more dull sermons; let words that are burning
>   Tell us that Liberty's name is divine.
>   God's cause our call, Heaven if we fall;
>   Does not your Gospel preach Freedom for all?
>
> Soldiers, see Italy's proud banner waving.
>   What! will ye shrink from an Austrian foe?
> Still for our life-blood their sabres are craving,
>   Still their flags flaunt in the vale of the Po.
>   Soon shall they hear vengeance is near,
>   Better die free, than like slaves live in fear.

Peasants, come trooping from each little village,
    Leave the plain golden with billowy grain ;
Vineyard and field must this year lack their tillage ;
    Better be waste than the German's domain.
            Wide your arm sweep, deal your blows deep,
            Goodly and rich be the crop that you reap.

Romans ! whatever your rank and your station,
    Princes and peasants, and children and old,
Think of the wrongs of our down-trodden nation,
    Think of what glories our fathers have told.
            Theirs though the might, ours is the right,
            God and His angels before us shall fight !

As Irene sang from her soul, her beautiful voice
and animated countenance might well delight her
soldier audience, who applauded frantically, starting up from the ground, waving their hats, shouting
and gesticulating as she concluded, and sending
up a deputation to thank the songstress. Their
evvivas pursued the carriage as it drove away.
Luigi hoped to be in Rome ere nightfall with his
detachment, but Signora Olivetti did not wait for
his escort. She thought it best to avoid such a
sensation as would have been created, had she
returned surrounded by the Garibaldi legion.
Irene had had the two foreigners for listeners, as
well as the soldiers and peasants. Their plaudits
mingled with those of the Italians, but little did
she guess that the French officer was an old
acquaintance, and as little did Colonel de Crillon
recognise in the young cantatrice that little
maiden whom he had encountered in the Bosco,
and forgotten years ago.

CHAPTER XVI.

L'è rivvenuto il fior di Primavera,
L'è ritornato la verdura al prato,
L'è ritornato chi prima non c'era,
E ritornato il mio innamorato."
RISPETTO.

COLONEL DE CRILLON had business in
Rome. He had been despatched on a confidential and semi-political mission to ascertain how matters really were going there, and what were the
sentiments of the French residents towards the new
régime. Before they left the little inn, he had made
Luigi's acquaintance with soldierly ease and good
fellowship, and the supposed Austrian turned out
to be a Pole, a nationality that at once recommended
itself to the volunteers, who had served with the
gallant Kamiensky and his Polish battalion in
Lombardy. Moreover, the poet Mickiewitz had
joined the liberal side so heartily at Rome, that his
countrymen were in high favour with the people.

Colonel de Crillon and his friend rode to Rome
with the Garibaldi detachment, and were witnesses
of the astonishment and amusement which ' the red
demons' created as they trotted through the streets.
Heads crowded together at doors and windows,
and Luigi was infinitely diverted to find himself
unrecognised, and yet producing such a sensation.
His spirits had been rising to their highest pitch
from the moment he had found himself within sight

of St. Peter's; he looked round in the streets as if
he needs must soon see some of his own family,
and presently a short, stout personage, with a
ruddy face, bright black eyes and white hair, came
down a side street, wondering at the commotion
which he perceived before him in the Corso—
caught sight of the cavalcade, and stopped short
to gaze, in amazement. Luigi recognised his
father, took off his hat to him, waved it over his
head, and shouted, ' *Viva* the Signor Ravelli!'
His soldiers, as great madcaps as himself, instantly
caught the joke, waved their hats and joined in the
shout; then, with a hearty, universal laugh, all
galloped out of sight towards the quarters appointed for them, leaving Signor Ravelli in a state
of blank amazement. But some light dawned at
last; the fierce wrinkles between his eyebrows
relaxed, exceeding satisfaction diffused itself over
his face; he burst into a short chuckle, and set off
homewards at unusual and undignified speed.

The general sensation had not yet reached Casa
Ravelli. Still and tranquil as usual sat its mistress.
No presentiment that the dear son, for whom she
was even then praying, was close at hand, had
thrilled through her, nor changed the perfect calm
of her countenance. It was the meek, passive,
abstracted look of a cloistered nun that dwelt on
her face, wife and mother though she was.
Human interests seemed not to exist for this
woman, whom all the devout of her acquaintance
regarded as a saint, while they spoke, awestruck,
of the contemplative, holy life that she led. In her
secluded, monotonous existence, meditation and
prayer entirely absorbed her. She fully carried out
the exalted ideal life conceived by St. Dominic,

when he devised the rosary, with its long meditation for each bead. Outside her quiet room the
world surged like a stormy sea, but its sound
never reached her ear, its spray never flung one
drop upon her brow. She led the life rather of a
recluse in distant ages than that of a woman of
the restless, agitated nineteenth century. Married
young to a husband twice as old as herself, whose
love showed itself by angry, ceaseless jealousy, she
soon resigned herself to as secluded a life as he
could have wished; but he had never gained her
affections, which were speedily absorbed in those
religious practices in which alone she found peace.
Two children were born and died; her heart followed
them into heaven. She was entirely devoted to her
confessor; a machine in his hands; the teaching of
her Church was followed out by her to the utmost.
And who shall say that a true and simple heart shall
not be accepted even though it have not learned
aright? In Signora Ravelli's face was the look
of peace achieved—that peace, attained through
much sorrow, which indeed 'passeth all understanding.' Several years after the death of her second
child, Luigi was born, and only what concerned
him now moved her. In any matter that touched
that affectionate, reckless, unstable son she was but
a weak woman after all.

When Signor Ravelli came in she raised her eyes:
hasty movements and hasty words always entered
with him. Moving here and there while he spoke,
he exclaimed, 'Well, well, signora, the world might
be turned upside down without your finding it out!
Here am I come home expressly to bring you news,
and you do not so much as ask what it is!'

'Tell me now, then,' said the wife, as he paused

and gave her for the first time an opportunity of speaking. 'Is it good?'

'You must divine, signora, you must divine, I say. Come, come, make haste!'

'You have seen Signora Olivetti? She has heard from her husband?'

'Signora Olivetti go to Jerusalem! and her husband too! Stay, stay, stay; now I think of it, I want to invite the signora and the little one to spend the evening with us. Immediately— where is Bernardo? Yes, we must have the bride here this evening. I mean to settle when the wedding is to be—Luigi will be coming home, eh?'

His wife looked up now, a flush rising to her cheeks. Till now she had worn an absent, patient look; her thoughts were elsewhere; it was an effort to listen to her husband. Now there was life, interest, agitation. He observed the difference.

'Ah, she lives now! See! one would think she expected that young good-for-nought of a son of hers to rise through the floor! Why, you do not expect him yet, eh?'

'What do you know about Luigi, signor?' she asked, pressing her hand on her throat where the pulses were beating visibly.

'Why, do you suppose I have seen him in the Corso?'

'It would be too much happiness,' she answered, with a deep, self-reproachful sigh, as the ever-haunting fear that her maternal affection was excessive, arose as usual. 'I love him too well, it binds me to the world.'

'Folly!' said Signor Ravelli, out of patience; 'does Heaven give you affections expressly that you may renounce them? Too much happiness!

Why so? Why should I not see him if he is here?'

'But is he? Tell me, I beseech you; I must know!' said she, rising hastily with joined hands.

Signor Ravelli was delighted. 'How——' he began again, when the door was partially opened, and a voice said with feigned formality, 'I am here to incommode the honourable signora.'

She turned abruptly with a cry of 'Ah, Heaven, it is he!' and would actually have fallen with joy and surprise if Luigi had not sprung in and clasped her in his arms. Mother and son embraced as if they could not bear to let each other go, and it was some minutes before Signor Ravelli, who walked round them, fuming and laughing, could obtain a fair view of Luigi, whose delinquencies he had quite forgotten. 'What a barbarian it is! What will his bride say?' he exclaimed, regarding him joyously when the first agitation was past and mother and son sat together, Signora Ravelli's trembling hands clasped in Luigi's, her eyes greedily perusing his face, and his fondly study-ing her countenance, while he gave an outline of his many adventures, with much more mirth and enjoyment than penitence, or even re-gret for the failure of the campaign. Between each pause Signor Ravelli ejaculated something about Imelda; Luigi instantly saw the beseech-ing look of old days come over his mother's face; and though all that day he had been planning a meeting with Gemma Clementi, he could not grieve father or mother by betraying any reluctance to meet Imelda; besides, he was so happy to be at home again, that he would have kissed a stone if he had heard that it came from a Roman wall. 'And

when the wedding ?' broke in Signor Ravelli again.
'We must cage this wild hawk now we have got
him back. Ah, you young scrapegrace, we have
kept that sugar-cake, that little bunch of violets
safe for you—when shall it be, eh ?'

'When the fighting is over, perhaps, my father !'

'Fighting, fighting ? what fighting ?' demanded
Signor Ravelli, fiercely, gathering his eyebrows
together.

'What are we here for? We were told that
France and Spain, Austria and Naples, were combining to restore Pio Nono.'

'Ah, my son, what a sin has been committed
towards the Holy Father !' sighed his mother.

'Old women's tales,' replied Signor Ravelli.

'What are we here for, then ?' repeated Luigi.

'To amuse the people, I suppose ; a fine show
for them you are, you rascals. Have you not a
respectable uniform among you ? And where are
the rest of you ? Garibaldi is not come.'

'He will be here to-morrow. You are very
much mistaken, signor, if you think there is no
fighting in prospect—nothing but play. I recommend the Provisionary Government to look to the
gates and the walls.'

'You recommend, forsooth ? Do you hear how
this young cock crows, signora ? What do fair-
weather, toy-soldiers like you volunteers know
about it ?'

Luigi looked at his father in utter surprise.
To one who knew what the volunteers had endured,
this jesting tone was a shock. He answered, with
unusual gravity,

'If sleeping on the bare ground, being half-
starved, and risking life fifty times a day, is to be a

fair-weather soldier, we are such. Have all the
Roman volunteers returned safe, signor ?'

'Ah, the poor Cardellas!' said his mother.
'Their old father, Luigi!'

Luigi's eyes were full of tears as memory
recalled to him the long list of dead whom he had
known and loved. He rose hastily.

'Whither away now, young sir ?' demanded his
father, with imperiousness more assumed than real,
for the thought of the childless old man had moved
him also.

'To see Nota. I hear he is at Palazzo Clementi.
I have not seen him since I helped to carry him to
a wagon, more dead than alive.'

'You will stay here, *signor mio*. Nota is safe
and well, and can wait, and we shall have visitors
presently.'

Luigi pressed his mother's hands fondly, rose,
made an arch and resolute bow to his father, and
had bounded down the stairs almost before Signor
Ravelli realized what he was about. The father
stood looking after him from a window, half laughing, half storming, and in fact enjoying the feeling
that his unmanageable son had returned to enliven
the dull house. He turned when the light figure
was out of sight, to address his wife, but she had
vanished into her own room; and, when he opened
the door he saw her on her knees, her face upraised
to the crucifix on the wall, with such a rapture of
joyful tears, that he was silenced and withdrew
softly; a strange mournful feeling taking possession of him for a few moments, he hardly knew
what; but an impatience of the passionless, monotonous life he led with her, a perception that she
had deep affections which were all sealed to him,

all given to Heaven and her son. He got rid of it after a time, and returned to his old well-satisfied belief, that women were only grown-up children, who must be watched and kept by force out of mischief, and that the very best of them was not capable of being a friend and companion to the dullest man in the world.

Luigi soon reached Palazzo Clementi, meeting on the way Colonel de Crillon. They lifted their hats as they passed each other in sign of acquaintance; and 'A fine young fellow,' crossed the mind of the Frenchman; while, 'I should like to know what that man's business is here,' glanced across Luigi's. He stumbled the next instant upon his own lieutenant, humming a line of Irene's song, and gazing round him with great interest on the mighty city hitherto known to him only by name.

'Ha, Fava! you here? better lodgings here than on Monte Suelo!' cried Luigi, as he passed.

'Not likely to blow away as yours did, into the valley of the Chiese, captain!' returned the other, pointing to the massive walls of Palazzo Clementi, under whose archway Ravelli was disappearing. He paused as he sprang up the broad staircases, and cast glowing looks towards the apartment of of the contessa, revolving once more the possibility of a visit there that evening. But he dared not trust himself nor Gemma in an unexpected meeting. While he stood devouring the windows with his eager eyes, the outer door opened; two ladies appeared in opera cloaks—Gemma and her aunt going to a party. The latter was speaking, the other following, with a pale, discontented, listless face. Luigi made a spring towards them; Gemma saw him, uttered a half-smothered cry, the blood rushed scarlet to her cheeks, she was absolutely transformed with joy, but her aunt was too much engrossed in recognising and questioning Luigi to observe her or to guess what was expressed in the quick look exchanged between them.

'You are going to Signor Nota,' said she, when her curiosity was satisfied; 'we will not detain you, then; but you come to us to-morrow evening, is it not so? even in these sad times we have our usual *società*. Come, Gemma. Why, it is a wild beast! what a costume, what a black beard! Should you have known him, child?' she asked when they were out of his hearing; and Gemma, palpitating all over with joy, replied, 'Oh, assuredly not, dear aunt.'

'You look all the better for the surprise,' said her aunt, looking at her; 'it has given you a certain colour; I was afraid you were losing all your beauty. You are growing really old; you are twenty-two and still unmarried; it is a scandal; you had better make up the Bible with some one!'

'Here is the New Testament, if you will find the Old,' returned Gemma, between mirth and scorn, as her aunt quoted for the hundredth time to her that proverbial expression for a marriage between an old man and a girl, which in its irreverent satire is no bad specimen of what Roman wit usually is.

'We are worse off than ever now that monsignore is gone. These atrocious republicans.'

Luigi had watched them out of sight, exultant in his good fortune, and then betook himself to Vincenzo's apartments. How familiar was everything around—the long corridors overlooking the quadrangle, the orange-trees in tubs, the range of

wall-flowers and stocks in pots on the highest
story; nay, even the network which confined
Madama Cecchi's hens claimed a look from him—
all these well-known objects made the experiences
of the past year seem strangely visionary to him.
Closing his eyes as he waited for admittance, he
recalled the night-watch on the hill-side, the leafy
cabin that had sheltered him, the wide landscape
on which his eyes had looked for so many weary
days from the Bergamasc hills. He seemed almost
to hear the swift river rushing past burnt and
deserted villages, and winding through the valley
towards the majestic mountains in the distance;
the sentinels' call came to his ear, the groups that
lay round the watch-fires with song and jest appeared before him; the bustle around the humble
stable which served as head-quarters; stars glittered overhead, wind howled among the trees,
foretelling a tempest. Luigi hastily opened his
eyes and looked round with a start, fearful lest
his vision should be reality, and Rome still be
divided from him by half the Peninsula. Menica
opened the door at this moment, and her pretty
face was an agreeable assurance that he was indeed
in Rome.

'Why, 'tis he! Fie, signor!' she cried, remon-
stratingly, but not very angrily, as he took the
readiest way of testifying that it really was himself.

'For once, pretty one! I am a soldier, you
know, and soldiers have certain privileges—you
are more of a rose of May than ever! Is Signor
Mori at home? and your master and the padrona?'
said Luigi, entering Vincenzo's room, while Menica
retired to the kitchen, laughing and shaking her

head, pausing and looking after him, while he cried, '*A rivederti!* there is no day in the week like the *Domenica* [Sunday]. Here I am, Vincenzo!'

'Welcome, indeed,' cried Vincenzo, glad but not surprised, as of course Irene had reported her encounter at Santa Chiara. 'At last! Let me look at you. Are you glad to see us again, friend?'

Luigi's dancing eyes answered the question. Irene came out of her room to welcome him again. She looked sad, and he remarked it.

'I have just had a note from Madame Marriotti to tell me that she leaves Rome to-morrow,' said Irene; 'I expected it; but she says I am not to go and wish her good-bye; it would only distress us both too much.'

'Madame Marriotti!' repeated Luigi, with a sort of perplexity; 'I declare to you I feel as a ghost might do who revisited the world after years and years of absence. I have lived so utterly in a different world this last year, that I can't come back to yours, where I find you speaking and acting as if nothing had happened! I am ready at every moment to order a tree to be cut down for firing; and when I saw Fava just now, I nearly told him to send out a party to lasso an ox for supper.'

'Lasso? are you a wild Indian?'

'The commander-in-chief is,' replied Luigi, laughing; 'and from what some of the men who came with him say, I suppose we are all much like a war-party in America.'

'The Spaniards call us *Caraibes* already!' said Vincenzo.

'Devoted thanks to them! When? why?'

'You have heard of their proclamation?'

'Not I. Are they helping to cook the broth at Gaeta?'

'All Europe seems combining against us, and England deserts us,' said Irene.

'Let them come, then. The day has no flavour without a little fighting in it. But my father scorned the notion of a siege.'

'It is impossible, is it not?' cried Irene; 'Pio Nono is too good, too gentle to hire foreign bayonets against his own people; he will not return to Rome through a breach in its walls!'

'As for his words, if they are roses, they will blossom; if they are thorns, they will prick,' said Vincenzo; 'he speaks roses, but they prick strangely, Irene!'

'"Heaven keep us from one who kisses us before, and claws us behind,"' quoted Luigi.

'There is a party who mock at the idea of a siege,' continued Vincenzo; 'but that will not prevent it; and, if it come, I shall almost rejoice, for we shall show the world that we can resist unanimously, and are not the mere republican faction they take us for.'

'Hum—I actually do not know what politics are in the ascendant.'

'Tending towards a republic, since all our overtures to Gaeta are rejected.'

'Why! you would not have the priests back!'

'No,' said Vincenzo, emphatically; 'only under certain conditions.'

'Rather Mazzini!' added Irene.

'Are there any priests left? What has become of Monsignore Clementi?'

'Fled, it is said. It would be at the risk of his life, if he showed himself here. The people

are furious against the priests, especially the
Jesuits, because they hinder all attempts at conciliation at .Gaeta, but we have Padre Rinaldi and
Ugo Bassi and others, and Leone is fully employed.'

'What does he think of things?'

Vincenzo shook his head. 'Ill.'

'And Cecchi?'

Irene shivered and looked away. Vincenzo,
who did not know half as much about Cecchi as
she did, answered readily, 'We see nothing of him
now; he shuts himself up alone when he is indoors
—he is strangely morose. And his wife—she has
taken a devout turn!'

'No!' cried Luigi, with a hearty laugh.

'It is too serious to laugh at,' said Irene; 'she
declares that a vision of her patron saint appeared
to her, and threatened her with unimaginable tortures, unless she should repent and convert her
husband; and ever since she has been perfectly
miserable, though the old spirit breaks out still
sometimes, and I think some great event would
rouse her again. It is such abject superstition!
I think all fear and no love is as bad in religion
as in government—only fit for slaves.'

'Leone! I hear his step,' said Vincenzo.

'I knew it was he before you did!' said Ravelli,
who had seen Irene's eyes brighten.

Leone had not been at home since the morning,
and therefore was not aware of the return of his
friend. As he caught sight of the guest, the
sudden, bright Italian smile flashed across his dark
face, and his welcome was full of the warmest
affection. But Luigi was startled by the worn
and serious look that soon settled on his face;
the weariness stamped on it so unlike the old,

vivid, changing expression. It made the light-hearted soldier realize, as he had never yet done, how much had been won and lost again in the past year. His trade had been fighting, and, beyond beating the Austrians and devising hare-brained expeditions, he had concerned himself little of late with anything, risking his life a dozen times a day as much in frolic as in patriotism. The hardships of his volunteer life had neither saddened nor sobered him. When the disastrous end of the campaign forced Durando to retreat into Piedmont, Luigi had rejected the armistice and joined Garibaldi, and had Garibaldi been forced to lay down his arms, Luigi would no doubt have offered to serve in the battalion of Bersaglieri which young Manara was forming in Piedmont. He had come gaily to Rome with his company, rejoiced to see it again, but without ever reflecting what the consequences of a siege would be. It was far otherwise with those who stood apart, watching public events, and a new view of them was given to him by the eager conversation that followed Leone's appearance.

Leone accompanied him when he left Palazzo Clementi, asking many questions. After their parting Ravelli dwelt long on the changed aspect of his friend, which hardly brightened even at Irene's side, and found himself looking round and calculating the possibility of a successful defence. Mentally he surveyed the points of probable attack, slackened his pace and mused, wondering whether any real preparations had been made. 'I would wager there is nothing but flags and flowers and tricoloured cockades,' thought he contemptuously, enlightened by his experience of actual warfare, which had taught him to disdain all the noisy demonstrations that had formerly seemed to him like substantial success. 'But who is there to besiege us? The Neapolitans? Pshaw! Poor wretches who are dragged out to fight with their pockets full of charms and rosaries? France? Surely one republic will not attack another? French honour is not sunk to that! Austria— perhaps! Why the very babies would stand up to fight the Croats—what is that old story Leone spoke of—some rascally king whom thirty cities leagued to bring back to Rome—we shall see!'

He entered Casa Ravelli while still plunged in thought unusually deep for him, and was re-called to other things by the voices that reached his ear; his father's banter, his mother's soft tones, and the grave voice of Signora Olivetti. One other he listened for and heard not—but Imelda was there. She was by his mother's side, watching intently for his step, full of tremulous joy that made her forget how wearily the days had passed without him, and brought a haze of tears into the soft dark eyes that glanced up shyly and lovingly when her betrothed husband entered.

All rose to welcome him; his mother's sup-plicating look was irresistible; and he could not meet Imelda merely with a cold formal greeting, but as that fierce ardent face of Gemma's rose before him, he inly vowed that come what would, this cruel entanglement must end. But for a little while it must continue; he could not spend his first evening at home in discord, nor greet Imelda by informing her that their engagement must end. And he might well be reluctant to intro-

duce any jarring topics—home was so pleasant,
the company of women so agreeable after his late
life! How wild and adventurous it sounded, told
as they all sat together—what a change from the
tempest-swept hill side! Imelda listened silently,
trembling as she heard of sallies upon the
enemy, excursions in disguise into villages held by
the Austrians, of swimming across the wild torrent
of the Caffaro, and of videttes close to the enemy,
who hung or shot every volunteer they could get
hold of. How she sympathized with the young
Milanese who, seeing himself cut off from his
regiment, tore the flag he bore and hid the pieces
in his breast, that they might escape the enemy,
whatever might become of him! How she rejoiced
when he re-appeared safely three days afterwards!
All anxiety had vanished; she had a most entire
and child-like belief that all must go well now
that Luigi was come.

CHAPTER XVII.

O révolutions!   J'ignore,
  Moi, le moindre des matelots,
Ce que Dieu dans l'ombre élabore
  Sous le tumulte de vos flots.
— cette tempête est lourde,
  Aux princes comme aux nations.
Oh! quelle mer aveugle et sourde
  L'un peuple en révolutions!

VICTOR HUGO.

RAVELLI for once was steadfast in his purpose. After an evening spent with the Clementi, during which he could only exchange a few hurried words apart with Gemma, and felt himself a very Tantalus during the hours which he passed in company with her, yet separated from her by all the barriers of rank and ceremony, he made up his mind to confess his love to the count, whose eye had been on them the whole time. He asked Clementi to take a turn with him in the corridor, and his hurried manner was so unlike his usual gay and dashing carriage, that it already half betrayed him.

They lighted their cigars and walked up and down, Clementi coolly waiting, and making now and then some slight remark, to which Luigi assented without knowing what he said. He could hardly fear a repulse from the young patrician who had a hundred times mocked at his own title, and had long ago thrown himself into the foremost rank of

Red Republicanism, yet so strongly were different ranks divided in Rome, that the rich plebeian, even in those democratic days, felt as if he were offering an affront to the noble, impoverished Clementi by aspiring to the hand of their daughter. He could tell nothing which the count's lynx eye had not seen long before, but a slight shade of surprise appeared on the young noble's face, and he answered Luigi's declaration in the full soft tones which could convey, when he willed it, the keenest sting, 'Of *my* sentiments you cannot doubt;' and Luigi, instantly remembering that he had the approval of several other people to gain, stopped short, and gave him time to add with a careless smile, 'I am sorry for that pretty little *sposa* of yours. Did she take it much to heart?'

'You are the first person to whom I have spoken,' Luigi answered, with more anger than he could explain to himself.

'You do not imagine that I suppose you have spoken to my sister? How can you figure to yourself that I could so suspect my friend? or my sister? I trust your honour as my own!' exclaimed Clementi, ingeniously misunderstanding Luigi's words, and assuming an aggrieved air. 'You wrong me indeed. Besides, I know that she would instantly have told me.'

Luigi was completely out of countenance, feeling as if he were a thorough villain, and unable to make the confession which sprang to his lips, since it would inculpate Gemma. He coloured deeply, passed his hand impatiently over his forehead and was dumb, while the count's dark grey eye watched him with inward amusement. It was a cat playing with a mouse; Luigi was at no time a match for

the keen, clear intellect of Clementi, and least of
all now, when he was smitten through and through
by these slender, stinging arrows, from which he
had no possible way of escape. Count Clementi
resumed: 'If indeed your father consents, and the
Olivetti give up their claims, I can only——' He
paused, and Luigi answered almost against his will,

'It was to you that I determined to speak
first.'

'Do you mean that your relations do not know
of this?'

'Exactly,' said Luigi, fast losing his temper.

'Then in fact you are still engaged to the
Olivetti?'

'That engagement shall be broken the instant
you give me your consent.'

'But, till it is!' said the count, in his most
melodious accents, 'till it is, my friend!' and the
intonation conveyed a delicate reproach which said,
'Can you expect an honourable man like myself
to promise my sister to the betrothed husband of
another, and without the knowledge of his family.

If Luigi were not acute, he was generous and
honourable, and detested double-dealing, though he
had been led deeply into it by Gemma's all-powerful
influence. He perfectly understood Clementi's
unuttered meaning, took his hand and said, 'You
are right, and I am wrong. No more of this now;'
and though they parted without one atom of a promise having been extracted from Clementi, Luigi
was convinced of his sympathy, and heartily
ashamed of having laid himself open to such a
reproach as his friend had mildly implied. Clementi
remained pacing up and down the corridor. A
very peculiar smile came to his lips as Luigi

left him, and he murmured to himself an old distich :

> ' Il mondo, di Noè gli è proprio l'arca
> Di bestie assai, di poche uomini carca !'

' But truly I find even more fools than knaves in it ; or men who are half fool, half knave, and then they are yet more easy to manage !'

Luigi returning home late, found that his father had been asleep for hours ; so that he was forced to delay the explanation until morning, but he firmly resolved that not another day should pass without one. A great desire to consult his mother came upon him, but he refrained, feeling as if it were a sin to trouble her calm existence with his feverish, stormy hopes and fears ; and moreover should he draw her into the business, she might be made to suffer for it. Luigi foresaw a tempest, and knew it would be safer to be able to say she knew nothing of his wishes.

While Luigi, with a clouded brow, was revolving these thoughts the next morning, a messenger reached him from Garibaldi, who had only a few hours since arrived in Rome. The indefatigable general had already formed a scheme for taking up his head-quarters at Rieti, which he intended to fortify, and remembering that Captain Ravelli had been educated as an engineer, he summoned him to hold counsel over the plan, made rapid notes of his observations, and ordered him off instantly to survey the old classic town, the Queen of the Sabine land, as its inhabitants sometimes proudly called it, built at the foot of mountains, in a rich plain full of vineyards. The swift Velino rushes by the town, which is a nest of quaint red-roofed houses, guarded by several towers and a citadel.

No more joyous spot is there on earth than Rieti in the vintage season, when all the population swarm forth from their hive to gather in the rich purple and amber clusters and heap them into wagons drawn by great meek-eyed oxen, or pile them in panniers on the backs of asses, which the children have crowned with leafy garlands snatched from the vines. Half-naked boys, graceful as fauns and brown as satyrs, perch themselves in the trees to which the vines cling, and throw down the grapes with jest and song to the laughing girls below: matrons in picturesque red boddice and snowy headgear superintend; children frolic round and steal grapes; spare and swarthy men complete the scene, and over all is a turquoise sky—radiant sunshine—everywhere laughter and song!

But in winter Rieti assumes a wilder aspect; sudden storms dash upon it and turn the clear Velino into a roaring torrent which sweeps wildly away all that falls on its surface, and tears at the banks as if it would drag them down after the large stones that it rolls along its bed. Rieti was rather in its winter than its summer aspect when Garibaldi resolved to establish himself there, though seldom had so exquisitely sunny and mild a season been known as the winter of '49; but summer or winter made little difference to the hardy chief, all whose plans were promptly conceived, and as promptly executed. No officer of his dreamed of delay or hesitation, and though never did orders come to Luigi at a less welcome time, he did not attempt to steal a moment for private affairs, and could only hurry to Palazzo Clementi to tell Vincenzo of his destination, with a hope that the news might reach Gemma and explain his disappearance. He bade his mother remember that he was only going fourteen miles from Rome, and comforted himself as he rode off with the thought that he should soon find an opportunity of returning for a day or two.

In this however he was entirely mistaken. His active commander employed him ceaselessly, and not only Luigi, but every one of the 2000 volunteers whom the honoured name of Garibaldi soon called together, was continually occupied. Rieti was fortified, and the troops drilled, disciplined, and inured to forced marches, exposure and hardships, which taught them that war was no game to be met as a gay band of picadors encounter a fierce bull in an arena, with fair ladies sitting round to 'rain influence and judge the prize,' but a stern and formidable thing, requiring patient endurance, as well as the lofty enthusiasm which brings volunteers together and makes them capable of sudden, daring enterprises, but which is apt to flag and repine during inaction and expectation.

1849 came amid increasing gloom. In spite of the absence of the Pope, the Christmas ceremonies were taking place, but the lower classes missed the usual magnificent pomp, and innumerable timid and scrupulous consciences were racked by fears that Heaven's anger must rest on the city that had frightened away the Pope; while others, though not troubled by scruples of conscience, looked forward to the future with dismay, and trembled at the possibility of war thundering at their very doors. Sicily was still struggling single-handed, fiercely but despairingly, with Naples; Venice held out, imploring succour from Piedmont, where Charles Albert was gathering his forces for a new campaign. Rome once more contributed largely to the war, but not with the exultant spirit in which she had lavished men and money in 1848. Now it was with stern self-devotion, full of foreboding, and more as a sign of adherence to the cause of Italy than with the expectation of success. Forebodings how soon realized! On the 30th of March the armistice between Austria and Piedmont expired; Charles Albert had marched to the village of La Cava, near the confluence of the Po and the Ticino. Thither Radetsky advanced to meet him. The old fate pursued the Italian arms; mistakes, treachery, and misfortune seemed to combine against them; a defeat was sustained at La Cava; and then came to Rome the tidings of Novara. Novara! what unutterable anguish and despair is contained in that fatal name! What Italian lips can speak it calmly? All ended with that day. Countless lives had been thrown away, a fair land laid waste by fire and sword, hearths made desolate for ever; all the stormy passions let loose which, though seas of blood be poured upon them, are not quenched, but burst out again and again. The tidings were to Rome like the shock of an earthquake. Close upon them followed the abdication of Charles Albert. The campaign was already ended, and North Italy, with her soil soaked with the blood of her best and bravest, sank again into the hands of Austria.

And meanwhile, since the Court at Gaeta would listen to no propositions, but ceaselessly protested, called on the Powers of Europe for aid, and schemed for an unconditional return, a new step became necessary at Rome, and a republic was at last proclaimed. It was directed by a Triumvirate, consisting of Salicetti, Montecchi, and Armellini. Mazzini and Gaffi soon replaced the two first. The Mazzinian faction was but small, but a settled government had become all-important, for disorder was fast gaining ground; several convents had been pillaged, much violence displayed, and the feeling of hostility towards the clergy as a body was intense, though personally many were popular. The strong hands of the triumvirate checked the growing anarchy; the moderate liberals knew well it was no time to protest against the new form of government, but looked on mournfully, and regarded the pomp and demonstration with which the republic was proclaimed from the Capitol with something like contempt. Such of the clergy as had remained in Rome could not keep or accept office under the republic consistently with their duty to the Pope. They resigned their posts, but for the most part they made no public protests, and went on their way quietly, working, as Padre Rinaldi had said, while it was yet day, but with heavy hearts, for the path of duty was hard to see, and the night was closing in already. Unhappily, not all conducted themselves thus discreetly; there were friars who came and went and played the spy in disguise, emissaries from Gaeta to those of the Pope's party who were still, openly or secretly, in Rome. Wherever they appeared discord sprang up, and the popular feeling towards them was made on several occasions fearfully manifest.

The new government might well have its hands full of work. It had an extensive territory to rule, corrupted by old abuses, innumerable offices to fill, formerly occupied by ecclesiastics who had resigned them (and men had to be found capable of filling them), the finances were exhausted, everything was in a transition state; all that Pio Nono had found it impossible to deal with was now thrown on them; add to this, enemies were crowding without the walls of Rome and corresponding with enemies within. That the republic should have done all it effected is no small praise; what it would have accomplished had the play been played out none now can say. Well had it been if the Romans had been allowed to try a little longer whether they could govern themselves.

CHAPTER XVIII.

But by the yellow Tiber
  Was tumult and affright;
From all the spacious champaign
  To Rome men took their flight.

*   *   *   *   *   *

I wis, in all the Senate,
  There was no heart so bold,
But sore it ached, and fast it beat,
  When that ill news was told.

Macaulay.

ON the morning of April 26th, two steamers
slowly entered the port of Civita Vecchia.
The sea was unquiet—that smiling, treacherous
Mediterranean! there had been rough weather for
several days, and the two vessels had been detained
in their progress from Porto Fino; the passengers, who had suffered severely, were standing
crowded together on the decks, casting eager
looks towards the land and the town, which rose
up all around the old port, and glittered in the
sunlight. They were all soldiers, all Italians, some
600 men. There were deserters from Austrian
regiments, to whom death anywhere was prefer-
able to falling into the hands of the Croats. These
were mostly bronzed and bearded men, of mature
age. Others on board had not seen their twentieth
year—the boy heroes of Milan, who had escaped
from their colleges in the famous '*Cinq Giornad*'
which freed her, and became soldiers by instinct.

They had seen hard service since; they were all exiles now—the poor remains of the Lombard Bersaglieri, on their way to Rome. Conspicuous among the groups on the deck of the largest steamer was a remarkably handsome young man, who seemed to be some twenty-four summers old; his broad hat and plume shaded bright dark eyes, and a sweet, finely cut mouth, half concealed by a dark beard. He wore the cross of Savoy, and a tricoloured ribbon was fastened on the breast of his uniform. He was pointing out the different objects in the view to his companions, clustered round him with an affectionate deference which marked him, in spite of his youth, as their leader. And in fact he was Luciano Manara, the hero of heroes in the Five Days; the first to strike a blow on Ponte Tosa; the gallant commander of the volunteers. Beside him was his secretary, Count Emilio Dandolo, several years younger than himself, who had shared the perils of both campaigns with him; Enrico Dandolo, a tall, slender, near-sighted youth, was on his other hand, a scholar who had thrown down the pen for the sword; and leaning against Count Dandolo was a lad still younger, whose gladsome, gentle features and caressing manner had something so feminine and attractive in them that none could wonder that young Emilio Morosini was the darling of the whole company.

As the steamers advanced nearer to the land, a considerable commotion was observable in the town, and suddenly Manara's eyes kindled, as with an exclamation he directed the attention of his companions to a number of frigates which had not long before entered the harbour, and

were slowly disembarking troops. There was a
kind of universal low cry of 'The French!' on
board both the steamers; a silence followed, full
of expectation and displeasure. The sight of those
fourteen frigates boded no good to Rome.

The strength of Civita Vecchia was all outside show; she made no effort to prevent the
French from landing; her dismay and doubt were
mute; General Oudinot quietly took possession
of the place, and when Enrico Dandolo was despatched to him, as a matter of form, with a
request that the volunteers might disembark, he
returned an absolute refusal. Manara listened to
the message with incredulity; then, with a scorn-
ful smile, said 'I should really like to hear that
myself;' and he went on shore to demand an
audience of the French general, who professed to
have come simply to mediate between the Pope
and his subjects, and inaugurated his arrival by
so singular a step. The cutting irony with which
Manara requested an explanation of his refusal
did not propitiate the general, already at a loss
how decently to explain his conduct. 'What
have Lombards to do with Roman affairs?' he
asked angrily.

'And pray, General, what have gentlemen from
Paris to do with them?' retorted Manara, and the
discussion waxed hot and hotter, in spite of the
intervention of the Governor of Civita Vecchia;
Oudinot seeking to extort Manara's promise to remain neutral, Manara haughtily refusing to pledge
himself one way or the other to the foreigner who
dictated to Italians on Italian soil. Meanwhile
the tempest-tossed soldiers crowded together on
board the steamers were growing momentarily

more impatient to land, and when a rumour of Oudinot's refusal reached them they broke into such furious indignation, that in a little while they would have been actually swimming to shore, permission or no permission, had not Manara returned. He was still quivering with excitement and anger from his encounter with Oudinot, but conqueror in a measure, for he had succeeded in gaining leave to disembark at Porto d'Anzo—once the classic Antium; and thither the steamers instantly proceeded.

The last few weeks had been spent in feverish activity at Rome. Many there still believed that the French would not interfere except by diplomacy, and counted confidently on the honour and sympathy of France; but others pointed to past events, reminded their fellow-citizens of Napoleon and Venice, and supported Avezzana, the Minister of War, in all his preparations. It was known that the Neapolitan army was preparing to march on Rome, and none could tell what the next movement of the victorious Austrians might be. Garibaldi had left Rieti, and fixed his quarters in Rome, at the convent of San Pietro in Montorio, whence the monks were obliged to go, and take refuge in the Capitol, a less exposed residence. The city was awaiting with a sort of incredulous expectation the appearance of the French; and the preparations for a siege formed a new excitement and diversion to the citizens, to whom any new thing was always welcome, whether a procession or an execution. Now, at all events, if never before, Rome was united. So hated was the ecclesiastical government, that men of every shade of political opinion combined against its restoration;

whether Mazzini should rule or not, had become for
the time utterly indifferent; resistance, as long as
a man was left to fight, was the universal resolve,
especially if Pio Nono were to be brought back by
foreign allies. Yet, while there was a ceaseless
buzz and stir of preparation throughout the city,
the shops were all open, friends met as usual.
Though barricades made several streets impassable,
and uniforms abounded as once the clerical habit
had done, it was almost impossible to believe that
in the nineteenth century a siege was at hand; it
sounded like a tale of the Middle Ages to speak
of the siege of Rome! Once before had the
City of the Seven Hills been assaulted by a French
general; she was destined to see another advance
against her.

Tidings of the French at Civita Vecchia, of the
reception which the Bersaglieri had met with, flew
to Rome, and when after a weary march across the
scorching Campagna, from Albano, in that almost
unparalleled hot spring weather, they entered
Rome on the 29th, the whole city poured out
to meet them with frantic applause, and to look on
those who had delivered Milan, and faced all the
hardships in 1848 and 1849, of which the Romans had heard through their own volunteers.
Something of a smile appeared on the faces of the
Bersaglieri as the throng flocked round them and
filled the air with acclamations; but martial discipline prevailed, and they entered the city without
making any response to the crowd, who, suddenly
chilled by conduct so unlike their own beloved
and noisy demonstrations on every occasion, grew
silent, and gazed after them with wonder and displeasure. Avezzana passed the Lombards in re-

view before they entered their quarters, where the wearied soldiers longed heartily to be. As the concluding '*Viva Italia!*' burst out, which ended the review, and Manara having thrown off the cares of office for a while, was talking with his companions, two hands were suddenly laid on his shoulders, and a voice cried, ' Well, major! not cut to pieces yet? Welcome to Rome!' and turning, he recognised Ravelli, whom he had known well while they both served in Upper Italy. Leone was near, too, a less intimate acquaintance, but well known by his fame as an *improvisatore* to Manara and the two Dandolos, who came up to join in the recognition. Much was said on all sides in the first few moments; then Luigi asked the true history of the detention at Civita Vecchia. Manara gave it, with comments from Emilio and Enrico Dandolo. Luigi heard with an outbreak of wrath; Leone with startled looks. He was one of those who believed in the French; too generous himself to suspect perfidy in others, he expressed his confidence in them, and Manara replied with one of Alfieri's ironical lines—

' Di libertà maestri i Galli !'

' How do our preparations seem to you ?' asked Luigi.

' Too like Milan,' answered Enrico Dandolo, sighing.

' You are right, Enrico,' said Manara, looking round with a clouded brow; ' too many flags, too many shouts, too much play here, friends. It will not work !'

' Wait till evening, and you will see a different

scene,' said Leone; 'you will not despise us then; you see us thrown into commotion by your coming. Where are your quarters in the Piazza of St. Peter's? By drum-beat you will see all quiet. Our chief preparations are about that part.'

They went thither, and the Basilica rose for the first time in their lives before the eyes of Manara and his company. But the glorious temple obtained scarcely a glance, for the soldiers' minds were occupied in noting the military preparations which had turned the vast piazza into a camp. Cannon were there; arms were piled at every corner; fires flickered up, round which men were cooking; others sat polishing their arms, or lay stretched on the straw which had been thickly littered down. Porta Angelica was open, and thronged by those going out and in, driving sheep, oxen, and loaded wagons. Batteries had been erected, and both a fine regiment of the line and the Carabineers had their quarters at this point. Two more regiments were located in Piazza Navona; the volunteers held the walls; the National Guard was at its respective quarters. Manara's eye glanced over the scene with satisfaction. Instead of a confused and noisy multitude only, the Lombards soon found they had come amid a noble and resolute people; they smilingly recanted their first hasty judgment, and awaited with cheered and brave hearts what the morrow might bring.

Manara found his way for a little while to Palazzo Clementi, under the guidance of Leone, who was equally desirous of introducing one whom he admired exceedingly to Irene, and of introducing his betrothed to Manara. The attendance at Irene's weekly *società* had been greatly diminished

by late events. Foreigners had fled from Rome;
many natives, too, were absent; her engagement
at the Teatro Regio was closed, and she had as
yet avoided making another. Only intimate
friends assembled in her *salon*. Clementi and his
sister were there; Signora Olivetti came; Luigi
appeared for a short time; Madama Cecchi came
in, excited out of her late depression by her
patriotism, which when fairly roused defied even
her spiritual terrors. All these formed an anxious,
eager group, asking for information from each
other, and reporting whatever had come to their
ears on the all-absorbing topic of the French and
the Bersaglieri.

The entrance of Leone and Manara caused a
great sensation; Irene was proudly presented
by Leone to the young leader of the Lombard troops, who looked with admiration at her
noble countenance, and then turning to Vincenzo,
made friends with him at once, with a manly
tenderness and compassion for the invalid, whose
bright eyes and smile spoke so cheerful an accep-
tance of his fate.

The general absorbing thought was put away
for a little while by Manara's asking Irene to
sing. All were glad to listen and be refreshed
by turning away from the harassing, exhaust-
ing dwelling on coming events. She took the
least warlike song that she knew; she was
weary, and had not spirits for a martial one
that night, and no doubt all shared in the same
feeling, for there was universal silence and a look
of quiet gravity on the faces that had glowed so
eagerly a little while before. Clementi's eyes
were fixed on Irene; for once he was off his guard;

for once a doubt of the success of his plans crossed his mind, unaccountable enough, for all seemed progressing to his heart's desire. Manara had leant back with closed eyes, absorbed in the sweet and soothing tones; he looked up suddenly as they ceased, and caught Clementi's gaze on Irene. It betrayed much to him; he met Leone's eyes and smiled, and that smile and glance towards the count suddenly flashed a new light into Leone's mind. He regarded Clementi compassionately, wondered at his own long blindness, and felt that he had often unconsciously caused him acute pain. He trusted his friend's honour as he trusted that of the French!

Luigi had not attempted to speak to Gemma apart, and an angry red glowed on her cheeks. She could not understand his conduct. He had not long returned to Rome, and had been too fully employed in his engineering capacity to have an hour to bestow upon his private affairs. With new but resolute self-command, he refrained from all intercourse with her unknown to her family; he would seek her no more until he could do so openly.

Irene left the piano, and the conversation began again. Vincenzo was pointing to a paragraph in a *Moniteur*, which had somehow reached Rome; Manara looked over him and read aloud, 'France cannot suffer herself to be enfeebled by the rise of a neighbouring power from which she derives no advantage.' It was in a speech on the Italian question, and a visible sensation was created by it in the *salon*. One or two voices asserted it to express but the opinion of a small faction; others scornfully declared the French had always been, and always would be, false to Italy, and bitterly alluded to Pio Nono's having called them against his own people. Manara was struck with the hostile vehemence with which Pio Nono was named; Clementi remarked in reply, 'We should welcome him among us if he were about to take possession of one place.'

'Where ?'

'The one that awaits him among his predecessors in St. Peter's.'

'The French enter our Rome!' cried Madama Cecchi; 'we will do like the women in Milan first—we will throw our tables, our pianos on their heads! I have filled my bags long ago.'

'And I !' said Signora Olivetti, alluding to the sacks full of earth which each family was expected to furnish to aid in the fortifications.

The acute anguish which shot across Manara's face at the mention of his beloved Milan, the city which he above all had contributed to make free, now lying again in chains, moved Irene deeply.

'Ah, pardon !' she said, as if in apology that it had been named.

'I have children there, whom I may never see again,' replied Manara, simply.

She looked up, surprised that the young soldier should be already married. He smiled, guessing her thoughts, and sitting down by her side, told her in a low voice much about those dear ones whom he could seldom bear to name. Irene's music, the sight of relations living happily together, had charmed him into a softer mood than he could often afford to indulge in. 'Thank Heaven, we shall have some fighting soon !' he exclaimed at last. She looked at him inquiringly.

'Ah, you do not understand,' he said; 'but we exiles must ever be doing something to keep us from feeling how empty our hearts are. Yet even a battle loses half its worth to exiles; to other men victory is the road to peace, to their homes, where the wife, the mother, the children are. To us—no! Yet it is much to strike another blow for Italy!' His fingers played with the tricoloured ribbon on his breast.

'You are certain, then, that the French will attack? All the residents here have protested against armed interference on the part of their Government.'

'Most certain, and that before many days are over. Thank Heaven, a way is opened to us in the midst of all the shame and misfortunes which have befallen us, by which we may show at least that we did not deserve them! The truth is, Oudinot is self-deceived; he fancies the city to be oppressed by the small Mazzinian faction and eager to be delivered.'

"Mazzini has few followers, but we have only one thought now, to defend our city.'

'And you have prepared in earnest; I saw houses knocked down, trees felled——'

'Ah, our ilexes! But the Committee of Public Safety judged it necessary. Yes, half the beauty of Rome has been destroyed; but "poor and free," as some of the people have chalked up on the walls!'

'I wished to ask whether that priest chance to be here who was with your volunteers; I have seen him many times confessing the dying as calmly on the field of battle as if he had been in his own confessional at Rome. It was a tall, spare figure, dark glowing eyes, a stern pale face.'

'Ah, you have not seen him smile, or you would not describe him thus! Padre Rinaldi. Yes, here, and ever occupied—he and Leone.'

'He does not fear republicans?'

'He has no need. None have who do not glide in disguise from Rome to Gaeta and back, with their wallets full of treason,' said Vincenzo, catching the question. Others heard what he said, and Manara saw that a sensation had been created by his words, which he did not understand. He looked for explanation at Irene.

'Have you not heard?' she asked in a low tone, and shuddering.

'Those two poor wretches!' said Signora Olivetti, drawing nearer.

'Those Jesuits!' said Clementi.

Manara made a sign of negation.

'They were not truly Jesuits,' Irene said, hurriedly; 'it is said not—no one really knows— the people were frantic then from having found out that there was a plot to deliver up the city to the Neapolitans. It was concerted between the Court at Gaeta and some unknown persons here. Papers were seized, but the bearer (a friar) contrived to escape before the contents were understood.'

'After that, every priest in disguise was held a spy, of course?' said Manara.

'Yes, signor; though many are only poor lambs who have put on the robe of a laic from timidity,' said Madama Cecchi.

'A heated horse and a friar unfrocked were never good for aught,' said Clementi, drily.

'Then, one day there were found two men lurking in a vineyard. They said they were vine-dressers, but a cry got abroad that they were spies—Jesuits; it spread like wildfire; the people seemed to swarm up out of the very ground like locusts to seize them. They were beaten, dragged, lacerated; they were forced by this very house, bleeding like an "*Ecce Homo*," in the midst of that furious multitude, who screamed, howled, surged in the streets. I saw the face of one of those two poor wretches. Oh, Heaven, that look!' Irene covered her face with her hands, shuddering all over, and there was a general suppressed movement, but no one spoke till Manara asked, 'And then?'

'They were dragged to the bridge of St. Angelo —it is said one was still alive and shrieked as he was flung into the river. I cannot believe it; I cannot think life would have lasted till then,' answered Irene, falteringly; then casting her hands from her tearful face, she exclaimed, 'Oh, signor, do not judge my Romans by this! You know what a mob is; what tigers the populace always are; but think, we had been all but betrayed, we knew not by whom, and that uncertainty martyrized us doubly! We knew not whom to trust, whom to doubt. You cannot guess what wreck, what desolation the unconditional return of Pio Nono would bring—there would be such vengeance as would make the streets run blood! Oh! all Rome has lamented that deed; we ask Heaven every day on our knees to forgive it.'

'It was an evil deed, much like those of the Croats,' replied Manara, thinking of horrible scenes which he had witnessed in Milan; 'but not like theirs, done in cold blood.'

'The pillage of convents was another objectionable action,' said Clementi, with a glance at Madama Cecchi, whose alternate patriotism and piety infinitely amused him.

'Yes, signor,' said she, very sharply; 'it was a bad action, and the republic has put a stop to it. It was infamous to see the rabble strutting in holy copes and albes, and velvet and silks on which they had laid their unsanctified fingers; silks worth many *scudi* a yard, such as we never have been able to buy for our church in this parish. When I think of it my heart sinks as if I had been following my mother's funeral!'

'What do you say to the confiscation of ecclesiastical property and the carrying off of bells from the churches to make cannon, signora?'

'I say it was a good action, a holy action; all done to defend one's country is holy, Signor Conte; and as for the bells, I say blessed be the Government, for I was daily awakened by the one for early mass at the little church yonder.'

'Ah, dear signora! what blasphemies you are talking!' said Clementi, and the padrona's face fell, but the patriotic spirit triumphed again.

'No, signor, pardon me; it seems to me that no one will be shut out of Holy Paradise for loving his country.'

'We are expecting Padre Rinaldi this evening,' said Irene to Manara, who had risen to go; 'you will stay for his coming?'

He willingly sat down again, and she told him of several colleges and museums which Padre Rinaldi had saved from the populace by his remonstrances, in the disorderly days before the Provisionary Government was well established, when the whole city was like a seething cauldron. 'But to him they ever listen,' she said; 'and if he had been at hand before the tumult grew such that no single voice could be heard, those two had not been massacred!'

He entered soon after, and was instantly surrounded by the assembled guests, eager to hear all he said. The mournful, austere look which he had worn of late had given place to a cheerful expression; all he said encouraged those who were gathered there, the defenders of Rome. Madama Cecchi was wonderfully inspirited by his tone, and forgot for some time that her confessor assured her—though he was a good man and loved Italy, after all—that Providence was against Rome.

The few words which Rinaldi spoke kindled new fire in the hearts of all the men there; they felt now, not only resolute to die on the walls, if needful—*that* they had been all along—but inspired with hope that Rome might resist successfully. On one brow alone no flush came; no spark lighted in the dark grey eye; Count Clementi listened with an artificial, assenting smile, but his powers of dissimulation drooped and failed before the eagle glance of the priest, who, he knew, saw through him as no one else had ever done; doubted him, but could not yet convict him. In his presence Clementi could never assume enthusiasm. While he listened apparently to what was passing, his mind reverted to the awful tale of which Irene had attempted an outline, and he felt a cold creeping chill as he reflected how deeply he himself had been concerned in the plot which had exasperated the Romans.

Those papers had been coming to him! What if his agent had not escaped—had betrayed him? And while his mind was thus engaged, his sister's was as busy in another direction. To her the siege was nothing; the state of Italy a trifle; the whole world for her was contained in Ravelli— Ravelli who was gone with an ardent look towards her, but no more! She sat apart, biting her full red lip, her face clouding tempestuously; she was indifferent to everything now, and impatient to take leave, since he was gone. On her, too, fell the eye of Padre Rinaldi; her secret was no secret to him; he looked pityingly on her for a moment, then gave a glance at her brother which seemed to read his very soul, and he felt as if he were detected, about to be proclaimed aloud a traitor, and could only by a great effort maintain his haughty composure. To Irene, Padre Rinaldi turned with a very different air; she and Leone were two who refreshed him in his daily strife with the world; those eyes that never feared to meet his; that noble brow and sweet smile of hers told, he knew, a tale as frank and sincere as if she had been owning her inmost feelings at a confessional. The heretic Irene was dear to him as if she had been his child—she and her lover, the young poet whose nature would have bidden him lie on Hymettus watching the amethyst and rosy lights kiss its marbles, and listening to the bees humming all day long in its thyme—but who had sacrificed his leisure, his life, his best hopes to his country. Leone and Irene were the two whom Padre Rinaldi loved best in the world; they had found a home in that visionary, austere heart of his which seemed all devoted to his Church and his country.

Manara was forced to go at last, though he would fain have stayed.

'You will look on our house as your own,' Vincenzo said to him as they parted, and Irene's smile enforced the invitation.

CHAPTER XIX.

Alors tout se leva.   L'homme, l'enfant, la femme,
Quiconque avait un bras, quiconque avait un âme,
Tout vint, tout accourut.   Et la ville à grand bruit
Sur les lourds bataillons se rua jour et nuit.
En vain boulets, obus, la balle et les mitrailles;
De la vieille cité dechiraient les entrailles—
Et de son râle affreux ameutant les faubourgs;
Le tocsin haletant bondissait dans les tours.

Victor Hugo.

SLEEP hovered somewhat shily over many pillows that night, but morning broke without any new events, and the Romans could rise and laugh half scornfully at the fears and expectation that had been excited in vain. Irene was standing at a window, looking out with some anxiety on a gloomy sky. Rome, another Heliopolis, scarcely looked its true self without its sunshine, which lends it such a glory, and speaks in a poetical language of colours all its own and untranslatable into any other. Irene looked wistfully out; a ray of light would have seemed such a good omen to her. She had in full measure the Italian sensitiveness to outward impressions, the same shrinking from gloom and harshness in any shape which showed itself so strongly in the ancients by their studious avoidance of words that might imply an ill omen, and the constancy with which their poets ignored the stern and rugged aspects of nature.

Irene and Vincenzo were alone together; Leone

was with the regiment to which he had joined himself; Cecchi still belonged to the National Guard;
both were at their posts, and the whole palace
contained scarcely one man.

As Irene gazed idly out, one of those solitary
thoughts that sometimes float into the mind, un-
connected with anything that was there before,
crossed her almost startlingly, a sudden perception of how different must this Rome seem to
the countless strangers who came to visit it from
what it did to her. To them—a world-renowned
past—to her, a living, struggling, suffering present. She, living there, accustomed all her life
to its wonders, had never been able, intensely as
she loved her birthplace, sufficiently to abstract
herself from it to be able fully to comprehend how
it appeared to foreigners, and still less could she
of late do so, when even Vincenzo's artist friends
had ceased to speak of anything but politics. All
the emperors put together were not just then
half as important as Mazzini.

She turned from the window to Vincenzo, and
was beginning to speak in the words of a game
which she had learnt at Florence and had introduced with great success among her aquaintance,
'Mona Luna, Mona Luna, give me counsel——'
when the palace suddenly seemed to shake, the
air to reverberate with sound; a startled cry from
half the inhabitants of the palace was lost in the
roar—the first cannon-shot had been fired! Now
the great bells of the Capitol and Monte Citorio
added their voices to the thunder of the cannonade
and the sharp, constant discharge of musketry.
Irene sprang to the window and leant out; Vincenzo hurried to her side; heads were bending from

every casement all along the street, and agonized
exclamations intermingled and were lost in the
shouts below, and the tramp of feet, as from every
door patrician, burgher, and artisan rushed out to
the walls. It was a scene to be beheld, to be shared
in, rather than to be described—the impassioned ges-
tures—the storm of voices—the strange weapons—
each man brandishing whatever he had first caught
up—the rush and tumult—the women waving scarfs,
veils, handkerchiefs from the windows—the roar of
cannon—the dread, the hope, the inexpressible
agitation—the sudden conviction that that which
had seemed but an exciting vision was a most
terrible reality—the thrills of terror for those dear
ones in peril, and the suffocating indignation
against the invaders, perjured and without a
shadow of excuse as they were—all this can but
be remembered years after with the same thrill
that shot through heart and soul on that 30th of
April, when the siege of Rome began.

The street was left suddenly empty; the throng
had rushed through it, and strange loneliness succeeded the heaving, hurrying scene of a moment
before. All was silent in the long street, but shouts
were heard in the distance and the boom of cannon
continued near St. Peter's. Irene could not leave
the window, and like her, matrons and maidens
still leant hour after hour from their casements,
listening, watching, calling to each passer-by for
news of the fight. Now prisoners passed, under a
guard; then a wounded man was borne by, a sight
which made them shrink and tremble; now a
thicker discharge of musketry filled all with alarm
and expectation; then a pause would excite the
same sensations, which grew more intense as time

passed. 'How goes it? what is done?' voices would call to some one hurrying by. 'Well—excellently—the Garibaldi legion have driven back the French,' was the exulting reply, the last words half lost as the speaker's rapid stride bore him speedily out of sight, and hands would be clasped and thanksgivings uttered. Next four men carrying a wounded comrade to the hospital would appear at the end of the street, and all bent from the windows in anxious suspense: 'Who is it? who is it? is he badly wounded? Ah! the poor fellow! I do not know him;' or, 'Oh, Holy Virgin, it is Modena, or Viola, or Galentini,' or some other friend or acquaintance, for whom at this moment all the sympathy of near relations was felt.

While sharing with the rest the watch that fluctuated between hope and terror, Irene received a note from the Committee of Aid for the wounded, summoning her to the military hospital which had been established in the Trinità de' Pellegrini. With a very few exceptions only married women had been appointed to undertake the charge of them; but Irene had earnestly desired to be admitted, and Count Clementi and Padre Rinaldi without any difficulty had obtained permission for her; her knowledge of several languages made her valuable, and she was a person of note; her *salon* had been completely the rallying-point of one party among the liberals, so that it seemed fitting to give her a prominent part. Her duties, it seemed, were to begin at once. She gave the note to Vincenzo, and prepared to go, and a strange expedition it was to undertake when the air was full of smoke and shot, and the streets

brimming over with agitated crowds. She half
doubted whether Maddalena would venture to
accompany her, but the woman drew her shawl
over her head and showed herself ready at once.
Irene threw her arms round Vincenzo's neck, and
went.   He, who could not fight for Rome, still
leant at the window, his heart with those at Porta
Cavalleggieri, and watching with keen anxiety
every sight and sound that came within his ken.

Irene's way to the hospital was lengthened by
the barricades, which obliged her to take a devious
course, or avoid them by passing through houses
and court-yards.   She found many wounded men
had already been brought in, and there was a considerable number of women there ready to aid as
best they could, but greatly in want of a director.
Irene saw that she should be obliged to remain
all night, for there was much to be done, and her
habits of command at her theatre made her able
to assume the authority to which the others at
once bowed. *Regolatrice* of a hospital! it was a
strange new employment for her, inexperienced
as she was. Nothing was yet well in train; all
were new to their work, unused to each other,
highly excited and anxious, uneasily conscious of
how weighty was the labour they had undertaken,
and horrified by the ghastly sights that were
continually brought before them. Irene did her
best to make a clear head and ready wit atone for
her lack of experience, gave her directions briefly
and decidedly, tried to foresee what would be
wanted, and availed herself of all the knowledge
possessed by one or two of her assistants who
had been previously used to helping at a hospital.
She had not realized how terrible gunshot wounds

were, how much suffering she should have to witness and endure; she tried not to feel, but only
to think, till her pulses would throb more calmly
and her voice sound more steady; and the incessant
call on her attention from her assistants, all requiring precise orders, was no small help, though
the dread that among those bleeding, mutilated
forms continually brought in, she should see some
familiar face, was continually agitating her heart.
As she was giving out some stores, a voice spoke
her name; turning in terror, she saw a mere
child had just come in, and recognised a cousin
of Imelda's. 'Filippo, my dear boy, you here!'
she exclaimed in astonishment; 'are you much
hurt?'

'No; I could not help going to the walls,'
replied the boy, as she supported him, while a
surgeon examined his bleeding arm; 'they locked
me up at home, but I got out on the roofs, and
down by the walls of the convent near; there is
an acacia—ah!'

'Did I hurt you, my lad?' asked the surgeon,
kindly; 'it is almost over.'

'Hurt! I did not complain,' said Filippo, indignantly, pressing his lips hard together, however.
'And I got to Porta Cavalleggieri, and there—
oh, such a fine sight! the French driven back pell
mell, fighting like demons! a poor fellow of ours
dropped just as I got there; he had his leg broken.
Doctor, I hope there will be a scar on my arm?'
he asked, very anxiously. The surgeon laughed
kindly, and did not disappoint him by a cruel
negative. Irene was wanted in a hundred other
places, but she could not leave the boy till his
arm was bound up. He leant his head against

her, and with his other hand pressed her fingers on his forehead, where large drops were starting, for the pain was severe, though he would not own it. 'Is that man here or in the other hospital? He was put into an ambulance, and as he could not fight any more, I asked him to give me his gun, and I shot—I did, I assure you—several times, before this rascally bullet hit me. Ah, why would they not let me volunteer into the Garibaldi legion? All the ground was covered with dying men; it was a magnificent sight, only they groaned and looked dreadful, and that made one's heart ache, though I believe most of them were Frenchmen. And just as I was aiming at a great fellow I got shot myself, and, if you will believe me, Signor Nota saw me, and came through a thunderstorm of shot to me; it was sweeping the whole road, and he knelt down by me and lifted me up, and carried me quite gently and coolly across out of fire, and all our men cheered him. Well, it is done, doctor!'

'Yes my friend; and now I should recommend you to go home; for neither I nor the signorina have any more time to spare for you.'

'Well, I go. What will they say to me? I thought I had better come here and be looked to before returning home. But I really must find that carabineer and tell him it was not my fault that I lost his gun. It fell as Signor Nota was carrying me, and I could not ask him to stop, for he would have been shot, without doubt. I think I will go back to seek for it.'

'Nonsense, Filippo, you may buy him another; but I am certain that some one else is using it by this time. Your carabineer is not here; he must be at the Bene Fratelli. Promise me you will go home,' said Irene, kissing him with a full heart. 'One moment; what did Signor Nota do when he had got you safe?'

'Rushed into the *mêlée*, I suppose; I do not know. *Addio*, dear signorina. I hope you will see me here again soon.'

Irene could not help smiling, but she had to leave the little hero to his fate and attend to more serious cases. Many beds were already occupied by wounded men; on the pale, contracted faces of some resolute endurance was stamped, but others gave way utterly, and broke into groans and complaints unchecked and heart-rending. As Irene turned from Filippo a man was brought in by four comrades, wounded to death. A faint moan escaped him as they laid him down; she went to his side and saw death already in his face. 'Farewell, comrade,' said one of those who had carried him in, lingering after the other three had hurried back to their posts; 'how goes it now?'

'*Viva Italia!*' muttered the poor fellow, almost inaudibly. His friend looked at Irene, shook his head and went, dashing some tears from his eyes. The surgeons were all employed with other cases; Irene leant over the dying man, seeing his lips attempting to form a word. 'Water!' she divined rather than heard; she held it to his mouth; he swallowed a little with difficulty, opened his dimmed eyes, and feebly moving his right hand to the tricoloured ribbon on his breast, murmured, 'For my wife.'

'She shall have it, I promise you. Where shall I take it?' Irene answered.

'To Via——' the voice failed, the eyelids fluttered, the lips ceased to move; he was dead before the priest, who was hastening towards the

bed, could reach it.   Irene pressed her hands upon
her eyes ; some of the horrors of war had come
very near her, but she must not linger by those
who were beyond her help ; she turned away, with
keen regret that at least she could not fulfil the
poor fellow's last wish.   He seemed to be a Tras-
teverin of the lower class, a fine handsome man,
scarcely of middle age ; his uniform was smeared
with powder and blood, and pierced through and
through with balls.   As cases more or less serious
thickened, Irene and her fellow-workers were more
and more occupied.   They were all thankful when
Padre Rinaldi came in, and at his name some of
the wounded, too, half raised themselves, eager to
attract his notice.   He had been all the morning
at the Bene Fratelli, where was a staff of other
ladies, full of good will, but most inexperienced.
Signora Olivetti was among them, using to the
full all the medical knowledge she had gained by
attending the sick in more peaceful days.   Padre
Rinaldi brought calmness, method, and experience
with him ; Irene felt as if half her responsibility
were lightened from the moment he appeared, and
as she watched him bending over the sufferers,
consoling and cheering them, she could well understand the passionate devotion with which he had
inspired the volunteers, whose dangers and hardships he had fully shared.

Late in the evening she hurried back to Vincenzo for a moment, inhaling the air outside the
hospital with refreshment, though still the reek of
blood and heavy stifling blue smoke seemed to
hang in it.   The cannon were mute, but their
boom still sounded in her wearied ear ; still she
heard groans and saw faces convulsed with agony

rise before her aching eyes. The streets were as full as ever, soldiers were marching through them; friends were meeting again with ecstasy, women imploring the passers-by to give them news of some who came not home; sometimes a mounted officer dashed past; new barricades were rising, those who were building them worked with a desperate energy—how unlike the idle sauntering with which the Italian labourer mostly toils! Just where Irene and her maid wanted to cross, a barricade was being formed; a deep trench had been dug across the pavement, and on the mound of earth formed on one side carriages, chairs, logs, nay, even the splendid coach of a cardinal, were being rapidly piled up into a barricade by a triumphant crowd. Irene had to turn back; another stopped her progress at the next turning, and she was hesitating in perplexity, when with great courtesy two of the men at work threw a table across the gulf, helped her over and saw her safely on the other side. She felt as if all the impatience to know how matters had really gone, which had been forcibly dammed up all day and only tenfold increased by the flying reports which reached the hospital, now rushed over her like a flood. She flew up the staircases with winged speed, darted past Menica who let her in, and into the sitting-room. Vincenzo met her before she could ask a question, 'All well—all glorious—the French repulsed, Leone safe, 500 prisoners, a triumph; we raw recruits have utterly smashed them, Irene.'

Irene could only reply by a burst of tears, but quickly recovering, she asked for particulars.

'They came up in disorder,' Vincenzo continued, with triumphant exultation, 'shouting hurrah for

luncheon in the Piazza of St. Peter's! They thought
to walk in at an open gate; Garibaldi and the
Carabineers charged them, drove them back, though
they resisted furiously; there has been hard fighting,
but we won the day gloriously—completely! Garibaldi has pursued them towards Civita Vecchia, and
that is all I know, except that Leone, who told me—'

'Leone!   Oh, where is he?'

'He could not stay, he only rushed up for a
moment.   Ah! I knew you would be terribly
disappointed, darling.'

'Never mind; and I must go back to the hospital directly.   Well?'

'He says new barricades are being created everywhere.'

'I can testify to that.'

'And the city is mad with joy. If the French
assault again, they will simply be more thoroughly
beaten than before. Pray Heaven they may, the
rascally traitors! Is not this fine news for Oudinot to write to Paris? We Caraibes can fight, it
seems.   I trust Garibaldi will drive them all into
the sea at Civita Vecchia.'

'Leone was safe?'

'Yes, quite—quite; rather grimy with smoke
and powder, but looking more like our old Leone
of three years ago than I have seen him since
Rossi's death. Ravelli had several shots through
his hat, and Donati was rather badly wounded by
a French sabre; but I know of no other disasters
among our own friends. Some of our people have
lost relations, I fear, but our loss is nothing compared to the French. You look tired, dearest;
this has been a hard day for you!'

'Oh, not as hard as to have stayed here doing

nothing but watch! I am very glad of this coffee, though,' said Irene, as Menica opportunely entered with a cup for her, and stood waiting while she drank it, to have the benefit of the conversation.

'Have you heard anything of Clementi and the Bersaglieri?'

'The Signor Conte has been here,' Menica interposed.

'Yes, he came in for an instant, sadly distressed about the contessa; the sound of the cannonade seems nearly to have terrified her to death. Manara and his troop were placed with the reserve and took no part in the fray.'

'What is that?' said Irene, looking across the street into the open windows of the opposite house, which their windows commanded. 'There is grief there!'

They could see that a man in uniform had just entered the room. A woman started up to meet him and gazed into his face with a look of speechless inquiry. He shook his head and covered his eyes with his hand. The windows were wide open; Irene must have heard if a word had been exchanged, but the gesture was enough; and the woman fell insensible at his feet. He hastily raised her, lifted her to a sofa, and seemed to summon attendants, who tried long to restore her to life, while he stood by motionless, his eyes bent on the ground. Animation at length returned, and unrestrained hysterical weeping told that with it had come the knowledge of some irreparable loss.

'Our triumph has cost her very dear!' said Irene, deeply moved; 'do you remember who it is that lives there? I wonder what relation they have lost ? Poor, poor people ! Oh, in how many, many houses to-night there must be mourning !'

Very strange at this moment did it seem to hear Madama Cecchi laughing in her room on the other side of the wall—her old hearty laugh, which was by no means over when she entered the apartment of the brother and sister.

'Ah, my signorina ! You are returned ? It is a consolation to see you ! *Viva i nostri !* You have heard all the story, *signorina mia ?* And I have had a visitor, Paoli ; you know that poor fellow, Signor Vincenzo ? I would not say he had a *baiocca's* worth of courage——well, he has just been with me, and says he, " Signora, you have heard of the barricades at Porta Cavalleggieri ; do you know what I have done ?" " No, speak !" " I dare not, indeed I dare not !" " Come, come, speak !" " Did they tell you of the French officer on a grey charger who fell first of all ? *Giusto !* I did it, signora. I never had a gun in my hand before, but I bought one, and stood behind the sacks, and when he came on, shouting ' Advance !' and waving his sabre to his men, we all fired, and he went down ! I cannot say, you know, for we all fired, but I believe my shot hit him !" The poor man looked so pleased and so frightened, signorina, like an innocent baby. So I put on a face of one who is scandalized and said, " And do you feel no remorse when you think of that poor man, *Raffaele mio ?*" " Do not ask me, do not ask me, signora." " Come, tell me ; I am a woman of honour." And he, " Well, then, I would do the same again. Hush, signora ! for charity's sake ! tell no one. I did not know

what was in me!"   And I, " Ah, *Raffaele mio,*
remember the proverb, ' Let him who has a straw
tail keep from the fire' !" '

And therewith Madama Cecchi once more burst
out laughing, and her audience could not but join
her.

CHAPTER XX.

But one sad heart, one tearful eye,
Pierced deeper through the mystery,
And watched with agony and fear
Her wayward bridegroom's varied cheer.

Scott.

SO complete was the check which the French had received that it did not seem impossible that Vincenzo's wish respecting their fate might have come to pass, had not the Triumvirate recalled Garibaldi, with a hope that this forbearance might propitiate the French Republic, and end the war at once. The Plenipotentiary Lesseps arrived from France, and about a month was spent in diplomatic conferences, during which of course there was an armistice, and the French freely entered Rome and visited the inhabitants in the most brotherly manner. Meanwhile Garibaldi and several companies of volunteers went out to attack the Neapolitans, who, some 20,000 strong, were now at Albano and Frascati, apparently waiting to see the Romans and the French fight. Garibaldi's name alone was nearly enough to put them to flight; the expedition was almost a frolic; and news of such easy victories came to Rome as raised the spirits of all to the highest pitch.

As no new cases were brought to the hospitals, Irene's duties grew light; she was only obliged to spend part of each day at the Pellegrini, to see that her directions were duly carried out. She went thither with daily increasing thankfulness that the siege had ended so speedily, for even this taste of war had made all realize what its horrors might be; and the result of Lesseps' conferences with the Triumvirate was awaited with intense anxiety. Each day before she left Palazzo Clementi, Irene used to glance at the windows of her opposite neighbour, and many times she saw the black-robed figure sitting alone, picking lint which was wetted by her quietly dropping tears. It was a picture of resigned sorrow which never failed deeply to move Irene, and she knew that that house contributed more lavishly than any other to the wants of the hospitals, when night by night the carts went round soliciting supplies. There was no acquaintance between her and the mourner, but they often exchanged looks, sympathizing on the one side, grateful on the other, which made almost a friendship between them.

Irene went to the Pellegrini one day towards the end of May, bearing a bunch of lilies of the valley in her hand, knowing well how refreshing their purity and fragrance would be to those lying in the hospital atmosphere, which notwithstanding every care was most oppressive in that hot weather when spring was fast passing into summer. She felt it overpoweringly as she entered, and was obliged to pause for a few moments to grow accustomed to it before she advanced. All was now in perfect order, and there was no lack of attendants; the sufferers fared as well as was possible, but fever was greatly increased by the heat, and Irene knew that many there would never rise from those pallets again. Some were sitting up, taking food; others lay looking round with hollow, anxious eyes and wasted features; others lay sunk in stupor like the death into which it would soon pass. The nurses were quietly moving to and fro, and a priest as usual did not fail to be in attendance, with unwearied, unweariable zeal.

Irene presently advanced, and visited one bedside after another, bringing cheerfulness with her, and rewarded, oh, how well! by the looks of love and reverence which followed her. She who had had all the Roman musical world at her feet was now in a very different sphere, and did her work with as brave and gentle a spirit as ever, always true to herself and her womanhood. She did not confine her ministrations to the hospital only; for to one invalid she brought news of a mother, too old and feeble to visit her wounded son, but rendered satisfied and happy by obtaining news of him from the *regolatrice* herself, and who had sent him by Irene's hands a little token of remembrance. Another she soothed by an assurance that a friend was supporting the family whose means of subsistence ceased with his illness. A third rejoiced in the Gazette which she brought him wherewith to while away an hour. Where she had nothing else to give, kind words at least were never wanting; words treasured up by those manly hearts which rejoiced in wounds they had received ' for Italy.'

Amongst the Italians some French were scattered, and it was satisfactory to perceive that there was no ill-will between the late enemies, but rather the honest respect which one man feels for another who, he knows, has done his duty.

Irene's handful of lilies had grown smaller and smaller as she advanced from bed to bed, leaving one here and another there, where wistful eyes had lingered beseechingly on the fresh pure blossoms. She had only one left when she came to a pallet where a French soldier was lying. An officer of his own nation, who had obtained permission to visit his sick countryman, was sitting beside him. Irene saw that the invalid had a visitor, and was passing on, when his *'Bon jour, mademoiselle!'* entreated her to pause. She came back and inquired in French after his welfare; heard he was soon to leave the hospital, and smiled in acknowledgment of his warm thanks for the kindness he had received.

'The beautiful flower!' he said, looking at her last lily.

'I must not give it to a French republican,' she answered, gaily; 'it is a royal flower;' but she held it to him as she spoke, and he took it eagerly, inhaling its perfume, and laying the cool broad leaves against his hot cheeks. Irene saw his companion's eyes fixed earnestly upon her, with a kind of recognition; and remembered him as the French officer whom she had seen at Santa Chiara. He saw that she did so, and made a movement as if to claim acquaintance. The wounded man noticed the mutual dumb acknowledgment, and said,

'You are acquainted with Mademoiselle Mori, my colonel?'

'We have met before, my friend, and I have the advantage of knowing her name,' said Colonel de Crillon. 'May I make mine known to mademoiselle? I have heard so much of her from my

comrades here, that I might almost flatter myself
that I know her already.'

'I have spoken to her of my dear master, often;
is it not so, mademoiselle?' said the invalid, eagerly;
'here he is!'

'Yes; but you have never called him anything
but "my colonel," and "my good master,"' said
Irene, smiling, but rather unwilling to be forced
into an acquaintance with a French officer.

'*Mais, mademoiselle!* It is the Colonel de
Crillon!'

'Colonel de Crillon!' exclaimed Irene, colouring
vividly, and looking so startled that master and
man might well be astonished; and the latter was
beginning to weave a magnificent romance out of
her evident knowledge of the colonel, when,
recovering herself, she continued, 'This is not your
first visit to my Rome, monsieur?'

'I was here lately for a few days.'

'And once before!'

'It is true,' he answered, much surprised; 'for
a short—too short—a time some years ago, mademoiselle.'

'And once on a Sunday evening you visited the
wood on the Pincio—the Bosco.'

'I did—I did,' he answered, suddenly remembering it, 'and doubtless, mademoiselle, you can
tell me the fate of two poor children to whom I
caused great misfortune. I see by that allusion
you know them.'

Irene paused in mischievous enjoyment of his
eagerness; she saw that he had not the faintest
suspicion who she was.

'Their name?' she asked, demurely.

'I have forgotten it—with shame I acknowledge

it. I entreated a physician here to send me
information of them, but he never did so ; his time
no doubt was infinitely occupied, and many events
crowded upon me, so that I too ceased to think of
the incident, but now the whole scene rises before
me. I should like to know whether that poor boy
recovered. To this moment, I assure you, I think
of that day with pain.'

'No ; he is a cripple still, and always will be,'
Irene answered sadly.

'Ah, I feared— And the little girl ?'

'You have quite forgotten what she resembled,
monsieur ?'

'I recollect that she had magnificent eyes—
veloutés—eyes like a deer's, or——' he smiled as
he looked for an instant at Irene's, the only equally
splendid eyes he thought, that he had ever seen.
'It was her only beauty, at least that night, for
fear and tears do not embellish.'

Irene smiled archly and said, 'I think she was
called Irene, monsieur ; her memory was almost
as faithless for faces as yours, it seems, but at
least she remembered your name, and even had a
fancy that your face was that of a friend when she
saw you at Santa Chiara.'

'It is impossible !' exclaimed Colonel de Crillon,
examining with amazement and incredulity the
features of Irene, still rather more brightly coloured
than usual, and so much changed and ennobled
since her childish days by mind and thought that
he might well be excused for his unbelief.

'It is true,' she answered ; 'I am Irene Mori,
and you asked after my brother Vincenzo.'

'Ah, mademoiselle ! what happiness—behold

you rewarded for your goodness to me!' exclaimed the invalid, greatly delighted.

Irene and the colonel both laughed a little, and the latter said, 'I only brought you misfortune in our former meeting, and I fear not many agreeable associations with this one. But believe me, had it depended on me, this assault had never taken place. I derived, from my late visit here, the strongest impression of the unadvisability of any armed interference; but as my representations entirely failed, nothing remained for me but a soldier's duty, obedience, reluctant as I was to fight in this cause.'

'Oh, it has seemed so hard to fight against the French, in whom we have always hoped! We have suffered so much—Such glorious dreams! Such a dark awakening! But we are all to be friends for the future—this good Lesseps!' said Irene, recovering her joyous tone—'all must go well since it is confidently asserted that he has signed a treaty of peace.'

Colonel de Crillon was silent, for he had reason to doubt whether Oudinot would allow any such treaty to be binding, but he had no right to express his private opinion.

'I must not linger; it grows late,' said Irene, perceiving how the daylight was waning.

Colonel de Crillon took advantage of her assurance that she bore the French no ill-will, to say, 'Is it permitted that I visit your brother? Would he allow one of the enemy to claim his acquaintance?'

'Yes,' said Irene, cordially; 'I answer for him. You will find his apartment on the third floor of Palazzo Clementi, if you will give him the pleasure of a visit. Signor Mori—all know where he lives.'

'When am I most likely to find him at home?'

'Always,' answered Irene, her bright eyes growing sad; 'he is not able to climb those stairs without too great an effort. Adieu! Adieu, M. Marot!' and she glided away, leaving master and servant equally full of pleasure and interest, though not quite of the same kind, since Colonel de Crillon's feelings were only admiration and agreeable excitement at this unexpected rencontre, while Marot had already planned a marriage between his master and his kind nurse, forgetting, in his enthusiasm, the fact that the lamps which shine in the opera-house at the feet of a cantatrice, form a line of demarcation between her and the rest of the world which Colonel de Crillon was not a man likely to overlook. Irene had been singularly fortunate in having many valuable friends who cared nothing for that bar. To them she was Irene only, the dearest and best; and even in general society her name stood so high and her tact and good sense were such that she had made her own position; so that even in the houses of the exclusive nobles she was looked on as friend and guest, not merely as one from a different sphere, tolerated that she might amuse the visitors. But Colonel de Crillon knew too little of Roman society to be aware of the estimation in which she was held, and in the eyes of a Frenchman an *artiste* seldom indeed holds an exalted place. He could not but respect Irene from all that he had heard of her, and from her own air and tone; but very far indeed would he have been from contemplating the bare possibility of such a *mésalliance* as that which had occurred to the active imagination of worthy M. Marot.

Irene went from the hospital to Casa Olivetti,

where she knew that she should find friends assembled, as it was the evening on which its mistress received her weekly *società*. She had not much time to spare, since she hoped to find Leone at Palazzo Clementi, spending at least one hour in rest. At Casa Olivetti she found some dozen friends; among them, Ravelli, Gemma, and Signora Clementi, but Clementi himself was absent, no unusual thing in these busy times. Irene asked Gemma where he was, and heard that Mazzini had summoned him to a private interview. Gemma added, that he had bidden her to tell Irene that a courier was about to start with despatches from Mazzini to Siena; and that if she had any letters to send, they might go quickly and safely by this opportunity.

'Oh, thanks!' said Irene; 'I wish very much that a letter should reach England soon and safely; I find from one that came to me to-day from Mrs. Dalzell, that she has not received any from me for several weeks. I will go home at once and write, if you will excuse me, dear signora.'

'Assuredly; lose no time, *carina*,' said Signora Olivetti; and Irene, as she kissed her, was so struck by the careworn look on her face, and the convulsive pressure of the hand which she held, that notwithstanding her haste, she paused to discover the reason. It was easily perceived. She read it the moment she noticed Luigi's flushed brow and compressed lips and the defiant manner in which he was devoting himself to Gemma, openly, as he had never done before, to the visible astonishment of Signora Clementi and the other guests. And Gemma, perplexed, confused, yet triumphant, seemed to dare and set at nought all remarks; while in Imelda's wondering, startled eyes, Irene saw that even she began at last to comprehend and suffer. Irene's look towards Luigi was so earnest an inquiry, that he, longing to vent his excitement, started up and accompanied her downstairs, where Maddalena as usual was waiting, but discreetly kept at a distance, when she saw that something serious was passing.

' 'Tis done, Irene! You know that I would not have thought of myself at such a time—of even her—you know it! but the Fates would have it; my father gave me the opportunity to-day, and I told him the whole story then and there!'

'And he was very angry.'

'Angry! beside himself rather! But as I live, he shall learn that I am no child; if I cannot obtain his consent, I will do without it—of Clementi I am secure. He cannot give me his sister under these circumstances, but he will let me take her. I asked him the question, and though he scarcely spoke, I feel, I know—yes, all may and shall see that I love her!'

'But not now, Luigi, not here!'

'Now and here—would to Heaven it had been all said and done years ago!' exclaimed Ravelli, in no mood to be reasoned with. 'Long ago you counselled frank dealing; here you have it, and now blame me!'

'Poor Imelda!' said Irene to herself, with a suppressed sob. 'Poor little one! as innocent and as easily broken as my lilies!'

Ravelli heard the sob, though not the words. 'Irene! you are talking to a man who has been driven half mad—I do not know what I say or do. Waste no words on me; it must all come to day-

light now. What! would you have me marry
Imelda while I love Gemma? There! good night.'
He ran up the stairs again, and Irene, with irrepressible tears falling unseen under the shadow of
her hood, went home.

Ravelli was already beside Gemma; and her
aunt, doubtless thinking he had gone at least far
enough, was about to summon her to her side;
when a new guest came in with authentic tidings
that a treaty of peace had been definitively signed
by Lesseps, subject to the revision of the French
Government, but securing in all cases a further
armistice for fifteen days.

In the exceeding joy and commotion caused by
this news, Gemma was unnoticed for a few moments,
during which Luigi bent down to her, and said
in a whisper, 'I must see you this evening
in the garden—at midnight.' She replied only
by a look; her heart beat high with mingled
expectation and alarm; she cast a triumphant,
malignant glance on her shrinking rival, whose
downcast eyes were now full of tears. The next
instant Imelda looked up into Luigi's face, and
in the reproach of that gaze was an expression
that told that the child had become a woman. Luigi
winced, but stubbornly put down the pang that
went through his heart, and threw himself into
vehement discussion of the news that was engross-
ing the company. Signora Clementi called Gemma,
who obediently sat down close to her, and did not
attempt to exchange another word with Ravelli all
the rest of the evening.

When the guests were gone, Imelda bade her
mother as usual good night. Signora Olivetti
held her child's hands and looked in her face in

silence. Never before had Imelda felt a sorrow without throwing herself on her mother's breast and finding comfort. She would fain have done so now, but something withheld her, and though her lips trembled, and she turned pale, and shrank from the earnest tenderness of that gaze, she only repeated ' Good night, dearest mother!' and Signora Olivetti let her go with a half belief that she did not even yet quite realize the pain in store for her. The mother said to herself, ' To-morrow! Not to-night. Let her sleep one more night in peace!' But when later she went, as she never failed to do, to look at her sleeping child in the little bedroom opening out of her own, she found Imelda asleep indeed, but a tear slowly stealing over her cheek, and her long eyelashes very dewy. Her mother stood and looked at her with unspoken anguish written in every feature. One or two scalding tears dropped upon the hands which she had pressed together—tears, compared to which Imelda's, though they seemed to the poor child as bitter as tears could be, were but the drops of an April shower which the sun and the breeze would soon disperse.

CHAPTER XXI.

When trembling stars look'd silvery in their wane,
And heavy flowers yet slumbered, once again
There stole a footstep, fleet, and light, and lone,
Thro' the dim cedar shade; the step of one
That started at a leaf, of one that fled,
Of one that panted with some secret dread.

MRS. HEMANS.

BEHIND Palazzo Clementi was a garden, accessible only through the inner quadrangle, and appropriated solely to the owners of the palace. It was surrounded by high walls, shutting it off from the streets, and was divided by an iron screen from the quadrangle. A passer-by in the streets would only have seen the lofty walls, over which orange-trees raised their glossy leaves and golden fruit; and the dilapidated old vases containing aloes and standing at intervals along them. No one could have suspected what a charming garden was contained within. The ground was so high inside, probably raised artificially, that had any agile climber once reached the top of the wall, he would not have had to spring down more than a few feet. From the quadrangle, the garden was reached by two semicircular flights of steps, leading to a long rather than broad parterre, laid out in formal flower beds with a fountain rising out of a miniature lake in the centre, and a *casino* or summer-house at the further end, consisting of several rooms adorned with frescoes—a delightful summer retreat. But the charm of the garden was the *pergola*, a covered walk with roses clustering thickly over it, and within, a double row of orange and lemon trees, forming an avenue, through whose screen no eye from without could penetrate.

Once or twice before, Gemma had ventured to meet Luigi here, when Count Clementi was absent from Rome; but such trysts were doubly dangerous, since she was too far from her apartment to be able to return at a moment's warning. On this evening she would have risked anything, for Luigi's conduct told her that a crisis in their fate had come. When he whispered ' The garden !' she recollected with dismay that almost from the day of Pio Nono's flight, Clementi had kept the iron gate locked; and that no one but himself had ever entered the *casino* for months—why she knew not, though she had a shrewd guess. She had watched him enter the garden stealthily at night more than once; and curiosity had kept her on the alert till he returned, which was not till a very late hour. She did not in the least think that he had been looking at the moonlight glittering in the fountain, nor enjoying the fragrance of the orange blossoms, nor even that he went to meet any one either young or fair. She had a strong conviction that Clementi was resolved, with all that intensity and fixedness of purpose which she knew full well, not only that the Revolution would not succeed, but that it *should* not. She believed that he had kept up a constant correspondence with Gaeta, and that in the *casino* plans were concerted which steadily thwarted every movement of the republicans. Gemma was perfectly certain that Clementi could have told the very hour on which the French attack was to be made, and that copies of every one of Mazzini's despatches were forwarded to the Court of Pio Nono.

While Rome believed that Monsignore Clementi had fled months before, his niece was as certain that he was concealed in the *casino* as if she had had a glimpse of those violet stockings which he fondly hoped his present exertions in the Pope's behalf would soon give him the right to dye scarlet, or as if she had beheld his liveried attendant waiting openly for him at the garden gate. Long ago she would have betrayed both him and the count had she dared, and sometimes a vision crossed her fertile and perverted mind of fabricating some tale which should lead Ravelli to believe that she had but just discovered her brother's treachery; but she had not of late had one opportunity of speaking apart to her lover, and the horrible death of the two wretched spies made her tremble and hesitate lest such should be the fate of Pietrucchio. She now hoped to avoid the temptation to betray, by hearing—of what she knew not—but of some happy turn of fate. The garden! It was a perilous rendezvous; but the *pergola* was thick, Clementi was engaged elsewhere; there never were lights visible at night in the *casino*. The locked gate? But Gemma said to herself that she *would* conquer that obstacle; at the worst, she could speak to Luigi through the grating, and her spirit only mounted exultantly as the peril came more clearly before her. That night she defied fate and fortune. Luigi was remarkably light and active; he had never found any difficulty in scaling the wall by means of the trees which grew in a tall group outside. He would not fail her, and certainly she would not fail him. She listened with edifying contrition to Signora Clementi's lectures as they went homewards, and assured her that it was only to torment that silly child Imelda that she coquetted with Ravelli. Her aunt was conscious that her surveillance was apt to be lax, and spoke with proportionate anger; and Gemma found a good excuse for immediately retiring to her room in the pretended tears which this severity called forth. She ascertained that Count Clementi had not returned; doubtless he was still with the Triumvirate.

Midnight was announced by a great clock somewhere not far distant, each stroke resounding heavily in the silent air. She stole from her room, glided into the corridor like a guilty ghost, down into the quadrangle; she had reached the iron gate. Her white dress, and the white opera cloak which she had not thrown off, added to her ghostly appearance; her face was colourless, making a startling contrast with her raven hair and burning dark eyes. She leant her face against the iron gate and listened. It moved and creaked; she shrank back in terror, but all was still again; overhead the clear stars shone; the fountain plashed, the white orange blossoms exhaled their exquisite perfume; a nightingale sang among them. Behind her the palace rose dark and huge and massive. She listened as if she had been all ear; the gate clinked again, and looking closely, she saw that the lock had shot but not caught; too hasty a hand had turned the key; the iron tongue was outside its case; the gate was unfastened. In a moment she was in the garden; she glanced towards the casino. All was dark, without a sign that it was inhabited; nor the faintest token that might wake Luigi's suspicious. With relief she entered the *pergola*, where the starlight only penetrated sufficiently to make all shadowy, but not dark, or here and there glided in where the rose trellice was less thick, and made a mirror of a glossy leaf, or kissed a cluster of fragrant snowy blossoms. There Gemma waited breathlessly. She heard in a little while the rustling of swaying boughs—a leap, a quick step—Luigi's arm was round her; his voice was uttering protestations of love so vehement and impassioned, that it was easy to see that he was excited beyond all self-control. She heard them unchecked till a thought crossed her mind, and striving to release herself, she exclaimed, with instinctive caution, in a low voice, ' Why have you neglected me then these many weeks? Are you daring to play with me?'

' Play ! This is earnest, compared to which life and death are play, Gemma! Listen—I have heard, one hour ago, from certain authority, that that dog Oudinot will refuse to ratify Lesseps' convention. May he die by a cord! He is not worthy of a soldier's death. Then, then Gemma, if we are defeated—if—all things are possible! Garibaldi will never submit; he will cut his way through the enemy, he and his men and Annuccia his wife !'

' Luigi, you frighten me !' she murmured, really terrified by his violence.

' Then I had best not say what I came for—I had other things to say when I bade you meet me here, but they are gone ! I can't recollect them, I only know what I have heard since. Well, I will be as composed as yonder urn if you like, but listen; I am one of Garibaldi's men; I too will sooner be torn to pieces than live here to see the monkish robes in our streets again, trampling our freedom under their sanctified feet; forging heavier chains for us with every word that those meek lips of theirs utter. Never, no never will I see that—as I am an Italian. I swear it as I believe in our cause. But you, but you, Gemma! my Gemma! my own! best loved of all I have on earth, what is to become of you? Annuccia goes with her husband; will you follow yours? Am I dreaming, or is it true that a woman laughs at danger and poverty beside him whom she loves? Is it all utter selfishness, or am I right in deeming him a fool who leaves the girl he loves because he fears want and hardships for her? As for me, to leave you would be to pluck up my life by the roots—why should I think it easier for you?'

'No, no, no; anything but leave me; you shall not, you shall not, Luigi;' and she clung to him convulsively.

'Then be my wife, and my fate will be your fate, and if I go alone—No, I could not expose you to such a flight as that would be, my darling—at least I will find some sort of a home for us both, and I will send for you, love, never fear. I am talking like a lunatic! Ah, never shrink from me, I know my own plans. All may be well, we may hold out, but for every reason I must be able to claim you as my wife.'

'But how—who?'

'Meet me to-morrow at San Nicolo, and I will find a priest who will marry us. You need not fear Clementi; I have spoken to him; he knows it all ; I cannot tell you the story now—another time, when I am myself. That perjured villain Oudinot!'

'Knows! Clementi knows!' repeated Gemma, ready to sink into the ground.

'Yes, knows; do you think I would steal you, silly girl? He knew long ago that I loved you.'

In one instant Gemma reviewed her position, took her resolve, and answered, 'I will be there, Luigi.'

'That is right! that is my own dearest, best,' he exclaimed, catching her hands and covering them with kisses.

The two stood near an opening in the *pergola.* A sound as of a softly opening door startled them ; footfalls were distinctly heard ; they shrank further back, Gemma striving with frantic but dumb terror to drag Luigi where he could not see who was passing; but he resisted, confident in the deep shadow in which he stood, and eager to see who could be in the garden at this time of night. The steps came from the *casino* ; two figures slowly passed, speaking in tones so low that they were inaudible in the *pergola.* The two were vaguely seen in the starlight ; one seemed young, the other taller, more ample in form, but both were shrouded by long cloaks. As they neared the gate, Luigi advanced more and more, full of confused marvel and suspicion. They halted at the gate and turned the key ; a rustle in the *pergola* startled them ; both suddenly looked back and Ravelli saw distinctly, unmistakeably, the faces of the Count and Monsignore Clementi. He stood petrified—then bounded out like a wild beast, but the lock was turned, they had disappeared into the palace. With a cry, hoarse, inarticulate, scarcely human,

he was by Gemma's side again; she had dropped
on her knees half dead with terror. Clenching
his fingers on her wrist, he forced her to rise and
asked in a voice which no one could have
recognised, ' What is this ?'

She could not utter a syllable.

' Answer me!' he thundered; ' are you a traitor
too ?'

' Kill me at once,' she stammered out.

'Speak! Do you hear me ? Yes, speak, speak,
say what you will, love, I shall believe you! Forgive me, I know you are innocent !' he exclaimed
with a sudden imploring change of tone; 'I do
not suspect you—I am mad, quite mad—I must be—
is it not so ? That was not your brother, nor Monsignore Clementi, but two demons trying to cheat
me. Dearest, speak to me !'

But she could not. All her powers of dissimulation had entirely failed; she could make no
attempt to work on his present mood.

' Come into the light !' he cried, after a
moment's mute waiting for an answer. ' Let me
see your face ;' and he compelled her to come forth
where he could study her colourless, convulsed
features, her trembling lips vainly seeking to form
some answer. Guilt was in every lineament.

' Ah, ha !' he said, with an indescribably taunting,
wild laugh, after examining her countenance for
an instant; ' this comes of trusting a woman !
You have deceived so many—why not me ? Why
not the one who loved you, trusted you entirely,
as, please Heaven, he will never trust man or
woman again! Once will suffice for a lifetime!
The play has been well acted, upon my honour!
And now kindly tell me how long your brother
has been on such excellent terms with monsignore?'

'Always!' she gasped out, entirely powerless under his indignation, more terrible now that it took the shape of irony than even before.

'And you have known it—always!'

'Yes; I dared not—dared not—'

'Dared not!' he repeated. 'Gemma, I loved you! Fool that I was! Oh, double, treble fool! Brother and sister alike!'

'Poniard me, Luigi; only do not look, do not speak so,' exclaimed the unhappy girl, trying to throw herself on his breast, but he held her off with a hand inflexible as iron. 'No, never! never more! traitress that you are—false to me, false to your country. But because I did love you, I do not curse you now; I did! I do so no more. I esteem you as I would a snake that had nestled to my heart and stung me. An honourable man can feel in one way only for traitors.' He looked again in her face, as if wondering whether this could be indeed his own Gemma. She clasped her hands in voiceless supplication.

'Farewell, farewell love, and trust, and faith,' he said; pressing a sudden kiss on her lips, 'that is for the one whom I used to love and believe in. When? A long while ago, I think! She is dead, and now I have another love to win, whose name is Vengeance. Farewell all that is past and gone!' and with one spring he had freed himself from her hands, reached the wall; and the sudden movement of branches, ceasing instantly, told that he had accomplished his headlong descent. Gemma did not know it; she had sunk down in a deadly swoon the instant he had released himself from her clasp. He rushed on, he knew not whither; purposeless, beside himself, actually insane for the moment. He did not know how long it was before he found himself in the midst of a patrol, answering their demand for the password of the night by some incoherent speech and a furious struggle, which, of course, excited their suspicions and caused him to be surrounded and detained. He grew more collected, but the word, which he had known well enough some hours earlier, was entirely gone from his recollection; he could only give his name, and ask where several officers were who could answer for him. The patrol obliged him to go with them; he knew he must submit, and did so, for his self-command began to return; but only one thought was clear, to denounce Clementi—denounce him publicly—and when a friend chanced to meet him in his forced round, he burst out at once with his tale so furiously and incoherently that friend and soldiers alike thought him mad. He repeated it, however, with so much persistence that a murmur among the patrol told that he was beginning to gain credence. All recollected the indubitable knowledge that was shown at Gaeta of each minute circumstance which had occurred at Rome—the suspicion which had long existed that there were traitors within the city. It seemed a revelation, a certainty, almost as soon as the mind could take in what he meant.

'This is news of life and death; report it instantly to the Triumvirate!' exclaimed his friend; and the patrol made no opposition whatever to his going. He had at all events convinced them. The hour of five sounded; he knew not how much time he had spent in the garden, nor in that wild course through the streets, nor with the guard; all was still reeling in his brain.

It was a hard matter to awaken the suspicions
of the Triumvirate, when after some delay he
obtained an audience. They trusted Clementi
like themselves, and would consent to no more
active measures against him than to summon him
before them, rebuking Ravelli sharply for having
spread a suspicion against him so incautiously.
Unless Gemma's absence had been perceived, he
could have had no warning, and doubtless would
come, believing himself to be summoned on political business. Ravelli, enraged at this tardy
dealing, rushed out of their presence, and long before their messenger was despatched, had reached
the apartment of the Mori, where he found Leone,
Vincenzo, and Irene, just assembled, for it was still
early morning. His entrance, his first words, prepared them for some astounding intelligence ; his
passionate story was half told, half guessed, and
struck them dumb, but he seemed possessed by a
spirit that would not let him rest for an instant,
and was gone almost before they could ask one
question. He was already at Clementi's door.
Well was it for the count that he had left his
room early on private affairs. His uncle had quitted
Rome that night in profound secrecy for Gaeta.
Ten minutes afterwards, he returned, just escaping
an encounter with Ravelli, and, knocking at Vincenzo's apartment, walked into the room, where,
mute, incredulous, horror-stricken, sat the friends
who had just heard of his treachery. He entered
with his unvarying calm demeanour, softening into
a smile of greeting, which died away at once as
their eyes turned upon him. No one spoke or
stirred. He stood still by the door, surveying
them. He knew as well as if they had told him

that, in some incomprehensible way, he was detected. A hot flush mounted to Leone's brow; he rose hastily, and began words which the cool, musical voice of Clementi cut short. 'What! tried, condemned, executed already, without appeal! Is that your meaning, friends?'

'Traitor that you are!' exclaimed Leone, precipitating himself towards him; but Clementi moved slightly aside, saying, 'Would you strike a guest, signor?'

'Before we call you our guest, hear me,' said Vincenzo, rising; 'Count Clementi, you are accused of treason. Leone! stand back; I am in my own house.'

'Accused of treason?' repeated Clementi, calmly and inquiringly.

'Such a tone is answer enough! What honourable man would stop to dally with such a charge!' cried Leone.

The count maintained unchanged composure, while he weighed in the lightning-swift balance of thought whether it availed to deny. In that instant the horror and aversion in Irene's face overturned his self-control.

'Turn from me if you will, Irene! none have ever loved you as I have. For you I have toiled and planned; all else has been as dust in the scale. I have loved you—loved you, as those who put first what they call their country,—dumb idol that they rear and break!—as such as they never dreamed of! What is your love, Leone Nota, compared with mine? I knew her before you did, staked all I had for her, spent life and honour for her. Irene, you know it!'

Leone's face flushed, he trembled with sup-

pressed passion, blighting words sprang to his
lips; Irene turned full on Clementi, with noble
anger on her brow—

'I know only that you are a traitor!' she exclaimed.

'This quarrel at least is mine,' cried Leone,
losing self-command, as Clementi gazed on Irene
as if she alone existed for him, and he had forgotten the charge brought against him. 'Do me
the honour to follow me, count.'

But at that instant, a sound which had been
gathering without, unheeded by those within, suddenly forced itself upon their ears; a bellow more
like that of a furious ocean than a human cry; a
wave of sound which, commencing afar, was taken
up by hundreds of voices all blended into one; a
hoarse roar, through which the words seemed to
rise to Heaven—'The traitor! the traitor! give us
the traitor!'

All the street was surging with a furious throng,
heaving, rolling through it, struggling to reach
the palace, yelling out execrations—'Death to the
traitor!—death to the traitor!'

Clementi was no coward, but as that shriek
came to his ear, his whole frame seemed to shrink
and cower; his olive cheek took a ghastly tint; he
stood immovable; his ashy lips muttered, 'My
turn!'

'Oh, no more blood; no more!' cried Irene, all
her feelings suddenly changing. 'Leone! Vincenzo!'

The tramp of feet on the stairs was heard; the
mob were rushing towards the Clementi apartments.

'Speak to them, Leone!' she implored.

Clementi held out his hand to her; 'All is welcome, since you will regret me, Irene.'

'No! Not the hand of a traitor,' she answered, in extreme agitation; 'but to see a human being—another—!'

'Escape by the roofs,' exclaimed Vincenzo, hastily opening his door, which communicated with a small outer staircase leading to the highest story. 'Go!'

Clementi gave one look on Irene, turned, was gone. She stood upright, with panting breath and fixed eye; Vincenzo put his hand over his face as though to shut out the very spot where Clementi had stood. Leone abruptly rose: 'This people must have no more blood on their heads,' he muttered, and the next instant was heard darting through the outer door.

There had been an ominous sullen pause without, as if the crowd were awaiting the return of those who had forced their way into the Clementi apartments. A yell of disappointment followed their return, and a search ensued in the garden, where only Gemma was found, crouching on the ground.

Another short pause, and then a wild scream of exultation from a thousand voices told they had caught sight of their victim. Count Clementi knew it, as he fled across the palace roof and sprang on the next, every sense concentrated in the effort to escape. He was paralysed for an instant, paused, saw the Tiber gleaming not very far off, thought of the fate of those other spies, and fled again, madly, headlong, from roof to roof, now seen, now lost, now seen again by the crowd below, and urged to more frantic flight by perceiving that some of his pursuers had scaled the roofs and were following fast. Now he reached the last house in the street—a convent—a roar of triumph from below showed that the crowd were ready ; he could see the faces glaring up at him like those of demons, the hands outstretched to clutch him, though as yet far above them. Behind came on fast, fast, pursuers over the roofs—below heaved the throng. Some feet lower than the roof, the street was spanned by a covered passage leading from the convent to the church. Without an instant's hesitation he dropped upon it, lay stunned for a moment, but gathered his senses with a desperate effort. A scaffolding projected from the half-repaired building ; he scrambled on it, how he knew not, saw a wall near, sprang on that, almost within reach of the crowd, thence climbed to another roof, and paused a moment. His purpose had been foreseen ; his enemies had ascended the roofs ahead of him and rushed back upon him. He dashed off the foremost, who tottered with a curse against those hurrying after ; a balcony was just below, Clementi sprang down into it, knocking down, he knew not whether man or woman, who had hurried to it to learn the cause of the uproar. A shriek followed him as he darted through the open window, dashing over chairs and tables as he fled—into a corridor, down a staircase, across a street. A church stood open ; he precipitated himself into it, and fell, breathless, bruised, nearly senseless, on the steps of the high altar. The sacristan, seeing a man rush in for refuge, closed and barred the doors, not a moment too soon, for before the last bolt was drawn, the mob were thundering at them, and those were days when even a church would not always protect a criminal. Not a soul replied to their summons ;

only the hard breathings of the hunted man were heard through the building; the sacristan was on his knees shaking as if in an ague; crash after crash resounded on the doors; the crowd were beating them in with heavy weapons. Sobs like a hunted stag's burst from Clementi's breast; he lay prostrate, helpless, death in its most ghastly shape waiting for him. A fresh yell and a creak of yielding barriers told that the last defence was giving way; a wilder shriek of joy proclaimed it doubly.

But out over the tumult rang a trumpet voice, a voice that might have reached the ear of death itself, and well nigh have called back the soul. Every word was audible, every one of those eloquent tones—the uproar lessened, lessened, sank, was hushed, till only that voice was heard, speaking of love and mercy, both human and divine. It ceased and a perfect silence ensued; then those same tones, which gradually had changed from persuasion to command, bade the church doors be opened. The trembling sacristan rose from his knees and obeyed. Not so much as a silken thread divided the traitor from those lately thirsting for his blood.

Padre Rinaldi entered the church with a crucifix in his hand; he bade Clementi rise, took him by the hand, and led him straight through the crowd, to the carriage in which, at Leone's summons, he had himself hurried to the spot. Not a voice was raised, not a murmur heard in all the crowd, who stood around, with contrite, downcast looks; but Clementi could not lift his eyes, only moved unconsciously along, and sank back in the carriage incapable of even comprehending that he was saved. The crowd watched it disappear, ere they moved; then slowly, mutely dispersed.

CHAPTER XXII.

Borne down in conflict !   But immortal seed
Deep, by heroic suffering, hath been sown
On all her ancient hills : and generous hope
Knows that the soil, in its good time, shall yet
Bring forth a glorious harvest !   Earth receives
Not one red drop from faithful hearts in vain.

MRS. HEMANS.

ERE the next morning, Clementi was far from Rome. Proofs of his guilt were found in papers and letters, but the Triumvirate were unwilling to award to one still so powerful the death which he had deserved. The contempt and hatred of all his fellow-citizens seemed punishment enough for the detected spy, who could injure them no longer. Perhaps if they had known the full extent of his treachery, his fate might have been different. As it was, he was conveyed in profound secrecy out of the city, free to go whither he would. He had yet to learn that Heaven smote him, though man did not. He might hasten to Gaeta, full of revenge, revolving new schemes, resolute as ever to win Irene, but one blow had fallen which no subtilty, no wisdom could avert. His mother, whom he loved deeply, could not recover from the shock which his awful peril had given her. Even before he left Rome, the frail invalid was dead.

But Clementi's treason itself was driven out of

the Roman mind almost immediately by the news
that Oudinot actually refused to ratify the convention of Lesseps. In a letter sent by him to the
Triumvirate on the 2nd of June, he announced
that Lesseps had overstepped his powers; that his
own private instructions forbade the armistice to
be extended; that hostilities were about to recom-
mence, but that in order to give the French residents time to quit the city, he should defer the
attack—one day.

' Who shall tell the fury, the consternation
throughout Rome when this letter was published?
Who shall tell how it increased tenfold when on
the next morning it was found that the French
had surrounded and seized the advanced posts
around the gate of San Pancrazio? Oudinot had
promised to defer the assault on the city, but had
made no agreement concerning the advanced posts.
Such was his explanation.

From that moment, the Romans fought at a
fearful disadvantage. The battle had shifted from
Porta Cavalleggieri to Porta San Pancrazio, and
raged there fiercely, ceaselessly. The cannon,
silent for a month, began to thunder again; the
French batteries replied; and ruined houses, tot-
tering walls, wounds and death, told day after day
how desperate was the defence. Lesseps had
returned to Paris in towering indignation, vowing
to appeal to his Government. In this appeal lay
the last hope of the Romans.

Day after day the citizens flocked to the walls,
defying death, wrestling hand to hand with despair,
seeming only to multiply as man after man fell. So
it lasted for three weeks; all felt that the strife
was hopeless, but all chose rather to die than yield.

Alas! so many did indeed fall, that it was wonderful that Pio Nono found a liberal left to dread when he returned. They threw up new fortifications, and strengthened their batteries; day and night were spent on the walls; Rome was resolved at least to utter one loud unanimous protest against her tyrants, if she could do no more.

By the 27th of June there was a breach in the walls. Here the last struggle must be made. Villa Savorella, the head-quarters of Garibaldi, lay in ruins. San Pietro in Montorio, the palaces below, the *casini*, the houses all around, were well nigh battered to pieces. The Trasteverini had suffered fearfully; many of their homes were utterly destroyed, and the Government offered them a refuge in the deserted palaces of the cardinals; but without complaint or murmur with one accord they remained in the front of danger, worthy citizens of Rome. Not a house in the whole city was safe from shot and shell; not a roof so sheltered that a bomb might not bring destruction on the heads of all beneath.

The 29th of June ended amid heavy rain. Around the breach were gathered those who remained to defend it, standing blinded by the storm, knee deep in mud, and diminished momentarily by the fatal, frequent shot and projectiles. The night was wild and gloomy, lighted but by the fiery course of the bombs through the air. The Romans were there to resist, not to conquer—there in vain! In vain, for towards morning the French assault was made, in thick darkness, amid tempest above, tempest below, shouts, incessant discharge of musketry; a hand-to-hand *mélée*, confused and fatal beyond description. In that assault, among heaps of slain, fell young Emilio Morosini. His companions scarcely knew it as they struggled at the various breaches now made practicable.

In Villa Spada were gathered Manara and a few more of his comrades ; here they had barricaded themselves and fought like wolves, amid the smoke, the shot, the glancing balls that rebounded amongst them from ceiling and wall. Manara looked round and saw a young Lombard beside him, whom he had supposed to be on a sick bed. 'Hallo ! what brings you here with a broken arm ?' he exclaimed.

'I shall make one more !' replied the brave fellow, who was there to die, if not to fight.

There too was Leone, and as Manara spoke, he staggered and put his hand to his breast. 'Touched?' cried Manara.

' 'Tis a trifle,' Leone replied. 'Beware of that chasseur, friend !'

'You have all the luck! I am not to have a scar in memory of Rome, it seems,' cried the young leader with bitter gaiety, as he took aim from the window at the enemy pointed out to him. One instant too late! the chasseur had fired ; Manara made a sudden step forward and fell on his face. A momentary slackening of the French fire allowed his friends to lift him through a window and bear him to an ambulance, where many others lay dying. Leone and Dandolo bore him thither, and a surgeon, his friend and fellow-citizen, hastened to him, but only to find that death was at hand. Bending over him, Dandolo whispered, 'Think of God !'

'Oh, I do much!' he answered, earnestly but very feebly. The *viaticum* was brought. Then after giving to Dandolo messages for his family, he looked up and saw the tears which blinded his friends.   With his old playful smile he murmured, 'So you are grieved that I die!'   But none could command voice to answer, and low but calmly Manara added, 'I too would have had it otherwise.' Morosini was dead, but this he did not know; Enrico Dandolo had fallen long before.   Leone was leaning against the ambulance; Manara turned his eyes to him and uttered his name; but no answer came, and with a deep sigh Leone sank down on the ground.   His wound was not the slight matter he had supposed in the excitement of the fight; and at least he was spared seeing his friend die.

At this same moment there was a group on the roof of Palazzo Clementi.   Irene, the padrona, and even Vincenzo had contrived to ascend thither at daybreak, and with telescopes were gazing towards the walls, where only a confused struggling mass was visible.   To venture on the roofs was so full of peril, that the Triumvirate strictly forbade it, but orders were set at nought in the suspense and agony of those last days.   They looked with eyes strained and misty; they saw nothing clearly —could not even distinguish the French from the Italians.   'Those are our men at the bastion!' 'No, French!'   'No, no, look again—the French there! it would be ruin!'   'That is a fresh breach since yesterday!'   'Heaven help us!'   'Listen to the uproar!   My husband is sure to be in the heart of it.'   Such were the confused exclamations interchanged between the watchers.

'The spy-glass is the first sign of the cross with me of a morning now—the first thing I think of,' said Madama Cecchi.   'Ah! all saints help us!'

Her loud scream was answered by a hundred voices; a shell came curving through the air full on the opposite house; a huge cloud of smoke and dust rose up, flames burst through it; from the neighbouring houses the inhabitants rushed out; all was helpless terror and destruction. In the quadrangle below was wild hurry and dismay; all were flying from the upper rooms to the ground-floor, seeking imaginary safety in the storehouses. At the same instant rang out a tocsin. Irene clasped her hands above her head in sudden, utter despair. 'Oh, then Heaven has quite deserted us—that is St. Agostino, and the French must be entering Rome!'

Three days however passed in sullen inaction on both sides. The French could now at any moment have taken the city, but they remained without, while complete uncertainty and confusion prevailed within. Not a barricade was as yet thrown down, the regiments remained at their posts, and crowds filled the streets shouting for war, which all the experienced knew was in fact over.

On the 3rd of July the Government announced further resistance to be impossible, and formally opened the gates. That same morning, Garibaldi, aware of what was at hand, gathered his men in the Piazza of St. Peter's, and told them that he at least would not live to lay down his arms; he was about, he said, to throw himself into the mountains; he had nothing to offer them but hunger, peril, and war. 'Let him who loves Italy follow me!' he shouted, and accompanied by 4000 brave hearts, he passed through the city, and dashed out at the gate of St. John Lateran.

Slowly the tidings of the surrender spread

abroad, so slowly that half the city still expected another assault.   In the afternoon the
French entered what seemed a region of the dead.
Through deserted streets the 12,000 invaders
marched with fixed bayonets.   The siege of Rome
was over.

The first certainty that they had entered was
conveyed to Palazzo Clementi by about a hundred
men entering the quadrangle, where they were to
be quartered.   A bomb would have been welcome
compared to such a sight.   In the utmost alarm
all who had taken refuge in the storehouses of
the ground-floor rushed back to their apartments,
and awaited in unspeakable suspense what was to
ensue ; but even in that moment it was noted,
and never pardoned, that the Clementi apartments were instantly placed at the disposal of the
French.

Neither Leone nor Cecchi had been heard of
for three days.   Irene and Vincenzo had remained
in their rooms, and so had Madama Cecchi, careless now of their fate, since Rome had fallen and
those they loved with her.   They did not even
hear the fresh confusion; Madama Cecchi was first
warned of what had occurred by a French officer
knocking at her door to inform her that every
one who had a spare bed was to take in a soldier
or two.   She faced him with blazing indignation,
which in no way disturbed the courteous tone of
the intruder.

'I have no room !'

' Here is a sofa, madame,' said he, looking in.

' A friend sleeps there ; and if I had a hundred
beds, they are not for Frenchmen.'

' If I were a Garibaldi man, I am sure madame
would find room for me.'

'This is my house, monsieur, and I receive whom I please,' she retorted, fierce as a tigress.

' Where is the husband of madame ?'

' I know not.   I command here.'

' Ladies always do so, wherever they are,' replied the officer, with a bow.

' Monsieur,' she broke out, enraged beyond endurance, ' we are in the hands of Frenchmen, who profess to support liberty, equality, and fraternity; I do not understand what they have to do with a foreign republic, but I know this—if you come in, I go out.'

At this point, when even the urbane Frenchman was foiled by her red-hot indignation, another officer came in.   She turned on him fiercely— 'Sir! this is not an inn!'   He passed her, saying, ' Pardon, I seek friends,' and went straight to the apartment of Vincenzo and Irene, who had heard the angry colloquy.   They were standing together, each seeming to support the other; Vincenzo nearly beside himself at his want of power to protect his sister.   She recognised the new comer at once— ' Colonel de Crillon!' but she made no friendly movement.

' I come only to ask if I can be of any use or protection to you—I can at least prevent any one from being billeted upon you,' he said, with such unmistakeable kindness and good-will, that Vincenzo replied, ' I accept that offer gratefully ;' and he looked at his sister, feeling that it was indeed a valuable one.

' This will secure you,' said Colonel de Crillon, tearing from his pocket-book a leaf, on which he had written a line; ' and now I intrude no longer.'

' Oh, monsieur !' cried Irene, starting forward,

'stay; do you—do you know anything of a volunteer—Leone Nota? It is possible you may have
seen him—'

'Nota, the *improvisatore?*'

'Yes, yes, the same.'

'No; I have not seen nor heard of him lately.'

'Are you sure?' she asked, startled by his tone.

'On my word I have not. But I trust he is
no relation of yours?' he added, with grave con-
cern.

'I am his promised wife, monsieur.'

'Ah! pardon me. Then doubtless you know
better than I do, why he is peculiarly obnoxious to
the Papal Government, as I believe he is.'

'Only because all who have Italian hearts are
obnoxious to it!' she cried.

Colonel de Crillon shook his head. 'It may be so,
or he may have powerful enemies; but I chance to
know that he would not be safe for a day in Rome.
I should use such influence as I have in vain for
him. Use all that you possess, mademoiselle, and
urge him to escape while he can.'

'He has not been heard of since the assault,'
she answered, leaning her face down upon a table
near and pressing her hands convulsively over it.

Colonel de Crillon said no more; he felt that to
leave the brother and sister alone was the truest
kindness. In the passage he encountered Madama
Cecchi, stately and fierce.

'Mademoiselle Mori may have spoken to you of
me, madame?' said he.

'Mademoiselle Mori knows no one of your
nation, monsieur!'

He passed out, and found the officer in the corridor who had attempted to billet himself upon

her. 'Ha! De Crillon!' said he, 'here you are; how have you escaped the claws of that virago ?—it is a she dragon! I wish you were billeted there, with all my heart, since you say you have friends there; as for me, I would rather sleep in the courtyard below.'

'Well, change rooms with me,' said the colonel, well pleased; 'mine is yonder.' And so it was settled, and the change enabled him to fulfil his kind desire to protect Irene from annoyance In the courtyard below, the soldiers were already established, and lighting fires, the smoke of which would have been a serious grievance to the inhabitants of the palace, had not all been too full of graver matters to think of it.

Towards evening another knock came to Vincenzo's door. Menica slowly opened a chink of it in fear and trembling. Her scream of joy brought Madama Cecchi. 'Where is my husband ?' cried she, as soon as she saw who it was. But no answer could be given; nothing was known of Cecchi's fate.

This was Leone, though so much altered as scarcely to be recognisable, and Irene threw herself on his breast. He sank down on the sofa, holding her close, while she sobbed for joy, quite worn out with suspense and suffering. She suddenly lifted her head and exclaimed, 'You must not stay one moment; fly, fly, now, instantly, Leone; you are not safe here one instant. Think what a Roman tribunal is! If you love me, do not linger !'

'My cause is before a higher tribunal,' he answered faintly, but with a light in his eyes more like the look of a conqueror than that of a vanquished man. 'Dearest! I cannot live to see our Rome fallen.'

The words were uttered with difficulty. Irene started up and looked in his face. 'Leone, Leone! And I!'

There was such appealing desolation in her voice and face that it wrung Vincenzo's heart. Leone sought to draw her back to his side. 'Love, they thought me dead—I hardly know how I revived; but when I heard that the enemy were in our streets, and thought of you, alive or dead I must be beside you, Irene. But what can I do now I am come? Protect you little more than if I were still in the hospital! At least, however, we have met again, though it is only to part, my dearest."

She wrung her hands and sprang to seek Madama Cecchi. 'A surgeon instantly. Leone is here; he is very ill—dying; my Leone is dying, dying!' she repeated wildly.

Madama Cecchi was sitting sunk in apathetic despair; she hardly seemed to hear. 'Whom can we send?' cried Irene, desperately. 'Menica?'

'Oh, dear signorina, I would die to please you; but to venture among those French soldiers!'

Irene could not ask it. She felt, too, that if Nota's present abode were betrayed, he might be undone. There was none to aid, and none to be trusted.

So some days passed, and the city maintained its eloquent gloom. The French realized at last what they had absolutely refused to credit— that the defence was the act, not of a small tyrannical faction, but of a people. There was scarcely a woman in Rome who was not wearing mourning for a relative—scarcely a house which was not full of terrified forebodings, for a day of reckoning with the priests was at hand. In many palaces and private houses, soldiers had taken up their abodes, to the daily and infinite tribulation of the owners, who not only chafed and fretted at the yoke, but suffered from the free manners of the soldiers, though on the whole the discipline maintained was admirable. The women in Palazzo Clementi held them, however, in horror, and not a maid would venture down unprotected to fetch wood or water, or go forth into the city. Menica's beauty was a real misfortune to her, and she appeared in tears before her mistress, after having most reluctantly ventured down to the fountain one day; a soldier had kissed her—a frog of a Frenchman, she exclaimed, with abhorrent emphasis, which showed how trebled the offence was by his nationality.

Madama Cecchi started out of her now habitual apathy like a tiger. 'Log of wood that you are, girl, do you not wear a *spadone?*'

Menica put her hand up to the silver dagger in her hair, now long and thick again, with a look of intelligence, and when a half tipsy Frenchman attempted to catch hold of her the next day, she made no ado, but snatched out the *spadone* and struck him in the breast with all her might. Without waiting to see the result she fled back to her mistress, and told her what had happened. It brought Madama Cecchi to life again, for she perceived the danger that the girl had run into, and quickly made up her mind that she and Menica must be gone. She announced forthwith to Irene that they were about to take refuge with friends at Ostia. Irene heard, and felt the loss of her padrona as an additional drop in a cup of trial then very full, but could not remonstrate;

and they went, returning no more for many
months, when fever and cholera had quite driven
the soldiers from their unhealthy quarters at the
bottom of the well-like quadrangle.

Madama Cecchi's weeping farewells to Irene
were interrupted by the entrance of Gemma; it
was the first time for a month that she had been
outside her door. That month had changed her fearfully; she was haggard, though her eyes shone
with fever; her features were pinched, her hands
wasted, her very voice unlike itself. She almost
forced Irene into her room, and exclaimed 'For
charity's sake, tell me, do you know anything of
Ravelli? Tell me, Irene, quick! speak!'

'Only that he is gone with Garibaldi,' answered
Irene, regarding her with mingled pity and aversion.

'Gone! gone!' repeated Gemma. 'Ah, who
comes here now?' and like a guilty thing she
fled behind the curtain which hung over a door, as
footsteps came near. Irene was not quite deserted;
Signora Olivetti thought of her with affectionate
sympathy, and not only ventured out to see her,
but conquered her own reluctance to taking Imelda
out of the security of her home, and brought her likewise, believing that the little one would be the best
comforter. Irene welcomed them eagerly, but with
alarm, knowing who was hidden near, and dreading
above all things lest Gemma should discover that
Leone was in the palace. Vincenzo was by his
sick bed; they could venture to have neither
physician nor attendant.

Amid all the sorrowful and gloomy faces,
Imelda's countenance looked like a vision of peace
herself. She nestled close to Irene caressingly, while

her mother said, 'My poor Irene! are you left here alone?'

'Menica's old mother has promised to wait on us, dear signora.'

'But that is miserable! we came to persuade you to return with us to our house, dear child—you and Signor Mori.   Come!'

'Thanks! thanks!' said Irene, with starting tears; 'one feels the value of friends now, but we cannot; we must stay here.'

'But why, *cuor mio?*   Tell me, Irene, have you news of Signor Nota?'

Irene glanced round with anguish and terror which warned Signora Olivetti that her question was imprudent, though she could not guess that Leone had returned weary and wounded, only to die—that his betrothed was racked with fear lest his very deathbed should be violated by the vengeance of his enemies.   Poor Irene! those were days which went near to break her heart. Signora Olivetti, with tact and skill, did not wait for her answer, but pursued, 'We met Padre Rinaldi, who bade us tell you he would soon be here. Even now he thinks of all but himself.'

'His sentence of exile has come already!' said Irene, and then, as if the words struggled forth against her will, she added, 'Oh, those are happy who lie dead under our walls! Manara is secure now, Dandolo and Morosini are safe, too—Donati is with them, Viola, Campana, Guerrieri, all gone! but those who remain—prison and exile for them! I would rather know them dead, too, than see those free hearts languishing in prison—prison for such as they! Oh, this life is very hard to bear!'

What could be said when all felt alike? Signora

Olivetti could only show Irene the utmost sympathy and affection. When they were about to go, Imelda said, with her pretty, childish simplicity, 'Dear Irene, do you know that we have heard from Luigi? At least, his mother has a letter; he is in Tuscany, safe so far; he could only write just a line; but, Irene, he bade her tell me he had learnt much in the last month, and that I was to forgive him. I cannot think why he said so; but imagine his recollecting me in all his haste! Irene, I was so silly, so miserable, some time ago; I thought he loved Gemma Clementi instead of me, but you see I was wrong.' She looked very happy and glad as she spoke.

'Ah, Imelda will be happy, after all!' thought Irene, with a thrill of generous joy that drove away her own grief for a while. They went, and she hastily sought her first visitor.

Gemma was gone. Every word had reached her like a death-warrant. All was dizzy, whirling in her mind; she dashed out into the corridor, down the stairs, almost over some one whom she did not see. She stood in the open street, amid the driving rain, on the bank of the Tiber. One thought had filled her; she looked hurriedly to sky and earth, grey alike; the dreary street was empty. She clasped her hands with a wild gesture over her head—another instant would have seen her plunge into the tawny waters, but a strong grasp caught her. She struggled fiercely, like a mad creature, for a few moments, then stood passive and exhausted in the hands of Padre Rinaldi, whom she had darted past on the stairs without recognising, without even seeing.

'Be still, mad girl!' he said, in a low deep voice;

what! is this life unendurable, and would you enter on another which has no end?'

She looked up vacantly in his face; the passion fit had passed and left her worn out. All power of volition had gone; she let him lead her, without asking whither, to a neighbouring convent. The doors opened at his word, and she was admitted. There she lay on a sick bed for months, between life and death.

She at length returned to her family, and afterwards married; but in those hollow, gleaming eyes and passion-wasted features, the most careless eye could read a strange tale. She became noted for her ascetic devotion, and gave continually and largely to a convent, where, it was rumoured, she had once spent many months after some startling event in her life, but her history was fully known to none, though all were well aware that the Countess Gemma was an unhappy woman.

Colonel de Crillon did not forget Irene. Had he not used his great influence in her behalf, she and Vincenzo would have suffered for the part they had taken in politics; and, as it was, a prohibition was passed by the head of the police when Pio Nono returned, against the reappearance on the Roman stage of the young actress whose name might recal to the Romans their days of liberty. It was an unnecessary precaution! Irene was dead as a Roman cantatrice; her life had passed into another channel; Rome was to see its favourite no more.

The French officer proved a loyal and unwearied friend to her on many occasions, as long as their paths lay together, and he did more than defend her at a distance. It was with hurried and anxious steps that he came one day to her door and asked for her. The old woman, who was now their sole attendant, opened to him, but perplexed by the foreign accent, stared at him uncomprehending, and finally called Irene. She came, pale as death, her eyes heavy and dim, and stood silently awaiting what he had to say.

'Mademoiselle,' he hurriedly began, 'I told you that I could not protect Signor Nota—I ask nothing; I wish to know nothing about him; but as a friend I warn you that his retreat is discovered. If you can communicate with him—I do not ask where he is, remember—tell him he will be seized immediately unless he conceals himself elsewhere. I told you that he had a powerful enemy!'

A light broke from her eyes; a flash of mingled sadness and triumph.

'Thanks, kind friend!   He has escaped.'

'Ah! that is well!' said Colonel de Crillon, much relieved.

'Yes, he has escaped.   Will you follow me?' she said.

He did so, with sudden misgivings.

She entered a room where lay a still form with features fixed in changeless repose. The sound of her gliding step and of the soldier's tread did not reach that ear, brought no change on that pale face. Yes, Leone had escaped. In the land where he had taken refuge, slave and patriot are alike secure; under the shadow of its King all are safe; no tyrant can pursue his victim thither; and no earthly monarch dare assault that realm; for the lord of it is Death; and Irene laid her head down on the heart that should never beat any more, even for her, even for Italy—and murmured, 'I thank Thee, my God! I thank Thee!'

CONCLUSION.

TWO years later there was exhibited in London a panorama of Rome. Few visited it so often and with such interest as Mrs. Dalzell, who was then residing in London. In one of her visits she was struck with a young foreigner, who stood gazing upon it with an intensity which showed that no passing feeling was roused by it. Only his dark profile was visible to her, but in it and in his attitude was a depth of melancholy which was striking and painful even to a careless spectator. She asked a question concerning him in an under voice of the showman who stood by. He shrugged his shoulders—'There has hardly been a day that he has not been here. Leicester Square, no doubt.' The Italian roused himself the next moment and looked towards Mrs. Dalzell, who had an impression that she knew him, but hesitated to identify this worn and saddened man with the gay youth who once had passed a summer afternoon with her party on the turf of Villa Borghese. Time had not, however, altered her, had not ruffled her smooth brow, nor dimmed her blue eyes, nor brought a grey hair among her soft braids; and in the sweet Roman Italian which she knew so well, he said at once, 'Does the Signora Dalzell remember me?' 'Signor Ravelli!' she exclaimed, with cordiality, which called the sudden Italian smile over

his countenance. He had been one of those very
few of the Garibaldi legion who reached a safe
asylum. Arrived in Paris, he clubbed his finances
with the slender means of four other refugees,
and in a Parisian garret they lived more cheerfully
than perhaps would be easily credited. But ere
long the exile's longing for home awoke, and he
found his way for awhile into Piedmont, to be at
least nearer to his birthplace. Passing through
Geneva, he came strangely and unexpectedly on
some slight traces of Cecchi, who had courted
death madly in the siege, but in vain, and afterwards disappeared. He had fled to Geneva, but
even the doctrines of Calvin soon grew as abhorrent
to him as those of Rome, and he went on a fancied
mission of preaching from place to place, proclaiming frantic doctrines devised by his own
disordered brain. He wandered about Switzerland
and Piedmont for a time, and then was seen no
more, and whatever his final fate might be, it was
never known at Rome.

Luigi had now arrived in London, to aid, as far
as he could, his fellow exiles less well off than
himself. He at least need not have suffered from
poverty; for his family transmitted money to him
constantly, though their resources were crippled
by the heavy fine which Luigi's part in politics
brought upon them. All he had to spend speedily
went to relieve old friends—there were but too
many who needed it; but those who were on free
soil were fortunate, for others had met with a sadder
fate. Mrs. Dalzell asked after one remembered name
and another—'Dead—shot by the Austrians—
in prison—disappeared'—came the answers, till she
shrank from asking more. One name was upper-

most in their minds, but neither could trust themselves to speak it, though when both paused and were silent, each knew that the other was thinking of him who lay in a lonely, unmarked grave in the Roman cemetery. Unmarked, but not unhonoured, for long after those who had best loved Leone had left Rome, that grave was still strewn, as the anniversary of the siege came round, by unknown hands which no spy could ever succeed in detecting, with flowers forming the three colours of Italy. All around the gate of San Pancrazio rise dark green mounds above the bones of the Romans who fell there, for Pio Nono had no sympathy with his Romans, but reserved it all for the French, to whom he raised costly monuments; but the ground where patriots lie is hallowed for ever—holy as the consecrated earth where Leone sleeps. The secret of his resting-place is kept deep in many hearts, though only the priest and the woman who loved him above all things on earth stood beside it when he was laid there. But still the Romans call it, in hushed tones, when only the trustworthy can hear, ' The Grave of our Poet !'

Luigi could not speak of his lost friend, but he asked after Irene. Mrs. Dalzell gave him the last letter she had received from her, and bade him come to her house to read it. Those hospitable doors were always open to him from that day, and he gained an insight into English manners and English tones of thought such as few foreigners attain. At that house he met sensible, earnest-minded men, from whom he learnt what freedom truly meant. When, after another year of exile, the united wealth and interest of the

Olivetti and Ravelli families succeeded in obtaining permission for his return, he did not refuse to accept it, but went back a wiser man, with views that had become more sober and more practical, though the patriot heart beat high as ever. Imelda had not married ; she was faithful to the love of her childhood, and in her he had the most true and affectionate wife that ever man was blest with.

He did not find Vincenzo and Irene in Rome. Irene's love had combined the constancy of the north with the passion of the south, and after Leone's death she drooped as if heart and spirit alike were broken. Vincenzo's own deep grief was put aside by anxiety for her, and gratitude and affection for him seemed the one thread that still bound her to life. All Rome was full of mourning and desolation, fines and proscriptions. Fathers, mothers, wives called for sons and husbands, banished, killed, imprisoned ; liberty lay dead in a double chain, and every improvement that the republic had introduced was swept away, destroyed as completely as the stately road that it had commenced beside the Tiber—as if by this wholesale sweep the recollection of all that had come and gone could be effaced from the minds of the Romans. But the brother and sister lived, for a time apparently forgotten, in their corner of the old palace ; the storm had overwhelmed them and returned no more. It might however have been otherwise had they had no protector ; for Clementi, though absent, was still powerful, and might yet have tortured Irene through Vincenzo. He never dared to return to Rome. Crushed as the Romans were, not a babe on its mother's breast, to use Madama Cecchi's energetic expression, but would have had a dagger for him had he reappeared; and still with abhorrence they point out Palazzo Clementi as ' the dwelling of the Traitor !'

When life began to reassert itself in Irene's breast, it was in a wish to leave Rome, but she remembered her brother's frequent assertions that he could not live elsewhere, and did not utter her desire. It was Vincenzo himself who first proposed to go. Rome was no more Rome to him in the mist of blood and tears that shrouded her. His friends were banished, proscribed, dead. Padre Rinaldi had been long since sent into exile. Vincenzo became eager to take his sister away. His thoughts turned to Mrs. Dalzell and their father's English home. They went there, and later to Germany, whence Madame Marriotti had been incessantly writing to beseech her pupil to come to her. After a time Irene returned to her profession. The world has since learnt her name; she has won fame such as never visited her even in the radiant visions of her childhood; she is loved and honoured in private life by those who have the privilege of knowing her and the brother who is wrapped up in her. She is devoted to her art and is happy; but the gladness of her girlhood perished in the siege of Rome; and deep in her heart lies the thought of Leone; only Vincenzo and her art can find a place there besides. But those who see the calmness and peace on her fair brow would find it hard to believe how stormy was the youth of Irene Mori.

THE END.